THE BEST OF
VOLUMES 1-5

Other Cutting Block Books Titles

+Horror Library+ Volume 1
+Horror Library+ Volume 2
+Horror Library+ Volume 3
+Horror Library+ Volume 4
+Horror Library+ Volume 5

Butchershop Quartet I
Butchershop Quartet II

Tattered Souls
Tattered Souls 2

Coming Soon

Cutting Block: Single Slices

Advance praise for
+Horror Library+: The Best of Volumes 1-5

"I starting reading the *Horror Library* series when the first one came out years ago and haven't missed one since. Each volume was a darkly wonderful blend of practiced pros and daringly original newcomers. When I heard they were going to try to put the best of the best together for this collection I was, frankly, a little skeptical. I didn't think they could do it without putting out some 400,000 word monstrosity. But I'm happy to say they not only proved me wrong, they blew me away. Looking back over the last ten years, I challenge anyone to find a better collection of stories anywhere. The *Horror Library* series is as good as horror gets, and these truly are the best of the best."

-Joe McKinney, Bram Stoker Award-winning author of
Dead City and *The Dead Won't Die*

"When I pick up any volume in the *Horror Library* series, I know I'm going to have a wonderful reading experience. I've loved every one, and highly anticipate each new release. Now this new book has compiled the best of the best, and no horror fan should miss it. Every story inside is an absolute winner!"

-John R. Little, Bram Stoker Award-winning author of
Miranda, *The Memory Tree*, **and** *DarkNet*

+Horror Library+: The Best of Volumes 1-5
First Edition Trade Paperback, May, 2015
All Rights Reserved

Published in the United States by
Cutting Block Books
an imprint of Farolight Publishing, a division of
Farolight Entertainment, LLC, Winchester, VA.
www.cuttingblockbooks.com

Editor:	R.J. Cavender
Layout and Design:	Bailey Hunter
Cover Art:	*Freak Family*, by William Smyers, based on a photograph by Parker Neely

ISBN10: 0996115900
ISBN13: 978-0-9961159-0-2

THE BEST OF
VOLUMES 1-5

This book is dedicated to the late Horror Writers Association president Rocky Wood.

A leader, a scholar, a mentor, and an inspiration to so many. Your memory and standards live on in the very best of our endeavors.

You will be missed, sir.

R.J. Cavender and the +*Horror Library*+ family

+HORROR LIBRARY+ : THE BEST OF VOLUMES 1-5

TABLE OF CONTENTS

+HORROR LIBRARY+ : THE BEST OF VOLUMES 1-5
TABLE OF CONTENTS

A Note from the Publisher

"There are more things in heaven and earth, Horatio,
Than are dreamt of in your philosophy."
—Hamlet (1.5.167-8)

Our world is full of things that we don't understand. As bards and prophets are fond of pointing out, many of us walk around in a metaphorical fog, neither noticing nor comprehending the wonder, for example, of a mountain vista, or warm sand under our toes, or a crackling fire on a chilly evening. Yet even when we notice them, all of these images can, and often do, obscure deeper realities. If we could clearly see what was shimmering just below the surface of our daily lives—for example, what lurks beneath a nearby underpass, or what's behind the dullness in your classmate's eyes, or why that TSA agent is looking at you funny— if we understood those sorts of things in their fullness, then we may very well fall prostrate on the floor in terror, waiting for Reality to turn Its terrible gaze away from us once more. Like Jack Torrance in *The Shining*, we might decide that we'd rather fall sleep at our typewriter, than awaken to the truths that would be revealed to us if, of course, we only knew where to look.

The book you're holding is full of stories that try to give shape and expression, each in their own way, to the deeper mysteries of life. In these pages you'll find starving people and hungry ghosts; silent invasions and mysterious travelers; burning lovers and patriotic cannibals. It's a book where gas stations aren't what they seem, and neither are door-to-door salespeople. It's a book where the end of the world doesn't have to be, well, the end of the world.

These stories all appeared at one time or another in the Bram Stoker Award® nominated *Horror Library* anthology series. Our esteemed editor, R.J. Cavender, has selected them as being representative of the very best stories published by that series. Similarly, the cover image on this book follows in the long tradition of *Horror Library* covers, featuring a striking image that nearly jumps off the page at innocent passersby. This one is called "Freak Family," by William Smyers, and is based on a stock photograph by Parker Neely. We welcome William and Parker to our own "freak family" of *Horror Library* contributing artists and authors.

As you settle in to read these stories, remember: not all that is fiction is fictional, and not all that is true is transparent. And a good thing, too. As Shirley Jackson once observed, no one can stay sane for long in conditions of absolute reality. I'm honored to have been able to bring together an all-star team of writers, and to present to you this "best of" anthology as a sure antidote against those real-life terrors that prowl the earth during the day, seeking the ruin of souls. Like Jackson's larks and katydids, we will dream the horrors away, at least for tonight.

    —Patrick Beltran
      Winchester, VA

Foreword

by Lisa Morton

The *Horror Library* series is important.

Let me clarify that: These books are not going to offer a cure for cancer or feed thousands of starving children. It's unlikely that any of the volumes will ever win a National Book Award (although they have been nominated multiple times for the Bram Stoker Award), or become bestsellers anywhere outside of a very specific list on Amazon. But here's what they've done and will continue to do: They provide readers with superb, carefully crafted horror stories that prove the horror genre is alive and well, and they offer an alternative marketplace for writers who live in the great gray zone outside of New York publishing circles.

Probably no other genre has had such a troubled history as horror (and there are many who will tell us that it's not really a genre; I respectfully disagree, but that's a topic for another day). The same genre that gave the world *Frankenstein*, *Dracula*, "The Black Cat" and "The Call of Cthulhu," *The Haunting of Hill House*, and *The Shining*, is now frequently dismissed as "torture porn." The same bibliophile who just finished *House of Leaves* or *The Lovely Bones* will deny having any interest in "blood and guts stories."

And this is a step up from about twenty years ago, when every Internet horror forum (remember forums? They were how we fans communicated in the days before Facebook and Twitter) was full of posts that asked, "IS HORROR DEAD?" The horror boom of the '80s had become the droughts of the '90s and '00s. The Big Five publishers virtually stopped producing new horror novels; where there'd once been dozens of small horror magazines, only a handful were still around; chain bookstores did away with horror sections, and the few anthologies that came out each year were almost all entirely populated by well-established old pros who'd been invited to contribute by the books' editors. The e-book indie scene was still in the future, as was the social media that would assist writers in building their fan-bases.

It was a tough time to be a newer horror writer. Trust me, I know—I was there.

I was luckier than a lot of my peers, because I made my first few sales to major anthologies; my background as a screenwriter gave me a nice "in" with editors who happened to also be movie buffs. However, as one of those newer prose writers, I was anxious to make sales and started looking around for more markets.

I joined the Horror Writers Association (HWA), and made some new sales through markets listed in the organization's newsletter and forum. And I discovered that horror had a vital, even thriving small press.

I started both reading more of those small press books and writing for them, and realized that these books were often very different from what the majors were putting out. The mass market paperbacks with the colorful, frequently amusingly-cheesy covers that passed for Big Five horror anthologies usually held stories that seemed to place plots and clever twists over unusual ideas and rich language. Fortunately the small press didn't play by the majors' rules; the best of them—like the *Horror Library* series—elevated originality and craftsmanship over formula and stereotype. Best of all, the small press anthologies weren't closed; they were open to submissions from those of us who hadn't yet graced the *New York Times* bestseller lists. Competition was understandably tough, but you knew that if you got in, you'd work with a great editor (like R.J. Cavender and Boyd Harris) who'd make your story gleam, and you'd be in the company of horror's best up-and-comers. It was both a training ground and a way to build that fan-base, and even kept some of us in meals. These books gave careers to newcomers, opened readers' eyes to the wider possibilities of horror, and kept the art of horror fiction alive.

And that's why they were—and are—important.

Long live *Horror Library*!

Lisa Morton is an award-winning novelist, screenwriter, Halloween expert, and president of the Horror Writers Association.

The Puppet Show

by Rick J. Brown

Mark Petrov's face was chiseled like death itself, a blessing of sorts, since it would ensure his survival.

At the bus stop, Leyna squeezed his hand. Her fragility never escaped him, so that he couldn't let go of her—not here, not anywhere. He wished he could wear her like a backpack, never losing sight of her. In this polluted air, she could disappear no less than twenty feet from him, forever lost behind a curtain of smoke the color of rust and bruises, where a Refurbished might stalk and capture her. How could he cope with that loss? In this world gone surreal and alien, she grounded him in a reality he priced to no end.

He bowed his wiry frame over the curb and counted the cobblestones. Those he could see. The foul-smelling smog, coughed daily by the Grinding Machines, swallowed the rest. He made a game of this, partly to track the thickening of the mist, partly to indulge in a number game. Perhaps this was not dignified of an aficionado of numbers and patterns, but it kept his mind busy. And in this simple act of faith that numbers always tell, he kept looking for clues wherever he could find them. There was hope in this. And it was all he could do to try to figure out The Grinding Machines, and whether the aerial release of human byproducts would ever stop.

The bus parted the smog in bellowing clouds, clanking its way down toward them. This brought color to his pale cheeks and he cracked parched lips into a smile long overdue. He knew how excited Leyna was, and if she would experience only one thing that a child *should* experience, it was this show.

"Is this it?" she squealed. "Is this it, Daddy?" She'd never ridden on a bus. He pointed to the electronic sign above the windshield that said, "THE PUPPET SHOW."

She stared at him in puzzlement. "I can't read, Daddy."

He shook his head impatiently. "You've seen this word before. What am I teaching you the alphabet for?" She delegated too easily, not realizing that her smarts might one day save her. She needed to hone her skills.

"Try harder."

She squinted, then burst into hops on the sidewalk. "Yes! Are we going to be able to take one home? Please, Daddy? Please?"

"A puppet? I don't think so, Leyna."

The bus screeched to a halt and they climbed up the metal steps. The stench was worse inside. The copper smell of blood and odd sweetness now mixed with the odor of sweat, feet and feces. The driver hunched over the wheel, hair in disarray, and unshaven. His bloodshot eyes ringed with skin folds the size of handbags, were testimony to eyestrain from peering into the smog. He gave them an impatient head tilt toward the back, and the doors rumbled shut behind them.

They walked down an aisle strewn with crumpled paper, stomped Coke cans, and old beer bottles with half-torn labels. In the first seat on his right, a sizeable woman in a soiled gown cradled a baby that screamed while a streak of saliva ran down her hand. Beside her sat a small boy, the Incredible Shrinking Man in his giant overalls, hair the color of rust and wild like campfire. To his left, an old man who seemed crooked at every turn of bone held onto the handlebar in front of him with a vacant stare. He sat beside a little girl who methodically banged her foot against the metal divider. A dark substance—probably a homemade substitute for the long-gone chocolate—caked the corners of her mouth. The rest of the bus was essentially a repeat of the first row. No one stood. They passed some faces marked with apprehension and restlessness. Some peeked ahead, craning their necks.

They insisted on glimpsing the invisible: landmarks of the old world buried in smog.

He sighed when he found two empty seats on the back couch. They were on either side of a young woman spruced up with erotic charm from the simplest of things: a turquoise silk blouse sewn-up at several places, and white jeans still hugging her thighs but thinning and graying at the knees.

Mark and Leyna stumbled toward her as the bus lurched forward, yet managed to keep their hands to themselves. He didn't want to have to touch the handlebars. He was sick enough, but proven not to be contagious. He didn't need an incurable disease he could pass on to Leyna, courtesy of a new wave of fools who tried to get sick to avoid the Grinding Machines.

The young woman was considerate enough to skew over and make space for two adjoining seats. Mark nodded in thanks, let Leyna hop on one side, and sat between the two. He knew he didn't have to worry about Leyna touching anything. She was well-trained.

"Daddy?"

"Yes?" He self-consciously adjusted his shirt and counted the buttons (there were seven, as always). He'd been too weak lately to rub his fast dwindling supply of soap onto the fabric, and with renewed embarrassment, realized it was rumpled and soiled.

Leyna startled him. "How many seats on the bus?"

"Forty-six." He didn't need to count them.

She giggled. "Are you sure? I'm gonna count them!"

"Go ahead." But he looked at his hands now, self-conscious about them, too. They were cadaverous. The bones popped out under the stretched skin, making ridges with too many shadows. It scared him. He still wanted to live, if only for Leyna.

The bus bumped along, negotiating every turn with the passing shadows of leafless trees.

"You're okay, Leyna?"

She frowned and slapped him on the arm. "Stop asking that!"

He laughed. "Okay, okay."

"She's truly adorable," the woman beside him said. She was exotic, with slanted eyes and high cheekbones of Eastern ethnicity. Yet, the deeper tone of her skin and lips hinted at Latin heritage—an extraordinary mix that made her brown eyes sparkle amidst a glow of golden hazelnut. She couldn't have been older than twenty, plump just enough to soften the curves—a jewel in a world where the young and healthy were now as rare as diamonds.

"I can only agree," he smiled, "but I'm her dad, you see."

"No, no," she said coyly. Her hand was doing a lot of the talking. "She is beautiful. How old is she?"

He turned to Leyna. "It's okay," he said. "Tell the lady."

She showed an open hand, fingers sprawled.

"She's been doing that all morning She turned five today."

"Happy birthday, Leyna!" She turned to Mark and extended her hand. "I'm Nathalie."

He took it before he had a chance to wipe off his own, wishing he could strip off its boniness along with the sweat.

Nathalie nodded toward Leyna. "Shy?"

"That's an understatement."

"And I bet," she said, "that she can't stop talking when she gets to know you."

He chuckled. "Do you have any of your own?"

"I was too young before the Invasion. Now it would be absurd." She recoiled, as if she realized what she'd just said. Her eyes shifted nervously between Mark and Leyna. "You seem like a good father," she said. "She'll be fine."

"It's just a puppet show," he said, hearing the apology in his voice. "And I'm not letting go of her if the earth splits open."

They rode in silence. The smog redoubled its thickness, a forewarning that they were getting close to the Grinding Machines. The bus suddenly hushed, save for the crying baby up front. Before long, he heard the Machines' incessant screech and rumble, like un-oiled metal disks rubbing gravel. The passengers' gazes shifted to the floor, the seats in front of them, and their hands. Mark didn't have to see their faces. He'd seen them before.

Eyes would glaze over, throats would gulp, probably running dry, lower lips would curl in, and hands would wring—the nervous discharges that came with dread.

Images would run through their heads. For some, they brought guilt; for others, despair; and for the rest, sheer terror. Who would be fed into the Grinding Machines next? Were people pulled at random? Was there a pattern? And what would it feel like? For Mark, when he heard the shrill sounds of abrading machines, it was inexorably linked with images of flesh tearing, slouching and granulating, with blood running down gutters to feed a giant cauldron of human pulp. *And out comes another Refurbished.*

The Grinding Machines ran in a circle that enclosed the city, with little gaps between them, so that once heading downtown, they couldn't be avoided.

You could shut your ears and look away, but you could never shut out their scream.

For the better part of his life, Mark had lived in a predictable universe—one ruled by order that, if he really put his mind to it, he could glimpse right out of chaos. There were numbers, numbers everywhere. The magic of the modern world, they sparkled like gold amongst it and dispelled its mysteries. Except for the Invaders.

An elderly lady sat two rows up, in a seat facing them. "Does she know yet?" she said. She had breasts like two giant bullets that bounced under a loose nylon top. She gazed at him with sleepy eyes, as if the ride made her groggy. "It will happen very quickly, you know. It will be subtle."

This was fact and unpreventable. Yet, he couldn't fathom why she would bring it up. It was unnecessary and obscene. The horror he felt at her callousness compelled him to look away and reach for Leyna's hand. He didn't have it in him to argue with the old hag.

They only take the young and the healthy, the flyers had said. These brave messengers regularly passed new ones around, whenever they learned something of importance that they glimpsed when spying on the Machines. But lately, the messages had become ramblings, less grounded in fact, and more fashioned out of fear and despair, with a growing obsession with false prophecies.

He retrieved a pack of Camel Lights from his shirt pocket, having long ago overcome the inhibition to smoke in public. No one cared anymore. The smog and its filth were far worse. He lit it and took a long draft, then blew the smoke as he tilted his head back, letting the calming rush take him to a better place that reminded him of a steaming bath when hot water was still available. "They'll kill you, someday," he said, "is what they used to say."

In front of them, heads bobbed in unison. The road was cratered with potholes. A man sporting a single tooth turned around and smiled at Leyna. Mark instinctively reached for her, then tried to hug her despite her complaints. She pushed him off, and he pushed back teasingly, then tickled her for good measure. She giggled and tried to run off, but Mark's reflexes kicked in and he grabbed her wrist before she made it down the aisle. Now that she felt comfortable, she was a bundle of energy. And this only pained him. In the bright green dress she wore for the occasion, she looked like an emerald brushstroke in a dark, macabre painting.

He felt Nathalie's gaze on him. She searched his eyes. "I went to a show like this," she said, "not too long ago. They're magicians, puppeteers, professionals out of Las Vegas, traveling circuses, things like that. They know how to put on a good show. It's admirable they do it for free now. I think it takes their minds off the Invasion. They really put their soul into it. She will like it."

"Oh, I don't doubt it. I made dolls out of cloth and buttons, even puppets out of paper and strings for her. She's crazy about them. She has a drawer-full now. Compared to mine—professional entertainers? Can't wait to see her face."

After a while, Nathalie added, "You know, you have that look."

"Oh?"

"I don't mean to pry. But before the Invasion, I'd say you were a teacher, maybe a professor or something."

He considered this. Maybe it was his eyes, the way they pierced and pried, although he didn't mean for them to. Maybe it was his Russian heritage, his nonchalant demeanor.

"I'm a mathematician. A bad one at that."

She winced. "Why do you say that? I'm sure there's no such thing as a bad mathematician."

"I failed at the only job I've ever had. I was part of the group at the Orion Search Center, a division of SETI. I tried every damned algorithm known to man. None of them worked."

"What are those? The algorithms."

"The thinking was that language based on mathematics is universal. We tried deciphering a pattern in the language of the Invaders. When we failed, we constructed our own message and sent it back. We never got a response. You wouldn't believe the pressure we were under. People with machine guns guarding the exits. We had to find a way to communicate any way possible."

"The Invaders were a serious threat."

He found that he was out of breath. He must've explained this a million times. Yet, people didn't get it. *Why would you want to talk to them? They're evil!*

They're killing us! They're the devil!

He caught a glimpse of the old woman staring at him, a smirk on her lips.

Leyna leaned across Mark and craned her neck at Nathalie with adult seriousness. "That's when Daddy got sick!"

"*Shhhhhh,*" Mark said. "That wasn't the question, Leyna."

"Sick?" Nathalie said.

"Leyna's been on my back about it. If you know of a doctor who's working pro bono—hell, who's even still *working,* you'll make her happy."

"It's the smog, isn't it?"

"That's what I hear. I know I'm not the only one."

"*They've been talking to us since day one!*" They both jumped and turned to the big-breasted lady.

She glared at them. A bump in the road loosened a white strand of hair from the bun in the back of her head. Her eyes beamed unrestrained spite, glistening deep in a halo of darkened skin. "You guys in your big towers with your big fancy computers don't get it, do you—you don't get it and you never will I reckon because you're thick in the head."

She forced a smile. "Yeah, they've been talking, all right. You're just not listening."

Nathalie put a hand on his arm. It felt warm, and he liked it.

The bus came to a stop and deflated with a *pshhhhhh.* They stepped out, reentering the smog, and the bus driver took the lead to guide them across the street. Mark felt apprehensive about crossing because there was no way to tell whether a vehicle might suddenly burst out of the fog and plough through them like bowling pins. Few people drove anymore, but some of the ignorant ones still did.

Finally, a giant drape striped blue and yellow broke out of the fog. The visibility was better vertically, so that the tent seemed to climb forever, paling to nothingness a hundred feet up or so. But once inside, the air was crystal clear. Mark breathed more easily. Tendrils of fog crawled low to the ground.

"The smog is heavy," Nathalie said. "When there's no wind to circulate it, it falls to the ground."

He felt her stare on him again, which lasted long enough that he had to acknowledge her. She pinched her lips, seeming to say, *did I just say something smart? Something that might impress you?*

They squeezed between two rows of seats, trying to avoid stepping on people's toes, and sat beside a heavyset lady who dipped enthusiastically into a pack of Doritos. She munched loudly while staring at the empty arena. He almost asked her where she'd gotten the prepackaged snack, but imagined she'd been prepared with wholesale boxes stacked to the ceiling—gathered in the few hours during the supermarket rush before they closed forever.

He turned to Nathalie, hoping to catch her gaze on him. And he did. She had fake eyelashes, but the number of strands in the right eye didn't match the number in the left. A silver necklace followed the curves of her breastbones with twenty-eight visible links. All this he got in a flash.

She blinked twice as he scanned her face. Pressured to say something, he opened his mouth to speak but found he had nothing to say. She smiled weakly, eyes drifting to his lips. His mouth dried up, and his heart galloped. He felt apprehension and fear, all this mixed with an urge to kiss those full lips. There were six lone, fine hairs at the end of each eyebrow. He wondered how many crowns she had.

"How many stripes?" Leyna caught him off guard this time, but he took a moment to let the new environment sink in. The stadium around the arena was perfectly concentric, with seats arranged so they sat exactly between the two down from them. Four hundred chairs in all. Seventeen empty seats.

More than likely, ten buses outside. The lights dimmed, and something waddled out of hidden curtains. Seventeen camera flashes sprinkled the stadium like diamonds before stopping abruptly.

"Forty-eight." He yawned and she slapped his arm.

"You cheated!" She said.

Without looking, he grabbed her hand and squeezed it three times. *I love you.*

She squeezed right back. Three times. He squeezed again, twice, then once, and once again. *Tickle time!*

She giggled, then squeezed twice. No!

"Are they going to be like your puppets, Daddy?"

"I doubt it."

As the figure advanced, still hidden by the darkness that cameras no longer obliterated with snapshots, Mark began to feel ill at ease. It was obscenely big, and dragged itself rather than walked. He'd been distracted when the cameras lit it, but the audience had apparently seen enough.

Spotlights snapped it into reality. Mark held his breath, as much for himself as for Leyna. What he saw was grotesque beyond description: a bloated lump of flesh, shaped to give a passing impression of an obese human figure, beamed at the audience. It was a thirty-foot tall puppeteer carrying two smaller versions of itself, two live fleshy horrors suspended on strings like greased dough balls. All three creatures were awkwardly designed in the crude human form typical of the Refurbished: two glistening puffy cheeks, a beaked protrusion carved in the likelihood of a nose. They leered with lips the color of liver through a jagged hole cut to give a rudimentary semblance of teeth.

"I don't know what's going on," Nathalie muttered, "but that's not the show I expected."

He didn't want to look at her, see the fright on her face, the validation of his own.

"They can come into our houses if they want," he whispered so Leyna wouldn't hear. "They can grab us off the streets. Why the charade?"

Mark finally found the strength to check on Leyna, whose face had gone expressionless, lips slightly apart, gaze darting across the creature. He scanned the tent, hoping to glimpse signs of protests, but found only confused fascination. Clearly, no one knew whether to stay or leave. Mark sat on the edge of his seat, heart pounding, ready to spring and run the moment things turned ugly.

On closer inspection, he could now easily pick out several of the traditional Refurbished. Like the giant and his puppets, they were parodies of the human shape. They sat there, inconspicuous in their immobility. In the early part of the Invasion, they'd been chased, killed and burned, but their numbers only grew. Finally, they stopped appearing altogether. But here they were, insidious as ever, partaking in a silent chorus of open mouths that doughnuted their faces.

As the monster pulled strings at random, raising wobbly limbs, the Refurbished stretched their mouths even further. Finally, they uttered a piercing shriek that felt like a needle digging into a root canal. Brief clinks of shattering glass popped all around him: watches and eyewear were breaking.

The monster of the arena slowly turned to face the audience, the leer on its face taking on a strange, inquisitive appearance.

Something was happening here, leaving Mark frustrated as to what it was.

The concern on Nathalie's face matched the general, growing uneasiness that permeated the air. It was as if the entire tent breathed fumes that could blow up with the accidental strike of a nail. People were on the brink of darting out to howl their pent-up terror. They were just waiting for the first person to shout fire.

Mark agonized over a deciphering frenzy. He tried counting the pulls of strings by the monster—a musician directing a symphony playing a silent melody; the shriek of the Refurbished provided a background chant—but no, he couldn't detect a regular beat, a pattern. He tried extracting a sequence, maybe one that repeated, and searched the underlying algorithm—something like Morse code— but nothing repeated, nothing seemed contrived.

In his peripheral vision, he saw a blurry shape staring at him. It was the elderly lady from the bus. With the knowing eyes and that smirk, it was clear what she was saying: *I told you so.* As she turned back around, he noticed that locks of hair dislodged from her scalp and stuck to her pullover, leaving cranial spots that glistened pink like burned skin covered with medicated gel.

He reached to his own scalp. His hair was still firmly attached. Suddenly, the Refurbished stopped screaming.

People looked at each other, but no one said anything. It was the silence before the storm. Something was about to happen, and Mark took a firm hold of both Leyna and Nathalie's hands, ready to bolt.

The Refurbished slowly turned to the audience, and in a guttural voice like a forced whisper, pronounced in unison the first utterance to ever breach their lips.

Hello.

Over the hush, nervous shuffling could be heard clear across the arena.

Everyone waited for what was to follow. Yet nothing came. The puppeteer had stopped pulling strings, the Refurbished had returned to their previous blank stares, and that was that.

"What, that's it?" Nathalie whispered. Mark winced. He feared her voice might disrupt something. But the monster and its puppets turned and left.

Mark let go of both hands to wipe his own on his jeans and burry his face in them. The chatter volume steadily rose as the spectators slowly disengaged from their trance.

Mark shrugged. "So...they were just saying *hello.*"

"So..." Nathalie parroted in shock, "that's what the Refurbished are for? They're translators?"

Mark suddenly had a vision of the Grinding Machines regurgitating flesh puppets: interpreters programmed to capture and translate the language of the Invaders. It was outrageous, yet there it was—they had just clearly communicated a simple greeting. There was strange hope in that. It wasn't *we will kill you all*, or *we will enslave you*, or *you will obey us*. It was a simple *hello.*

"And what if," he said, "they had much more to say to us? Won't they need a new batch of humans to process through their Grinding Machine to say it?"

Finally someone screamed, then a child across the stadium followed suit until it infected the audience, reminding him of the nocturnal canine frenzy before the Invasion. Mark rose to his feet in the middle of a cacophony of screams, hands grabbing and pushing, people tripping over seats and themselves. Nathalie's hand firmly in his, he strained to hear what people were screaming about.

"What happened to him?" Female voice. "He was sitting right here!"

Male voice. "Oh my God! She's gone!"

Female voice. "I told her not to go anywhere! Please please please please, Mary Ann where are you?"

As the realization of what was happening dawned on him, he spun toward Leyna and found only an empty seat. "LEYNA!"

He searched for her frantically in the aisles, screaming her name, but the panicking audience carried him toward the exit like a tsunami. He pushed his way through the crowd, but lost more ground than he gained, and finally spilled outside.

The emerging crowd eventually thinned. With still no sign of Leyna, he fought his way back inside. He found himself among a couple of dozen people in the arena center, some on their knees, face in hands, some running around to look under seats. But she was nowhere among them. He scanned the tent for the exit taken by the monster, but couldn't find a single break in the tent material.

A hand rested on his shoulder. It was Nathalie. Without enthusiasm, she said, "Let's look for her outside."

* * *

For months, he looked for Leyna. He looked for her where the world was slowly unwinding, losing its familiarity, and shrouding her—at least in his mind—like the strange world of *Alice in Wonderland*. He frequented bars where the last drops of booze were freely distributed, churches, and the dreary, candlelit hallways and classrooms of high schools and universities. There, various groups met regularly to organize plans of action. But his questioning only met the knowing stares of the demoralized. They were veterans; they knew people were never recovered. He looked for her in buses that also ran freely, and for free. He looked in parks where prowlers, shielded by the smog and the conspicuous absence of law, were unstoppable. He looked in alleys where the homeless now cherished the diseases and mental illnesses that rendered them untouchable. Sometimes a Refurbished would crystallize out of the fog with fear on its doughboy face, or maybe an unknowable emotion inherited from the aliens. He would peer at the thing, at the absence of eyes in the malformed crevasses, to wrench some recognizable feature that would tell him that Leyna was in there, somewhere, lost in the cellular soup of a dozen, a hundred—a thousand?

But the only certainty was the faraway sound of the Grinding Machines playing in the background like eternal thunder. And one day, as he fell to his knees in front of one of them, its tall walls without doors rising in the smog, he screamed. Because he knew he would finally search no longer.

One morning, he found Nathalie sitting at the edge of the bed as he woke to her touch. She used a sponge soaked in cold water to cool his face.

"Did you have bad dreams again?" she said. She didn't use the name *Leyna*.

But the way he avoided her eyes said it all. She lay down by his side, and he breathed deeply. The weight on his chest was heavier than usual, the fever had come back, and he'd lost more weight. The weakness he had felt when moving about he now felt upon waking, and all he could do was ride the fatigue until he fell into a slumber.

Nathalie curled up to him and rested her head on his chest. He knew what she was doing, but the Illness wouldn't spread. It would kill him, not her, and she would eventually be alone, waiting for her time at the Grinding Machines, waiting to dilute into the human ocean.

Her instructions once he was gone were simple. There were razors in the cabinet and a bottle of vodka to ingest for a cottony departure. Of course, neither Mark nor Nathalie knew with any certainty whether she would have time to take that route.

Blue and yellow canopies had gone up throughout the city, a clear sign that a new message was to come—the impulse to count them had evaporated with Leyna's departure. He gathered that the people most likely to venture in the tents would be the curious: the physicists, the psychologists, the mathematicians, and the linguists; people with cameras and equipment; people with a desperation greater than their fear.

In the middle of the night, Mark often woke up in sweat. His worst dream resurfaced again and again—a child without a face crouched by a writhing mass in the grass, holding a kitchen knife over it. The bulk was a cat, skinned and bloody. Every time the child removed some skin, the cat shrieked. Every time the cat shrieked, the boy turned its face to Mark, as if asking for a translation. Mark screamed, "It's not talking to you! It's crying in pain!" The boy stared eyelessly for a moment, then went back to the cat to cut some more.

Whatever the Invaders were trying to say must've been of enormous importance, for they were killing life by the masses to do it. Perhaps Leyna, with her inherited love of numbers, might pass on enough enthusiasm about patterns to bring attention to a new means of communication for the aliens.

But for now, with the distraction of numbers out of the way, Nathalie looked splendid and carried a subliminal message of her own that needed no encryption: *I will be here with you, no matter what.*

In Nathalie's embrace, Mark daydreamed about what that next message would be. He also wondered if there was anything in that message that would have something recognizable of Leyna in it. And even though the likelihood was slim that a recognizable pattern would emerge, there might still be a coded question in the strange voice of the Refurbished. One that only she and he would know, like a particular pattern from their hand squeezes. He would wait, however long it took.

He would wait for anything.

How many seats in the tent, Daddy?

How old am I now, Daddy?

Anything at all.

The Exterminators

by Sara Joan Berniker

"Hon, you awake?" Richard shouted up the stairs.

Yawning, Molly struggled to shake off the dream that still ensnared her: Samantha's dwindling cries; Richard's shining smile; the silent beach and a sky filled with stars, each worth a wish.

As she dressed, she noticed the bottle of sleeping pills on the windowsill: Richard was having the dream again, too. This was getting weird. They were going to have to have a talk.

"I've got to go, Molly! You up?"

"Yeah, Richard."

"Good, then I'll let them in."

"Who?"

Down the hall, Samantha began to cry, obscuring his reply.

So tired she could barely walk, Molly went into the nursery and picked up the wailing baby. Samantha's forehead felt a little cooler, but that didn't mean much. She could tell from those snotty, labored gasps that her daughter was still sick.

In the silence that fell when Samantha paused to gulp a breath, Molly heard voices downstairs: more contractors, she guessed. They'd been taking bids for remodeling the kitchen, and lately the house had been crawling with burly men in tool belts.

Molly hurried down the stairs, smiling at the waiting men as she jiggled Samantha to try and ease the cries that came in out-of-breath bursts.

"You and your husband called?" the taller one said. "I'm Grady. This is Stan."

She blushed under Grady's unblinking gaze. He wasn't a bad looking guy, with those muscular arms and straight white teeth. "You're here to look at the kitchen?"

"No, we're the exterminators." He held out a clipboard. "Just need your signature…"

19

Exterminators? Had she and Richard talked about this? Who could remember? For weeks, Molly had been running on weird dreams and too much caffeine. Richard must have called them because of the ants in the pantry. They'd charge a bundle, these guys, and that meant another raid on the vacation fund. They were never going to get away, never going to get a break.

Molly felt warmth on her neck, and when her fingers came away they were wet with milky spit-up.

"A signature, Mrs. Bindley?"

"Yeah, just give me a sec." She shifted Samantha to her other arm and dabbed at the mess, the smells of used milk and talcum powder making her dizzy. The dream had been so real this time. Every part of her craved to be back on that sandy beach with Richard at her side, the two of them rapturous under the canvas of glittering stars. If only Samantha would stop crying for two fucking seconds so she could think straight…

"Here, let me," Grady said, holding out his arms. "Don't worry. Kids always take to me."

"You'll be sorry," Molly muttered, trading the squalling baby for the clipboard. She stared at the contract, unable to make sense of it; she wasn't much good before her first cup of coffee, and the writing was so very dense. "Wasn't my husband supposed to take care of this?"

"Yeah, he did. Put your John Hancock beside his, and we'll be good to go."

Molly looked up, startled at the sudden silence: Samantha was *smiling*. "I guess she likes you."

"Yeah, I'm good with babies. That's why they hired me."

For the life of her, Molly couldn't grasp how being good with children was linked to being an exterminator, but Grady had the kindest eyes she'd seen in a long while. No sense in looking stupid by asking. She squinted at the contract, a mess of legal jargon gobbledygook, and found her husband's cramped, hurried signature. Using the pen tied to the clipboard, Molly signed her name.

"There you go," she said, handing it to the other man. "Let me show you where the ants have set up house. You'll have to excuse the mess; Richard didn't tell me he'd called you."

"You both called us, Mrs. Bindley," Grady said softly, but Molly didn't hear him—she was busy wondering if she should offer them coffee and whether they could tell she hadn't bothered to put panties on under her jeans.

It wasn't until she reached the kitchen that she realized the men weren't following her. She turned just in time to see them cross the front lawn toward a white van, Samantha's little hand waving over Grady's broad shoulder.

"*Wait!*" Molly cried, running through the hall and out onto the porch. Stan climbed behind the wheel, while Grady opened the van's back door and placed Samantha inside.

Stumbling down the stairs, she saw that the van's interior was crowded with racks of big guns and cruel-looking spiked mallets.

"Stop! Stop!"

Grady stared at her. There was nothing threatening in his gaze, only mild confusion. "Ma'am?"

Molly sprinted across the lawn, her breath coming in harsh bursts. *"Give her back!"*

"Shit, not again," Stan said. "We don't got time for explanations. That last one put us forty minutes off schedule."

"There's no need to be upset, ma'am," Grady said. "Everything's in order. She'll be fine."

"Sure she will," Stan said, winking. "Tell the nice lady what she wants to hear."

"We'll bill you in two to four weeks, Mrs. Bindley," Grady said, ignoring his partner.

"What? No, the *ants!* That's why you're here!"

"I didn't say that."

"Give me my daughter back!" Molly reached for the van's rear door, meaning to wrench it open and rescue Samantha, but Grady held her back, smiling patiently as if she were an ill-tempered child.

"You signed, ma'am," he said. "You and your husband both. Have a nice day."

Pushing hard, he sent Molly sprawling to the ground, then climbed into the van. In the moment before the engine growled to life, Molly heard her daughter laugh and wondered when she'd last heard Samantha sound so happy.

The van roared away from the curb.

A Chainsaw Execution

by Stephen R. George

A chainsaw execution is an ugly, messy thing. That's the point. At least, that's what my brother Grayeyes says.

To deliver a death so horrendous that it can never be forgotten. Its aftermath to linger in the minds and affect the actions of those who witness it; but even more so, to affect those who only hear of it. In their minds to take on a significance far beyond its admittedly ugly reality. The details, blown up to nightmare proportions, become the thing itself. Those details are what really matter, says Grayeyes. Putting a chainsaw to somebody who deserves it, if anybody can ever be said to deserve such a death, is one thing, but putting the saw to somebody who does not, that is pure genius, that is the poetry of kings. Those are Grayeyes's words. That is the kind of death that resonates forever. It makes the condemned a figure of nearly unbearable pity—it makes the executioner a figure of terrifying legend.

The man tied to the chair in the garage of the derelict North End house was named Lisandros. He was the leader of a Chicago gang called Tráiganos. Lisandros was Hispanic, maybe Mexican or Puerto Rican. I couldn't tell. They all look the same to me. His skin color was nearly the same as ours. We could have been brothers. Maybe we all looked the same to them. All us redskins.

His eyes were impossibly black. In one a tiny flaw glowed like a nugget of gold, and beneath that eye a deep scar on his cheek curved like a crescent moon. If not for the scar, he would have been a handsome man. Tráiganos had expanded north of the border a month ago, cutting first into our cocaine, and then into our prostitution. My brother had called for a meeting. Lisandros had been foolish enough to accept. Now he sat bound in a chair at the back of a derelict garage, in a country not his own, looking from Grayeyes to me to his own four men who were standing at the back of the garage with shotguns pointed at their heads.

Lisandros, like my brother, was a small man, wiry, muscular. His power came from his eyes, burning, focused. Those eyes moved slowly from my face to Grayeyes's face. If he knew what was about to happen, he gave no indication.

There was a tattoo on his neck, just visible above his collar: a black skull with its tongue reaching out of its mouth and slithering into one of its eye sockets. They said Tráiganos means "Bring us." Bring us where? Bring us what? I don't know. We all had something like that. On my right forearm, as on my brother Grayeyes's forearm, as on all our men, was a dreamcatcher. A dreamcatcher is supposed to catch the bad dreams, to let the good ones through. When I was a child on the reserve, I had one hanging above my bed. I remember staring at it as I listened to my mother cry for hours in the dark. I have never known one to work.

The atmosphere in the garage was thick and sour, as if the air had become heavy like stale cigarette smoke. It was as if a bad spirit had come in there with us, was hovering at the edges of things, waiting. Our voices seemed to echo, sounding not quite like us, as if the walls were made of tin.

"You want a piece of what's ours, you're going to pay with a piece of yourself," Grayeyes said to Lisandros.

He bent down and picked up the chainsaw from the floor. Lisandros's expression did not change. He must have known what was coming.

"You can do this?" Lisandros said to Grayeyes.

"Fuckin' rights I can do this."

Grayeyes looked to me. I shook my head.

He spoke to me in a low voice. "Don't you chicken out now, little brother. We don't come down hard on this, we never hear the end of it."

"He doesn't deserve this," I said.

Grayeyes grinned. "That's the point."

He pulled the starter cord and the chainsaw roared. One of Lisandros's men screamed. He was clubbed with the stock of a shotgun and collapsed to his knees. My brother Grayeyes didn't notice. He turned to Lisandros, stepped closer, and brought the blade down on his shoulder. Blood sprayed, the saw roared.

It went on for what seemed like hours, but was only minutes. Cutting a man to pieces with a chainsaw is not an easy thing; not to watch, not to do. I could see that even Grayeyes, who has no heart, was troubled. More so, because Lisandros would not die, not right away. Without his left arm, he spat in my brother's face, the spittle clearing a sheen of blood down Grayeyes's cheek. Without his right leg, he laughed, a high cackle that cut through me more than the roar of the saw.

The only screaming in the room came from those of us who watched in disbelief, including me. When it was over and Lisandros was finally dead and quiet, the only sound was the retching of Lisandros's men, and ours.

My brother let the chainsaw die. He dropped it on top of the pieces of his enemy. He turned to face us. In the light from above, his eyes flickered, points of flame in his blood-soaked face.

I thought he was going to speak, but it was one of Lisandros's men whose voice broke the glassy silence.

"Let me bury my brother," he said.

His eyes were on mine. I turned to Grayeyes. Grayeyes nodded.

We unbound the four men. Silently, they gathered the pieces of Lisandros.

Grayeyes kept a foot on one of Lisandros's arms, the right arm. "This I keep," he said. "To remember."

They picked up everything else. One by one they left, until all that remained on the floor was a sea of blood.

Grayeyes surveyed his abattoir. "Burn it down," he said.

And we did.

* * *

My brother was right. The memory of that day had found a place in my mind forever. I could not sleep. I kept seeing Lisandros's face looking at my brother. I kept hearing the screams, the roar of the saw.

But Grayeyes, too, suffered. In the weeks that followed he slept little. At night, in our home beside the rail yards, I listened to him tossing, turning, moaning. Sometimes he would get up, open his bedroom door, and stand there. I could see him from my room, drenched in sweat, gasping for air. But I said nothing.

Once, in the morning, he said to me, "I can't stop thinking about him. Tough bastard. Can you imagine?"

My brother was also right in that Tráiganos moved south again. We got our drug trade back, they left our girls alone. The message had gone out. *Don't fuck with us.*

But they didn't need to be here to fuck with us. They were here in my brother's mind, in his dreams. At night, he started screaming. His dreams, I knew, were haunted by the roar of the saw, the sudden grinding noises as the blade bound in bone, blood spraying. He slept little. He began to look sick.

A chainsaw execution is an ugly, messy thing. It is a death that can never be forgotten, not by those who witness it, not by those who hear of it. And apparently, not by the executioner. By mid-summer, Grayeyes never left the house. At night, he tossed and turned and cried and screamed, haunted by that night in the garage and by what he had done.

But it was more than that. I know that now.

He burned Lisandros's arm and buried the ashes, but that wasn't enough to clear the memory from his head. The dreams got worse. His waking screams became louder, and longer.

There came a night when I woke to silence. Although I could not see in the darkness, I felt that I was not alone. There seemed to be shapes in the room with me, slithering between shadows. I could not get out of my bed.

Suddenly, the darkness was pierced by my brother's screams. Not the screams that marked his waking from dream to reality. This was worse. I heard him speaking, pleading.

Then I heard the terrible sputtering roar.

I could not move. The roar filled the small house, filled my head. The screaming reached a pitch that was inhuman, and then stopped. But the roaring of the saw went on for a long time. It must have stopped at some point, but I was not aware of it. My bedroom window became pale with dawn, and I saw that I was alone. The house was silent.

A dream, I thought. Only a dream.

But when I opened Grayeyes's bedroom door, and saw what they had done, I fell to my knees and threw up. Then I wept.

In the first week of June, we buried what was left of Grayeyes. They left everything but his right arm. Like him, they wanted a trophy.

By mid-June, Tráiganos was back on our territory. My men looked to me to make a decision, but it was Tráiganos who moved first. They called for a meeting. A meeting in a public place.

To refuse would have been cowardly, and dangerous. That was not an option. But I am not a stupid man. I was well protected when I finally found the courage to go to the park on the designated day, at the designated hour.

He was waiting for me there, sitting on a bench, his face turned up to the sun. His men, like mine, hovered at the edge of our vision, watching, wary. He turned to me as I sat down, and he smiled.

"So, we are done with the silliness?"

For three heartbeats I said nothing. Then, I nodded.

He held out a hand for me to shake. I clasped it and squeezed. He squeezed back, firm and strong.

My heart was pounding. His grip had a terrible, aching familiarity to it. I fought the urge to look down, but I could not. His hand, gripping mine, seemed to be a slightly darker shade than the skin of his face. The skull on his neck seemed to be smiling at me. The gold fleck in his eye seemed alive in the afternoon sunlight. The crescent moon scar on his cheek seemed deeper than it had that night in the garage. The dreamcatcher on his forearm bulged as the muscles beneath the skin squeezed.

"Is time for us to put this behind us," he said. "Time to do business, yes?"

I nodded yes, yes, yes, but I could not find the strength to speak until my brother's hand released me.

I Am Meat, I Am in Daycare

by Cameron Pierce

When Ted Branson called to ask the rate for Susan's daycare service, she didn't realize his child was a hunk of meat. But that's what the man who introduced himself as *Mr. Branson, but call me Ted* was dragging into her home.

"Should I put him with the other kids, or will you take him from here?" Mr. Branson said.

"Mr. Branson...Ted," Susan said, "I can't take your child. I'm sorry, it's just not..."

Not what? Susan wondered. She was paid to watch kids, and if this loon wanted to pay her for watching a hunk of cow, she would do it.

"I don't see what the problem could be," Mr. Branson said.

Susan smiled. "Problem? None at all. Bring your son this way and I'll introduce him to the other children."

"His name is Scotty," Mr. Branson said.

"Excuse me?"

"My son's name is Scotty," he said.

"Oh, of course," Susan said. "His name is Scotty."

For the first time, Susan was glad the two-, three-, and four-year-olds she watched were, without exception, idiots.

She led Mr. Branson into the living room. The man dragged the hunk of meat behind him like it was a reluctant child. Where the hell had the meat come from anyway? Maybe it was just a large rib-eye steak, but Susan had never seen rib-eyes that size. Ever. She watched the six children watching *Alice in Wonderland*. "Everyone," she said, "I'd like you to meet Scotty."

Haley, a little blonde girl, turned from the television and waved both hands in the air. More like calling for help than waving hello, Susan thought.

Normally, there were over ten pages of paperwork to fill out for a new child, but since Scotty wasn't really a child, she skipped it and concerned herself with getting Mr. Branson the hell out of her home.

"Well," Mr. Branson said, "I'm already late for work, so if there are any forms to sign, I'll fill them out this evening, around five. Thanks again."

He walked out of the living room. Susan heard the front door shut.

Easier than expected.

She heard the door creak open. "I forgot to tell you, Scotty's allergic to chocolate milk," Mr. Branson called.

The door shut again. Susan stared at the meat child.

Allergic to chocolate milk…

She expected to have an easier time lugging the meat into the kitchen. It couldn't have weighed more than fifteen pounds, but felt like fifty, maybe more. When she picked it up, legs, which she hadn't seen, uncurled from the thing's red underside. Susan recoiled before hurrying down the hallway into the kitchen.

She returned with oven mitts.

None of the other children said anything as Susan dragged the meat into the kitchen by its legs. Susan wondered what the little idiots would tell their parents about Scotty, the new boy, or if they would even remember someone new at all.

Scotty was too heavy for Susan to lift onto the kitchen table. Instead, she slid him into the corner, right beside Mr. Rat's food and water. She emptied the water bowl in the sink and cursed her husband for the empty bottle of Jack he'd left out on the counter. She understood how much he loved Mr. Rat. She loved Mr. Rat too. They'd gotten the cat over ten years ago, before they were even married. Still, the cat had been dead for a month. Leaving food and water out was a harmless means of coping, but if a parent were to see the empty Jack bottle and complain to the daycare board, she could lose her business.

Now that the bowl was clean, she searched the fridge for chocolate syrup. She realized it was no use. They were out of milk. Instead, she grabbed one of her Atkins chocolate-flavored protein shakes.

It was close enough, right?

Susan popped the tab and poured the liquid into the bowl. She set it on the floor beside Scotty. "Drink up," she said, but who was she kidding? Of course he wouldn't drink up.

She lifted the bowl and tilted it just enough so that a small stream dropped onto the meat. Nothing happened, so she poured more. Then she let the whole thing spill.

Still, nothing happened.

Susan left the chocolate-soaked Scotty on the linoleum floor and walked out of the kitchen. She peeked into the living room to make sure the kids were still alive and watching the movie.

While they seemed no less alive than before, Susan screamed when she saw these *new* children. She collapsed on the floor and covered her head. A nightmare, a very bad…

"Mrs. Mackery," said Charlie, the oldest boy she watched.

Susan looked up. Her insides tightened. A trail of red ran from the sofa where Charlie had been sitting to where he stood. The child didn't seem to notice that he was skinless. How could he be alive? How could he be without skin?

"Mrs. Mackery," he said.

"What is it, Charlie?" she said.

"That new boy, he hurt me."

Susan glanced at the other children. She looked at the cable box. 1:11 glowed green. How could it be over an hour past noon? Mr. Branson dropped off Scotty around eight. In that time, she'd done nothing but drag the meat into the kitchen and pour the chocolate shake over it.

Something moved in the hallway. She looked at the children again, taking count. One was missing? Who? Haley.

"Haley," she called, "Haley!"

The toilet flushed. Then the sink ran for a few seconds before the bathroom door opened. "Haley," she said.

The thing that scuttled into the living room was not Haley, even if it wore her face. It grinned, but the skull beneath didn't smile in sync with the loose-hanging little girl face, and Susan wondered if more than one mind somehow existed behind that hideous thing.

Susan awoke in the dark room. Her husband stood over her. He stared down, squinting, and she wondered how long he had been there. He held out a hand and she took it in both of hers.

"Where are the children?" she said.

He pulled her to her feet. "I came home for lunch. You were passed out, so I called all the parents. Are you hungry? I cooked dinner."

Her stomach grumbled. Susan wrapped her arms around her husband. "It was a terrible day," she said.

He kissed her cheek and walked out of the room. Susan followed. She tried finding the words to explain what happened, starting with Mr. Branson, but her mind felt foggy, scrambled.

When she entered the kitchen, Mr. Branson stood from his seat at the table. "What the hell is he doing here?" she said.

Her husband opened the oven and pulled out a tray stacked with burnt meat. He turned around. "Ted is my new partner. We're going into a sort of business project together."

"What business?" she said.

Her husband and Mr. Branson responded together. "Your new husband," they said.

Susan left the kitchen, passed through the lightless living room, and pressed her face against the door. She looked through the door peep. Outside stood Mr.

Rat. No, even if that thing on the doorstep wore the face of their beloved cat, it couldn't have been. Not Mr. Rat, not with his head on the body of a little boy.

He held a platter of meat. All six of the children she watched stood around him.

"Can we come in now?" said Mr. Rat in the voice of a boy no more than six years old.

Susan looked into the eyes of Mr. Rat. Something was behind them, something familiar but terrifying. Two hands wrapped around her belly from behind.

"It's just me," her husband said. "Don't tense up like that."

She wanted to step away, but there was nowhere to go. Her husband kissed the back of her neck. "What's the matter with you?" he said.

"Nothing."

"Nothing? If nothing's the matter with you then why the hell are you letting our guests sit outside in the cold? We've got dinner to serve."

He tugged her inside and waved for Mr. Rat and the kids to follow. "Mr. Rat, take the kids in the kitchen. I'd like to speak with my wife alone."

Mr. Rat gave them two thumbs up and shuffled into the kitchen. The children followed close behind, as if they were afraid of what might happen without Mr. Rat's supervision.

Susan was crying now. "What the hell's going on?" she said.

Her husband said, "Don't get upset over this. You've got no goddamn reason to cry, you know that? I should slap the shit out of you, that's what a sensible husband would do. I know you've wanted us to start our own family for a while now, and talking with Ted, I realized that we'd have enough money, that we could support a child, if we introduced a few extra workers to our home."

"But where did you meet him?" Susan said.

"Meet who?"

"Ted Branson."

"I met him nowhere special."

Susan buckled over. She pulled at her hair and rolled around on the carpet, at her husband's feet. "Nowhere special," she said, "nowhere special. For God's sake, what does that mean? Nowhere speci-"

He slammed his foot against her mouth, cutting her off. Susan bit her tongue and tasted blood. Despite the pain, she wondered why her husband wasn't wearing shoes since he'd just arrived home from work.

"I didn't mean that," he said. "All I want is for you to understand that we can finally start a family. I want you to be happy. And if it's really that goddamn important to you, I met Ted in the grocery store years back. He was shopping for a child. I never mentioned him to you, then ran into him again a few weeks ago. He was looking for a daycare service."

Susan looked up at him. Was this really her husband? He'd never been abusive, at least not overly so. Never anything like this. And she'd always considered him the more rational of the two of them. She thought of Mr. Rat's death. Had it really impacted him this much?

"Ted and I decided that since Mr. Rat might have trouble acquiring a job, he's the best candidate for fatherhood. Ted and I will provide financial support while Mr. Rat stays at home with you and the child. With Ted in the family now, you don't even have to run a daycare service. We'll be the perfect family, honey. Don't you think?"

Mixed in with the children's laughter in the kitchen, Susan thought she heard something meowing. No, it couldn't be. And this man could not be her husband. This house could not be hers, either. She was somewhere else. *This isn't my life, I cannot be Susan.*

Everything grew quiet in the other room. Susan listened to herself breathe. Her heart felt ready to explode.

"It's dinner time," her husband said.

She didn't fight as he pulled her to her feet.

Maybe she didn't want a family anymore. Or maybe she did, just not this one. But she loved her husband, even if he was no longer the man she married. Susan also loved Mr. Rat, just not the one in the kitchen.

Her husband guided her toward the kitchen and the stench of burnt meat.

"What would it be like," she said, "to start a family with the ones you love if they're no longer who you thought they were?"

"You should ask Ted about that one. He says he's a philosophy professor."

The children broke out in laughter. Was Scotty among them? Something was meowing. Had to be meowing. Susan stepped into the kitchen, followed by her husband. She wondered how much time would pass before she no longer tasted blood in her mouth, and what, exactly, would be served for dinner.

Trapped Light Medium

by Sunil Sadanand

In twenty minutes, a middle-aged man wearing a blue suit and a black overcoat is going to walk into this office and kill everyone. His name is John Newcomb and he's mad because accounting screwed him on his last check. They were fifteen dollars short. He has a sawed off, twelve-gauge Mossberg tucked beneath his coat. He's on his way right now. He's taking the bus. I got in by making an appointment with the manager at G&J Mercantile. In a couple of seconds, I'm going to go into the bathroom and wait out the storm.

When he's finished killing all the people in the office, he's going to put the barrel of the shotgun into his own mouth and blow his brains all over the receptionist's desk. But she won't notice because she's one of the first people this gentleman is going to kill.

"Excuse me."

"Yes?"

"Will it be very long before I can meet with Mr. Howard?"

"Well, he's kind of busy right now, but he said that he'll definitely meet with you."

"Any idea how long?"

"I really can't say, sir…maybe twenty minutes?"

In twenty minutes you'll be a stain on the carpet, sweetheart but—

"All right, well, is there a restroom I could use here?"

"Straight down the hall, first door on your left."

"Thanks."

"You're welcome."

I go into the lavatory, lock the door, sit on the toilet and wait. I check the film in my camera. Fuji Velvia for sharp saturated slides.

I put my ear to the door and listen. The hectic office sounds go on for a while, and then fifteen minutes later chaos erupts.

"Mr. Newcomb," says the voice of the receptionist. "Can I help you with something...I didn't know you were...Oh...Oh, my god!"

Boom

The explosion is like a thunderclap. People scream. I hear the sounds of glass shattering and desks overturned. A man screams for help. There's the sound of plaster breaking apart as the scattered shells rip through the walls.

Boom, boom, boom

Newcomb shoves cartridges into his weapon and blasts away like some possessed robot. The madness goes on for about ten minutes. I hear a woman sobbing before she is cut off by an explosion. I hear the sounds of boots crunching down on broken glass. Some people are moaning and making pathetic gurgling noises.

Silence

There is one more thunderous blast and then a thump—the sound of Newcomb's broken body crumpling to the floor.

I wait even though I shouldn't. I have about two minutes before the cops arrive. My hands are shaking and my palms are clammy.

The camera almost slips from my grip.

I open the door.

Carnage

Blood everywhere—staining the walls, all over the desks, all over the carpets. Papers, phones, staplers, and desks are broken and in pieces, strewn about the floor. Bodies are everywhere. Some of them still twitch. There's a guy draped over a busted copier, which keeps bleeping and spewing out paper.

Another guy is slumped across the desk with the phone still clutched in his hand. Newcomb blew off the top part of his head.

Click, click

The phosphorescent flash of the camera briefly illuminates the office. The receptionist doesn't have a face anymore. Only a few bloody strands of sinew attach her head to her neck.

Click

Now Newcomb. Another nasty head shot, mouth opened into a perpetual scream. Little pieces of teeth and skull sit in a sticky pool of crimson amidst empty shotgun shells and a pile of paper clips. That's going to be a good one.

"Shit."

Sirens

A few more pictures, and then I'm gone, out the back door.

* * *

We're in a coffee shop in DC. Trendy, white, teenage hipsters sip unpronounceable variations of the mocha blend. Hair and clothes fashionably unkempt, they lounge on the sofas talking about politics and MTV, often using both words in the same sentence.

Meredith carelessly runs a hand through her dark hair and chews on the end of her glasses.

"I'll give you three hundred for the whole lot of them," she says.

"Why so much?"

"Clerks going postal isn't that uncommon nowadays, and some of these pictures are simply too graphic for our publication."

"That's what you always say," I reply, "and then in the next issue, I find every one of those pictures in there."

"Three hundred," she says. "Take it, or leave it."

"Don't have much of a choice, do I?"

She hands me a check under the table, and then she does something strange.

"Hey," she says. "How do you get these, anyway?"

This line of questioning is highly irregular. We've been working together for almost a year now, and suddenly she's curious?

"Excuse me?"

"I mean, how do you get there before the cops come. How do you know these things are going to happen?"

"I'm a psychic," I reply, ready for the usual look of poorly suppressed hilarity, mingled with a healthy dose of contempt and skepticism.

"You don't look like the Tarot card and crystal type."

"I'm not."

"Well, if you're a psychic, then what am I thinking?"

There's one I haven't heard before.

"It doesn't work that way," I say.

"Ever see a ghost?"

"No, I don't think there's such a thing."

"Can you talk to the dead?"

"What is this—twenty questions?" I say.

She looks away disappointed.

"Look," I tell her. "I can't see things that happen thousands of years later, and so I don't consider myself some sort of prophet. I can't look at your palms and see if you're going to have a happy life, or marry the man of your dreams, and I can't read your mind. I don't know whether the world is going to end, and I have no idea whether or not your dead Uncle Harry is happy in the spirit world. Okay?"

"Okay, okay, sorry," she says. "Sensitive subject, point taken."

"I don't mind talking about it," I say. "Just don't make it into a joke, all right?"

"Yeah, all right."

A few people are staring at us. I guess I must have raised my voice a little.

"So where are we meeting next?" she says.

"I don't know yet."

"Well, try to get something a little more sensational next time, like a school shooting or something."

She winks, pats me on the arm and heads out the door.

"Yeah."

* * *

Hollywood Beach, Florida. I'm on the boardwalk sipping a margarita, watching young girls in bikinis frolic around on the beach. It's like an episode of *Baywatch* out here. The sun is resplendent; the sand is white, the water crystal clear.

In fifteen minutes, a gang of Haitian drug dealers are going to come careening down the street in a black van. The cops are going to be after them—they've already shot out one of their tires, and one hundred feet away from where I'm standing, the driver is going to lose control of his vehicle.

It will veer out onto the boardwalk, sparks flying from the axle, and roll over one and a half times. Then it will skid into a stoplight, which will come crashing down on top of it.

The van will explode like a landmine sending pieces of burning shrapnel in every direction. But that's not the worst of it. Two of these gentlemen are going to escape the van and start shooting it out with the cops. When it's all said and done, there will be at least thirty people dead and twice as many injured.

"Hi."

"Hey."

She's been staring at me for the past ten minutes or so. I've been staring back. She has black hair, dark eyes and a deep tan. She's vaguely familiar.

Cuban chick.

Cute.

I've seen her before.

"You don't look like you're from around here," she says. She has a charming, crooked smile and a faint trace of an accent. She rolls her R's a little bit.

"I'm from everywhere," I say.

"Here on vacation?"

"Yeah, sort of."

"With your wife?"

"Not married."

"Oh."

Awkward silence.

"So…you come here often?" I ask, immediately realizing what a clichéd, idiotic thing that is to say. But sometimes clichéd, idiotic things are good icebreakers.

She laughs, but it's not mocking…not exactly.

"Not really," she says. "I live in South Beach. I'm just visiting my cousin."

I hear the sirens wailing in the distance. I look at her and she takes an involuntary step backward, probably because of the sudden gravity in my expression. She looks behind her quickly and then turns back to me biting her lower lip in consternation. I'm about to do something highly irregular.

"Look," I say. "You ought to get out of here right now. You hear those sirens?"

She nods slowly.

"In a few minutes something terrible is going to happen, and if you don't leave, you're going to die."

"What? Are you crazy, man?"

"No, I'm not crazy. Please just listen…"

"Whoa, take it easy, buddy."

"Look, just get out of here," I say.

"Jesus, all right, just tell me you're not interested, spare me the bullshit."

"I'm not…"

"Whatever, I'm sorry to have bothered you. Adios."

She walks away and then turns around and stops as she hears the shrieking tires. The van barrels through a fruit stand and skids out of control. She is paralyzed with fear. My head is throbbing.

I yell out to her again, but I can't hear my own voice because of the sirens and my heartbeat pounding in my ears. People scream and run for their lives, but she just stands there.

The van goes into its roll and is about a quarter-way through the first rotation when it plows into her. Just before it hits her, she looks back at me and our eyes meet. People are screaming and crying, the van is on fire, the cops are yelling out orders, and the sirens howl and shriek like starved wolves. Two men holding submachine guns crawl out from beneath the wreckage. Their eyes are wild and filled with madness.

My headache is gone, and the sheer beauty of the chaos expanding all around me is spellbinding. I'm in the quiet center of a maelstrom. The van explodes and, almost magically, the camera materializes into my hands. The Haitians start shooting.

As do I.

* * *

"People don't know anything about psychics," I say.

Meredith thumbs through the photos, wrinkling her nose in disgust at a particularly garish picture of a mangled Haitian crushed to pulp beneath the weight of the van.

We're in a dimly lit bar in Miami. A television hung over the bar is showing baseball highlights. The place is more or less empty. The bartender is a blonde-haired goddess with low cut pants that tantalizingly reveal the topmost portion of her pink thong. She looks bored. If she is aware that I'm drooling over her, she's either unaffected by this or playing it cool. I suspect the former.

"My theory is," I continue, "there are probably a lot of people like me in this world, but they just don't know how to cope with their talents, and most of them end up in a loony bin. Probably think they're crazy. They don't know they're psychic because the media portrays extra sensory perception all wrong.

"It's not about moving objects with your mind and reading tarot cards. It's not that clear cut. It usually comes to you in drips and drabs at first, and then one day it just hits you with astonishing clarity. At least that's how it works with me anyway—"

"I like this one," Meredith says.

She's referring to a picture of my Cuban girl with a hunk of metal sticking through her chest. Her eyes are wide open, vapid, like a fish.

"Horrific incidents," I say, "circumstances of extreme trauma, bloodshed, mayhem, chaos, death—these are the things my mind seems drawn to. It anticipates situations in which catastrophic incidents will take place, reaches out and then plugs into a wave of collective cognizance—nasty little slices of the human experience. Fleeting glimpses into the time-stream continuum, fragment-by-fragment, piece-by-piece the images form like a puzzle in my mind's eye, only complete when I arrive at the scene of the carnage."

"Have you ever tried to stop it?" she asks, sipping at her gin and tonic.

"What do you mean?"

"Have you ever tried to prevent these things from happening?"

Pause.

"Well?" she presses.

"Yes."

"And?"

"Let's just say that there are a lot of people who believe in free will, just like there are a lot of kids who believe in Santa Claus. Sometimes it's nice to comfortably slip into a delusion, especially if many other people, who may pretend to share your views, are there to validate your false belief system. But it's all bullshit, and on some level, everybody knows it."

"Why do you do this anyway?" she says. "I know it's not for the money."

"You really want to know?"

"Try me."

"It's for the same reason people read your magazine," I say. "I like it. It is always violent, it is always bloody, and it's always breathtakingly beautiful. It's for the rush I get—the moment of anticipation mingled with the absolute knowledge of what will occur, yet it always shocks me, there is always something I did not foresee, some implication that my mind did not fully grasp. Human beings find a sublime beauty in death and in chaos and wanton destruction, though most people would never admit this to themselves at the risk of seeming like sadists or unmentionable bastards.

"But ask any of these people why they like action movies so much, and why the newspapers and media are only interested in stories of a violent and graphic nature. Why? Because people like it. They like to watch it. America is a country full of voyeuristic perverts. Don't believe me? Turn on the television and thumb through any of the fifty or so reality programs circulating the networks at any given time. Hell, turn to any news station. It's just a cataloguing of violent events occurring within a proximate position of your current location. And you can call me a bastard if you want, I know what I am, and I know what I'm not. It's all for the art, you see...all for the art. Everything else is secondary."

"You're a bastard," she says. "But then, what does that make me?"

"A bitch?" I offer.

"You're funny."

"I've always thought so."

"I'll give you five hundred for these," she says as she polishes off the rest of her drink.

"I guess so," I say.

"You know what I think?" she says.

"That I'm starting to look more attractive with each drink?"

"Some psychic you are. I think that one day you're gonna see something so bad it'll make you want to stop doing this."

"I've seen it all, sweetheart."

"You've never seen a ghost. My friend is a psychic—she says that real mediums can see ghosts."

"Does she happen to have a one-eight-hundred number?"

She gives me the finger and then smiles good-naturedly. She hands me the check and then gets up to leave.

"I'll see you when I see you," she says. And then she's gone.

* * *

I've been having these nasty little visions lately. I've been seeing them for almost a month now. That's a long time for me. I have a horrible headache, worse one I've had in years. Today is the day when the proverbial shit will hit the fan.

I walk down a few blocks, and a moron cab driver almost runs me over as I cross the street. I turn left down Fortieth and come upon it shortly. Nasty looking piece of work—real run down and decrepit. Only a matter of time before the city does away with it...

...A woman bound and gagged, long blonde hair, bright blue eyes. She's naked. The silver gleam of a steak knife. Wide, filthy room; scurrying rats, boarded up windows, grime and soot-covered walls and floors. Bodies hung upside down like cattle in a slaughterhouse. The woman's eyes widen in terror. A dark silhouetted figure...

"Jesus."

My headache borders upon mythic proportions.

I see the building looming above me.

Here we go.

I walk up the stairs and enter. There's a stench like blood and rat feces. I startle a couple of pigeons, and the sound of their wings flapping almost makes me jump out of my skin.

Thick layers of dust coat every inch of the foundation's crumbling brick and mortar structure. I find a stairwell and start ascending. It's on the top floor.

It's as cold in here as it is outside, but I'm sweating like a hick virgin alone with a drunk uncle. I reach the top floor and he's there.

He's standing with his back to me.

There are five bodies hanging upside down, gently swaying back and forth like piñatas. Only a few rays of light penetrate the darkness, leaking in through holes in the wooden planks that cover the windows. It's not exactly pitch black in here, and the lens I'm using will work in this poor lighting. The stench is unbearable. I wonder how long these bodies have been up here quietly moldering.

I take a step forward and he spins around. I can't make out his features from where I'm standing.

"Don't worry," I say. "I know who you are. I'm not here to interfere with your work, and I'm not gonna call the cops."

I can hear his heavy breathing. He takes a faltering step forward.

"I'm an artist," I say. "Like you. I'm an admirer of your work."

He stops moving forward and lowers the knife. I raise my camera.

"Do you mind?" I ask.

He stares at me for a long time. I stand there motionless, waiting for some sort of reply.

"How did you find this place?" he says. His voice is high-pitched, nasally. Though I can't see his face now, I've seen it before. He is a small, nervous-looking young man with thick glasses and acne scars covering his forehead. He is young, hasn't even graduated high school yet. If the police profilers only knew how off the mark they were.

"Look," I say. "I won't take any pictures of you. Keep in the shadows and I won't see your face. I just want to see the bodies. If you don't want me to do this, I'll leave right now, and no one will find anything out from me."

"Maybe you'd like to join them," he says.

"You can kill me, but I've got six people waiting for me downstairs. I don't come back in ten minutes, they'll come up here, take you down, and then they'll call the cops. They've got guns, and they've got pictures of you, so even if you get away, they'll send your name and information to the police. They'll be all over you. Like flies on shit."

"What kind of sick shit are you into?"

"Isn't that sort of a funny question, coming from you?" I ask.

He stands there and considers this for a moment, and then just like I knew he would, he takes a step back and disappears into the shadows. It's not because of my threats, which are as hollow and as empty as this man's soul.

It's because he's proud of his work.

He wants me to see it.

I enter the room. Something becomes evident rather quickly. This guy's not your typical killer. He's the worst one I've seen in years. And I've seen some bad ones.

This guy shows no preference for age, gender, or race. He hates everyone and everything. He has stripped all the bodies of clothing and sliced them from chest to groin. He has pulled their entrails out, eviscerated them, and then stuffed them into their orifices.

There are teeth marks on the inner thighs of his victims and around the genitalia. He has skinned some of them. And he did it all before they died. How do I know?

I look down to my right and see the girl bound and gagged, quivering in the corner. I know how she is going to die. I've seen every last detail of her death. The vision has haunted me for over a month. It is going to be terrible. He will act out every one of his perverse desires upon her innocent flesh, and when he's finished she will resemble a shapeless mass of blood and pulp, and he will keep her alive and suffering for as long he can. She looks up at me and pleads for help with her eyes. I aim the camera and snap off the last picture. I turn to the shape in the shadows.

"Thank you," I say.

"Anytime."

* * *

We're in an Italian Restaurant on Fifth Avenue. I'm working on a bowl of fettuccine Alfredo. Meredith is three-quarters of the way through a bottle of red wine.

"Do you use a digital camera?" she says.

"No, I'm not into the whole digital camera and camcorder thing. I think a photograph is the most powerful trapped light medium. I use a 35-millimeter that accepts interchangeable lenses and allows manual iris and shutter speed settings. It suits my purposes just fine."

"These are awful, by the way," she says.

I've arranged the pictures in sequential order. The first snaps are of the oldest victims, the ones whose bodies have become unrecognizable due to decay and mutilation.

Then we go to the fresher corpses and then finally—

"He just let you take the pictures?"

"Yeah."

"Nice guy."

"Not quite."

"Six hundred," she offers.

"Are you kidding?" I say. "The FBI would probably give me more than that for these. By the way, you're going to have to blur out Blondie's face. The cops are still looking for her."

"Hmm, I don't think we'll use that picture."

"Probably shouldn't."

She stares at it for a second and then looks up at me. Her face has visibly paled. That one has gotten to her.

"How do you live with yourself?" she asks me.

"How do you?" I say.

"I drink," she replied.

"I see."

"Seven hundred and fifty," she says with a tone of finality.

"Deal."

She downs the rest of her drink and gets up without saying goodbye.

* * *

A man named Reginald Collins has just sliced his wrists with a broken shard of mirror glass. He is a paranoid schizophrenic with complex delusions of grandeur.

"Daemon," he mutters, rocking back and forth with his hands around his knees.

He keeps saying that. Daemon. Over and over again, while his life seeps out of his severed arteries and soaks his blue hospital slippers.

Prior to slitting his wrists, he killed two nurses, three other patients, and an orderly. He locked the door to the ward and pushed a desk in front of it. So now, I'm stuck here with him. The other patients have all hidden away in their rooms or cells or whatever the fuck you call those padded domiciles and are screaming out inanities.

"Daemon."

Yeah.

This is not good. I don't know how I'm going to explain this to the cops and the doctors. He hasn't seen me yet, but I'm not too worried about that. The guy is weak and weakening by the second. I figure this may be my last chance for a photo opportunity. I get a good angle and take his picture.

His head snaps upward.

His eyes are sunken and red-rimmed. They widen for an instant, and then something bizarre happens.

They narrow and I see the recognition in them. It is undeniable.

This guy thinks he knows me.

He smiles.

The lights buzz and flicker and then they go out. They've cut the power. It's not completely dark in here, though. There is another light on somewhere—I can see it down the hall. The loonies are screaming their heads off.

"I know you," he whispers.

"How do you know me?"

His eyes go blank. His head pitches forward. He forces himself to look back up.

"There are Daemon in my room," he says.

"There's a daemon in your room?"

"Not a daemon," he says. "There is no such thing as a daemon. When they come, they come in legion."

I don't know what the appropriate response for that is, so I keep quiet.

"You'll see," he says.

I turn around and look for the source of the light. It's coming from a room down the hall. Collins's room.

He says something else, but I can't quite make it out. In a couple of minutes, he'll be dead.

I start walking toward the room without even realizing it. The light draws me in.

I enter. The first thing that hits me is the smell. Collins has smeared shit all over the walls. Of all the foul places I've visited in my lifetime, this is among the worst. This room is like a rat's warren—a haven for some festering pestilence. It is unbelievably cold in this room. Not imagined cold, but biting, stinging, you can see your breath type cold. Weird little symbols and crude stick figure drawings cover the walls and floors.

A dim light glows in the corner of the room. The light is colorless and swirling, and as I stare into its depths, I feel this queasiness in my stomach, as if I am standing on a high precipice and staring downward. A numbing fear creeps up from my bowels and holds me there.

I hear something. Whispering. Not one voice, or two voices, or ten, but hundreds of raspy whispers echoing in my ears, and this wave of nausea rises in my stomach and I can taste the bile.

Then everything goes black and I feel nothing.

* * *

"They took all your film?" she asks.

We're in a pub filled with drunken Irishmen singing along to a Garth Brooks song. The cigarette smoke is so thick I can barely make out Meredith's face.

"I'm going to be called back as a material witness," I say.

"You don't look too good," she says. "Was it that bad?"

I say nothing.

"If I didn't know better," she says, "I'd say you look like you've seen a gho…"

"I don't know what that thing was," I reply. "If it was what Collins said it was, then it kind of makes sense that it was there. Certain people and places draw certain things to them. It's a magnetic pull, a force of nature, and there really isn't much you can do about it. The world is not a nice place. It's a freak show, a fucking carnival. Good is an unquantifiable and abstract concept, and evil in all its multifarious gradations is the only reality."

"A little jaded, are we?"

"Conduct a survey," I say. "Ask a hundred people if they've ever heard of or seen anything that was evil. Then ask the same or a different group of people if they've ever seen someone or something that was good—that was entirely devoid of any negative or harmful qualities.

"Are you aware of the economic theory of Pareto optimality?"

"No," she says. "Please enlighten me."

"Basically, it is a situation in which you can't achieve success without in some way taking from or hurting someone else. Every so-called good thing has this quality, from the roses and vegetables whose presence ensures that other plants won't grow in the garden, to the air filled with innumerable microorganisms which perish every time you draw a breath.

"Evil—destructive energy—has a variety of forms and gradations, but it's everywhere, all pervasive, omnipotent, and either you can succumb to it or try to understand its savage beauty. The purpose of my work is to find a manifestation of this cosmic, primordial force in its purest, most unadulterated form and capture it—immortalize it in a picture."

"You have a rather idealized view of your work," she says.

"You're just another voyeur, and one day you're going to look back on your life with sadness and regret."

She pauses to guzzle her beer. She wipes the fizz off her face, and then looks up at me triumphantly.

"So," she says, "is it safe to say that you and I are through working together?"

The jukebox has gone on to play some U2 song. The Irishmen are going nuts. One of them gets on top of the bar. He's so drunk he can't even stand without swaying. In a few seconds, he's going to come crashing down on top of it, maybe break his arm, and his comrades seem to be eagerly anticipating this, nudging each other and pointing up at him.

"If I have one regret in my life," I say, "it has to do with that thing in the psychiatric ward—that hoary light infesting Reginald Collins's disheveled, shit-smeared cell."

"Yeah? And what's that?"

I peer at her through the veil of smoke, and I don't turn my head even as the crash of a heavy body and broken beer bottles resounds above the din of noise and music. Everyone in the bar roars with laughter.

"I wish I had taken its picture."

Apple

by Marc Paoletti

The airport was the perfect place to kill her. In the crush of people, she'd never see it coming.

Was he worried the country was at Threat Level Orange? Are you kidding? Fuck Homeland Security, you could throw all the money in the world at technology, but if you had losers running the chem-sniffers and X-ray machines and face recognition software, you were screwed, and at JFK, you couldn't throw a Filet-o-Fish three fucking feet without hitting a loser. These twelve-dollar-an-hour ghetto kids barely old enough to drive and white-trash remainders who couldn't hack the postal exam were given uniforms and were all that stood between passengers and total catastrophe.

John Doe knew this and watched the black woman walk toward him through the international terminal. She'd flown all the way from Ethiopia and was the mayor of some tiny province, like the title she held there meant anything real over here. The U.N. was having a summit, about what, who gave a shit? The U.N. liked to pander, got off on making countries they raped for raw materials feel like they had clout, go ahead, give us your opinion, we're interested, really, say all you have to say, because later you'd better lay back and relax and act like you enjoy what we're doing to you.

So he didn't know exactly where she was from or what she stood for, not that it mattered. All he knew was the faceless guy who'd left a suitcase full of cash behind the Bald Eagle strip joint on Court Street wanted her dead.

She wasn't close yet, but she was within a clear line of sight. She wore some glorified housedress with white tribal markings on it that hung to her ankles and swirled around her body as she walked. She moved with the carefree recklessness of someone who thought she had nothing to fear. He looked at her clinically as he looked at everyone and all things when he was on a job. People were simply that—man, woman, boy, girl. Things, they were just things, even if they posed a threat. The clinical distance allowed him to keep focus and react appropriately with ruthless precision, had allowed him to rack up the best win/loss ratio in the business.

Around the African woman a throng kept pace, ninety people, maybe more, all disembarked from the same transoceanic airliner, all heading for customs: A gaunt woman wearing a sheer sweater the color of menstrual blood; a man in an ash three-piece suit; a gaggle of tittering Asian girls with pigtails and fine clean bones, all wearing white blouses and blue skirts; a boy no taller than three feet with a smiley-face watch around one wrist and string tied around the other that led up to a green helium balloon that bobbed with every step. Plenty of others made up the human herd, all shapes and sizes and colors, a seething mass of bodies, nobody visible or in the same place for very long except the woman's bodyguards. Let's not forget them. Two men, marching on either side of her like movable walls of muscle, skin the color of pitch, wearing navy suits and mirrored sunglasses. Their jackets bulged at the right breast. Obviously, they'd been cleared to carry weapons.

He didn't give a rat's ass. They could carry fucking Stinger missiles for all he cared. The woman would still die. All he had to do was wait for the beep.

* * *

His father was a teacher, and starting at seven years old, he watched his father work. He was home schooled and traveled with his father to a different country every year. This year it was Bolivia. Last year it was Sudan.

It was 8 a.m. sharp, and at seven years old, the toes of his Adidas barely scraped the floor as he sat in the elbow desk. The classroom was crescent-shaped and antiseptic smelling with a stage placed up front and a white tiled floor that sloped toward a center drain the size of a 45 rpm record. Florescent lights hummed. The brown-faced men sitting around him that first day, dressed in khaki uniforms with small colored ribbons on the lapels and shiny black holsters at the hips, patted his head and called him *asesino pequeño*.

His father stood before the officers, wearing his blue powdered surgeon's gloves and a white lab coat over a charcoal business suit. Next to him on a metal table, angled up so the whole class could see, was a naked man, strapped down spread-eagle by his wrists and ankles. The man was very thin and his flesh was the color of sun-damaged leather. There was a patch of brown hair covering his chest between the nipples that mirrored a patch at his groin. Thick black-rubber dental stoppers had been wedged between his teeth and kept his mouth stretched open. The man whined softly, and the noise reminded John of when he'd come upon a dog once that had been struck by a car and lay in the middle of the street with its hindquarters crushed. The dog made the same noise that the man was making, and listening to it made John squirm. Didn't the man want to be here? Was the man afraid?

His father pressed a button on his jeweled watch—beep—and then said to the class, *Let us begin.* There was a rustle of paper as the officers opened notebooks and readied pens. John watched his father produce a long-necked plastic bottle from the pocket of his lab coat. The bottle was filled with a liquid that glimmered like diamonds in the greenish fluorescent light. When his father stepped toward the table with the bottle, the naked man began to scream through his fixed-open mouth. The sounds were panting and hollow, like gusts of wind through a rusted chimney flue, and then his father pushed the long neck of the bottle deep into the man's throat, causing him to gag violently, a hard grating sound that made John jump in his chair.

John expected the man to cough the bottle free from his throat like he coughed up aspirin sometimes when he didn't swallow right, but his father held the bottle fast, making the naked man gag harder and then swallow, swallow, swallow. John watched the level of glittering liquid in the bottle sink lower and lower in jerks and starts as the knot in his stomach drew tighter. His thoughts were a jumble. Did his father know he was hurting the man? *Daddy*, he began, voice tiny and overshadowed by the spectacle, *Daddy*, he tried again, a mouse, tiny in his seat, no use.

His father held the bottle in place, and when it was empty, he pulled it free, the tip trailing thick mucus, and then stepped back. *Please*, the naked man said, voice garbled by the dental stoppers. *Please.* John counted twenty-two pleases before bloody vomit exploded from between the man's lips. The man vomited so much and so hard that the stoppers sloshed free and his body and the table and the white-tiled floor around him became coated and dripping. The officers around John leaned forward, eyes feeding on the red.

All leaned forward, that is, except one, John noticed. He had dark thin eyebrows and yellow teeth, and he turned his head away from the man on the table and kept it turned away while the others watched and scribbled in their notebooks. John thought he should help the man on the table, but the adults weren't doing anything, so he sat absolutely still and tried to will his stomach ache to go away as the officer with thin black eyebrows stared at the wall.

Please, the naked man said, word bubbling crimson, and his father held up a second bottle filled with blue liquid. *Tell us what we want to know*, he told the man, *and this will stop the pain and heal the damage.* The man did. The man spat out a stream of words and bloody spittle and after he was done, his father pressed the button on his watch again—beep—and then slipped the bottle back into his lab coat and watched the man vomit black and purple this time and die.

That's how it's done quick, his father said, locking eyes with John, and then went on to explain to the class that the first bottle contained salt water and ground glass, and the second bottle had water and food coloring only, no magic elixir, just a ruse to offer the prisoner hope and produce the desired result. His father pressed a wall buzzer, and two uniformed men thick with muscle emerged from a side door and took the dead man away, then returned moments later with another naked man who they strapped struggling to the table.

His father demonstrated a dozen methods per day for weeks at a time, sometimes months. John came to realize that women withstood pain better than men, and children took the longest to die. From the age of seven, John watched every demonstration without fail, and learned.

* * *

John looked at his watch. Any second now, and he'd hear the beep.

The African woman marched along like she didn't have a care in the world, and although John resented her peace of mind, it was much better than the alternative. If she were the toy-poodle-type, the jittery look-over-her-shoulder-who-the-fuck-are-you? type, this would be much harder since her paranoia would protect her. But she wasn't jittery, she was joyful, and her joy would make killing her easy.

The woman took long flowing steps in her African-print housedress as her bodyguards tried to hustle her along. Their body language said it all…move your ass, c'mon, *move your ass*. But with respect, of course. They were the help and their heads would roll if she went down, but it wouldn't do if they pissed her off and lost their jobs that way either, so they each gripped her gently by the elbows and tried to guide her, to hurry her up, but it was like wrangling a creature made of pure light, unfettered by the concerns of the world. Her expression beamed, and her eyes darted this way and that, taking in the sights of this foreign airport, a shithole by any standards, but her manner told him that she was the type who appreciated the new simply for being new.

She took a few steps more when it seemed, suddenly, that she *did* have a care in the world. Her eyes fixed on the little boy with the green helium balloon. In the swirling crowd, she'd noticed that no adult stood by him long enough to be a parent. Her face sagged in concern, and then she stopped beside him, mid-stride. Motherfucker, she stopped, nearly screeched to a halt, stopped so fast she even faked out her bodyguards. They stopped a half-step later, *What the fuck is it now?!* dripping from their faces.

John sucked a breath. Didn't this bitch have enough cocksucking to do at the U.N. without saving lost kids? Her idiotic concern could throw off timing. Ruin everything. And there was precious little he could do about it. She was only fifty feet away now, well within striking distance, but if the plan were blown, it wouldn't matter one fucking bit.

The woman knelt and spoke to the little boy, rubbing his arm as she did. The balloon tethered to his wrist bobbed from side to side as people hurried by. *Where are your mommy and daddy?* the woman asked. From this distance, he could read her lips. *Where are they, honey? Are you lost?*

Fuck this bitch and her fucking country and her fucking useless visit to the U.N.

The little boy stared at her, mesmerized, and then looked around the airport, at the thick crowd of people, his eyes following one, then another, then another with a lost blank look on his face before he turned his head and looked directly at John.

Don't look at me! John tried to send the thought into the little boy's head with the force of a .38 slug. Don't push her attention my way! Don't you fucking do it!

The woman kept asking, *Where are your mommy and daddy, Where are your mommy and daddy*, not letting the kid go. John took a step forward, moved for the first time since the African woman made her entrance, and by doing so was already taking a risk. Motionless, you're nearly invisible to the human eye unless you're in direct line of sight. But the eye is calibrated to movement, and sure enough, no sooner had John taken that step than one of the bitch's bodyguards zeroed him. He was hoping the guy would be like the worse-than-useless X-ray screeners, but this dude had training and locked onto him like Bill Clinton peering into a teenage girl's bedroom window while the woman yammered away clueless, trying to save the fucking world one-kid-holding-a-balloon at a time.

Time was short, John could feel it. Too short.

The woman wasn't moving, and now he'd have to perform the strike himself, fuck, do it himself, up close and personal and fast. He was ready to do it, of course—he was a fucking professional, educated in torture and killing—but he hadn't wanted to resort to Plan B. He'd been hoping for success just as his father had hoped for success when he'd shown him the ropes by giving that naked man in Bolivia a ground-glass smoothie.

He fingered the hypodermic needle in the pocket of his long coat, kept walking. The syringe was filled with plant extracts—the mixture unique, impervious to antidote, purchased from a Nazi octogenarian in Argentina—that would scream through her blood and burst her heart like the meat balloon it was in record time and without trace. Pretend to bump into her, that was his plan, bump into her and jab-push the syringe into her bicep, not the best place to jab since the skin was tough there and the needle might break, but it was the most exposed part of her body and would have to do. In less than a minute she'd start seizing, and by then he'd be deep in the crowd and away.

He controlled his pace, not walking slow but not walking fast either, and popped the plastic stopper off the needle, releasing its point. Fifty feet, forty feet, thirty-five, and the woman still chattered at the lost-looking boy. Now John wanted her to keep talking, keep saving the fucking world so she'd stay distracted and he could do what needed to be done.

At thirty feet away, the bodyguard that zeroed him made it his business to act. He moved in front of the woman and little boy, stood fast. His face said it all: I don't know who the fuck you are or if you're really a threat, but if you are, you gotta get through me.

Motherfucker, John thought. Motherfucker.

He'd have to angle around the wall-man, maybe pretend like he was coughing and lunge and hope he'd strike the target. His likelihood for success had gone from ninety-eight percent at first to seventy percent when the black bitch decided to save the kid, down to what it was now, fifteen percent if he was lucky. But he couldn't abort the mission, he never could, once he committed to a job, he committed to it. He could not deviate from the plan, even if it meant capture. He could not. He could not.

John closed on the guard, sweeping around wide to get a last glimpse of the target before he angled his shoulder and bulled his way past the man, and that was when he saw the boy point. A chubby finger protruding from a chubby fist at the end of a chubby arm. Following the trajectory of the finger, John realized the boy was pointing at the men's bathroom. My daddy's in there, the finger proclaimed, don't worry about me, lady, my daddy's taking a piss and will be out directly, so don't worry, go to the U.N. and save the world, don't worry about me.

The woman's face relaxed and she smiled, but not all was beaming and bright. There was a slight furrow in her brow, one that clearly said she didn't approve of a father who left his little boy alone in a crowded airport no matter how close he might be, but she stood regardless, conscience eased, or maybe not wanting to create an international incident over some strange kid, who gave a shit? What mattered was that she stood and started to move again. The bodyguard that blocked John's way must have sensed her movement because he fell back and took his place by her side.

The African mayor became a free-flowing spirit again, a creature of light, bodyguards at either side with the little boy left behind in the swirling, seething crowd, maybe just an afterthought to her now, and in the next moment, in the very next moment, in the nick of time just like in the movies...John heard the beep.

* * *

John knew memories had impact. He was very fucking aware. Growing up, the first time he touched a woman—really touched a woman and elicited a reaction—was when he was twelve years old and his father invited him to kill one with a power drill. He could not say no. He always did what his father asked, the command burrowing into his brain, compelling him to act, compelling him, compelling him. After witnessing so many of his father's demonstrations, after seeing his father's power over others, he was driven to perform such an act when ordered. He could not say no. He could not. His father had been teaching in Syria, and the woman had been accused of talking to a man other than her husband in public, so her honor-bound siblings—older sister and two brothers—brought her

49

to his father, who had her stripped naked, hogtied, and placed in a ceramic tub with claw feet. His father plugged the drain and filled the tub two inches deep with battery acid before asking John to join in. John thought about that woman whenever he talked to or saw any other woman since: her red, stretched-open mouth as the acid burned her naked flesh, her wide-eyed disbelief that a child was about to murder her, the whir-bite-whir as he pushed the drill into her ear. He thought about her as he thought sometimes about the officer in Bolivia with the thin dark eyebrows and yellowed teeth who wouldn't dare look, wouldn't dare look.

But as deep as the memory of the Syrian woman ran, it didn't run nearly as deep as the effect Susan used to have on him. Susan. He'd met Susan in Chicago, in Wicker Park, on one of those cold crisp days that makes your cheeks just as cold and just as crisp, but somehow, even though your cheeks are that cold they warm right up when someone gently lays their hands on them. It was one of those cold crisp days, years after his father had died peacefully of a stroke in his sleep, and John had moved on from what he was taught to a worklife in construction. Framing and drywall and welding, he was good at his job, good with his hands because of what he'd been taught, but what had been systematically forced into his psyche, the precise application of torture and assassination and horror, had slipped under and away, like a shark into dark water, and incredibly never once broke the surface until the Japanese man came.

But before the Japanese man there was Wicker Park, and John was drywalling a two-story walk-up, and Susan was the new assistant to the contractor who'd come to check the crew's progress. They weren't talking ten minutes before he leaned forward and kissed her, laying his cold hands on her cold crisp cheeks, making both hands and cheeks warm and inviting and soft because it was precisely that kind of day. Susan had dark eyes and chestnut hair and held such pure beauty that his memories of the Syrian woman were pushed away almost immediately, and forever after, too.

Six months later, he and Susan were married on a grassy hill overlooking a lake. Six years after that, a year ago today, John was visited by a slight Japanese man, no taller than a step-stool, who came to his worksite and told him to lay down his tool belt. Do I know you, John asked, and the Japanese man who had cruel, thin eyes and soft hands and dragged his N's the slightest bit said *no, John, you don't know me, but I knew your father.* John told the Japanese man to get the hell away, that he had a good life now filled with love and glory and light, but the Japanese man said, *you work for me now, John, you are the apple that drops close to the shrub, that is the expression, yes? You are the apple and will do what I say*, and John could not say no when ordered like that, he could not, he could not, he could not. The Japanese man said, *you work for me now, John, you work for me right now, and I want you to start with your wife right now, but I want you to spare your son.*

* * *

John heard the beep, but only because he was listening hard, and even then, it was almost lost among the voices and loudspeakers and rolling luggage clatter of the disembarked herd. It was a tinny sound, nowhere as richly luxurious as the beep of this father's watch, but it was the beep from a watch just the same. The black woman took another step, and then John saw her slap the back of her knee like a scorpion had stung her. She whirled to see the source, but the crowd seethed around her, bucking and flowing, making everyone and no one a suspect—the exact reason he liked to hit targets in the airport. The crush of people rushing to this gate or that beat the hell out of a fifth-floor depository window. John looked on with satisfaction as the bodyguards scanned the crowd with her, knowing in their guts that something terrible had happened.

The woman was still rubbing the back of her knee when her skin, which was blacker than black, the black of tar, the black of space without stars but somehow not empty in that blackness but poignant and full, paled, turning the color of campfire ash. She turned ash-white, the color of a true spirit as her spirit drained away, and then she collapsed hard, face-first onto the tile, her mouth constricting like a hooked fish, issuing noiseless yelp-yelps.

John looked at the convulsing African woman and saw the hogtied Syrian woman there instead and felt his stomach clench like he was seven years old again, as it always did when he pulled off a job he was ordered to perform, and he couldn't banish the image of the African woman or the Syrian woman with memories of Susan because the last time he'd seen Susan, he'd decapitated her with an ax.

As the bodyguards rushed to the collapsed African woman's side, John walked backward slowly, smoothly, fading into the crowd in case the bodyguard who'd spotted him before got desperate for a suspect, or wise. He made his way to the door of the men's bathroom and waited until the little boy who'd almost been saved rushed up, green balloon bobbing. John leaned over and pressed a button on his smiley-face watch—beep—and said, *That's a good boy, son, nice and quick and precise, the part where you pointed here, toward the men's bathroom, was very very good, that's how it's done. That's how it's done.* The boy dutifully handed over the hypodermic needle, plunger depressed like John had made him practice a hundred times over, jab-push, jab-push into the back of the knee; his son was a smart boy for one so young and caught on fast.

John slipped the used hypodermic into his coat pocket where it lay with his own. *That's a good boy*, John said again, *and now it's time to go.* He took his son by the hand and led him away from the crowd gathering around the dead African woman and her wailing bodyguards. John tried to tell his son more about what he'd done right and what he'd done wrong, but his son would not look at him, would not look. Instead, the boy stared at the fallen woman, still noble in death even though her spirit was gone, stared at her like the young officer with the dark thin eyebrows who couldn't bear looking at all the red. John hoped that someday he'd have the courage to look away himself, someday, someday, before his son was pulled in too deep, before his son was given an order he was old enough to understand and could not disobey, someday he would have the strength not to do as ordered, not today, but someday soon, he hoped, someday soon.

Next Stop, Babylon

by John Mantooth

She watched as the bus crested the hill and cut a silver blur across the burnt landscape. Her name was Tamara, and she had survived when the rest of her family had passed into eternity or oblivion, whichever came after death. Her husband, Terrance, had died in the fields, toiling to bring forth fuel from the red earth. Her mother and father had died in one of the subway attacks—a bomb or a terrorist or a derailing—she could no longer remember which. Her brother disappeared with the wind, and her sister died last winter giving birth.

Tamara shuddered as the bus drew closer. When Terrance had been alive, they'd had a car, and he had taken the bus, but she had sold the car months ago for next to nothing. Now she saved her money for bus fare, and waited in the South Alabama heat for a bus without air conditioning. But that wasn't all. She could tolerate the heat. What she hated, what she dreaded, was the bus itself. The driver. He frightened her most of all.

Once Tamara had asked her seatmate if she thought the bus driver was strange.

"Strange?" the woman, whose name Tamara did not know, said. "No. Just broken down. All of ours talk gibberish. I've heard up in New York that those things are spit-shined and polished every day. I've heard those robots never say anything that isn't interesting." The woman had nodded her head vigorously before falling silent again.

But Tamara knew the difference between gibberish and something, well, something more sinister.

She took a deep breath as the bus slowed and the air brakes hissed and locked. The door creaked open wide, a sideways leer, inviting her in. The robot's head swiveled on his neck and he gazed at her through slits that weren't eyes as much as razor blades, cutting her skin, peeling her open like a husk of corn, laying her wide with sharp strokes and exposing her naked center. She wanted to turn and run back to her house, but that meant certain death. The sweepers would come and take her temperature and find her healthy but useless, vigorous but lazy, unworthy of breathing the oxygen, consuming the fuel, or riding the bus.

So she kept her eyes down and stepped onto the bus. She did not look as she placed the coins in his slotted hand. As the robot shut his hand over the money, sucking it down into his belly, a silver fingertip grazed her hand and she felt sick inside. "Welcome," the bus driver said, "to the last stop."

Tamara hurried past, sliding into the first available seat. She closed her eyes and counted slowly, until she convinced herself that it was only her imagination, and that if Terrance were alive, she wouldn't even be worried.

"The damn government will be by today," a voice next to her croaked. Tamara opened her eyes and saw she was seated next to Missy Faye. "Be by today to take my check and slit my neck. The damn government will be by today to feel my cooter and bug my computer."

Tamara looked to see if any other seats were available, but the bus driver announced that they should fasten their belts. "Next stop, nowhere."

She glanced around the bus to see if anyone else noticed the ominous words. The man across the aisle from her slumbered, a shiny coat of drool sparkling on his chin. In a seat in front of her sat a woman and her baby. The baby, mercifully, slept. Tamara couldn't bear to think of babies awake. It always made her feel better when she saw one sleeping rather than languishing in this world. The mother was silent, her head lolling from side to side in the rhythm of the road, though the bus had not yet started to move.

No one but me, Tamara thought. It is only my fear.

"...break my mind and realign my spine. The government, lawsy mercy. The government."

Tamara closed her eyes. This was the easy part. The hard part came later.

She slipped in and out of sleep for miles, never missing an ominous proclamation from the bus driver: "Today is fair and dark. Tonight there will be a slim chance of moon and the rain will be full. Franklin Thomas! This is your stop. On this date in history the great state of Alabama slipped between the cracks. The low tide is pulling us out to sea, and the undertow is making us forget." She opened her eyes and watched the bus driver's steel-trap mouth clanging out prophecy and stop times, trivia and destinies.

Missy Faye slept beside her, her mouth slackening out into a formless bag, and her words turned to breathing, her eyes rolled back like hard, soulless marbles.

"Next stop, Babylon!" the bus driver said.

The bus groaned to a stop, red dust exploding into the air. The driver jerked the door open. "Wendell Patrick this is your stop," came the voice. He never got this part wrong. Of course, this was the essential part, Tamara thought. So many people sleeping or drugged. They would miss their stop without the bus driver telling them. Then the sweepers would come in with their questions and their guns.

She wished the government had just kept the real bus drivers. She would never understand why they had bothered to send all the robots down here to southern Alabama. Tamara remembered Mr. Ayers, the fat old man that had driven the bus before they sent the robots on their silver, terrorist-proof buses. He had whistled while he drove, and nodded politely at her each morning. Told her to have a nice evening each afternoon.

But this bus driver—with his vibrato voice and soulless eyes—this bus driver had never been right. He had never even been like the other robots she knew, which had always left her feeling cold and lonely no matter how many other people were around.

She looked at him, using the big rearview mirror in the front of the bus. He was looking back, all jagged metal teeth, smiling at her.

The bus lurched. "Arlie Sherman!" he shrieked. "This is your stop."

Robots don't smile. This thought and she closed her eyes again. Better not to think.

"Missy Faye! This is your stop." Missy Faye jerked awake and continued babbling as if she had never stopped. "The government gave us silver buses with bots so the terrorists can't shoot us full of hots. The government took my guns away, sent me a robot that can't think like my pistol on a bad day. Senators, congressmen, the Governor, the President, robots all rot." She climbed off the bus and went along her way on Main Street, which was mainly deserted these days, except for the women like Missy Faye who picked up trash and swept the gutters free of rats.

Tamara watched her amble down the sidewalk. "She should be retired somewhere," Tamara muttered.

The man beside her was awake now. He grunted his assent. "We should have all retired by now."

"Edward Smile! This is where you get off."

One by one they left her, until she was alone with the driver. Tamara sunk down in her seat. She hoped he wouldn't look at her.

"Next stop, Oblivion!"

Oblivion. What did that mean?

She straightened up to see the bus driver, and he saw her right back through the rearview mirror. She stifled a gasp. I'll make it today just like the others, she told herself. Except each day lately she's noticed the bus driver acting more and more strangely.

"A few more miles," she said beneath her breath. Her stop would come soon, and he would thrust open the silver doors and shout her name. She had made it so many other days. Why not today?

Her nails dug into the vinyl seat.

"On your right, just out your window," the bus driver said pleasantly, "You can see the fields of death. Men toil day and night only to die! We are all driving into oblivion." Then his head swiveled until she could see those razor blade eyes. Tamara pushed back in her seat, trying to escape his line of vision. Those slits, the way they narrowed on her—she looked away.

The bus sped up.

"What are you?" she said, her eyes still shut tightly.

"There are ghosts in the machine and ghosts in the government and ghosts online," the driver said. "Ghosts on the moon, ghosts under the sea, ghosts everywhere for you and me." She could have sworn that he cackled.

Her stop was on the horizon. Beyond that she knew there was a vast wasteland where the sweepers took the bodies of the useless people.

"My stop," she said.

She forced herself to look at him. The steel-trap mouth was grinning at her. "Your stop is coming right up, Tamara Teasdale." The bus sped up.

"Look at the road!" she said.

As in answer, the head swiveled a little farther around. He seemed to study her, and all she wanted to do was run away from the iron grin and the sharp, inhuman eyes.

"The road to hell is paved with good intentions," he said, his mouth moving in a garish parody of human speech.

The bus hurtled through the brown landscape very fast now. Her stop flashed by in a colorless blur. She got out of her seat and tried to run to the back of the bus for the emergency exit. Before she reached it, she heard it click shut. He had locked it. She couldn't even choose suicide, and somehow this was the worst. She would have to try to take the bus over. She turned back and saw the bus driver was no longer driving the bus. He stood in the aisle, his stilt legs planted like metal pegs, his narrow humps of shoulders squared in her direction, his mechanical mouth working back and forth from snarl to smile, from robot to bus driver to something more.

"Oblivion!"

She closed her eyes, trying to find eternity before oblivion found her.

The Garbage Collectors

by Ron McGillvray

The bus pulled up to my stop and I got off and began my short walk home. The same neighbors who'd ignored me this morning were all smiles and waves as I passed by. I waved back and smiled, but didn't stop to chat. I'd commented to my wife a few days earlier about how strange our neighbors seemed, but she told me it was all in my imagination. I crossed the street and couldn't help but look at the house where the early morning incident had occurred. In front of the house a van sat, crammed with boxes and small tables. More furniture adorned its roof. It looked like they were moving. I wondered if it had anything to do with what had happened this morning? Nah, they must have been planning the move beforehand. I was still thinking about the incident when I walked in my front door.

"Stephen, can you come in here please," my wife, Sarah called from the kitchen.

What now?

"Patrick's upstairs crying and won't come out of his room." She had a worried look on her face and she was fidgeting with some framed pictures on the mantle. Never a good sign.

"What's the matter? Is he sick?"

"No, something happened at school. I think some kids picked on him, but I can't get the whole story out of him."

"Was he hurt?"

"No, I don't think it was anything physical. Can you try talking to him?" She looked more than desperate.

"Sure. I'll go up there right now. It'll be fine," I tried to assure her.

I placed my briefcase against the wall and walked toward the stairs. As I passed my wife I stopped for a second to give her a kiss. I got the smile I was looking for and headed up the stairs.

I heard sobbing from the other side of Patrick's door. I knocked a few times before I finally let myself in. Patrick lay on his bed, his head facing the wall. He looked up briefly and I could see he'd been crying for a while. His eyes were puffy and red, and he looked like he'd been through the wringer.

"What a terrible day I had at work," I said, trying to commiserate with my son. "Looks like you had a bad one too. Want to come downstairs with me and have a beer so we can talk about it?"

That got a bit of a grin, but the sobbing started again. Without warning, Patrick jumped off his bed, ran over to me, and wrapped his little arms around my legs.

"Whoa there little buddy, what's the matter?"

"You wouldn't let anyone take me away would you, Daddy?"

"What are you talking about? Of course not. Who'd help me with the chores?" I tried to make a joke of it, but what he'd said hit me like a jackhammer.

"Some of the kids at school told me the garbage collectors were going to come and get me and there was nothing you could do about it," Patrick managed between sniffles.

"Garbage collectors? What are you talking about? Do you look like garbage?" I said, putting on my *Daddy knows best* smile.

"These are a different kind of garbage collectors."

"Slow down, son. Take it easy and take a big breath." I waited for him to calm down. "Okay, now tell me the whole story from the beginning."

Patrick seemed hesitant at first but then opened up, letting it all come flowing out. "Kids at school told me that on the night before garbage day the garbage collectors come out and hunt through people's garbage. They look for a sign that'll tell them which kid will be next to go to the Dump." Patrick took a deep breath.

"Oh really? And what happens to these kids who end up at the Dump?"

"They're eaten by the garbage collectors. It's what keeps them alive."

"I see. Don't you think the parents might have something to say about it?"

"The parents are the ones who give the kids to the garbage collectors," he cried, tears streaming down his face. "If the garbage collectors come, can you give them Kim instead of me? I promise I'll be good and do everything you guys say."

I felt a knot starting in my throat and a rage welling up inside. I wanted to go find these kids and give them something to really be afraid of, but I'd worked at keeping my temper under control and I wasn't going to blow all that hard work now.

"Don't worry, I have no plans to let either you or Kim end up at the Dump."

"Promise?" Patrick said, looking at me with pleading eyes.

"Yes I promise," I answered. "So are these kids sent away because they were bad?"

"No, the families do it to save their other boy or girl."

"What if the family only has one child?" I asked not so innocently, hoping to poke holes in the story.

"No one here does. Everyone in town has two kids. Haven't you noticed?" He stopped for a moment to catch his breath. "Danny told me, they only let you live here if you come with two."

What an imagination kids have these days, I mused. Then I asked, "Why wouldn't the parents just pack up and leave if they found all this out?"

"We can't leave. There's no way out of here," Patrick answered with all the conviction he could muster.

"Well we came here from somewhere, didn't we?"

"Yes."

"So if we came here from somewhere, we can always go back there, right?"

"I suppose," he said.

"There you have it."

"But they said people have tried to leave before and always ended up coming back."

"That's just nonsense. In fact I just saw the people about eight houses down all packed and ready to move. Where do you think they're going?"

"That's the Donnelleys. They have to give their son up tonight."

"The other kids tell you that?"

"Yes," Patrick answered.

"Well if these kids know so much, did they tell you what these garbage collectors look like?"

"They're like shadows. They're all black and hate the light. They have big glowing eyes," he said, tears once again welling up in his eyes.

I felt a cold sweat form on my back as I recalled the strange dream I'd had last night. I'd been looking out one of the bedroom windows when I'd noticed what I thought was just a shadow across the road. Hadn't they been going through the garbage?

In my dream I remembered a shadowy figure tearing through the neighbor's trash. Then out of the corner of my eye, I'd noticed another black figure glide across the street to join it. I watched them as they inspected the neighbor's garbage unaware someone was watching them. Suddenly, one of them turned to face me and I tripped over myself, landing on my ass.

I slowly picked myself up and looked back out the window toward where the dark figures had been, but they were gone. As I turned away, a movement caught my eye—a dark figure sat crouched on my garage roof, staring right at me.

I woke up drenched in sweat and immediately went to check on the kids.

I thought about the dream for a moment until an idea popped into my head. "Go get your shoes and your sister, we're going for a drive. I'll get Mom."

"Where are we going?" Patrick asked, between sniffles.

"I am going to prove to you, we can drive out of this town any time we want," I answered, trying to sound sure of myself.

A sudden look of relief washed over my son's face as he hurried into his closet to grab his shoes, calling out for Kim at the same time.

"What's going on?" Sarah said. "How's Patrick?"

"I think he'll be all right," I told her. "Some kids told him a story and it had him spooked. So we're going to go for a ride in the car to make him feel better."

Sarah looked at me strangely but grabbed her purse as Kim came marching down the stairs with Patrick right behind her.

"Okay, are we ready?" I asked.

"Where are we going?" Kim said.

"We're going out for dinner to a restaurant this evening."

"Which restaurant?"

"The first restaurant we come to outside the city limits. I'm going to prove something to your brother."

"Let me guess. He told you we can't get out of here, right?"

Her comment stopped me cold and I looked at her in surprise.

"Why do you say that?" I asked.

"I heard the same story today at school. They told me I'd never be able to leave the city and there was some evil force at work here."

"Who told you that? Did you overhear Patrick and I talking?"

"No I didn't hear you guys talking. Some losers in my class told me. There's a group of them who think they know it all, but they're nothing but brainless hicks."

"Well I have to agree with your description of the locals so far," I laughed.

"Stephen!" Sarah cautioned me.

"It's true, honey. The neighbors haven't exactly been welcoming."

"Maybe we should give them the benefit of the doubt," she suggested.

"Sure, whatever. I'm just venting."

"Okay enough of this," Sarah said. "Let's get going. I can't remember the last time your father offered to take us out, so we'd better get started before he changes his mind."

Everyone laughed as we headed out the door and piled into the car. I put the key into the ignition and started it up. "So far so good," I said with a big grin.

"Just drive," the three of them said in unison.

I backed the car out of the driveway and followed the tree-lined street to the first stop sign and turned right. I followed a winding road until we came to a major intersection. Sarah spotted the sign to the highway first and pointed it out. I made a quick couple of lane changes until finally we were on the highway.

"Here we are then. Well on our way and no problems so far," I said, more to Patrick than anyone else. "So tell me, Kim. What else did you hear about this place?" I asked as I pulled into the far right lane of the highway and settled in for the ride.

"It's just a bunch of nonsense," she said.

"Humor me, will you please?"

"Fine," she answered, exasperated. "Alison Crimble said there are things living in or around the garbage dump. I can't remember which."

"Go on," I prodded.

"Anyway, supposedly the dump is on some old forgotten burial site. The things buried there feed off the life force of children," she said as she rolled her eyes.

"And do you believe the story?" I asked.

"Of course not, duh."

"See, Patrick? Your sister doesn't believe the story."

Patrick didn't say a word but continued to stare out the window at the passing trees. The car was silent as we continued to drive down the highway. The sun still bright in the sky even though it was closing in on seven o'clock. The sound of the wheels on the road gave off a hypnotic hum. I looked over at Sarah and she seemed to be daydreaming. I took a peek in the rearview mirror and saw Kim sitting with her usual scowl. Patrick, though, seemed to be studying the outside landscape for something I couldn't fathom. Seeing this little trip wasn't helping my son the way I'd planned, I decided to strike the conversation back up.

"So tell me, Kim. How do these things manage to get the children they need?"

"Well, supposedly they go through the garbage at night and look for personal items. That's how they decide who they're going to pick."

"Going to pick?" I asked.

"Yeah, when they find the item they're looking for they leave a mark or something, letting the family know they've been chosen to give up one of their children."

"I see," I said with a smirk, looking at Sarah who didn't seem to find any of this amusing. "What if the family only has one child?"

"Actually, that's the only thing that spooked me. It seems everyone at school has either a brother or a sister. There doesn't seem to be any families with just one kid around here."

Once again the car went silent.

"Shouldn't we have reached an exit ramp by now?" Sarah said, breaking the silence.

"Not sure," I answered. "I got caught up in the story and wasn't keeping an eye out."

"Well it's starting to get late, and the kids are probably hungry. Let's find a place, okay?"

"Sure, no problem. Once we cross the city limit there's a restaurant on the other side of the highway. I remember seeing it when we first drove down."

"Who would you pick?" Patrick asked out of the blue.

"What?" Sarah and I replied at the same time.

"Who would you pick? You know, if they came to our house and left their mark."

"It's just a story," I said, beginning to feel exasperated.

"But just for fun, if you had to choose, which one of us would you send away?"

"The one who asked too many stupid questions."

"Stephen," Sarah scolded. "Daddy didn't mean that, he was just trying to be funny."

"Well I'm serious," Patrick said. "I want to know. Which of us would you pick?"

"Yeah, Dad. Which of us would you send to the monsters?" Kim piped in.

"Now they're monsters, eh? I thought they were garbage collectors."

"Funny dad," Kim said without a smile.

"Look you two, it's just a story. But for the sake of an argument, if it was true, I would refuse to give either of you up."

"Supposedly you don't have a choice," Patrick said. "One of the kids in my class told me a family tried that once and barricaded themselves in their house."

"And what happened?" I asked, keeping an eye on the road.

"The neighbors made the choice. They broke down the door and took one of the kids to the dump themselves."

"Is that what you heard, Kim?"

"Yeah, Dad," she said. "It's just a stupid story, right?"

"Of course, Pumpkin."

"You know something, Stephen?" Sarah said. "I know we've only been here around a week, but now that I think about it, everyone I've met so far has two kids."

"Not you, too."

"Don't you find it strange?"

"You're not helping the matter here, Hon. Have you seen any signs for an exit yet?"

"No I haven't," she said. "And it's getting late. The sun's already starting to set, and we should have hit the city limits a long time ago."

"Maybe we missed it when we were all talking," I suggested, trying to sound optimistic.

"Patrick," Sarah asked suddenly. "What happens to the child who's left behind?"

"Sarah." It was my turn to be indignant.

"It's okay Dad," Patrick said. "The kid that's left is given some sort of special powers."

"And what is this special power?" I asked, no longer hiding the fact that I was getting tired of all this.

"They wouldn't tell me," Patrick said.

"What about you Kim?"

"Same thing. They wouldn't tell me, but they said it's worth it and the family goes away to a wonderful place."

"A wonderful place, eh?" I muttered, tapping the steering wheel in agitation.

"Yeah, to make room for a new family," Kim said. "That's why you never see a family with only one kid."

"Jesus, Stephen. Step on the gas and get us out of here. This whole thing is starting to freak me out," Sarah pleaded.

I accelerated and took another look into the rearview mirror only to see the heartbreaking sight of my son crying quietly in the backseat. Rage began to flow through me again like a freight train. I couldn't recall feeling like this for some time. I'd battled with my anger management problems before and beaten it, so what the hell was wrong with me now? And where was the damn restaurant?

The sun was below the tree line, and I was sure we should be well out of the city limits by now, but the highway kept going on and on. There weren't even any bends in the road anymore, just straight highway as far as the eye could see. Once again the car fell silent and I wondered what everyone else was thinking. The fact I couldn't reassure them everything was going to be okay drove me crazy, but not half as much as the thought that all this could be true.

And the road went on.

We'd been driving for hours and nothing in the scenery had changed. There were no longer any other cars on the road either. Sarah had stopped badgering me to turn around and sat in her seat, mute, gazing out the window at seemingly the same trees we'd been passing for hours. Both Patrick and Kim were asleep in the backseat. What the hell was going on?

I felt like I was going to be sick, but there was no way I'd go see that therapist again. The thought of it got me even more upset.

"Sarah, are you still awake?" I asked, needing the comfort of another voice.

"Yes," she answered.

"Do you want me to turn around?"

"I want you to tell me what's happening," she said with tears in her eyes. She looked into the backseat at the loves of her life.

"I have no answers," I said. "I'm sorry."

"This can't be happening. This is all just some mistake, right?"

"I just don't know any more," I replied.

"Then let's just go back. We're not getting anywhere. Besides, once we get home we can call someone outside the city and get help."

"And what are we going to say?" I asked, sounding a bit more sarcastic than I'd meant.

"Let's just go home," she said.

63

I slowed the car down and looked at the dashboard clock. It was past eleven o'clock. My God, we'd been driving for almost five hours. This was madness. I decided we must have missed the exit. I did a quick shoulder check and turned the car around, heading back into town. My eyes felt heavy and I wondered if I'd be able to make it all the way without falling asleep at the wheel. As I drove along the dark, deserted highway I tried to find flaws in the stories the kids had told, but with what we'd experienced so far, I couldn't. I thought about my office co-workers and how they'd all seemed like good, decent people. I couldn't see any of them buying into this crap. I pictured each individual I'd met at the office and recalled how they'd all spoken with love when it came to their children.

The memory hit me like a tidal wave. Everyone I'd spoken with had shown me pictures of their two kids.

Two kids.

Just as my eyes started to close from exhaustion, I spotted lights ahead. I glanced at the dashboard clock again and saw we'd only been driving for about ten minutes in this direction. How come we hadn't noticed the lights earlier? I focused on the lights as we drove toward them.

I looked over at Sarah, but she was asleep. I decided to wait until we reached the restaurant before I woke them. I couldn't believe I'd started to buy into the kids' stories. I let out a little chuckle. I drove into the lit area and my smile turned to a grimace of horror when I recognized where we were. We hadn't found the exit at all. We were back in the town we'd been trying to escape. I looked at the dashboard clock and calculated the drive which took almost five hours one way took only fifteen minutes on the way back. I wanted to scream in frustration, but held it in for the sake of my family. Looking over at Sarah beside me and my two precious, sleeping children, I felt lost.

I exited the highway and found myself on the main street. I followed it through town, passing businesses and restaurants. As I drove along, the street became busier with other cars and people. Everything looked and seemed so normal. Just your average citizens going about their usual business. What was I expecting, I wondered? Should they all be wearing Druid costumes or something more befitting of a city that gave up their own?

I saw the sign I'd been looking for and turned left. I followed the road until it turned to dirt and continued on. I had a purpose now, because it just occurred to me, today was garbage day.

I followed the dirt road which became more and more bumpy. The road lead into a dense forest, and the trees were close to the road and seemed to grab out at the car as it passed by. Visibility became worse. Maybe this wasn't such a great idea. I looked around at my family, but they were still asleep so I kept driving.

Finally, I saw a clearing ahead. I slowed down and took another look at the dashboard clock. It was a few minutes before midnight. There was a bend in the road ahead so I slowed down. In the glimmer of the headlights I saw the sign.

Town Dump.

I stopped the car to stare at it for a moment, then continued around the bend. There it was.

A fiery glow from behind one of the mounds of trash lit up the area around it. I saw movement ahead and squinted my eyes in an attempt to see better. In the soft light of the dump's eerie glow, I spotted the woman who lived in the house which had had the packed van. I didn't think she'd noticed me, so I turned the lights off and drove a bit closer. She wasn't alone. Her husband was there as well. They were both looking at something on the other side of the fence.

"Oh my God," I whispered in horror, following their gaze.

Inside the dump's compound, a young boy around the same age as Patrick stared through the fence. The boy faced the two of them, rattling the gates, trying desperately to get out.

Their child?

Through the car window, I could hear the boy crying and pleading with the couple to let him out. The woman cried as well, but the man held her firm. I watched the boy beg for his parent's help while turning his head around constantly as if to see if something was coming up behind him.

I wasn't sure what to do. Instinctively, I wanted to plow my car through the gate and rescue the boy. If I ran down the parents, so much the better. But I had my own family to think of. This whole thing was insane.

At that moment the fiery glow brightened, lighting almost the entire area. I couldn't take my eyes off the pleading boy who now shook the fence even harder. The boy was in a frenzy. He tried to climb the fence, but something was preventing him from doing so. Something else caught my eye. From behind the glowing mounds of garbage, dark figures began to emerge.

I watched them in horror, but dragged my eyes away to look back at the boy. The young boy tried desperately to dig under the fence with his fingers, always looking behind him.

To my shock I noticed the parents walking away, turning their backs on their own flesh and blood. I felt nauseated and my head began to spin. There were too many emotions going through me at once, and I felt as if I were going to go mad.

The black figures closed in on the boy. He was back on his feet shaking the gate with both his little hands and calling out for his mother. A switch seemed to go off in my head and before I knew what I was doing, I had the headlights back on and the car speeding toward the gate. The boy started to run, the black ghouls closing in on him. Why hadn't I acted sooner? I continued to drive faster at a good ramming speed.

As the gate approached, my car's headlights lit the area ahead of me. I saw the terrified boy running as fast as his little legs could carry him over and around the garbage heaps, trying desperately to get away. The boy stumbled, and before he could scramble back to his feet, the black forms were on him. Unable to watch it any longer, I swung the car around, but it was too late. The image of the little boy was forever burned into my memory. I felt tears well up and I choked down the scream building up within me. Once again I was overcome with a myriad of emotions. But one emotion stormed to the top of the heap.

Rage.

I turned the car around and drove away trying desperately to work out a plan to protect my family. I spotted the parents of the little boy walking glumly along the side of the road. They didn't even turn when the headlights illuminated them. Just as well, I thought, as I gave the car a little gas and slammed into them. I didn't want to see their faces when I killed them anyway. I hated them for not warning me about the dump.

I hated them all.

I turned on the windshield wipers and gave a few quick bursts of wiper fluid to clean off the splattered blood now covering the glass.

I looked down at the dashboard clock. It was well after midnight.

"What's going on?" Sarah asked, startling me.

"Sorry Hon. Did I wake you?"

"No, I think I was having a nightmare. Where are we?" she said, still half asleep.

"While you were dozing, lazybones, I found our mysterious exit," I lied. "We must have passed it while we were telling our ghost stories. Everything's fine," I tried desperately to gain control of the rage I'd let loose.

"Why do you have the windshield wipers on?" she said. "Did it rain?"

"No, we hit an animal. It ran out from the woods, and I didn't see it in time."

"Are we almost home?" she said as if she hadn't heard my last statement.

"Yep. I just wanted to go check out the dump first," I answered.

"The dump?" she repeated, still half asleep.

"Yeah, it's just a dump. Nothing unusual there. I just had to see for myself."

"And you found the city limit and the exit we were looking for?"

"Yes and we can come and go from the city anytime we want. Just like I said."

That was all the reassuring she needed as she fell back into her interrupted sleep. I drove home and parked in the driveway. I nudged Sarah awake, and we scooped up the kids and put them safely into their beds.

"I guess I still owe you guys a dinner," I said with a smirk as we walked into the bedroom.

"Don't worry, I'll remind you," she said, smiling back at me. She gave me a kiss on the cheek. "Are you coming to bed?"

"In a bit. I just want to check out the front of the car and clean whatever blood's still on there. Don't want to freak out the kids tomorrow morning."

"Okay, don't stay up too late." Sarah got into bed. "Won't be long before you have to get up again."

"I'll be up soon." I walked over to the bed and gave her a soft kiss on the lips. "What's that for?"

"Just for being the best wife a guy could have."

I stopped in the washroom where I threw some cold water on my face and took a good long look at myself. I wasn't sure I liked what I saw. I walked into Kim's room and looked at her for a moment. I smiled and placed a gentle kiss on her forehead before going into Patrick's room and doing the same.

"Goodnight slugger," I said, and with tears in my eyes I walked from the room.

I went downstairs and followed the back hallway past the laundry room to the garage door. I stood there for a minute before finally opening it and stepping inside. I turned the light on, crossed the garage, and began clearing a spot on my workbench. I spotted the locked metal box I was looking for and carefully took it down from its resting place. I unlocked it with a key from my key ring and opened the box.

The revolver gleamed.

I took out the bullets, kissing each one of them before loading them into the gun.

I held the gun in my hands as I knelt and prayed, tears streaming down my face. Afterward I stood up and slowly walked to the door that led into the house. I turned off the garage light, opened the door, and entered the house.

For the last time.

Bound

by Alan Smale

Day after day they threw him into the sky, arms strapped to his sides, legs straight and lashed together with tight cord. The rough cloth of the bindings abraded his neck and wrists where his jumpsuit did not protect his pale skin. Layer upon layer of bandages prevented him from bending his legs or curling up into a ball. Bundled as tightly as any Chinese child, he was immobilized and helpless.

The schoolyard was paved with black asphalt and marked in fading yellow paint with the rectangular grid pattern of a game he couldn't identify. Not soccer. Not tennis or field hockey. The schoolyard was enclosed on three sides by a tall wall of brick, crested with slate and concrete. A soot-blackened church with a high steeple defined the fourth side of the square.

Bound and rigid, they threw him. He turned end over end, or spun like a top, or drifted stably to the peak of his narrow arc with a clear view of the sky, wall, or pavement. It all depended on the angle of his previous bounce, the spin imparted by the blanket they used to toss him, and the skill of the thirteen people who held the blanket, but they never cast him high enough to see over the wall.

When he flew up—terror. When he dropped back towards earth—frantic terror. Especially if he could not see the ground beneath, and did not know how far and fast he was falling, or whether the blanket remained stretched below him. He could neither help nor hinder, steer nor protect himself.

He was at their mercy.

His memory of his life before the schoolyard was hazy. He thought his surname might be Jackson, but perhaps this was a pun created by his subconscious: Jumping Jackson, muttered a sarcastic voice in his head. Jumping Jackson.

They'd toss him into space again and again, until he was close to vomiting. Somehow they could tell when his equilibrium was failing and stop the punishment. That was a shame. Puking over them would have been a kind of revenge; petty and gross, perhaps, but there was little else he could do to discomfit his tormenters. Also, he was curious to know what they were feeding him.

They wore overalls and hoods of plain black, and ski-masks to obscure their features. Always thirteen of them, but not always the same ones. Of any given group, between six and ten seemed familiar in build or body language. He'd hear whispers from his memory—this one perhaps a parent, that one a brother, here a lover, there a child, maybe a friend from college. Of course, he couldn't recall their names any more than he could be sure of his own, nor could he picture their faces. Yet he was firmly convinced that he was not being tortured by strangers.

As he arced upwards once more, Jumping Jackson thought perhaps today was the seventh since he had arrived here. A week of being hurled into the sky within these schoolyard walls.

"Is...this the seventh day?" His feet hit the blanket first, and then the rest of his body. It took the whole of the next bounce for him to draw enough breath to finish his question. "Six days...oomph...before today?"

None answered, yet as he spun he saw one of them flick her head towards him so familiarly that he wanted to kiss her, or slap her. Distracted, she did not pull her weight on the next flip, and he spun crazily across the sky, his view a blur. The blanket crew had to skip back several feet to be in place to catch him and whiz him upward again, this time so high that he almost came level with the wall's parapet—but not quite, not quite.

His nausea rose, and his throat spasmed. Seven days, then. Seven. He should try to remember that.

When they folded the blanket around him and carried him through the arched doorway into the church, he fell asleep, apparently of his own accord.

* * *

He regained consciousness as they threw him into the sky, bundled in his cocoon, arms strapped to his sides, legs straight and bound together. Instantly he panicked—he couldn't move! The rough cloth of the bindings abraded his neck and wrists. He screamed as he fell, to be silenced abruptly as his impact into the blanket knocked the wind from him. He sailed through space and tried to suck air into his lungs, bounced again, saw the squad below clutching the blanket's edges just before he hit one more time. They were in the swing of it now, and fresh, and for the next few times he flew up horizontally, not spinning, and he could count them. Thirteen in all and...surely two of them were family. A brother? A sister?

I am Jumping Jackson, he thought. They do this day after day.

I never see over the wall.

That church is the same church, its walls blackened by urban pollution, its spire pointing heavenward. Showing them the direction they must throw me.

And it's the eighth day of this torment.

The eighth day! Clutching at the knowledge, Jumping Jackson felt his panic recede. Whomp! He hit the blanket again, askew, and spun dizzily up into space, hung for an eternity, then the sickening fall back downward. He saw a flash of

69

yellow—surely the markings for a game of some sort, yet not one he recognized. For a moment his consciousness flickered, then he flowed back to himself again as the crazy rhythm echoed in his bones.

He tried not to let his body adjust. If he accustomed himself to this insanity, if it became acceptable, it might last forever. But if he stayed off-kilter and dizzy, it would stop. He remembered that if he was close to throwing up, they'd cease and take him inside for another interval of timeless sleep.

Jackson thrashed within his bonds. He moved only a fraction of an inch, yet in his victory it felt like he twisted and turned. Almost as if he was dancing. Almost as if he was winning. He spun in the air, his ground-church-wall-sky world a striping blur before his eyes. As the tears came, as the hugeness welled up in his stomach and throat, he shouted "You're my brother, you shit! My sister! And *you*, you bitch…I should have—oomph!—I…when I had the chance…"

They faltered, tossed him askew, ran to catch up. His gorge rose. He coughed, and heaved.

It stopped. They caught him and stilled him, and bore him to the door in silence.

He smelled their sweat, familiar and almost comforting.

* * *

He fuzzily swam up into consciousness. Black-garbed men carried him in a blanket into an area surrounded by high brick walls. No—some of them were women.

"What happened?" he said. "Am I ill? Was there an accident?"

Without warning, they stretched the blanket out between them and threw him into the sky:

—bundled in his cocoon, arms strapped to his sides, legs straight and bound together, rough cloth abrading his—

He was Jumping Jackson. This is what his loved ones and hated ones did to him, day after day. What they would do for the rest of his life. This was Day Nine of Forever.

Today the terror abated more swiftly than before. He relaxed in his bondage and let himself fly. Really, there was nothing else he could do.

Perhaps they'd break his neck by accident, ending his trial…But his head seemed to be held straight by splints and padding. And they were skilled with the blanket; when he fell badly they'd jerk it sideways as he landed to spill him onto his shoulder and make him take the brunt of the impact full-length.

He studied the sky. Was this truly the ninth day, or just the ninth time they'd brought him out in a single day?

The sky was the same, a cloudy gray. The climate of late fall, perhaps. In another thirty days of being thrown into the sky, it might snow. The asphalt of the schoolyard might grow slick with ice. They might drop him.

Or maybe the weather would mysteriously endure, just as the blanket and the bindings and the black clothes and the dark brickwork endured.

"What's the point?" he shouted, when he had enough breath. He crashed into the blanket again and met it feet-first with a shock he felt all the way up his spine. Immediately he had a blinding headache. "What the hell are you … oomph…trying to do?"

* * *

Up, down. Abraded neck, wrists. Gray clouds. Jumping Jackson. Day Ten.

None of yesterday's pain remained. They must be fixing him up overnight with some powerful drugs. Or maybe this was Year Ten and he'd naturally healed in his coma.

The repeated thuds dulled his thoughts. After a while he closed his eyes.

* * *

He came out of a thick, indistinct dream to find that his fraternity brothers were marching him out of the house on a blanket. But that made no sense. He'd graduated years ago. Decades?

Confusion turned to a blind, shrieking panic as they threw him into the sky, bundled in his cocoon, arms strapped to his sides, legs straight and bound together. The rough cloth…

Jackson screamed as the abyss yawned in front of him. Then he slammed back into the blanket and the black-clad men swayed with the force of it and threw themselves backward, jerking the blanket taut, hurling him up once more. The gray sky slid by his eyes. Dazed, he saw a church spire.

He screamed again. College was years ago and indistinct, the time in between an empty void. This wasn't hazing; this was just torture. Soon, he'd complete his second week of this absurd and painful ritual.

His face thudded into the blanket. His nose bent but did not break. His momentum reversed in a second, and Jumping Jackson flew back into the air.

And laughed, a strange hiccupping sound, for his lungs held barely a thimbleful of air.

Not hazing, but perhaps the principle was the same. A test to destruction, to measure his mettle.

They would not destroy him. Jackson was tougher than they.

Bounce, throw. Up again into the gray sky, not quite high enough to glimpse the world beyond the wall's crest, beyond this stupid schoolyard.

The schoolyard was their prison, not his. They were bound by it. And they were bound by gravity, but Jackson was not. He was above them all. They'd never break his will, and he would climb to heights they could never reach.

To survive he had to adapt. He must embrace this reality and make it his own. He must dwell on its freedoms—flight, absence of responsibility, immunity

71

from the crippling backache that must affect the others. He must ignore its negative aspects—powerlessness, danger, futility, nausea.

His terror dwindled. Surely this pattern must have been the same in his prior world, where his compatriots had worn no masks and he had worked with them as colleagues, cleaved to them as lovers, raised them as children. He must have had freedoms and constraints. This existence was no different.

To panic was animal. To accommodate, human. He would live and die a human, and that was how he would win.

He relaxed his whole body and allowed the bindings and splints and jumpsuit to control him and keep him straight, as they were designed to do. His eyes closed naturally as he hit the blanket, and opened again as he flew into the sky. He breathed in rhythm with the motion.

The riotous spinning eased. By declining to fight, Jackson was making their job easier. He was assisting his wives, lovers, and brothers in their task. Did they appreciate his cooperation? He could not think how to frame the question, quickly between bounces, without it sounding like a taunt.

They gave themselves to this backbreaking work, day after day. Jackson's was the easier burden to bear.

His nausea receded, and he began to enjoy the madcap sensations of flight. Surely he had felt this giddy abandon with some of the women below, under different circumstances.

Perhaps his acquiescence was impolite. A good lover should play his part.

The next time he came down flat, he jerked himself rigid as he left the blanket. It helped. Once he got into the swing of it, the Thirteen did not have to work so hard to throw Jackson to the same height, that tantalizing level just short of the wall's parapet.

Jackson could keep this going all day.

They got their second wind now, his lovers, his friends, his family. Their efforts redoubled, and he matched them. He called out to them, single syllables of encouragement. And they threw him higher still.

They were all imprisoned in this black yard, with nothing to see but the bricks and mortar of the wall and the spire of the church, but perhaps, just perhaps, Jackson could see over the wall, and recount to them what he saw. Share it with his family.

Jackson summoned his strength and gave it everything he had. A subtle electricity flowed between them all.

In his concentration, the final push seemed timeless. He floated down towards his brothers and they stood and waited. He landed sideways-on, shoulder and hip to the cloth, and felt them absorb his impact and bend almost to the ground. His heel grazed the asphalt through the blanket, and then they leaned and jerked, a superhuman pull, a gigantic effort from this masked but familiar clique. Up he went like a bullet, up and up, as if gravity had finally given up the struggle against the team that fought to vanquish it.

"Yes!" called Jackson in exhilaration.

He sailed up, and the wall fell below his eye level, brick by brick. He tilted on his axis very gently, came even with the crest of the wall, then his body was fully above it. Higher still, and now he could see shards of glass twinkling in the concrete coping.

His eyes raked the horizon in a single sweeping arc.

The church was the only building that still stood. Beyond, he saw the blackened remains of walls, shattered towers, smashed windows. Craters pocked a city wreathed in smoke. Houses and halls alike were wrecked and gutted. Legions of shambling and misshapen men picked and clawed their way between the derelict buildings, the rusted cars.

Time slowed as Jackson reached the top of his trajectory. His heart pounded in his throat, ice crystalizing in his veins. This, then, was the world beyond the schoolyard, the world they were locked away from.

He would tell his brothers and sisters and friends. They would face this adversity together.

A makeshift arrow pierced his shoulder and set him spinning. One of the shamblers, his reflexes quickened by anarchy, had seen Jackson appear over the wall and plugged him. Perhaps the shambler had heard his earlier shouting and had been waiting for him to appear. Jackson's shoulder blazed with pain. He squeaked out a cry, and heard an answering moan from the Thirteen below.

He fell, head over heels over head, and the wall came up like a cat's eyelid and mercifully screened his view of the devastated city.

Jackson tumbled back towards his family's loving arms, already dragging in the breath he would need to call out the truth to them. He spun lazily to face them.

The Thirteen walked towards the church door. The giant blanket lay crumpled against the wall where they had thrown it. Beneath him he saw only blackness, lined with the yellow markings of an unknown game.

As Jumping Jackson screamed and plummeted into the ground, not a single one of his family looked back.

Drawn

by Daniel L. Naden

How did it start?

I sit here with Teresa and Anna, huddled in the remains of our apartment, and I wish to hell that I didn't know. Around us our building is in ruins, walls and ceilings collapsed, two-by-fours poking jaggedly through the debris. Outside the noise of chaos and destruction continues. How did it start? Was it bad luck? Bad choices? I don't think it really matters now. I just want to hold my wife and my baby and wait for it to be over. When I close my eyes, it all replays. I see the day my daughter was born.

It was ten months ago.

At 12:03 PM, following nine hours of labor, Anna Marie Cooper came into the world, pink and bloody and squalling with gusto. In a flurry of activity, the nurses swabbed, tested, and weighed Anna, wrapped her up in a neat little bundle, and set her into Teresa's tired arms. Against the backdrop of the buzzing fluorescents, with IVs and wires tangled every which way from the odd collection of equipment surrounding the bed, Teresa and Anna looked like a gift of angels. Mother and child: the Renaissance painters never did the subject justice. It was like light had come into the world and settled on them.

Teresa looked as beautiful as I had ever seen her—an aching grace and peace that tugged at my heart more deeply than I would ever have imagined possible. Anna was a delicate flower, cradled in Teresa's arms. Tiny fingers clenched into little, chubby fists. A perfectly round face with a dimpled chin, a classic button nose and a shock of black hair. Her eyes...

Anna's eyes.

Well, that's where all of this really began.

Ordinarily, when babies are born, their eyes are a deep, dark shade of blue. They don't usually get their natural eye color for a couple of months, sometimes longer. Anna's eyes were auburn, a rich, almost-coppery color, shot through with flecks of black and irises that opened into pools of night. When she looked at you

74

with those eyes, you couldn't look away.

I stood beside Teresa, both of us looking at our baby, and we were spellbound. From a distance, one of the nurses was saying how sometimes babies are born with unique eye colors, assuring us that Anna's eyes were perfectly ordinary. While we listened to every word she said, neither of us ever looked up from Anna and her perfect, enigmatic eyes.

We were *drawn* to them—we simply could not look anywhere else.

* * *

Time passed for us like it does for all first-time parents. A lot of sleepless nights and hectic days, rotating through feeding shifts and messy diapers. We had smiles and laughter and tears and scores of other emotions that new moms and dads go through in the earliest stages of their children's lives. But even from the beginning, there were hints of the shadow to come.

The mobile for Anna's crib had been a shower gift. It was fairly typical—a collection of dangling moons and leaping cows on a carousel that could be wound up to play a lullaby. It was designed to be secured to the headboard by a clamp with a thumbscrew. At three months old, Anna had been giving us a bit of trouble with bedtime. She could keep herself awake crying for quite a while. Teresa thought if we set up the mobile, it might distract Anna and help her fall asleep. Anna had been fussy all day, so by her bedtime, we were ready to try it. I dug the mobile out of the closet and screwed it onto the headboard of Anna's crib.

Anna started crying as soon as I set her in her bed. I wound up the mobile, flipped off the light and pulled the door closed, waiting outside and listening.

Almost immediately, she calmed down, evidently fascinated by the new sound and sight. Every now and then, she whimpered, but seemed to be done crying. As I walked away, I heard a clatter and Anna started shrieking.

I opened the door and hurried to her crib. Anna was tangled up in the mobile, screaming in fear and anger. She didn't appear to be hurt. I scooped her into my arms as Teresa appeared over my shoulder.

"What in the world happened?"

"The mobile fell on her," I said.

Teresa arched an eyebrow at me.

"I put it up the right way," I told her. I was whining and not hiding it well.

We examined the headboard. The base of the mobile was still firmly in place. About four inches from the top, the plastic arm that held up the mobile had snapped off. I picked up the part that had fallen into the crib and examined it. The break matched the headboard piece exactly.

"See!" I said, sounding petulant. "It's broken. She must have pulled it down."

Teresa regarded me again, this time with a smirk. "Do you know how ludicrous that sounds? She's a three-month-old!"

"I don't know," I replied, deadpanning as best I could, "maybe she jumped..."

Teresa groaned in mock exasperation. Together, we tucked Anna into her crib and kissed her good night. I deposited the pieces of the mobile in the trash dumpster outside. We didn't think of the incident again until three months later when things began to fly around the apartment.

* * *

In retrospect, we should have known.

I can sit here and tell myself that we were new parents and didn't find it odd the way Anna always seemed to turn up with her favorite teething toy or the TV remote. Or how we'd hear her jangling the car keys that we *knew* we'd left on the table. I could try to believe that we didn't feel the pull on our arm whenever she saw her bottle coming. Or that we didn't notice how we simply couldn't turn away when she was looking at us. I'd really like to believe we were blind to what was happening with Anna. But I know I'd be lying.

We were happy to pretend that nothing was really odd or different with our daughter. That lasted until the day I came home from work to find Teresa in tears.

For me, the day had been ordinary. I got up and went to work before Teresa and Anna were up. I came home at the normal time, enjoying the unseasonably pleasant weather. The sun had fought its way free of the morning's overcast and left behind a bright, breezy afternoon. I specifically remember thinking that my life so far was turning out pretty good. It sticks out in my mind because it was the last truly carefree moment I can remember.

Teresa met me at the door of our apartment, her eyes red and her face splotchy. She pulled me in, quickly shutting and locking the door behind me. I heard Anna screeching from her bedroom.

"Oh Pat, I don't know what to do! It's Anna, she..."

"What's wrong with Anna?" I got two steps toward her room before Teresa stopped me. She clung to my arm with a death grip.

"No NO! Let me tell you. Anna was eating and...um...She...Oh God, how can I describe...?"

"WHAT?"

The words were suddenly pouring out of her. "I was feeding Anna...had her strapped into the high chair. She went through a whole jar of strained plums and I left to get another one and...and...well you know how cranky she can get when she's hungry. She was mad at me because I walked away from her. I set the empty jar on the counter and turned to pull another one from the pantry and when I turned back, the jar *wasn't there!*"

"What?"

"It wasn't there, okay? And when I looked up at Anna, *she* had the jar. She'd stopped crying and was busy trying to work the damn thing into her mouth!"

"So how did she get it?"

76

"I don't know! Well, I *didn't* know..."

She dragged me by the arm to the kitchen.

"I thought I might have left it close enough for her to reach, but I knew that I hadn't. I left it...right...here." Her forefinger stabbed at the counter. "So I took the jar back from her...you should have heard her scream...and I put it, very specifically, next to the sink. And I watched her."

Teresa paused, out of breath, trying to work up the nerve to tell me what happened next.

"Anna looked at me and it was weird. All at once I felt kinda sick to my stomach. Like something was moving around in there. It only lasted a second, and only while she was looking at me. Her eyes were weird. Focused. Scary. Then she looked at the jar and it just...*flew* to her."

"It *what?*"

She continued as if she hadn't heard me.

"Anna didn't really catch it. It kinda just dropped in front of her and she picked it up and started to work on it again."

"You're telling me that the jar flew to her."

"It flew, Pat! I saw it and I couldn't believe it. So I took the jar from her again and I held onto it. Tight. Anna looked at the jar and I could feel it pulling against my fingers and I tried to hold onto it. I was squeezing it as tight as I could but it didn't matter. When Anna looked at the jar, it went right to her."

I became aware of how quiet the apartment had become. Anna wasn't crying anymore. The silence was suffocating, choking the air out of my lungs. I saw my own fear mirrored in Teresa's dark eyes.

"How can this be?" I said. "I don't understand."

"Neither do I, Pat. I put her to bed...just left the damn jar with her. I was afraid to take it from her again. I was afraid...of her. What are we going to do?"

"I wish I knew."

* * *

The next morning, when Anna woke up, we tested her.

We started with some of her toys, showing each one to Anna and then moving them out of her reach. The teething ring flew out of Teresa's hand as soon as Anna saw it. I tossed the plastic keys on the floor and they scuttled across the carpet and rose into Anna's outstretched hand.

Teresa pulled out a squeaky ball and worked it a few times to get Anna's attention before hiding it behind her back. Anna squawked briefly, keys still clutched in her chubby fist, but the ball did *not* go to her.

"So what's that mean?" I said. "Did she lose interest, or is she just unable to get it?"

"I don't know." Her voice was flat, quavering a bit.

We moved up to bigger items. The remote control. A stuffed teddy bear.

She appeared to have misjudged the weight of the basketball, because it smacked her squarely on the forehead and left her crying and angry, but otherwise unhurt.

I tried holding onto a bottle of formula with both hands, using all my strength, just to see how much force she could exert against it. It was no good. The bottle flew to her from my hands, painfully splaying back my fingers in the process.

For everything we tried, when Anna wanted what we showed her, she could make it come to her. But she couldn't move the items that were out of her line of sight.

Eventually, Anna got sleepy and cranky. Teresa set her down for a nap. While she slept, we talked.

Together we debated the end of our world.

Even now, I remember it perfectly. The afternoon sun cast slats of shadows at odd angles from the window blinds, and the silence in the apartment had swollen into an almost physical thing. The weight of doom. I sat on the couch beside Teresa and cradled her hands in mine. I took a deep breath.

"We *have* to take her to the doctor," I began. "This is too big for us..."

"NO!" Teresa's eyes welled with tears. "They won't understand! They'll take her from us and turn her into some kind of freak show."

"How can we handle this? Do you want to gamble on what she might or might not be able to move? On whether or not she'll be able to pull the TV on top of herself? How can we keep her safe?"

"We'll just have to make sure we don't leave stuff lying around. And if we don't show her that big things can move, she won't try to make them come to her. It'll be all right. We just have to be more careful!"

"Listen to yourself, Teresa! How do you think we're going to hide this from everyone?"

"We'll teach her just the same as we'd teach her anything else. We already know that if we keep her from seeing something, she won't be able to get it. If she's trying to get something she shouldn't have, we'll simply hide it out of sight. We can take care of her. Please, Pat. *Please!*"

I knew better. To this day, I swear I knew better. Looking back at it now, I should have put my foot down and taken Anna to see the doctors or someone at the university—*anything* rather than trying to keep her with us.

But sitting there, I saw the anguish on Teresa's face, and I knew I would not change her mind. It was more than damning our daughter to a lifetime under a microscope: I would be damning our family, our marriage. She would never forgive me. To be honest, I would never have forgiven myself.

"I'm not going to give our baby away," she said quietly, almost to herself.

"I know. We'll make it work."

She cried softly on my shoulder and I stroked her hair as the shadows deepened around us.

"Everything will be all right," I told her.

I couldn't have been more wrong.

* * *

As Anna grew, she learned. And as she learned, it became more difficult for us to keep some pretense of control over her.

One day, with Anna safely strapped into her high chair, Teresa left the refrigerator door open while she was setting something on the counter. Attracted by the bright colors on the labels, Anna started "grabbing" things from the door. A jar of mustard. A ketchup bottle. The jug of milk. A carton of eggs. Most of the items she didn't try to catch, but was content to let them soar across the room and crash into the wall behind her.

Caught between getting to Anna and closing the door, Teresa eventually put her hands over Anna's eyes to stop the barrage. She spent a good part of the afternoon cleaning the kitchen and dining room, listening to Anna thumping objects off her bedroom walls from the prison of her crib.

Not long after that, Anna learned how to crawl and our apartment grew smaller and our problems bigger. Now that Anna could move throughout the apartment, our lives became even more harried; Teresa's days became an endless series of futile attempts to keep ahead of Anna's slow, but determined progress.

Months passed in a blur, a slideshow of images marked our passage into confusion and despair.

Teresa, her face darkened with dread, dragging herself out of bed in the morning. Teresa, her face smudged with fatigue, collapsing into bed at night.

My own sunken eyes staring back at me from the mirror; days spent at work and nights spent catching up on the housework that Teresa was unable to do.

Anna's bright inquisitive face, her furious wails, an apartment that resembled a battle zone.

And behind it all, Anna's eyes. Her beautiful, terrible eyes.

* * *

Don't get me wrong. It's not like Anna was some demon-baby bent on finding new ways to torture us. She was just like any other nine-month-old who sees stuff and grabs it and puts it into her mouth to taste or gnaw or drool on. Sometimes temperamental and sometimes achingly cute. She was our daughter.

But she was also different. For a long time, a forever spanning all of three months, we fought a losing battle. Distract. Move. Hide.

Not a very good way to define one's life, but Teresa and I wanted to believe that she would grow out of her baby phase and reach the stage where she'd know the difference between *yes* and *no*. That she would somehow learn to leave things alone.

Somewhere in its development, the average infant gains an understanding of the concept of "behind." Young babies lose interest in an object when it is placed behind some obstruction because they don't understand that it's still there. Eventually, they figure it all out…some kind of spatial intelligence that signals a new stage of development. It's all perfectly natural.

For Anna, this comprehension signaled the beginning of the end of our battle. She learned that when we "hid" something from her, it didn't simply go away. It was behind, but there was something in *front*. Usually one of us. She learned that she didn't have to crawl to change her line of sight. All she had to do was to move whatever was shielding it from her view. She learned that she could move us.

Just that quickly, our lives changed.

When we tried to stop her or distract her, she abruptly pulled us out of the way. When we tried to hide or put away what Anna wanted, the door or drawer simply opened.

The ways she found to exploit her talents grew almost exponentially. She learned she could unload the VCR tapes and DVDs from the entertainment center. She followed that by raiding the pantry and her old friend, the refrigerator. We lost dishes when Anna "explored" the kitchen cabinet where we kept them and crashed them against the walls and floors. Shutting Anna up in her room didn't work anymore because she figured out how to open the door.

We became little more than hermits: mentally and physically exhausted prisoners isolated in a cell of our own making. We were not safe taking Anna out of our apartment and we couldn't trust anyone to come in. We could not risk it.

The low point was the night when Teresa caught Anna sitting peacefully in her crib while her dresser floated around her room. Given Anna's talents, the display shouldn't have been too surprising. But it was the last straw. If she could "lift" something as heavy as her dresser, who knew just how heavy an object she could move. But there was something else: she dragged us around like rag dolls. How long before she was lifting us as well?

That night, while Anna slept, I moved as much of our furniture as I could from our apartment into a storage unit.

I returned home to blank floors and walls that echoed the noise of my arrival. Teresa sat on the empty carpet, lights off, holding a sleeping Anna against her shoulder. Teresa's face, in shadow, was dark and fathomless. As empty as the apartment. As empty as my soul.

We huddled together on the floor and waited for morning to come.

We were wraiths in our own home. Ghosts of the people we once were. Shades of lives we lost.

That was last night.

* * *

The sun rose this morning to a beautiful spring day.

In the early light, the depths of despair we'd felt in the night seemed distant and less foreboding. Our barren apartment seemed open, almost airy.

Together, Teresa and I watched Anna sleeping between us and without saying a word, we arrived at the same conclusion: We couldn't do this anymore. We needed help.

We looked ahead of us and saw Anna learning to walk. We imagined her in her terrible twos, the unreasonableness of the two-year-old temperament, mixed with the power of a god. We could envision the temptations and the horrors waiting for Anna outside our home, with an entire world of things that could get her attention...toys for the playing.

Worst of all, we were left with the haunting question: *how powerful was she?* And how powerful would she become?

It was beyond us, now. Perhaps it had always been.

I called the doctor and set up an appointment for 9:30. I told his receptionist that our daughter was behaving strangely and left it at that. There would be plenty of opportunities to explain Anna to the doctor when we got there.

* * *

We left our apartment. Teresa carried Anna down the stairwell while I ran ahead to get the car.

We had already talked about the best way for us to safely get to the doctor's office. Anna could move big things: the TV, furniture, even us, around with ease. Neither of us was sure whether or not she could move something as big as a car or truck, but I wasn't going to gamble against that chance. Just the thought of it gave me chills.

I pulled up to the curb in front of our building, but waited until there was nobody around and no traffic passing by, before opening the car's back door and giving Teresa the signal. She came out quickly, hand shielding Anna's eyes, in part from the glare of the sun, but mainly so that she wouldn't get a good look at anything around them. At the car, she strapped Anna into her baby seat, and shut the door.

It was then that we realized that the height of Anna's car seat allowed her a clear view out the car window.

"This is *not* going to work!" I told Teresa. "She can see too much."

"But we have to get her to the doctor."

"Imagine what will happen if she grabs someone...or some*thing*...while we're moving. People could get hurt. People could die. *We* could die."

81

"But we *have* to try!" Her voice, pleading and desperate.

"We could walk..." I began, but immediately knew that was a bad idea. "No. She'd see even more that way."

"What if I sat on the floorboard with her in my lap?"

"That'd do it!" I hugged Teresa. "But you'll have to ride in the back seat. I don't want Anna getting interested in my keys or the steering wheel."

"So...you think it will work?" she said.

I hugged her again. "Yeah. Let's get going."

We turned back to the car and two things happened, all at once.

Anna screamed. Not the pissed-off, "I didn't get my way" type of scream. She screamed in absolute pain. The type of sound that makes you drop everything and come running with your heart in your throat.

The other thing that happened was bizarre, but every bit as terrifying. The car window beside Anna exploded, showering all of us in a rain of shattered bits of broken and molten safety glass.

"ANNA!"

Teresa screamed and I ran to the car door, glass burning holes through my clothing, and tried to open it but the door frame had melted and warped, blistering my hands as soon as I touched it. I ran around to the other side of the car. Anna was shrieking now in agony and I threw open the door and crawled through to get to her. Then I saw her eyes...

God help me, I saw her eyes.

My baby's beautiful auburn eyes were a muddy, bruised color and the whites were shot full of red. The skin around her eyes was raw and beginning to blister. Blood leaked from the corners and traced streaks down her face.

"Oh my God, Anna! Hang on! Daddy's gonna get you out of here. Hang on!"

I fumbled with the buckle on her car seat. Teresa had come around to the other side of the car and was standing behind me.

"What's wrong, Pat? Is she okay?" Her words became a mindless litany. "Is she okay, Pat? Is she? Is she okay..."

"*I don't know, dammit!*"

I looked at her over my shoulder. Teresa flinched as if I had slapped her.

"Teresa, I don't know what happened, but we can't afford for you to panic right now. We've got to get Anna out of here and get her inside and it's not going to help her if you're freaking out!"

I turned back and gently lifted the seat belt over Anna's head. By then, she was howling and I was desperate to get her back into the apartment, but before I did, I took a quick glance, a snapshot in my head, through the empty space that had been our car window.

What had Anna seen?

I scooped her out of the car seat and sprinted Anna inside as fast as I could carry her. To be honest, I was worried about what Teresa might do when she saw Anna's eyes, but somehow, she had managed to get a little control over herself. She was right on my heels as I ran up the stairs.

* * *

Eight minutes.

I know it was eight minutes because I had glanced at my watch as I turned toward the car in the instant before the window exploded. It couldn't have taken me more than two minutes to get Anna out of the car and into the apartment and another minute until I was able to get it through to the 911 operator that my daughter was seriously injured.

Five minutes had passed. Teresa was holding Anna, still trying to calm her down. Three more minutes passed while I yelled at the 911 operator to hurry the fuck up. Then the first earthquake hit.

In the instant before everything started shaking, it darkened briefly outside, like the shadow of a fast-moving cloud passing overhead. Then the world convulsed. We flew around the apartment like rag dolls. The windows shattered and the walls cracked. The doors banged open and shut, splitting in their frames. Just when I thought I couldn't take any more and that we would be crushed as the building fell apart around us, it all stopped.

Suddenly, silence, echoes still roaring in my ears. Eventually, other sounds intruded: car alarms blatted in the parking lot; dueling police and fire truck sirens wailed. More chilling, sounds of fear and pain and anguish coming from the other people in their apartments.

I looked around. Teresa, pale, wide-eyed, had a small cut on her forehead, but otherwise looked okay. Anna didn't appear to have been injured further, but was lethargic and hung limp in Teresa's arms.

When the next wave hit, I just had time to drag Teresa and Anna into the kitchen and throw ourselves in the space between the counters before the roof collapsed. Then another wave hit. And another. They continued, each one worse than the one before, and each one shaking apart more of our home. By the time they stopped, our building *had* collapsed—very little was left standing. By some miracle, our kitchen stayed mostly intact, with the cabinets propping up part of the fallen ceiling. To a certain degree, we were trapped. I was pretty sure that I could move enough debris to allow us to escape. But I wasn't sure if I could do so safely, without accidentally making everything else fall in on us. So we sat. And waited.

Anna slept fitfully, cradled in my arms, while Teresa fiddled with the battery-powered radio she'd pulled from the cabinet next to the sink. The news wasn't good. Reports came in from all over the world. What we thought were earthquakes were actually shockwaves that came from somewhere in space—they really didn't know where, or even how. But the devastation affected the entire planet. Entire cities were leveled. Mountain ranges collapsed and the plains were now buckled and broken. Coastal areas had either fallen off into the oceans or had been swept away by tsunamis of unimaginable size.

Several hours later, we listened to the static-filled briefing from some NASA scientist, who kept talking about problems with the Earth's orbit…somehow it had *changed*. We couldn't hear the next part, but later a panicked voice said something about a "possible collision with the moon." After that, we lost the signal except for the words "drifting off into space."

Much later. Teresa had fallen asleep and I tried again to catch more news. Static had replaced most of the stations and I was about to give up when I picked up a signal. I could make out only a portion of it, but it was enough. The dead, hopeless voice on the radio discussed the significance of the "rapid sublimation of Earth's atmosphere."

I turned the radio off after that. I'd heard all I needed to hear.

* * *

So I'm sitting here, in the dim glow of a candle, watching my wife and daughter as the world slowly dies around us.

Anna's breathing has gotten shallower in the past hour. I don't think she'll make it through the night, and there's not a goddamned thing I can do about it. Maybe it's for the better, all things considered.

"How did this happen?"

Teresa asked me this question shortly before she fell asleep, and at the time, I told her that I didn't know. But that was a lie. I know.

What did Anna see?

I had taken only a brief glance out of the broken window of our car…a snapshot in my head…before I grabbed Anna and ran inside. But I remember what I saw…what Anna had seen from her view through the window. She saw the apartment building and, off to the right, some trees. Nothing much of interest except the sky above.

And the sun.

I think I knew, even then, what had happened, but I didn't want to admit it. It was too unbelievable. Too impossible.

What I knew then and what I know now doesn't matter.

Anna saw the sun and the earth was doomed.

Like everything else, the sun was drawn.

The Station

by Bentley Little

Derek looked impatiently at his watch, making a show of it, wanting Gina to know how annoyed he was getting. But she was focused on getting her shot and either did not see him or did not care. She crouched down in the sand, viewfinder to her eye, moving incrementally to her right as she tried to capture the sun shining through the thin crack between two boulders.

Why did her new hobby have to be photography? Why couldn't she have gotten into Sudoku or needlepoint, something that she could do in the car while they drove?

The bitch of it was, he knew she'd probably burn out on this before the end of the year, maybe before the end of the summer. It would go the way of all her other transitory passions: scrapbooking, flower arranging, sushi making, and of course that damned book club. But right now it was making his already too-short vacation a living hell, and he looked again at his watch and said loudly, "Hurry up! We have a long way to go, and if we don't check in by six, they won't hold the room for us!"

"Relax!" Gina called back. "That place has about a thousand rooms. And it's the off-season. We'll be fine."

She was right. Furnace Creek Inn was huge. And, other than themselves, who else was moronic enough to vacation in Death Valley in the middle of July? They could probably walk in without *any* reservation and get the finest room in the hotel. "Hurry up anyway!" he shouted.

"I'm trying!" she called.

Derek opened the car door, sat down in the passenger seat and consoled himself by looking at a map. Before Gina had gotten them off track chasing artistic landscapes down this side road, they'd been making pretty good time, and if they could get back to the highway within the next half hour or so, they should still be able to reach the national park by mid-afternoon. Although he'd done so a thousand times, he once again went over their itinerary, then flipped through the

AAA book at random, looking for future vacation destinations. When he glanced up again several moments later, assuming she'd had plenty of time to take her photo and was walking back to the car, he saw that she hadn't moved. She was in exactly the same position she'd been in ten minutes ago.

This was ridiculous.

Derek slammed the glove compartment shut and strode across the sand, ready to give her hell. Gina stood at his approach. "I was just going to come and get you," she enthused. "There's an old building out there. Look." She pointed past the boulders and down the sloping plain.

Oh no, he thought.

"It would make a great photo." She handed him her camera.

"Jesus Christ," he muttered, but dutifully looked through the telephoto lens. It appeared from this vantage point to be an abandoned gas station (*Esso*, judging by the shape of the sign's iron skeleton). He saw no indication of any cars or people. Derek handed back the camera. "Hurry up then and take a picture."

"Not from *here*!" She hit his shoulder. "I want to go down *there*!"

"It's already been—"

"I'll make it quick," she promised.

"You know," he told her, "if Death Valley was good enough for Ansel Adams, it should be good enough for you."

"That's the point," she said. "It's overdone. *Everyone* who goes there takes pictures. This is something new. I might be the only one to *ever* take photos of this."

"I doubt that," he said, but agreed to give her ten minutes at the building if they left *right this second*.

She beat him back to the car.

Derek drove quickly, stirring up a cloud of dust behind them. The road was not paved, and it was doubtful that it ever had been. Moreover, the barely extant trail ended at the gas station. *Odd*, he thought. Ordinarily, service stations were built alongside highways. They were generally not destinations in and of themselves. Something about that seemed wrong, but he told himself that since it had probably been the only gas station for hundreds of miles, travelers probably wouldn't have minded driving a couple of extra miles down a side road.

He pulled to a stop between an empty island and a closed garage door that had been seriously battered by the elements but surprisingly boasted no graffiti. There were no pumps left, only metal foundations embedded in concrete from which protruded sections of pipe and tubing. The two of them stepped out of the car. "Oh, this is wonderful," Gina said. "So many good angles and such high contrast with the light and shadow."

"Ten minutes," he reminded her. "Or I'm driving off without you."

He didn't like this place. That end-of-the-road thing bothered him, and there was something about the building itself that made him uneasy as well. He walked around the back of the car and looked at the closed garage door with its chipped paint and dents and inexplicable lack of graffiti. A small alluvial fan of sand had accumulated at the bottom of the garage door but the line of sand was too even, too perfect, and he didn't like that either.

He moved on to the office. The broken window had long since been boarded up but the door was gone, and Derek peeked inside. It looked pretty much as he'd expected. Chair. Metal desk covered with dust, yellowed papers and an ashtray. Table with an empty cardboard fuse display and a single broken fan belt. Bulletin board with tire ads and tame cheesecake calendar from 1955.

There was nothing that should not have been there. Yet it seemed wrong, all of it, and he was about to back away and tell Gina that they should go, when she pushed past him and into the office. "Whoo," she said, fanning the air in front of her face. "Stale." There was a closed door in the wall next to the desk, and before he could say a word, she had walked across the office, opened it and was peering into the darkened room beyond.

Derek braced himself for her reaction, because he knew somehow that there would be one.

And there was.

"Oh my God," she said, staggering backward, eyes wide, face drained of color. "Oh my God." Already he was moving beyond her to see for himself.

The room was dark and windowless, but enough light filtered in from the outer office for him to see that a single straight-backed chair sat in the center of the chamber, which, in contrast to the metal and glass of the rest of the building, had a floor, ceiling and walls made from rotting unpainted wood.

Slumped in the chair was the body of a dead man.

That would have been shocking enough, but it was *who* the man was that caused Derek's legs to wobble.

It was the president of the United States—although the president was supposed to be on a tour of Asia and Derek had seen him on the news this morning giving a speech at a banquet in Tokyo. He was dressed just as he had been this morning, in modified tuxedo, but his face was gray and pasty, his eyes wide open and staring. It could have been an impersonator, someone made up to look like the president, but Derek knew somehow that that was not the case. There was a charisma to the man even in death, a tangible regality that made the authenticity of his body without question.

Maybe the impersonator had been the man in Japan, covering for the president who had been…what? Meeting someone here in the middle of the desert? Visiting this abandoned gas station? None of the scenarios he could imagine made any sense, and that was what bothered him the most. If there had been an understandable *reason* for this, if there was even the thinnest plausible explanation for finding the president's corpse in the back room of this deserted desert building, then he would have not felt so utterly lost and so bone-deep chilled. But there was no hint of rationality here, and he was more frightened at this second than he had ever been in his life.

Derek turned, grabbed Gina's arm, and the two of them ran through the office, out of the gas station and back to the car. He did not wait for her to put on her seatbelt but took off in a clatter of gravel and a cloud of dirt. They drove straight back to the highway, bumped back onto the asphalt and sped north as fast as the Toyota would carry them, not speaking at all until, two hours later, they reached the tollbooth at the entrance to Death Valley.

Death Valley.

Appropriate.

They checked in at Furnace Creek just before a busload of German tourists arrived, and after hauling their luggage to the suite, Gina immediately took a shower while Derek turned on the TV, not wanting to be alone in the room with silence.

By the time Gina had finished her shower, he'd gotten the whole story. She emerged from the bathroom redressed, hair combed, and stopped in her tracks, staring open mouthed at the image on the wall-mounted television. *Death of a President*, read the words at the bottom of the screen, while a small live shot of a Tokyo hospital crowded with reporters sat in the corner of a larger picture of CNN's top pundits in Washington.

"He had a heart attack," Derek said. "This morning at a banquet. He died instantly."

She looked at him. "Is his body missing?"

"Not that I heard."

Gina took a deep breath. "What did we see?" she asked. "What happened out there?"

"I don't know," he admitted.

There was a pause.

"I want to go back."

"What?" He sat up straight in the bed.

"I want to take a picture of it," Gina said. "I should have photographed it the first time."

"No," he told her, shaking his head. "No way."

"*No one's* taken a picture of *that* before. I'll be the first. It'll be totally unique—"

"No. It's not going to happen."

"We're the only ones who know about it, the only ones who've seen it."

"We're not going. We're staying here. Take a picture of the sand dunes. Or rocks."

"We were there already and nothing happened to us. It's not dangerous, it's just weird."

"It's..." He struggled to find the right word. *Wrong? Evil?* Neither of those were exact, but either of them would do.

Her face hardened into obstinacy. "*I'm* going back. With you or without you."

The argument continued for another twenty minutes, but in truth it ended right there. It was late afternoon, and he got her to agree to wait until the next morning—*neither* of them wanted to be in that place at night—but at the crack of dawn, they were checking out and packing the car and driving back the way they'd come.

They reached the gas station mid-morning, and while the desert heat was scorching, Derek felt cold. Gina, too, was nervous, though she refused to admit it. She tried to act as though nothing was wrong, but her voice was quavery and her hands shook when she lifted the camera from the backseat.

They stood for a moment in front of the open door, looking into the office. The air was still, too still, and even in the bright midday sun, light spilled only into the front room, leaving that secret chamber in the rear, with its door that they'd left open in their hurry to escape, shadowed and dark.

He wished he'd brought a flashlight, but he hadn't.

Gina stepped in first, camera before her like a protective talisman, and he followed, moving past the metal desk and dusty table into the back room.

The president was gone, but there was another man in the chair. He, too, was dead, only the cause of his demise was immediately obvious: blunt force trauma to the head. The entire back of his skull had been crushed, and white pieces of bone could be seen within the matted mass of red blood and brown hair. His eyes were closed but his mouth was open, lips frozen in a scream of shock and agony.

"Do you recognize him?" Gina whispered. Something about this place requested quiet.

Derek shook his head, afraid to speak. His brain was trying desperately to make sense of this, to find reason in the irrationality. Was this heaven? Or hell? Was it some sort of way station to the afterlife? That made the most sense, given the fact that the president's body had disappeared and been replaced by the corpse of another, but if that were the case, bodies should have been appearing and disappearing every second. People were dying all the time.

On impulse, he stepped forward, reached out and touched the dead man's arm. The form was solid. He'd half-expected it to be some sort of incorporeal figure, a ghost or shade—after all, the president's body had been in full view of witnesses in Japan at the same time they'd seen it here—and the tangible reality of its existence made everything that much more confusing.

The room flashed with light as Gina took a picture.

Derek jumped, startled.

There was another flash.

Was the expression different on the dead man's face?

He couldn't tell, but there seemed some slight change in the cast of the features, and he backed away from the chair, heart thumping crazily.

"I'm doing this as quickly as I can," Gina said, as if reading his mind. "I want to get out of here. I don't like this place."

Derek beat her to it, ducking under her camera arm and returning to the office. She followed immediately, obviously afraid to be alone in the room by herself. "Let's go."

He hazarded one quick glance back. He could see only the legs of the dead man from this angle, but on the shadowed surface of the rotted wood wall was what appeared to be a face formed from the contours of the irregularly shaped boards, a disturbingly intense visage with eyes of mold, nose of shadow and mouth of woodgrain. It could have meant nothing, could have been coincidence, but in this place under these circumstances, he found that hard to believe, and he instantly faced forward and hurried into the sunlight, not daring to look behind him as he ran around the side of the car and got in.

They sped away—for the *last* time, he promised himself—and as the car bounced along the rough dirt road, he let out a huge exhalation of air, unaware until that second that he'd been holding his breath. Gina, too, sighed with relief, although it sounded more like a moan than a sigh, and she clutched her camera in her lap as though afraid someone might try to steal it.

"I should've brought the digital camera, too," she said. "Then we could have looked at it right away." She turned to face him. "What if the pictures don't come out? What if it's all dark or all light or that...thing's not there?"

He didn't answer. He didn't want to answer. And they hit the highway and headed south toward home.

* * *

The photos did indeed turn out, and Derek looked closely at the prints Gina had made, his insides knotted into a tight ball of cold. There were only three shots of the dead man in the chair, and they were so clear and real that he was immediately brought back to that horrific chamber. He could almost smell the dust, could almost hear the silence. In the first photo, a side view, Gina had focused on the head and upper torso. He could see that bashed-in portion of skull, could even make out blood that had dripped onto the collar of his shirt. From this angle, the open mouth appeared not like a scream but a grotesque deformity. The next was a full body shot, and it had a Whistler's Mother feel, only the portrait at the center of the composition was the corpse of a murdered man. Derek found himself studying the background, looking for that face on the wall, and wasn't sure if he was relieved or disturbed that he was unable to spot it.

But it was the third picture that held his attention. For some reason, the flash had not worked on this one, and the scene was far too dark. The dead man in the chair was little more than a silhouette against a smudged and grainy background. Yet even in the gloom, Derek could see what looked like a dress over the man's pants and slender feminine fingers pointing downward from the hanging arm on the side of the chair.

Gina had captured the corpse when it was changing from the bludgeoned man to a woman.

Maybe, Derek thought, the thing in the chair was some type of shapeshifting creature that absorbed the physical characteristics of the immediately departed, picking up the essence of the dead like an antenna.

No. He'd touched that last corpse. It had been human. And real.

It was the room and the gas station that was so wrong and evil, not the figures in the chair. They were pawns...or victims...or something...

The phone rang, and Gina picked it up. She didn't call his name, so it obviously wasn't for him, and he didn't pay attention at first. He kept looking at the photos, including one shot of the gas station taken with a zoom lens from the boulder area. But gradually he began to realize that her tone of voice was too somber and she wasn't saying much. He looked up just as she asked, "When did he die?"

Eavesdropping on the last part of her half of the conversation told him nothing, but finally she hung up the phone, stunned. "Sue's husband died. Heart attack."

His first reaction was shock—Jim was two years younger than he was—but fear beat out sadness for the emotion that immediately followed. He met Gina's eyes. "Do you think he went...there?"

She looked quickly away, but he knew she'd been wondering the same thing, and he glanced down at the prints in his hand, at that dark top photo where the man was changing into a woman, and he shivered.

* * *

That night, in bed, Gina turned to him just as he was about to roll over and go to sleep. "I've been thinking," she said.

He didn't want to hear this.

"About the gas station."

He remained silent, refusing to take the bait.

"Do you think everyone goes there when they die?"

"No."

"But who does? And why?" She moved onto her side, finding a more comfortable position. "There must be a way to find out, to test it. What if we knew someone was going to die?" she asked. "I mean imminently. One of us could wait with the person, and the other one could wait at the gas station, and we'd both have cell phones—"

Derek shook his head.

"Or, even better, we could take the person there! And when he died—or she—we could see what happens. Right at that moment."

He didn't like the direction in which this was headed, and he cut off conversation then and there, saying that he was tired and needed to sleep. But in his dreams, Gina kidnapped a little boy, drove him out to the desert, and strangled him in the back room of the gas station and watched with excitement as a carbon copy of the child appeared in the chair.

In the morning, when he awoke, Gina was gone. He gave her the benefit of the doubt, told himself that she was just exercising, walking around the neighborhood, maybe going over to Starbuck's to grab a latte. But when he saw that she'd taken his Toyota instead of her old Dodge, and when she hadn't returned after an hour, he knew what had happened, he knew where she was.

On her way to the gas station.

Derek had no idea if the Dodge would make it out of Orange County, let alone all the way out to the middle of the Mojave, but he had no choice but to follow his wife. He didn't pretend to understand what was driving her, the impetus behind her pilgrimage. But if he was completely honest with himself, didn't he feel it, too? The abandoned gas station terrified him, and if he had his druthers, he would never see or even think of the building ever again. Hell, he wished they'd never encountered it. But at the same time, deep down, there was an impulse to return, a barely acknowledged, almost subconscious desire to know what was happening in that back room, to see who was in the chair.

She had more than an hour's head start. Maybe two, possibly three. Even if he drove at top speed and the car did not break down somewhere on the way, she would be at the gas station long before he was.

What would happen when she got there?

He didn't know.

He was afraid to even think about it.

He drove as fast as the car would go, well over the speed limit, and it was only dumb luck that prevented him from getting a ticket. The trip seemed to take forever, despite his speed—wasn't that one of Einstein's theorems?—and it was nearly noon when he finally pulled off the highway onto the unmarked dirt road that led to the gas station. Shot shocks bouncing, he sped past the collection of boulders that had originally attracted Gina to this place, cursing both the site and the photography obsession that had led to her interest in it. Coming over the rise, he saw the forsaken gas station on the desert plain below.

And the red Toyota parked next to one of the empty islands, sunlight glinting off its windshield.

Derek's heart was triphammering in his chest, and he was filled with a cold fear far greater than any he had previously experienced. He honked the horn as he approached, hoping the noise would draw Gina out, but he saw no movement through the broken window or open office door, and his hands were shaking as he pulled next to the Toyota and shut off the car.

He opened the driver's door, got out. "Gina!" he called as loudly as he could. He was afraid to go inside the building, wanted her to come out and meet him, but he knew that wasn't going to happen. "Gina!" he called again, angrily this time.

Nothing.

The world was silent.

Derek slammed the car door, and the noise was flat, muffled by the oppressive heat and heavy air. He could still see no movement in the office, and the doorway to the back room was completely dark. He hurried in, wishing he'd thought this through more thoroughly and brought something with him. A flashlight. A weapon.

A weapon?

Yes, he thought as he sped past that by-now-familiar metal desk. *Just in case.*

He stopped in the doorway of the secret room. "Gina?"

He didn't know why she'd come here, what she'd planned to do or what had actually happened, but her body lay sprawled on the dusty floor, unmoving, one hand stretched out as though reaching for the digital camera that was just beyond her reach.

She was also in the chair.

With an involuntary cry of anguish, Derek fell to his knees and shoved his face next to Gina's. The skin of her cheek was cold, and her eyelids were frozen halfway over her pupils, as though she'd died instantly in the middle of a blink. He reached for her hand, grabbed it, but it too was cold. Limp and heavy at the same time. She was dead, but he had no idea how she'd died, and he looked to the body in the chair for clues. Other than the fact that she was sitting up instead of lying on the floor, however, there was nothing that to his eyes indicated a cause of death.

He was too stunned to cry, though he was having a difficult time drawing breath and a low continuous moan was escaping from between his lips. He knew that he should have expected this, but somehow he hadn't, and the shock seemed to have rendered him incapable of coherent thought.

He suddenly realized that the body in the chair could disappear at any time, replaced by the corpse of another, and he quickly grabbed this Gina around the waist and, with considerable difficulty lowered her to the floor. On impulse, he kicked over the chair and shoved it into a corner of the small room.

He turned to look at his wife. Both versions of her. Other than their postures, they were exactly the same, down to the half-mast eyelids and the partially open mouth. His gaze was drawn by the dull silver of the camera that lay just beyond the reach of what he considered Gina's *real* body. It was her digital camera, not her 35mm, and it dawned on him that if she'd taken any photos, he would be able to look at them.

Did he really want to?

It was not a question Derek even considered. He picked up the camera and pressed the button to scroll back through the last pictures taken. He overshot his mark and had to scroll forward through a series of photos taken on Mother's Day: Gina with her mom, unwrapping presents, eating at a salad buffet. The sadness was sharp and painful, bringing with it logistical and practical issues as well as memories. Then he was past the personal pictures and in the desert. The gas station. The front office. The back room. There was a child in the chair, a dark-skinned nearly naked boy who appeared to have died from malnutrition. And the last shot: the boy disappearing, Gina taking his place, both figures ethereal and nearly transparent.

Derek stared at the small camera screen, trying to figure out what was happening in the picture. As far as he could tell, the dead Gina had started to appear in the chair even as the real Gina was alive and photographing the scene. He had no idea how that was possible or what it meant, but Gina had not taken another photo. Whatever had happened to her had happened then or immediately after. He looked down at the body lying on the ground, arm outstretched. She must have *seen* something, because after she'd been struck or smitten or however incapacitated, she'd still attempted to reach for her fallen camera. Her last act had been to try and take a picture, and he was filled with guilt that he had ever belittled her passion.

His eyes went to the section of wall that resembled a face. The visage looked exactly as it had before, rotted wood and shadow and mold combining to create that disturbingly intense countenance. Only from this angle, the black eyes appeared to be looking straight at him with what could have been anger, could have been hunger.

He wanted to tear down this building, wanted to come back with a fucking bulldozer and raze it. He even considered running out to the cars, getting the tire irons out of each trunk and coming back to smash that chair and gouge out that face, whaling on the walls, ripping off those boards and destroying as much of the room as he could.

But he didn't. Instead, he looked down at the bodies of his wife, trying to read the expression shared by both faces. She *had* died in mid-blink, he decided, and that partial hooding of her eyes made it difficult to ascribe an emotion to her death. Body language said more. The sitting Gina appeared rapt, as though viewing or hearing something absolutely fascinating. The Gina lying on the floor and reaching for the camera seemed desperate to record something of vital importance. Neither of them appeared to be in pain, but while his wife had not died in agony, she had died, and he would probably never know why or how.

He walked over to the face on the wall and spit on it.

This close, it did not even resemble a face. The individual components looked like what they were: rot and mold, shadow and grain. But nothing was what it seemed here. He glanced toward the overturned chair in the corner, then walked over, picked it up and set it right again, in exactly the same spot it had been in before.

He should get out of here, drive back to civilization, call the police, make arrangements. But he looked at the two Ginas and knew he couldn't leave. No matter how much he hated this place. No matter how scared he was.

Like her, he had to know.

Taking a deep breath, he sat in the chair.

And waited.

After

by Kealan Patrick Burke

This time tomorrow, they'll be asking why he did it.

This time tomorrow, he'll be dead by his own hand, or from a nervous policeman's bullet. Either way, it'll be checkout time and the method by which David Hoffman leaves this world will "make no never mind" as his mother used to say. He'll be gone and finally, mercifully free of the torment, the rage, the hurt that has torn him asunder all these years.

This time tomorrow he'll be dead.

But first he's going to shoot up the school.

And because they'll want to know why he did it and he won't be around to tell them, they will try to tell the story of his life based on the details available, accrued via neighbors ("He was so nice…"), family ("There has to be some mistake; he would never do such a thing…"), the old notebook found under his bed ("Fiery stars shining in the ragged black sockets of my enemies…"), and those who suddenly know him in light of the tragedy but never claimed to know him before.

They will look for answers, because such things cannot be let lie without them.

* * *

His childhood was not a turbulent one, no matter what spin the media put on it in the days after his death. There was discipline yes, sometimes severe, but no worse than the punishment doled out to any other child who grew up in the Catholic faith, a religion insistent in its belief that harsh words are never enough. You must be physically and emotionally bruised so that, when the blood rushes back into the hollows in your body and mind, it carries with it an awareness of what you've done, why it was wrong, and why you won't be doing it again.

Catholic children rarely make the same mistakes twice.

His mother liked to use the wooden spoon, but with strict control. Every

96

whack across his backside was a measured one, borne not of anger, but of necessity. *One-two-three, now think about what you've done.*

His father, on the other hand, had no such control, and David came to understand after years spent curled up in a wailing ball after weathering his furious rages and the hard bite of the belt across his legs, or a fist across his face, that his father's punishments were driven by disappointment, partly in the boy, mostly in himself. Frank Hoffman's life, it seemed, had somewhere along the line derailed and brought him to a place he had not planned on ever visiting, and surely did not want to stay—a place where his wife showed him affection that was more dutiful than genuine, as if she were following guidelines set out in some marital textbook; his son tested his patience and temper at every turn, and his boss treated him little better than a dog. He felt he did not make enough money and yet drank way too much, cursed even more, and seemed to hate himself a little more each day. Despite it all, some of David's best memories were of spending time with his old man, the weary smiles as some piece of paternal wisdom—which would invariably prove to be false—was handed down. Nevertheless the boy loved his father, and when cancer claimed him, two weeks shy of David's fourteenth birthday, he stood at the edge of the grave and begged him to come back, or at least, to move over in the bed so they could lie side by side, as he had been allowed to do, somewhat begrudgingly, whenever a storm battered their old house, or the monsters began to poke their gnarled bony fingers against the underside of David's mattress. They would sleep together, Laura Hoffman snoring softly on the far side of the bed, and all fear would vanish, swept away in a nothingness that smelled of Brut aftershave and whiskey.

The body in the coffin smelled nothing like his father. It looked like a wax representation of him that had started to melt in the heat. In the year of agony it took him to die, he'd wasted away to nothing, and not even the mortician could restore that weight to his corpse. Only the queer plastic face with its expression of forced serenity suggested there was anything beneath that cheap suit but clothes hangers.

They put him in the ground and, as that final shovel-load of dirt was tamped down on his grave, the light in Laura Hoffman's eyes went out like a snuffed candle. She had loved him, it was supposed, but had never quite learned how to show it beyond looking after him. It was probably how she'd been *taught* to love: cook, clean, and minimize the amount of hassle your man has to contend with when he arrives home from work, and surely he'll know you care. Over the next year, she grew almost as thin as David's father had been while the disease fed on him. It was as if she was suffering on his behalf, showing sympathy, empathy, though he was no longer around to observe or appreciate it. And though she was never cold to her son, he learned to rely on nobody but himself. He cooked, cleaned up, got up on time for school, and never missed a day.

Perhaps if he had, his own life would not have derailed and delivered him to his death.

It started when he turned fifteen, an event that, like so many things, passed by virtually unnoticed by his mother. He celebrated it by staying up an hour later than usual and watching *The Outer Limits* on TV. Then in bed, came hostile dreams in which the world was shrinking around him, the stars coming ever closer until each one was as big as the sun and burned the skin from his face. Frequently, he once confessed to his mother, he was subjected to such terrors, the world rushing in to suffocate him, making him feel vulnerable, ill at ease.

Never popular in school, he seemed to possess one of those dispositions that attracted the worst kinds of people—those who so desperately needed an outlet for their own unhappiness and inadequacies that, without a target, they risked implosion. The simple name-calling—"Dickless Dave," "Homo Hoffman"—and the shoving, shouldering, and sneering, didn't bother him so much. Despite the unfortunate fragility of his physical appearance, he was made of stronger stuff than that. He had lost his father, after all, and still moved about in a sluggish shell of grief that kept him numb, insensate. But that protective shell, the blinds he had kept drawn down to shield him from the world, had an adverse effect too. So tucked away was he that it made listening and learning difficult. His grades began to fail, not because of laziness, but because David found it almost impossible to retain the information being fed him.

It was only a matter of time before the lackluster grades came to his mother's attention. He had managed to hide from her the report cards, having learned to forge the wild loops and jagged scratches that were her signature, but there was only so much he could do about the phone calls from teachers, and ultimately, his principal, who insisted that they meet and discuss the boy's future, assuming, as he put it, his mother still wanted David to have one at Denmark High School.

Evil dictatorial principals are stereotypes—after all, no kid wants to go to school, and much like bullies, a candidate for the blame is essential—but the genesis of stereotyping is fact, and Mr. Brunner fit it perfectly. He was a thin, bald, sallow-faced man who wore suits he would like to pass off as expensive, a facade foiled by the frayed hems of his sleeves, the inward curl of his shirt-collars, and a single button on his blazer that didn't quite match the others. He wore glasses so thick they made his eyes seem stretched and made entirely of water. Even thicker were the dark hairs that poked from his wide nostrils, as if small animals had nested in his nasal passages. His mouth was set in a permanent expression of disapproval, and it was not hard to imagine him as a baby, fresh from the womb, his lips turning down as he critically appraised the world into which he'd been thrust. He seemed born to find flaws in everything, a task at which he excelled and in which he seemed to delight.

Laura Hoffman agreed to meet Mr. Brunner, and at 4:30 p.m., half an hour after school ended and the rank of yellow buses had wheezed and coughed their way out of the parking lot, she met her son outside Brunner's office, her own expression much like the principal's, but with less energy behind it. She said nothing to David, just sat and waited, her hooded eyes on the posters on the wall opposite, each one telling her how to circumvent the latent strains of rebellion that come courtesy of puberty. To the remaining staff that passed her by, she seemed likely to crumble into dust under the weight of Brunner's words.

But the meeting was a brief and civil one, with the ordinarily overbearing principal appearing to recognize the delicate state of his guest. He restricted himself to the facts, his tones measured as he informed Laura that her son's performance in school was growing steadily worse and could not be allowed to degrade further. He proposed that Laura take a more active role in David's education by keeping in constant communication with the teachers (after it emerged that David had been signing his own report cards) and by encouraging David to focus more on his work at home.

During the meeting, David spoke little, and indeed seldom was he called on to give his input. Brunner and Laura had convened not to hear his thoughts or feelings on the matter, but so he could hear firsthand what he was going to be *made* to do, what he would have to do if he intended to stay in school.

Had they asked, he might have told them that leaving or being expelled would have suited him fine. An intelligent and astute boy, his inability to hold on to the information and recycle it to impress his teachers depressed him. Added to that, he was the target of two bullies, one of whom was a grade higher, the other a boy in his own class. It is unknown whether or not David's antagonists were aware of each other—though in the microcosm that is high school, it seems likely—and it matters little. Together they presented a tireless and complete assault on his already fragile mind, with one preferring verbal abuse pertaining to David's dead father, while the other taunted him with threats of physical violence. And though David rarely found himself in a fight with either of them, choosing instead to abide by his father's wisdom that ignoring the threat was better, there were occasions in which he was discovered crying, bleeding and bruised under the bleachers, his pants and underwear bunched around his ankles, his glasses cracked or broken, his books scattered around him, most of them torn, his backpack missing, taken by his assailant.

In lieu of a proper school counselor—considered a useless luxury in a school of sound and secure young boys, and therefore vetoed by the school board some years before—the teachers tried to get David to open up to them about his feelings and promised to punish the offenders. The boy refused the former and railed against the latter, claiming it would only exacerbate an already bad situation. For a while, his request was met, until the day he was found sobbing in the boy's bathroom with a bloody nose and urine all over his clothes. A meeting was promptly held in the auditorium, reminding the students about the consequences of bullying, with severe promises of suspension, expulsion, and perhaps even police involvement if anyone dared ignore the school's policies on such things.

For a brief period after the meeting, David was not picked on. Instead, he was avoided. His presence in the hallway was enough to trigger a dramatic parting of the crowd of students as if he had become Moses at the Red Sea. They watched him with contemptuous stares and muttered insults as he walked by, then jeered at him as soon as he was far enough away to be unable to tell from where it had come. Not that it would have made a difference. David had never 'ratted out' his tormentors and never would, but the interjection of the principal and teachers, the indication that they had been made aware of something rotten in the state of Denmark High, had been enough. David was made a pariah, outcast further, and he withdrew into himself, became a ghost haunting the high school halls.

At home, his mother tried to console him and reel him back from the dangerous precipice upon which he seemed to stand, but since her husband's death, her own resolve had buckled, leaving her ill-equipped to handle even the most rudimentary crises in her own life. The thought of having to counsel her boy out of *his* misery was overwhelming, and, she thought, beyond her means. Laura did, however, suggest taking him out of Denmark High and relocating him. His response was to shake his head and quote another of his father's adages: "Nobody ever got anywhere by running."

At night, he wrote stories, thinly veiled fictions based on his own experiences and accompanied by crude illustrations in which larger-than-life adversaries were vanquished in hellish storms of blood, rent limb from limb by equally overdrawn heroes. None resembled David, but all were clearly reflections of how he wished he was: omnipotent, a dealer of destruction, a creature of vengeance. In the margins of the pages, squiggles and scratches told the story of an unfair world forever growing smaller, fiery stars shining in the ragged black sockets of his enemies. *Every step*, he wrote, *brings the end closer.*

Time passed. The bullies, the scoffing students, even the teachers forgot about David Hoffman. He became just another face in the hall, unremarkable, unworthy of note unless he chose to be.

And at length, of course, he did.

Because although the boy faded into the mural of high school, he remained intrinsically aware of the mechanisms that had brought him to this point in his life—the hurt, the hate, the pain—and it festered inside him, lurking just beneath his gaunt face and hollow eyes, warring with his restraint and patience, eager to explode in an all-consuming fire of vengeance. But though he permitted himself the odd fantasy (later reproduced and documented in his notebook) of ultra-violent ends for his fellow students and their vapid-faced teachers, he kept a tight rein on his emotions and the venomous threads that stitched them together.

He could wait, because hatred is patient.

* * *

On the 10ᵗʰ of October, 2008 at 8:03 a.m., David Hoffman walked up the steps of Denmark High School. The door was not locked. He entered the building and stood in the cold, empty hallway for some time, perhaps reliving each and every hurtful moment he had endured here, perhaps possessed by a single moment of doubt in which he questioned the purpose of what he was about to do. If so, grim determination and homicidal resolve overruled it, and he carried on, chambering a round into his deceased father's shotgun—a gun Frank Hoffman had owned but never used—entering each and every classroom and opening fire. The sound was like a cannonade, echoing around the school, rattling pipes and sending vibrations rippling through the floor and walls. Plaster flew, glass shattered, wood exploded. David carried on, until he had visited every classroom, assassinated every vile phantom, by which time the cops were clustered outside, sirens flickering silently, stern voices filtered through megaphones ordering him to come out.

Only then did he find his way back to the main entrance, where he stood weeping as he looked out on the world. Without his realizing it, it had grown smaller still, trapping him inside the vault of his worst memories, recollections that had not fallen before his gun as they'd been meant to, but snickered and sneered when he turned his back on them.

The police would later say he looked like a ghost, an ashen figure behind glass so dusty it hardly reflected anything at all. His eyes, they would add, were the same.

* * *

And when at last David dropped to the floor and sat so that he could better execute his own suicide, jamming the barrel of the gun beneath his chin and screaming, it was the thing they would remember most: The day a forty-five-year-old man, for no apparent reason, went mad and took his own life in the doorway of a long-abandoned school.

Attempts would be made to unravel the mystery of David Hoffman's life, to find answers, because such things cannot be let lie without them in a world as small as ours.

Consumed

by Michael Louis Calvillo

If he learned anything, something, one thing, it was that his teeth were strong as hell. Limb upon limb upon bone upon gland, muscle after muscle after tough, tough muscle, slick, slimy nub after nub of indistinguishable biology: through all of it, his choppers held. They showed no signs of wear. They could, would, go on and on and on. Nathan, wide-eyed ever-stare, pictured them gleaming, gnashing, chewing, still in motion long after the gums, tendons, muscles and soft tissues that powered them had shredded away into wet webs of pulpy nothing.

He closed his eyes, not that it mattered. The bodies were still there. Bodies. Flesh. Blood. Bone. Prickly pieces, salty parts (genitalia he assumed, feared, gagged, choked), coiled, mushy greens and pinks and reds and blacks and here he was, mild-mannered Nathan at the bottom of it all, in the thick of it so to speak, mouth full, spitting decay sideways, refilling and then spitting once again.

Repeat.

So very many bodies.

His body, though gored and grimy, was holding up. Not nearly as well as his teeth, but well enough.

Well enough?

Yes, well enough, considering: hands bound behind his back, tight, thick, razor wire about the wrists and ankles. Zero cooperation. Miraculously, his limbs still functioned on his behalf. However, they bore no autonomy. Instead, they moved as one giant muscle. His mouth (more importantly his teeth) chewed away what it could, his head tossed the vile meat aside, and then his body jerked and bucked and wriggled its way upward. The process was slow and impossible, but Nathan pushed on, human worm, slug, a maggot with a good set of teeth and the unfortunate ability to ponder destiny, how he got here, and where he was going…If ever you find yourself abroad, tropical diversion, plushness so plush that the world looks soft, American antidote in the land of the ever present sun, thong back bikinis and alcoholic concoctions that taste like angel urine, if ever you

102

find yourself here, appreciate the contentment you have situated yourself within. Appreciate and ignore the dizzy tickle in your nose, the futile thought that this could be better, that things can always be better. Ignore, ignore, ignore. Remind yourself that you are already high, that things don't get much better. This is a land of beauty. This is unreal. This isn't the cutthroat, cocksure, dog-eat-dog, rat race of the cliché-ridden Americas. This is paradise. Using cocaine here would be an exercise in redundancy.

Listen to yourself.

Never engage the natives.

Never solicit them for drugs.

Never exude American ego, pride. Never head off into the rainforest with a Carlos or a Juan or a Hector. Never do these things or you might find yourself bound, forced to line up with others—men, women, children you've never seen before—at the edge of a deep, deep pit. Shots are fired, you are shot, or just startled by the blast, unhit, amazingly missed, falling anyway, feigning dead, plotting your escape. But the plan keeps getting tougher and tougher to realize because group after group of hysterical prisoners are being lined up, shot and dropped on top of you.

When the carnage is over and your murderers have started their jeeps and roared away, you are buried deep, oh so deep, in death.

Desensitized entirely.

Skinbilepusblood. The retching passes after a few hours. The smell becomes, for lack of a better word, familiar. Nathan adapts and eats because he must. Must. He closes his eyes and tries to invoke memory, tries to go inward and get free. He tries to place himself in the board room, AC on full blast, his associates looking at him with envy as Boss man pats him on the back and compliments him on his deal-sealing smile. He tries for recollection; respite in the cool center of his brain, but no matter how hard he flexes and strains for cerebration he can't escape the tactility of the pit.

It's nearly impossible to get past a world that impresses itself upon you so forcefully. Imagine the pressures of everyday life manifest, made real, physical, woven into hunks and chunks of flesh and bone. Imagine them poking and prodding and penetrating every inch of your skin. Nathan shifts and the world shifts back: haggard female torso beneath, fleshy breasts and bony ribs supporting his weight, a gaggle of stiff children flanking his left and right, lips blue, hands frozen like claws. And so it goes: above and below, on and on and on: anatomy without discernable structure: pink-brown-red, strands of dark, matted hair, bone, a thousand eyes, filmy, dead, staring, inviting him to eat and eat and eat, to rise refreshed, reinvigorated, reborn.

And when free? What then? What of where he has been? What of the flesh? How can he ever look at another human being in the same way again?

He can't, no way, not now, not ever, and this horrible thought stops him, gives the worm act pause and freezes his teeth. What would freedom, escape, a lung full of fresh air, do to his brain? Would it surge, effervescent lightning, animating him, plunging him, full force into the ecstasy of being?

Or would it burn?

Would it atomize, destroy, sear, melt?

Would it drive him backward, hungry for the pit, hungry for death, burrowing downward, mouth wide, black-heart open, soul dilated, ready, waiting, burning to eat and eat and eat?

Would it accelerate the rot?

The rot manifest. The rot eternal. The rot evident.

Constant. A dead spot in his eyes, a foul taste in his throat. The impetus of all desire, natural and unnatural, made big and shiny and evil, armor plating his brain, twisting his every thought toward darkness.

Nathan's physicality has been tainted; his physiology stained. The process of living, really a process of dying, would now arch and turn, forever changed, forever exemplifying decay, forever focusing, honing in on and centering upon death. If he actually made it, rolling up and out, on his back, searching the night skies, begging to be blinded and consumed by starlight, Nathan feared that the constellations and their exquisite beauty, their sacred glow, would be forever lost to him. Something inside told him that he would only be able to focus on the dark and limitless black that surrounded the world. Should he ever emerge from the pit, he was convinced his actuality would become one of shadows.

Cocooned within this temple of flesh, Nathan has become nameless.

Topside, priorities would shift. Snorting, spending, conversing, loving, logging on, clocking out, all of these things no longer possessed meaning.

Curbside, awash in a sea of people, the smell of hair gel, sweat, perfume, laptops, commerce, there would be no way to stop staring. No way to shelve this awareness, this understanding of the continual, constant internalizing, thinking thoughts like mold and for what? Everybody tastes the same. Everybody is the same inside: wet and funky and raw. Nothing more than intelligent fruit, genius vegetable, rational plant.

The point here then, is that there is no point. None. Beauty is organic, biological, it's blood and sperm and pus and sweat and bile and marrow, it's that cool, damp, nothing space in the very center of all things, its electricity and fire. It's everything but thought. Thought, that by which we became gods and superiors, is nothing but a senseless waste of energy. Thought does nothing but slow Nathan down.

Repeat.

Back to it.

Return of the worm.

The violence of Nathan's motion shifted the dead pit entire. He sank ever so slightly, crushing the torso beneath him, losing ground. Getting his teeth around what he figured to be either a hand or a foot, he readied himself. Closing his eyes tightly, he began working his jaw, jerking his body, intent on carving a bloody path upward, ascension, striving for some sort of pit-side enlightenment and the cool, unlit kiss of destiny.

Guarded

by Michael A. Arnzen

The security gate swallows you.

An alarm blares, louder than you expected, jangling your nerves. For just a second, everyone at the checkpoint around you freezes and time seems to halt while the horn rapidly bleats like the high notes from the *Psycho* soundtrack. Then three Transportation Security officers in starched white uniforms step forward and form a phalanx that blocks your path. The one on the left, a black woman whose jaws grind on a piece of Juicy Fruit, manages to lift a smile on one side of her face before asking you to step back. The white bread guy on your right wears his uniform like it's his nicest suit, and he primly steps forward, raising an eyebrow to dare you to resist as he pats the end of his metal detector wand in an open palm, a high tech billy club. The third has his hand open like a talon above his holster. "Step back," he repeats, Schwarzenegger-style.

You blush and apologize, exiting the gate while you check your pockets, avoiding the glares of the people in line behind you. The alarm finally switches off and you can hear some of them grumble and curse. Your hand hits something cold and metallic and you realize how stupid you've been. You drop your keys and a cigarette lighter into a plastic tub, and one of the officers shakes it around as if panning for gold as you step back through the gate.

The alarm blares again, annoying more than alerting—loud enough to erase your brain. The guards' eyes fix on you and you shrug your shoulders. "Maybe it's my belt buckle?"

White Bread waves you over with his wand. "Step over here, sir."

You walk over to a table behind a wall of clear, but thick, glass. The phalanx encircles you the entire way and two more guards join them, militarily alert. Your risk level apparently just went up a notch.

"Arms out," the woman says, chewing her gum between her big teeth.

You stand scarecrow stiff as they wand your limbs like you were radioactive. You watch as others pass through the gate. A few of the people who were in line

106

behind you toss angry glances your way; others avoid looking at you, as if eye contact might set off the alarm again.

You can't believe that you've been singled out like this. Plenty of people passing through the gate look more like terrorists and mad bombers than you do. People with scraggly beards and brown skin and beady black eyes and suicidally dour worry lines. People with bulky outfits and funny hats and bottles of God knows what kind of liquid. Compared to them, you might as well be Uncle Sam himself. You're just an average Joe. A regular guy. It's not fair.

"Shoes off," Juicy Fruit commands. You lift one leg at a time and try to control your balance as you slide off your sneakers. The concrete is as cold and hard as a prison cell floor when you step down on it.

One of the guards inspects your Nikes. He takes a deep sniff of one and you laugh.

"What's so funny?" White Bread asks, patting your kidney with his wand.

Your eyebrows furrow. You see a bearded man with a turban stroll through the security gate. "Nothing...I just can't believe you're wasting all this effort on me when clearly there are others who..."

White Bread pokes you this time and then turns you around so you are facing him and the other guards. "You have a grudge against the other passengers?" he asks.

Your feet feel cold and bony on the floor. "No, I just have a plane to catch. And I honestly don't know why you've stopped me when there are plenty of people just traipsing right on through the gate who clearly fit the terrorist profile."

"The TSO does not practice racial profiling anymore," Juicy Fruit says, that one-sided smile of hers lifting high enough to show the black-and-pink lining of her upper gums.

"Nope," White Bread confirms. "But *you* sure do think you're special, Mister. And special people are our business." He hands his paddle over to an officer on his left and then pulls on a pair of latex gloves. Every prison movie you've ever seen flashes in your mind. But he doesn't ask you to bend over and instead moves both of his hands toward your face. "Now open wide," he says, as if he were some kind of military dentist.

You clamp shut. It's instinct. The idea of having his fascist fingers probing around in your mouth makes you gag a little.

"Sir, I am just asking you to open your mouth. We need to check..."

You grind your teeth and snap your head side-to-side to mime your reply: *No. Fucking. Way.*

White Bread flexes his hands in front of your neck like he'll strangle you. You raise your chin defiantly, and he eventually shrugs. You detect a little smile, in fact. "Fine, we'll play this your way."

Juicy Fruit waves at a gladiator-type nearby, sporting a Kevlar vest and an over-the-shoulder rifle. The gladiator swizzles a toothpick between his lips and sizes you up with the pencil tip-thin pupils of his steely blue eyes. "What've we got now?"

His buzz cut seems to bristle when you grumble at him from behind your compressed lips.

"A defier," Juicy Fruit says, as if it were a real word. "He set off the alarm twice, but nothing turns up when we wand him. We performed a full pat-down and shoe check, but he's refusing oral inspection."

"Is that so?" Gladiator asks, his face an inch from your nose. His breath smells of stale wood and artificial mint and it even burns your eyes a little. But you're not going to open your mouth. You'd rather miss your flight than be violated by these human robots.

Gladiator smirks. Then he looks over at White Bread and winks.

Before you know it, you're being lifted off your feet and ushered behind another partition—an opaque pane of frosted bulletproof glass.

A place where there will be no witnesses.

You break your silent rebellion. "Okay, okay, you can check my mouth. My flight's leaving soon and I want to just get this over with."

They ignore you, carrying you toward a darkened doorway with a sign overhead that reads DEEP INSPECTION.

"What the *hell*?"

You receive a kidney punch for that one as you pass through the entrance, the hands beneath your underarms pinching you tight as the group of thugs lead you through a twisting corridor of partitions. You grunt and struggle, but then stiffen as you detect the sounds of other people up ahead.

You hear plaintive cries. The screams of children and grown men. And behind them: electric sizzles and spits.

You make a final turn and enter a room the size of a theater, illuminated with so much overhead fluorescence that it takes a minute for your eyes to adjust and recognize the nightmare in store for you.

For a second, it looks like some kind of factory floor. Shockingly shiny aluminum tables, dress-right-dress, fill the room. Strange machines pivot over them, with robot arms that pinch down at the bodies tied down on the tables. The tabletops are angled so that the feet are in the air and the heads are almost upside down, mouths twisted in agony. Pistons and tubes and wires dangle everywhere. You see sparks. Uniformed men and women operate each station, anonymous behind their hospital masks, overseeing monitors and keyboards beside the horrifying machines.

There are at least fifty of them.

Oddly, there are wide windows of glass that reveal the expansive field of the airport beyond. A plane takes off, as if leaving all of this madness behind. It seems unholy for so much mechanized evil to be so visible, so out in the open like this—and yet at the same time so invisible, so ignored. *How can they get away with this?*

You cry out for help and White Bread groans. "Oh, why don't you just do us all a favor and go back to playing mum?"

And you do, because you know that no one will come to your rescue. There are plenty of other people crying out for help and mercy and God, but no one seems to be paying attention. The machines bob and weave like you're on some kind of science fiction movie set. This place functions in such well-oiled harmony that it has obviously been in operation for a very long time. So you know there is no hope for rescue. You focus your attention on identifying an escape route. But there is none. The only way out is the way you came in, and there's nothing out there but more guards with guns and ammunition.

"Over there's a free table," someone says behind you and then you see what he is talking about: an empty operating table near the far wall awaits. A man with large glasses perched above his hospital mask stands nearby, tapping keys on a console.

As they lead you toward it, you scan the agonized faces of others who are being probed and lanced and photographed and electrocuted. The people are from every walk of life, every culture, every age, and every race. Unified in pain.

And, given the screams you hear, you are surprised to see so little blood. But there's plenty of scarring and bruising and burn marks to make up for it. Men and women—some of them young children or geriatric grandparents—writhe around you like insects crisping under a magnifying glass.

"What the hell is all this?" you ask, but they ignore you, stripping your clothes off of you like they are tailoring a department store mannequin. Then they lash your torso down on a cold table with a black ribbon of thick Velcro.

"Open wide," White Bread teases again as the officers pull your legs apart. The ankles are strapped awkwardly to the table.

The head of your table drops down, angling, lifting your legs above your head. Disoriented by this, you gaze out the large windows and see a plane take off and it looks like it is descending into a dark pool of night outside, rather than lifting up into the heavens. Then all light blots out as the robotic arms whir into place before you. The rubber tubes that run back from its fingers begin to jitter and chug like a cyborg's circulatory system.

It angles and moves closer toward your face. A needle slides out from the center of its palm.

You writhe and tug and scream.

And before you know it, it's already pulling back away from your neck, trickling a few hot droplets of blood onto your chin.

You have no idea whether it has taken a sample or has injected you with something of its own.

A second arm swings down out of nowhere and slowly streams a bar of light across your body, Xerox style, beginning at your feet, then washing over your groin, then over your chest, the table moving along with its actions automatically in sync. You can feel the blood droplets on your body fizzling dry beneath its beam. When the lamp reaches your head you're blinded.

You feel the light switch off. You blink as shapes and shadows slowly form around you. You hear a scream from nearby while someone else says something about a sandwich.

Then something pinches the nape of your neck. You feel a metal mouth gnawing its way into the back of your skull. The metal clicks, pops and scrapes between your ears, behind your head, and the itchy foreign wetness you feel sliding around beneath you is maddening.

But you're still alive.

And you hear the man operating the keyboard beside you call over White Bread. "Confirm," he says.

You can only see hazy shadows of form, but White Bread looks down at you, and you can tell he's grinning. "Are you sure?" he asks his cohort through the side of his mouth.

"He's a niner-niner," the faceless man replies somewhere beside you. "He's got the gene."

"I'm not a freaking terrorist!" you scream, struggling in your bonds. "I'm an American citizen!"

White Bread chuckles while you finish screaming. "Why do they always say that?" he asks the man beside him.

The faceless man peers down at you like a doctor. "There's no such thing as terrorism, sir," he says, swinging a new robot arm down in front of your face. "An ism is a belief. A mere worldview." He adjusts a dial. "And worldviews are always colored by genetics." He blinks twice as he takes a moment to size up your confusion. "To put it simply, sir, you have what we call the Defiance gene."

"The *what*?" You feel your blood boil. "There's no such thing!"

"Of course you'd say that, sir," he replies. "You Defiers always disagree. It's in your nature." He blinks again. "We're not going to argue with you."

White Bread is again requesting that you open your mouth. Only he's doing it politely this time.

You don't defy him. You obey, as if that meant something. You drop your jaw.

And then the machine moves forward like a fist that fingers your mouth open even wider than you thought possible with its sharp metal hooks. Seven-tined forks clamp grizzly into your tongue and you bite down on them. You puzzle over the flavor, which doesn't taste like blood so much as hand sanitizer.

It's the last thing you'll ever taste.

Obsidian Sea

by Kurt Kirchmeier

Trammel caressed the trigger of the flare gun, once again resisting the urge to squeeze it true. Although the sea itself had settled, the storm-kneaded waters flattening out like so much cerulean dough, a thousand black spheres continued to bob in his periphery, riding the waves like onyx balloons set adrift. Some had swelled to the size of bowling balls, while others remained no bigger than the hailstones Trammel had initially mistaken them for. He wondered now about the lightning, if perhaps he'd mistaken that, too.

For all his panicked rowing, for all his grunting and splashing and adrenaline-fed desperation, the mysterious spheres were no further away at present than they had been at the very outset. It was as though they were attached to the raft by tethers unseen, held in place by forces ineffable.

Well past the point of exhaustion now, Trammel simply slouched in the stern and waited, his arms and his back aching from exertion, the cool evening wind made cooler by the sheen of sweat on his skin.

Spent thunderheads patched the horizon like oblongs of rust; the ochre sun had begun to set, following the path his thirty-foot trawler had taken just a short while before.

Empathy. Trammel had named the boat thus to spite his father, who had attempted to impress upon his only son the belief that such a trait would get him nowhere. It seemed the old man had had the right of it, after all.

More than anything, Trammel had hoped to leave behind him sons and daughters of his own, children to carry his name as well as his spirit, but with his future hinging on the results of the single flare, of one small distress signal loosed at an endless sky, the idea of a living legacy was beginning to seem unlikely at best.

Unlikely, but not impossible; as tempting as it was to swear off patience and just let fly the brilliant projectile now, to follow up on the whistling shot with one last prayer, Trammel knew he'd have a better chance of being spotted after dark.

111

He shuddered at the thought of a whole night spent surrounded, a whole night spent listening to the eerie hum.

He'd failed to notice the monotone sound through the duration of his failed escape, but now that he'd become aware of it, he could hear nothing else. Low and deep and continuous, it brought to mind meditating Buddhists as heard from a distance. The Zen analogy, however, ended there.

He cupped his ears and took a deep breath, expelled the air from his lungs in a long steady stream. How the myriad globes could even float was beyond him, for they'd descended upon his trawler with a weight and fury exceeding grapeshot, puncturing the roof of the cabin, perforating both the deck and the hull. The sound had been deafening, a million miniature fists pounding on wood and fiberglass and cold Atlantic water, the hail and the spray and the fragments reducing visibility to virtually nil.

That he himself had somehow passed through the carnage unscathed seemed nothing short of miraculous. It was almost as if the violent rain of black had avoided him intentionally, as if it had made a conscious, premeditated even, decision to keep him alive. Why this would be didn't bear contemplation.

Every so often, a dorsal fin could be seen amidst the many orbs, a curious knife in the water, but never did the sharks stay long; nor did any of them see fit to drag one of the unearthly objects down for a little taste. Hungry enough to investigate, yet too wary to eat—probably not a portentous sign, thought Trammel.

The raft continued to rock, seconds turning into minutes and minutes giving way to hours. Darkness settled about the sea like a blanket, the crescent moon sheltering behind a thick bank of ominous cloud. The water was glass now, but no less sinister for all its lack of turbulence.

The spheres continued to encircle the raft, staring up from the midnight broth like a thousand obsidian eyes. Still no sign of another ship. Still no sign of the shore.

Trammel blinked hard and rubbed his eyes. Perhaps it was too much sun and too little water, or maybe it was the hours of physical exertion and compound stress finally catching up to him; whatever the case, the strange hum soon began to sound almost tranquil, a morbid sort of lullaby.

For a while he fought his weariness, frequently splashing water in his face and occasionally screaming into the empty night, but eventually the strain on his lids became too great.

Even in sleep, escape remained elusive.

Trammel's eyes had scarcely closed in earnest when he sensed a sudden otherness inside his mind. Like sentient probes, they assailed him, every memory they touched given life in the form of a dream. Lucid throughout, Trammel wondered what it was they were doing, what they were searching for.

They lingered long in his childhood, corkscrewing through recollected scenes like wisps of curious smoke, pausing now and again as though to examine the nuances of human interaction, the social hierarchy of man. And through the course of the million-shot slideshow grew an air of studious zeal and grim intent.

Trammel awoke to the sound of splashing.

Despite the absence of the moon, he could still make out those spheres that were nearest the raft, though no longer were they spheres at all. The once-black shells were now fleshy and misshapen, and contorting in a way that bespoke of life within. Life attempting to get out. Some bore singular arms at either side, groping hands paddling them in hopeless circles. Others raked at the waves with two.

One by one, they approached, the sickly white and almond tanned, the olive and the brown, skin-sacks of forming tissue and shifting cartilage, all of them flailing and thrashing at the tar-black waters, some with fully-formed fingers and some with only stumps.

Brandishing an oar like a club, Trammel reared back and swung at the first one to reach the raft. The oar connected with a sound like a tenderizer put to meat, the sickening wetness accompanied by the unmistakable pop of broken bones. The fleshy surface gave like an oversized grape, blood oozing from orifices that might otherwise have become nostrils and a mouth.

New hands clawed at his ankles, partially formed heads lolling on necks not yet strong enough to fully support them. Here and there a wide and searching eye could be seen, the sickle moon, exposed now, reflecting in rheumy stares.

Again and again the oar fell, but there were simply too many of them. Adrenaline soon yielded to exhaustion; Trammel collapsed to his knees. And saw a light in his periphery.

There, in the distance, a panning beacon. The shore.

He scrambled for the flare gun, found it within the grasp of pale fingers, being dragged overboard. A well-placed kick freed it from imminent submersion. Trammel quickly took it up and aimed it skyward, releasing its charge into the darkness.

Light washed across the ocean's surface like a veneer of shimmering crimson, bringing the countless beings into sharp relief. There followed an awful epiphany as Trammel looked out upon a living legacy gone horribly wrong. At once he understood why they'd so thoroughly explored his mind while he slept, why they had plumbed the depths of his experience.

They'd been searching for a suitable form, a subtle means by which to commence their invasion.

Many of them were whole now, arms propelling them toward the shore. Children. They were becoming children.

The Living World

by C. Michael Cook

Melissa emptied the cupboards and then the refrigerator. She put everything in the trash because she couldn't imagine putting any of it in her mouth.

Cereal, eggs, meat. Especially the meat.

She scanned the countertops, looking for anything she might have missed. She found the honey sitting next to the stove, and almost threw it away before realizing it was okay.

She could eat honey.

She fought with the lid then found a spoon. The honey was sticky and thick, so sweet it made her throat itch, and she swallowed one grateful spoonful after another. When it was gone she scraped the sides of the jar clean.

Tomorrow she'd tell Carrie about the honey and swear her to secrecy. Melissa could lose her job over it, her apartment and car and everything else. Then what? She could picture the whole thing ending with her back in Iowa, with her parents, at the farm, where everything, everywhere was destined to become food.

Beef, corn, milk.

Melissa loved working with the girls—and sometimes boys—at the hospital. They all arrived with at least one secret. It was the secrets that made them push the food around on their plates, or bring it back up in private, or rush it through their systems with pills, or refuse it altogether.

Secrets about the things they'd done, the things that had been done to them, the things they desperately wanted to do.

Melissa wasn't that much older than some of the girls. She believed this was why she'd been hired. The girls saw her as more of a contemporary, not exactly a counselor, even though she'd filled that role for over a year. Because she was young, they were more likely to be honest with her, more likely to share the secrets that made them want to be so thin, to starve themselves, sometimes even to die.

Carrie was different from the other girls. At nineteen she was a little older, her case more severe. She'd been pretty once, smiling from snapshots and school photos, with blonde hair and eyes blue as gas flames.

Her secret was different too. Different even from Melissa's. Once, Melissa had believed there was a door in front of her, one only she could see, and if she could only get thin enough, she'd finally be able to slip through it.

The passage would transform her, making her something both special and ordinary, perfect and unattainable. And then she'd be free to go, leaving her parents and the farm, her school and the little town around it, so far behind that no one—not even she—would ever be able to see it.

That was her secret, and it had been coaxed from her at a hospital two thousand miles and ten years away, by a woman named Marilyn, with curly brown hair and round hips like Melissa's. The secret was the key, she said, that could unlock the trap Melissa had created for herself, and eventually Melissa saw that she was right.

Eighteen months later, when Melissa finally did leave home, it was for college. She majored in psychology and earned her master's and came to California. Now she helped other girls unlock the traps they'd created.

But Carrie was still a puzzle. She didn't want to escape a troubled childhood or adolescence. She wasn't interested in distancing herself from a family that trapped and embarrassed her. She didn't care about the admiration of other girls or the attention of boys and men, or fitting in or standing out.

Carrie just wanted to stop eating. She'd been hospitalized, gotten better and worse several times before finally showing up at Melissa's hospital, wheeled in on a stretcher, refusing to open her mouth even to speak.

Her parents had tried everything, they said, she'd been seen everywhere. They didn't know what to do for her, but they wanted her in a hospital environment. She was destroying their family. There were two other children to worry about, and Carrie's illness was affecting them.

It was all in the folder Melissa's supervisor gave her one afternoon. Carrie stood five-foot-six and weighed 92 pounds. She had a BMI of 14.8, low blood pressure and heart rate, alopecia, every sign of advanced malnutrition. Her academics had been good and her IQ was high. "Scary smart," is how her supervisor put it.

"No one expects you to cure her," she said. Her supervisor was blonde, one of those women who polish themselves to a high gleam, and Melissa always felt dowdy in front of her, no matter what she did. "Just see if you can get her to talk," the supervisor said, catching Melissa's eyes with her own. "See what you can learn."

Later that afternoon Melissa led a group. The topic was how the girls and their friends supported their disordered eating habits.

One revealed, "We competed to see who could eat the fewest calories each day."

115

Another confessed, "We tried to be the one who could go the longest without eating anything."

Yet another, "We took pictures and video of one another, looking as thin as possible, and posted them on the Web."

They told about texting their weight morning and night, of passing along diets designed to trick their bodies into shedding just a few more pounds, sharing cocktails of supplements and laxatives, taking turns with trusted friends in front of the toilet while the other stood by in silent, supportive approval.

Melissa listened to them all, and now she had a new secret of her own: everything they talked about, everything they described, made her want to do those things again.

Juice, pastries, soda.

Carrie was too weak to move so they met in her room. She was nothing like her pictures. Now the skin hung from her bones like so much empty fabric, thin hair clung to her skull like it was wet, and her eyes, those brilliant blue eyes, bulged from sockets stained purple. She looked like a frail and frightened old woman.

The first time Melissa arrived, Carrie was watching TV. Melissa introduced herself and explained why she was there, then asked if Carrie would mind turning off the TV so they could talk.

Carrie's eyes never left the screen, even after two more requests. Melissa ended up turning it off herself, then spent the next forty minutes asking questions that Carrie left untouched. Toward the end of the hour she finally resorted to telling Carrie about herself.

Their next appointment was the same, so Melissa simply sat and watched TV with Carrie, curious to see where things might go.

The science channels were Carrie's favorites, especially the shows about animals. Over the course of a week or more they watched bears pulling salmon from rivers, owls and hawks plucking mice and rabbits from grassy fields, tigers separating the weak gazelle from the rest of its frenzied herd.

As it was on land, so it was in the sea. Shrimp scoured life from the ocean floor, fish ate the shrimp, bigger fish ate the smaller ones, and on and on, until it finally ended at the ocean's surface, with giant nets spilling their catches onto boat decks and beds of ice.

Day after day Carrie watched TV, not eating, not talking, and Melissa watched Carrie. She grew thinner and more frail. The lines of her skull emerged from inside her face. Veins stood out on her arms like worms beneath the skin.

Sharks, lions, wolves.

A week later Melissa's supervisor summoned her to a meeting with the administrative board. Melissa told them Carrie was making progress, even though she still hadn't eaten or spoken.

Someone asked if it was time to consider next steps.

Another replied that their hands were tied in many ways. Carrie was of legal age, able to refuse treatment.

Someone else wondered if a dedicated psychiatric unit, or even a hospice, might be a better alternative.

Another suggested contacting Carrie's parents, to broach the subject of having her committed. Then they could start tube feeding, right here, even without her consent.

Their businesslike tone said they thought she'd failed, or was in danger of doing so very soon.

"These are all good ideas," Melissa said, and every head in the room swiveled toward her. "But they'll all take time to implement." She managed to keep her voice steady and meet most of their eyes. "Given that, I'd ask that you allow me to continue working with Carrie, at least until another approach can be implemented." Outside the window a bird landed on a branch, a piece of something dangling from its beak. "I think I can help her. I just need a little more time."

They considered her request. It would only be a few days until something could be done. There seemed to be no harm in allowing Melissa to continue until then.

When the meeting was over, Melissa took the stairs to Carrie's room two at a time. The elevators were always busy because the stairs were off-limits for the girls, had been ever since someone discovered a group of them climbing up and down the flights, trying to burn off the calories they'd been encouraged to eat.

The TV was on when she arrived. An amoeba enveloped something on the screen while a voice described how the organism traps its prey.

Melissa looked down at Carrie from the side of her bed. "You have to talk to me," she said.

Carrie stared at the TV.

Melissa weighed her options, chose the one she estimated would have the greatest effect. "They want to have you committed," she said, "so you can be force fed. No choice. They'll put tubes down your throat and pump your stomach full of food. Is that what you want?"

Carrie looked at the ceiling and blinked back tears, then gathered a deep breath and let it out as though she'd just made a great effort. Her breath smelled sour and sulfurous, the telltale scent of her body burning muscles and organs.

Then, finally, she spoke. Her voice was weak and rusty, and each word sounded like a rock she had to carry up a steep hill.

Carrie said, "I want to tell you a secret."

Melissa kept her face steady. She sat down in the chair next to the bed and turned toward Carrie.

"Closer," Carrie said.

Melissa leaned forward and tilted her ear, close enough now to hear the meaty clicks of Carrie's throat as she swallowed.

She whispered, "Everything you eat is dead. Every time you eat, you put something dead in your mouth. Every bite. Every day."

Melissa sat back. It was as though Carrie had inserted the words directly into her ear. They itched in there like drops of water.

She'd met girls who worried over the calories or grams of fat in every bite. She'd seen them nurture peculiar likes and dislikes the way old women cultivate rare orchids. Others maintained strict vegetarian diets or obsessed about the preparation and cleanliness of every meal. But she had never, ever heard anything like what Carrie had just said. Had never even considered it herself.

She smiled and said, "That can't be right," and tried to think of an exception. Not meat or seafood. At the other end of the spectrum she discovered that every fruit and vegetable she could think of, from the moment it was picked, was as dead as any flesh. Grains, too. Even dairy products and eggs fit the mold, all of them dead from the moment they left the animals' bodies, their steady decline toward decomposition slowed only by refrigeration.

Melissa stood up. "That can't be right," she said again, unsure of what to do next. She walked to the door and rested her hand against the wood, then turned and said, "I'll be back."

She went to her office and typed "live food" into a search engine, then spent her lunch hour following the results. She saw video of factories where cattle and pigs were slaughtered and blood turned the white floors black. She read about sushi cut from live fish and served quivering on the plate. She watched Asians eating live octopus, the animals' systems in shock from soaking in vinegar and wine but still conscious enough to curl their tentacles over the mouths opening before them, fighting life's oldest insult with life's oldest instinct.

She passed the rest of the afternoon in a call-and-response argument with herself, seeking an exception she could bring back and present to Carrie. Surely not all food was dead. There had to be something.

And if not an exception, at least a line of logic that would neutralize Carrie's...observation. Melissa couldn't bring herself to call it a delusion, because the more she thought about it, the more it wasn't turning out to be very delusional.

Perhaps she could argue that it was only natural, that death was simply the currency of the living world, the grease that enabled every other wheel to turn. The weak fell to the strong, the large ate the small, the living consumed the dead. It was true, but it didn't make the endless cycle it described any less horrifying.

Steak, bread, cheese.

After work she drove home past restaurants, their bright windows framing couples and families gathered at tables, eager for the feast to come. She passed supermarkets and corner stores where people bought death to take home with them, or ate it right there beneath the fluorescent lights.

It was dark by the time she pulled into her parking space. She walked to her front door with insects humming in the trees and bushes around her, and birds swooping in the purple sky above. They were part of the cycle, too. Everything was.

She hurried to the safety of her front door and scrambled to get the keys in the lock.

At the sight of her kitchen Melissa's stomach felt sour and hollow. She hadn't eaten since breakfast, and even though she wasn't hungry—couldn't be, really—it was important to eat. Skipping lunch had been an accident. One missed meal, once in a while, wasn't a problem. Healthy people did it all the time, and usually overcompensated for it the next time they ate. But two meals in a row, especially when her nerves were humming and she was almost enjoying that familiar feeling of emptiness, the one that also filled her up, that was the slippery slope they warned the girls about.

She found a plate of leftovers in the refrigerator—a chicken breast, a mound of mashed potatoes, some green beans. She put it in the microwave and when it was done she sat down at the kitchen table with the steaming plate in front of her.

The potatoes seemed most appetizing, so she began with small forkfuls of those, paging through a magazine as she ate. This was something they advised the girls never to do, especially the ones who binged, because it kept them from concentrating on the meal and their bodies' response to it. But tonight she needed the distraction. Without it she wouldn't be able to eat at all.

The green beans were next. She ate one and then another, finding them stringy and tougher than she would have liked.

Finally, she started on the chicken breast, looking at it only long enough to cut a few pieces and spear one on the end of her fork. She put it in her mouth and returned to the magazine.

She swallowed two bites. On the third she hit something hard that made a squittering noise between her teeth. She stopped chewing and stood up from the table, her tongue darting around to isolate whatever it was.

She went to the sink and spit into it. The chicken hit the stainless steel with a metallic plop. And though she should have rinsed it down the drain then and there, she couldn't stop herself from examining it.

She'd bitten into a brownish lump shading to black on the edges, about the size of her fingernail. A piece of gristle, a bit of bone or tendon, passed over by who knew how many hands and across how many miles until finally making its way to her mouth. Yes, it was unappetizing, but it was also nothing more than a stupid coincidence.

And yet, this wasn't the first time. How often had she found something strange inside a piece of meat, bitten into an apple that turned out to be mealy, heard a news story about food that had spoiled or was unsafe to begin with? It happened all the time. She spit again, this time to get rid of the taste, before finally rinsing all of it down the drain.

Melissa returned to the table, her appetite gone. The potatoes had grown cold, the green beans gone drab and greasy. She picked up the plate and tipped it over the trash, scraping the surface with her knife and fork, then put everything into the sink.

She stood there, thinking back to Carrie and wondering again what to do for her. If she could find something that didn't fit, it would be good for both of them.

She opened the cabinets above her. The nearest held boxes of crackers and cans of tuna, bags of pasta and bottles of sauce. Melissa set it all on the counter, then stood on her tiptoes to pull more items from the back. She found soup, a chocolate cake mix and matching tub of frosting, bottles of olives and salad dressing. All of it once alive, but not anymore. Now it was just…preserved. It had to be because, well, it was true. It was dead, every bit, no matter how natural or processed.

The first thing she threw away was some take-out that had gone sour and fuzzy in the refrigerator. After that, things happened quickly. She trashed stuff that was merely old, or wouldn't eat anyway or never really liked to begin with. And with that done, it was easy to throw out the rest.

She filled one trash bag, then two. Even as she dumped cartons of yogurt and packages of frozen vegetables into a third, Melissa knew she was touching the outer edges of rational behavior. A reasonable voice told her she'd have to eat eventually. It was the only sane, sensible option. But there was another option, whispered to her like a girlish secret. She could eat only when she absolutely had to, as little as possible. And damn whatever problems it might create.

Coffee, spices, wine.

Three bags full and the cabinets were empty, their doors open. The kitchen looked like she was moving out. She checked again for anything she might have missed, and found the honey, next to the stove, left there after she'd made tea several nights ago. Back when Carrie still wasn't talking.

Melissa picked up the jar, turning it around in her hand the same way she was turning it around in her head, tracing its origins. It was flowers and pollen and bees, and none of them had to die for it.

Honey didn't fit.

She removed the lid and found a spoon. She dipped it into the jar and then into her mouth, and was soon scooping out mouthfuls of the stuff and chasing the drips with her tongue.

When the jar was empty Melissa felt satisfied and somehow calmer. Happy, too, because the honey would help Carrie as well. Maybe she could even get her to eat some.

It was past ten o'clock when she dragged the garbage bags out to the trash and returned to the apartment. She was tired, everything about her felt heavy. As she walked back to her bedroom, turning off the lights behind her, she hoped sleep would be easy.

That night she dreamed of flowers.

Thunder woke her earlier than usual. For several minutes she lay in bed, the covers bunched around her neck, listening to the storm, remembering the events of yesterday and last night, reconsidering everything she'd done and was planning to do today. It wasn't too late to step back from the edge she had walked right up to and was now leaning over. Not too late to eat something, anything, for breakfast, to go to work and talk with her supervisor and find something else to do for Carrie.

But as the minutes passed, the clarity and common sense of those first waking moments slipped away. She showered quickly, then dressed in front of the big mirror in her bedroom, glad for the first time that she was a little heavier than ideal. It would make the weight loss that much harder to notice. She could live on honey for a long time. And she could nurse Carrie back to health with it. No one needed to know how she did it, but everyone would know she had.

She stopped at a 7-Eleven on her way to work, running in and out of the rain as quickly as possible. Death was everywhere in there, lined up, on display. It made her feel as if something terrible was about to happen.

At the hospital she found a patient advisory waiting in her email. She opened it, her hand trembling on the mouse. During the night Carrie had suffered a seizure and then a mild heart attack. She was stable now, but still in and out of consciousness. Her parents had been contacted and authorized tube feeding, which had been installed. If Carrie didn't regain consciousness by that afternoon she'd be transferred to a nearby hospice.

Melissa grabbed the bag she'd brought with her and hurried up to Carrie's room. It was just after six, the halls still half-lit and quiet. In another hour they'd be alive with morning sounds of wheeled carts and girls' voices, but for now they were dark and mostly deserted. Melissa slipped into Carrie's room unnoticed.

Even in the dark the change in Carrie was obvious. She lay slightly askance in the bed, her arms loosely crossed over her bony hips. Her eyes were closed but her mouth hung open, pulled back from teeth that seemed too large. A thin tube snaked from behind one ear and into a nostril, carrying pale yellow liquid to her stomach.

Someone had loosened her gown and pulled it away, exposing the sharp angles of her shoulders. Electrodes studded her chest and led to a heart monitor standing guard on the far side of the bed. The machine tracked the sluggish beats of Carrie's heart in silent pulses of green light. The TV, thankfully, was off.

Melissa sat down next to the bed and whispered Carrie's name, hoping she would stir. She said it again, louder. Carrie's eyelids fluttered and finally opened.

"I know," Melissa said, smoothing limp hair away from her forehead. Carrie's eyes focused on her the tiniest bit. "I understand. But I found something." She reached into the bag at her feet and pulled out a jar of honey, holding it up so Carrie could see it in the gloom.

"It's not dead," she whispered. "Nothing dies for it."

Carrie lifted a hand and slid her fingers down the jar's front. Melissa removed the top, suddenly wishing she'd thought to bring a spoon. She searched the dark room for something she could use, but found nothing, so she dipped her index finger into the jar then brought it to Carrie's lips.

Carrie's tongue poked out, dry as a cat's. She took the honey from Melissa's finger, savoring its sweetness, and Melissa wondered how long it had been since Carrie had tasted anything.

Melissa dipped her finger into the jar again. This time Carrie suckled it like a child, hungrily cleaning every trace of the honey from it. Melissa recoated her finger and offered it again, enjoying the warmth and busy sucking of Carrie's mouth as she licked and swallowed.

They continued this way, rain pattering against the window, thunder rattling its frame, Melissa feeding Carrie, until a quarter of the jar was gone. Carrie finally pulled away, gasping and satisfied, then asked for water. Melissa poured some into a cup, and held it for her. Carrie drank, slurping and still breathing hard, as greedily as she'd taken the honey. When she was finished she dropped her head back to the pillow, gratitude shining in her eyes.

It was brighter in the room now, the color of things starting to appear in the morning light. Carrie opened her mouth to speak. At the same moment, the heart monitor began beeping like an alarm clock.

Melissa jumped at the sudden intrusion. The hospital staff would arrive in seconds. She leaned in to hear what Carrie wanted to say, but all she could make out were the words "everything" and "everywhere."

Nurses bustled into the room, turning on lights and making Melissa wince at the abrupt brightness. They traded looks with Melissa and then each other but said nothing. The on-call physician joined them a few moments later.

Melissa shrank into a corner of the room and watched as they surrounded Carrie. A nurse pulled Carrie's gown away, revealing deflated breasts and ribs like the bars of a cage. Someone began CPR, blowing into Carrie's mouth and pumping her chest with so much force Melissa feared it would collapse.

An orderly wheeled a crash cart into the room. The doctor gelled the paddles and pressed them to Carrie's chest, then someone shouted, "Clear!" Carrie's hips rose off the mattress again and again and again. Each time the heart monitor momentarily ceased its alarm, then took it back up again a few seconds later.

Melissa counted the attempts to revive her. At eight everyone took a step back from the bed and looked at one another, making the decision. She wanted to ask them to keep trying, just one more time, and if that didn't work, another and another. She could save Carrie. She knew how. She just needed a little more time.

The physician nodded. A nurse glanced at her watch and called the time of death at 6:39 a.m.

Melissa stared in disbelief, her gaze following the doctor and nurses as they left the room. The orderly packed away the cart and wheeled it out of the room. A few minutes later two nursing assistants brought in a gurney with a basin and some linens on top. Melissa watched, still in the corner, as they cleaned Carrie's face, her arms and legs and chest, and then her privates, with washcloths and towels, chatting the whole time as though they were doing dishes. When they were finished they lifted Carrie onto the gurney, draped a sheet over her and tucked it in, then fell silent as they took her away.

Melissa turned from the empty room. She dropped her head into the corner and allowed the tears to come, stifling her sobs with a sticky knuckle that still tasted of honey.

It was possible she'd contributed to Carrie's death, and every time she considered this, guilt tore a fresh wound in her chest. What was certain, however, was that she had been involved, drawn to Carrie's side at precisely the right time, the way predator and prey are drawn together at the moment of death. There to witness her end and hear those enigmatic last words.

Try as she might, it was impossible now to isolate those words from the noise and chaos crowding her memory, to give them some new meaning or put them together in a way that made sense.

Everything, she'd said. Everywhere.

Melissa wiped her eyes and faced the room again. The honey still sat on the nightstand, unnoticed and undisturbed. Melissa walked over to it, still shaking inside and out, and put the cap back on, then dropped it into the bag and left Carrie's room.

The rain had stopped. Now sun streamed in through the clinic's large windows, falling onto the hallway floors in bright rectangles. Once inside her office she e-mailed her supervisor, explaining what had happened and requesting the day off.

She drove home in gathering traffic, thinking about everything and everywhere. Each time a restaurant or convenience store appeared in her windshield she looked away, concentrating instead on the other stores lining the way back to her apartment.

Furniture, gas, clothing.

She unlocked her door and went from room to room, drawing the curtains, plunging the apartment into darkness. She entered the bathroom and began filling the tub, then undressed, leaving her clothes in a heap on the floor. When the tub was full she sat down in it, glad for the punishment of the too-hot water.

She sank to her nose, her skin prickling from the heat. Everything. Everywhere. She stared at the wall in front of her, turning Carrie's last words over and over in her mind, hoping to fit them together in some new way that would reveal Carrie's message. Her final secret.

Melissa let her eyes roam over the bathroom. She looked at everything, everywhere. Plastic bottles of shampoo and body lotions clustered together on a shelf above her. Towels and washcloths filled a rack above the toilet. A small arrangement of flowers sat atop one corner of the vanity.

The flowers were dried.

She remembered buying them fresh at a farmer's market one sunny Saturday morning, shortly after she'd started at the hospital. She'd tied the stems together, then hung them upside down, to go stiff and shriveled like something left in the desert to die.

The flowers were dead.

Dead when she'd brought them home and even deader now, sticking out of their vase like a clutch of dusty green skeletons, their arms and heads hanging down.

She looked again at the bathroom, and shivered despite the hot water.

The vanity was made of wood, of flesh stripped from trees that had lived and grown and died.

The towels and shower curtain were cotton, torn from plants that had produced it using only sun and water, each one alive, then snuffed out as soon as the fibers were harvested.

Every one of her shampoos and lotions, the ingredients of each, had their origins in the death of living things. Even the bottles—all of them plastic, produced from oil, borne from animals and plants that had died and rotted and been transformed by the darkness of untold millions of years.

She crossed her arms, pressing them against her breasts. She drew an unsteady breath from the steamy air, then closed her eyes and sank down into the water until it covered her head, squeezing her eyes shut against it and the thoughts tumbling through her mind like great boulders.

It took so much death to keep the world alive. The living world's appetite for it was infinite.

Wood, cotton, oil.

All of it. Dead.

Everything. Everywhere.

The Steel Church

by Charles Colyott

My friend, you would not tell with such high zest
To children ardent for some desperate glory,
The old Lie; Dulce et Decorum est
Pro patria mori.

         -Wilfred Owen

The siege continued on long past dusk, its constant strobe and battery and chaos becoming nothing more than an accompaniment to the ceremony at hand—the daily memorial. The clank and thrum of steel on steel echoed in the high ceilings of the chapel as the organized hordes entered. Company by company, the soldiers filed rigidly in and stood at attention before their assigned tables. Fresh from the front lines and still bearing the marks of battle upon grim faces and outdated, obsolete body armor, the men and women of the 14th battalion, tired, cold and hungry, stared unflinchingly at the faces of their fallen comrades upon the walls of the Steel Church.

Unlike the stained glass used in places of worship in the Old Days—windows long since destroyed by the Faithless—these walls, built solely of transparent plasteel tubing, depicted no gentle doves, no saints, no all-knowing saviors. These walls, every soldier knew, were their future. From chutes built into the trenches, the dead were deposited only to collect here, in the walls of the church; a murky sludge of blood and dirt, intact cadavers and disembodied chunks which drifted lazily through the pipes and columns of the place. Friends, lovers, and family—soldiers all—here to be remembered a final time.

The Chaplain, a triple-amputee in a barely functional spider-walker, mounted the pulpit amid the hisses and whirrs of his robotic transport. With a perpetual scowl of scar tissue marring the lower right quadrant of his face, the

125

Chaplain regarded the ranks of warriors before him. The ritual was old, older by far than the Chaplain, and had long since lost its pleasantries.

"Sit," the Chaplain barked, and the soldiers filling the church did.

As the lectern computer loaded the names of the day's fallen, the Chaplain gazed up at the razor-edged cross suspended above him that gave the church its name. Reflected in the symbol he saw bits of heroes, pieces of those who'd given their all for The Father. The sight always strengthened his faith, seeing them there within the cross. A small beep from the console informed him the list was ready.

He began reading the names, only twelve hundred today, and ignored the whining growl of his stomach. Since retiring from the field and taking on the mantle of Chaplain, he'd become soft; pressing the plastic valve of his colostomy bag deeper into his stomach to deter any further distractions, the Chaplain read on.

"Frater Samuel O'Reilly, go with God...Soror Stephanie Ingraham, go with God..."

He continued down the list and ignored the sounds of the repository behind him. As each name was read aloud, the corresponding soldier's dogtags, crucifixes, and any personal effects fell into the processing bin in the front of the lectern for washing, sorting, and eventual redistribution. When he'd reached the last fifty names, the combine engines fired up with a roar. Upon the recitation of the final name on the screen, the Chaplain announced, "You may rise."

The soldiers stood.

With a nod from the Chaplain, they formed lines at the sides and back of the enormous church. And as the valves opened and the combines began to grind, the Chaplain said, "As our Lord sayeth in the days of old, 'You do this in memory of me.' And so we do. But not in memory of Him, for He is with us always. Tonight we do this in memory of our brethren. We do this to take in and accept their strengths. We do this to shit out their weaknesses."

He watched as the plasteel pipes vomited forth frothy sludge into waiting bowls. At fifteen second intervals the jets ceased, the full bowls were removed to the tables, and a new soldier, with a new bowl, would step into place. The years had honed the proceedings down to a quiet, efficient, operation—far smoother and, in the Chaplain's mind, far better than the ruckus his father had told him about from back when *he* was a cadet, back before the siege began.

When the ranks had all returned to their seats, Frater Coulter brought the Chaplain his bowl. He prayed silently over it, confident that the rest of the battalion was doing the same, and, upon completion, opened his eyes and said, "Amen."

Grasping the spoon with the three fingers of his remaining hand, the Chaplain set to, shoveling the gruel into his wounded mouth without really tasting it. He'd blocked out that sense years before a Faithless shell took down his chopper at the Battle of Columbus. His heavy-lidded eyes glanced out over the troops; he knew the newbies from the vets on sight.

The newbies picked out the flecks of bone. They drew the strings of tendon from their mouths and stared with disbelieving eyes. They lost their stomachs on the steel floors. In each memorial, a few of the kids inevitably had to be taken to the field hospital. They were too green; they didn't know what it was, yet, to be hungry. They were wasteful.

They would learn.

The vets, on the other hand, scraped their bowls clean and asked for seconds they knew they couldn't have. Casualties were down; they were holding their position firm and the tide was turning, but it was bad for morale at mess time. Things would have to change—soon—or it would start to get ugly again.

Some tastes, once acquired, were hard to shake.

When the memorial was complete—the bowls placed in a receptacle for washing, the soldiers ushered out and back to the field, the plasteel pipes sluiced until they shone clear and clean once more—the Chaplain remained, alone, in the Steel Church. He looked at the cruel beauty of the cross and the battered, battle-scarred flag that hung beneath it. It still held together well, despite its injuries; the Chaplain figured they had that much in common.

He saluted the two beloved symbols with his gnarled hand and turned (after a bit of fiddling with his spider-walker's wiring) to leave. He belched once, loudly, and grimaced at the taste of gastric juice. He swallowed hard, wondering idly if the juice had been his own. The robotic legs of the walker sputtered and hissed and clanked upon the metal floor, echoing slightly in the vast and empty hall.

It sounded as if the barrage outside had more or less ended for the night.

The Chaplain whistled Taps as he rode back to his quarters.

It is sweet and right to die for your country.

The Apocalypse Ain't So Bad

by Jeff Strand

If you ask me, people are unnecessarily gloomy about the end of the world. And that starts with calling it "the end of the world." It's not like the planet exploded or cracked in half or melted or anything like that. The world itself is perfectly fine—it's just that almost everybody is dead.

Here's the thing: We all *know* that it was a devastating tragedy. Why keep bringing that up? Anybody you talk to, you literally can't have more than fifteen seconds of conversation before they've gotta switch the topic to the apocalypse. I'm not suggesting that it isn't a major news story; I'm just saying that it doesn't have to be the *only* news story. Know what I'm saying? It's been almost four months.

Believe me, I've got plenty to whine about. I'm pretty much on my own at this point. For a short while after humanity's 99.7% demise, I was traveling with a woman named Cyndi. Unfortunately, I sort of botched the timing on bringing up the whole "Hey, we've gotta repopulate the earth!" topic, and I found myself surviving on my own.

Sure, the mutants are a problem. (And, yes, they're mutants—it seems like some people want to call any non-verbal human with a messed-up face a "zombie.") But they go down pretty quick with a shot to the head, and c'mon, who among us thought we'd get the chance to open fire on real people without it being a felony?

Now, some survivors did have to defend themselves against mutated friends and/or family, and there's no question that it must've sucked. If you're one of them, you have the right to be mopey. That's not who I'm complaining about. It's the folks who had to shoot three or four mutant strangers, yet are acting like they had to drown their own mother in a bathtub. Three words: Get. Over. It.

Would I rather the plague not have claimed billions of lives? Of course. You'd have to be a fool or a psychotic to feel otherwise. But are those billions of people going to get right back up and return to their normal routines? No. (Especially because they're *not zombies!*) It happened, the streets are littered with corpses, so let's make the best of it.

Take Disney World, for example. The rides aren't working because there's no electricity. But admit it, haven't you always wanted to get out of the car in the Haunted Mansion and just take a look around on your own? I did that a couple of days ago, and it was an absolute blast. I even tore off a piece of the wallpaper as a souvenir. Could I have done that pre-apocalypse? No way! I would've been thrown out of the park. Hell, I even got to climb on the track of Space Mountain, and there were no lines anywhere. You don't need some guy walking around in a Mickey Mouse costume to have a good time.

Food is a trade-off. I won't lie to you—I miss steak. On the other hand, last week I brought home an entire shopping cart filled with candy. That sucker was overflowing, and I left plenty on the shelves.

I guess I just don't understand people who always have a negative attitude. Life in a post-apocalyptic world isn't anywhere near as bad as movies want you to believe. It's actually kind of fun. Now I'm going to head over to Barnes & Noble and pick out any book I want.

* * *

I got bit by a mutant this morning. It was my fault; I should've been paying closer attention to my surroundings. Got me right on the arm. It hurt—oh, Christ, did it hurt. Still, my gun was within reach, and I've always been ambidextrous, so I took care of him before he was able to actually start chewing.

Infection is a concern, I'll admit, but it's not worth getting all bent out of shape over.

Trust me, I'm not taking a lackadaisical attitude toward the bite. I cleaned the wound (which did, unfortunately, break the skin) thoroughly with antiseptic, and then I covered it with a bandage. I cleaned it again every half hour after that. Yeah, it stung like crazy, but that means it's working, right? When life hands you lemons, you make lemonade, and even though the antiseptic burned worse than pouring lemon juice into the wound, I wasn't going to let it bum me out.

I knew a guy who got bit. You wouldn't believe how much he carried on, and how much of a "Pity me!" attitude he had about the whole thing. Know what he did? He said "I don't wanna become one of those things," shoved his revolver in his mouth, and pulled the trigger. Can you believe that? I mean, who kills himself over a mutant bite?

Me, I don't care if I become a shambling, oozing, moaning super-mutant, I'm not swallowing a bullet. That's the coward's way out. Screw that.

* * *

Well, it's been five days, and the bite is almost completely healed. That's how it works. When you have an upbeat attitude, your body chemistry and immune system respond accordingly. Mind over mutant.

A lot of people would've just holed themselves up in their home or apartment after being bitten like that. Not me. Know what I was doing when the pain was at its worst? I was smashing up an abandoned Volkswagen with an aluminum baseball bat. That's not something I could do before the plague, and don't try to act all high and mighty and pretend that the idea isn't appealing. In this new world, boys can be boys, and I love it!

* * *

I miss my family. There, I said it.

This feeling started while I was in a pottery store, breaking pottery. Though I was being cautious and staying out of the narrow aisles, I suddenly felt a hand grab my wrist and yank me away from the shelf. It was the nastiest-looking mutant I'd encountered thus far, and I mean both nasty as in "disgusting" and nasty as in "mean."

There were four other mutants with it. The fact that they were less nasty-looking than their counterpart wasn't much of a consolation.

I immediately opened fire, pumping a bullet into the first mutant's nose. As expected, its grip loosened and I yanked my wrist free. Another shot and the mutant was missing a goodly portion of its skull, including essential brain components. It fell to the floor.

The other four mutants lumbered toward me. They aren't exactly speedy creatures, but they aren't *that* slow. I mean, it's not like you'd feel like a schmuck and be embarrassed to tell people if one of them got you. So I quickly scooted back through the aisle until I was well out of arm's reach, and then started pumping bullets into those reeking brutes. (Have you smelled one of those things up close? Oh, man, imagine the worst case of festering halitosis you've ever inhaled and multiply it by eighteen or nineteen. Foul. Foul, foul, foul.)

I got the first one in the chest, which didn't do any good. I fired again and got it in the chest again, which continued to not do any good. But the third shot was the requisite head shot, and the mutant dropped.

Something grabbed me from behind.

I screamed and spun around, getting a damn good view of another mutant's jaws coming right at my face. I jerked my head back just in time to avoid the no-doubt unpleasant sensation of its teeth digging into my eye, then pushed the barrel of my gun against its chin and squeezed the trigger. Much splatter resulted.

I spun back around and fired at the other three mutants. I finished off the first one in line, pulled the trigger again, and heard the always-disappointing click. Fortunately, I always carried two guns, plus a hunting knife and a grenade. I wasn't sure if it was a "blow things up" grenade or a smoke grenade (I'm not exactly a weapons specialist) but I kept it with me anyway, just in case.

I pulled the second gun out of its holster and fired, blowing a hole in the mutant's right hand and giving him an impromptu stigmata. Couldn't repeat that shot if I tried. I didn't try, because it was more important to kill them than impress myself. My next shot got rid of the mutant's ear. It howled in pain.

I took a few steps back, almost tripping over the dead mutant behind me but thankfully sparing myself that indignity. The two remaining mutants walked side-by-side down the aisle. They were both women, which sucked. There was a definite macho thrill to be found in blowing away ugly guy mutants, but shooting women—even grotesque mutated ones—made me feel like a jerk.

My next bullet shattered a pot. But my next two bullets after that got both of the female mutants in the head. Down they went. At least they weren't hot.

Then *another* mutant popped up behind me. How did I miss that they were having a frickin' mutant convention in the pottery shop?

Its teeth sank into my shoulder.

I immediately pulled away, which was a bad idea. A generous strip of flesh ripped off in the process. I fired four or five bullets into the mutant's skull before it hit the ground, and two more after.

I frantically peeked around the corner of the aisle, expecting to see a dozen more mutants coming at me with outstretched arms, but the store seemed to be empty now. My shoulder wound was bleeding profusely, and I plucked one of the mutant's teeth out of my flesh and flicked it onto the ground.

That's when I started to miss my family.

Sure, we had our little spats, but they never bit chunks out of me, and our quarrels never involved gunplay.

I pressed my hand against the injury, then quickly made my way out of the store and back home.

* * *

I'm a bit more cynical about the apocalypse these days. The bite really, *really* hurts when I use the antiseptic, and I'm seeing definite signs of infection.

I still think people complain too much about the whole situation, but the lack of qualified medical personnel is a pretty big downside. That said, I don't think that I'm going to become one of those creatures and I don't think I'm going to die. I do think that I'll be doing a lot of screaming for the next few days.

* * *

My shoulder looks like crap. It never stops hurting. I've got aspirin but it's not doing any good. I've gone on several supply runs trying desperately to find something stronger, but those goddamn scavengers have cleared out all of the painkillers.

Not gonna die.

Might have to cut my arm off.

I don't think it's possible to saw off your own arm. I think you'd pass out from the pain, and then wake up with a hacksaw imbedded in your arm. If the infection gets worse, I'll need somebody else to do it.

Is there a tactful way to ask somebody to perform an amputation? How do you even bring up the subject? I guess you could always leave the bite uncovered, and keep the hacksaw in plain sight, and hope that they put two and two together and make an unsolicited offer.

Of course, the whole arm-removal thing is a last resort. Don't want to chop my arm off and then have some guy find me lying in a huge pool of my own blood and say "Oh, gosh, I've got a pill right here that would've cleared that up."

Think I'm gonna scream some more.

Yeah, that sounds like a good way to spend the afternoon. Afterward I'll open a can of spaghetti.

* * *

Wow, my social skills have taken a beating since the world ended. I went out looking for survivors with medicine (y'know, for the whole arm thing). Found a family of four. Started shouting like a crazy person. I don't even know what I was saying. I know what I was *trying* to say: "Hi there, folks, I've had a spot of trouble and was wondering if you could spare some antibiotics?" But as soon as I saw them I got so excited that I lost my ability to form a coherent sentence, and the father calmly suggested, with the aid of his shotgun, that I move along.

I tried to give him the whole "I mean you no harm" speech, but he fired into the air and looked really damn stern. So I left. Couldn't find anybody else all day.

I try to continually think happy thoughts about my shoulder, but it keeps looking worse and worse. It's hard to move my fingers and elbow.

But, hey, it doesn't hurt as bad anymore! It's more numb than anything. That's a blessing, I guess.

I really think this arm has to go. Better than losing a leg. Can't walk very well with only one leg. You try to run away from those mutants with one leg, and you're almost guaranteed to fall on your face unless you've had a lot of practice hopping. Me, I'd rather lose an arm than a leg any day.

I'll be an inspiration. How many people can survive in a post-apocalyptic world with only one arm? Not too many. Amputees have accomplished many great things throughout history, and I will proudly join their ranks.

After I do some more screaming.

* * *

Know what? I think it's looking a little better. Not a lot better, but a little. Can't expect it to heal right up overnight. That would be wacky talk.

Starting to get tired of all this candy. Wish I had some pork chops. Think a nice meal of pork chops, baked potato with sour cream and bacon bits, and steamed broccoli would make my shoulder feel better. I've got the broccoli, anyway, but not the steamer.

Wish my family didn't live on the other side of the country. Sure, they're probably all dead or mutants, but it would still be nice to see them, if only for a brief visit.

Time for more antiseptic. Joy.

Almost out of it.

* * *

I've got to admit, I didn't expect to end up in a cage. Dead, maybe. Mutated, sure. Caged? Nope.

Thing is, there's something much worse out there than the mutants. Namely, a band of paranoid survivors, led by this insane gentleman named Sunshine, who are trying to rule this new world. I saw three of them walking down the sidewalk and I thought, hey, potential source of shoulder medicine! Having learned from my previous mistake, I took a deep breath, composed myself, and politely stepped into their path and introduced myself.

I remember a big wooden club swinging at my head, but the other details of the encounter are blurry.

Woke up with my hands and feet duct-taped together in a school gymnasium. About twenty other people were there playing cards and smoking cigarettes and just hanging out. The walls were lined with cots. I seemed to be the only prisoner.

Sunshine stood over me, his wild hair and facial scars a weird contrast to his serene expression. He ran his finger over my lips and asked "Are you one of them?"

"Do I *look* like one of them?"

Helpful hint: Sunshine and his band of followers are not admirers of sarcasm. When I woke up again, I was in a wooden cage in a classroom, and the rest of my body hurt even more than my shoulder. The posters on the walls indicated that it was a history teacher's classroom, which added an extra dimension of terror to my nightmare.

A little kid, maybe twelve, was crouched outside of my cage. "Got any aspirin?" I asked him.

He shook his head.

"Any chance you'll let me out?"

He shook his head again.

"Could you go get a grown-up so I can talk to them?"

He grinned. "I'm a grown-up now. I even get first pick."

"Of what?"

"Of what I eat."

133

I had the very unnerving sensation that this conversation was going to move in a cannibalism-themed direction, but I tried to play stupid to give myself a couple more moments of mental health. "What do you mean?"

"You're food. We're going to eat you for dinner tonight."

"I see." My mental health status dropped a few notches.

"Gotta cut off the bad parts first, though," he said, pointing to my arm.

* * *

My natural optimism faltered a bit after they duct taped me to the desk. I tried to let a smile be my umbrella, but it wasn't working. Though I explained to them all the ways in which their actions were poor ethical decisions, I wasn't being particularly coherent and my message didn't really get across.

Sunshine held a lighter flame underneath a knife that didn't look anywhere near sharp enough to do an efficient job.

I wept.

He began the unpleasant process. It took me a long time to pass out. With a better knife, I probably could've done the job myself. Live and learn.

* * *

The tile floor under my cage is spotted with blood. Though they cauterized the stump, it's still leaking a little.

I wonder what they did with my arm?

Apparently I get one more day to live before I become brunch. They're still finishing off their last batch of meat. The little kid—Toby—loves to sit outside my cage, licking his lips and rubbing his belly in an exaggerated manner.

I'm almost delirious from lack of sleep. Toby threw stuff at me all night. He'd get real close to the cage, and I kept trying to thrust my good arm through the wooden bars and grab him, but he always kept himself just out of reach.

Well, not always. I did get his collar once. He shrieked for help, and a couple of Sunshine's nutcase crew came in, pulled him free, and then beat the crap out of me.

Tenderizing me.

So this is how it ends. Tormented by a little brat, missing an arm, and about to become dinner.

I had a pretty good life before the plague.

The apocalypse sucks.

No...I'm not going to let these bastards take away my happy disposition. Screw 'em. I'll get out of this, somehow. Optimism. Optimism is the key. Nobody ever got anywhere with a can't-do attitude.

They can take away my freedom. They can take away my arm. They can take away my life. But they won't take away my smile until they eat my lips.

I try to smile. My lips are swollen from the beating and it hurts too much, so I abandon the idea.

* * *

I hear footsteps in the darkness.
They're coming for me.

* * *

Sunshine is a charismatic leader, with devoted followers who will obey his every command, even if it means marching to their death. However, the guy isn't very good at keeping everybody in the loop regarding crucial pieces of information.

Such as, my severed arm was for disposal. Not for adding to the soup.

A lot of people got really foamy-mouthed that night, and they started to prey on each other. They grabbed Toby and pulled him in half, right in front of me. I wanted to applaud, but...well, you know...

A couple of them tried to get into the cage. It took a while, but they finally broke the lock. I scooted past them and fled out of the classroom and down the hallway, where there was carnage galore.

It was disgusting, but it was a *good* kind of disgusting, y'know?

I saw what I think was Sunshine in a few chunks on the gymnasium floor. Not completely certain—he wasn't easy to recognize. The chin looked familiar, though.

I found a gun next to a body that was missing a few feet of intestine. Fully loaded. It was empty by the time I got out of the school, but I made it to the exit unscathed.

I ran home, went to sleep, and woke up feeling refreshed. Though I'm not suggesting that my stump wasn't sore, it was definitely a more pleasant feeling than being devoured. One arm was still one more arm than I would've had if that rotten little brat had gotten his way.

After a few days of relaxation, the swelling went down, and I could smile again.

* * *

I'm wiser now. When you think about it, this whole thing was a learning experience. I'm no longer that innocent guy breaking pots. I'm not saying I wouldn't rather have my arm back, but all things considered, I think this was good for me.

Again, people need to quit their bellyaching. The apocalypse ain't so bad.

Into The After

by Kurt Dinan

The room was little more than a cement bunker located in the back of an abandoned grocery store. Dad and I had stood third in line underneath the flickering fluorescent lights for an hour. No one could stop staring at the same white sheet that obscured the area near the front wall. Unseen spotlights backlit the makeshift partition, and the oversized silhouette of an empty chair shone through. I rocked back and forth on my heels, certain at any moment my nerves would give out and send me to the exit.

Dad motioned to the manila envelope in my hand and said, "Which one did you bring?"

"Hilton Head."

He smiled at the memory, but it died quickly, and he returned to his thoughts and vigil watching the chair. I'd chosen the picture of Mom in a flowered sundress from a rubber-banded pile hidden away in the basement where Dad wasn't likely to run across it. Most days he still couldn't even say her name; God knows how he'd react to unwillingly discovering her picture.

"*...in December of 2000, I took a job with security personnel at One World Trade Center where every day...*"

Ethan Stuckey's story played from a Peavey amp sitting on the floor at the front of the screen. His voice had been on a continual loop since we'd arrived, slithering into my ears and sending an uninterrupted chill through my body as if he stood directly behind me. Even after all the waiting, I still didn't know if I believed his story which had brought us all together. Dad accepted it though, and that was all that mattered.

Metallic knocking from behind the partition silenced all talk in the room. Burt, the bearded man who'd frisked us upon entry, stopped on his way around the screen and shut off the CD player wired into the amp. I held a breath to ten, hoping to relax. A deadbolt clanged open, followed by the scraping of metal across cement. Seconds later, the outline of Ethan Stuckey, stooped and hobbling, appeared. He moved in jerky motions toward the chair as if his hips had been broken and set improperly. As he passed the screen, his distorted shadow made it appear he was rising from the earth.

Burt reemerged from behind the sheet and knelt in front of the amp. A low static hum filled the room. Dad drummed his fingers against his legs. He had been anticipating this night ever since he'd transferred a thousand dollars for the two of us through PayPal. The guilt I'd experienced since helping him make the plans flooded through me again. I shut my eyes and swallowed hard, reminding myself that tonight was about saving Dad, not about my fears of a man some labeled a fraud and others called the boogeyman.

On the screen, Ethan's shadow lifted a microphone. When he spoke, his voice had the scratchy quality of an old blues album.

"You've all come tonight hoping for answers, and I can promise those to you," he said. "What I can't promise is that you'll necessarily like what you hear. That doesn't really matter to me. All of you have made a deal to hear the truth. Nothing more. What you do with it is up to you."

He lowered the mic onto his lap. Burt restarted the audio of Ethan's story, then waved forward the woman at the front of the line. I recognized her from a midnight showing of *The Lies of 9/11* that Dad had taken me to at an empty warehouse down by the shore. When she reached the edge of the screen, she paused as if reconsidering. I secretly hoped she would turn back, starting a mass exodus that would shake Dad from his waking coma. Instead, she turned the corner. I followed her outline projecting black on white until she knelt at Ethan's feet.

"I know I said it before, but I appreciate you coming along, Will," Dad said. His eyes were ringed by dark circles like he was looking up from the bottom of a well. "Maybe tonight we'll get some truth."

The irony wasn't lost on me. In the years since 2001, Dad had avoided the truth by turning our Hoboken home into a cave of wall-plastered newspaper articles and building schematics whose relevance only he understood. Even with no remains ever recovered, Mom was officially classified as deceased nine months after that September. For Dad though, no body meant Mom might have somehow survived, possibly suffering amnesia and living life elsewhere. He remained immobile in The Before, existing in a perpetual 2001 where he hibernated with footage of plane crashes, building implosions, and mystery jumpers. Meanwhile, I lived in The After, alone and feeling orphaned as if I had somehow lost both parents on the same day.

"*...a massive rumbling on the street like the ground was opening up. Then I was consumed by dust and ash, and there was nothing but darkness.*"

I recognized most of the people in line behind us. There was the wheelchaired man who'd been removed by Borders's security after initiating a shouting match with the author of *Conspiracies Debunked*. Past him, the woman who kept vigil at Ground Zero with a sandwich board covered with her daughter's picture. Then the blogger whose page *Among the Missing* Dad monitored daily. And the Diane Lane look-alike who brought her young son to the support group meetings. And on and on. Despite our common bond, no one acknowledged each other. Years of attending the same events brought recognition but not friendship, as if suffering alone equated to some sort of valor.

On the screen, the silhouette of the woman with Ethan convulsed as if overcome by a seizure. Then, after letting out a deep sob, she cracked him across the face with her hand. The sound echoed through the room. Burt was around the screen and on top of her in seconds.

I unconsciously stepped behind Dad. He showed no sign of my existence, instead watching with everyone else as Burt carried the woman, slumped and weeping in his arms, off to the man standing guard at the back of the room.

"...hundreds of shadowy impressions wandered about. No one had bodies or heads, but I could hear everyone talking. Some told what they'd eaten for breakfast, or how the contract language needed to be settled, or about the goal their kid scored..."

Next up was a man in a business suit. I wondered how his days at the office went. Did he spend work hours searching obscure websites for minutia while management debated how long they had to wait before they replaced him? Or could he sequester away his misery enough to work his job before returning home to ignore his children and resume his real quest? Books tell you there is no one way to grieve. When something terrible happens—something truly horrific—you change. For some it may be for the better, for some the worse, but anyone in horror's path is irrevocably altered.

For me, it had taken years of school suspensions and police run-ins before I moved into The After and accepted the truth that Mom was gone forever. Unlike other kids I knew who lost a parent that day, I never idealized my mom. She did the best she could but regularly missed my games and school functions due to long work hours. To compensate for her absence, she showed her love by celebrating birthdays and academic achievements with manic enthusiasm. As I got older, she even created what she called "our signal"—running her index finger over her earlobe—in order to initiate a form of closeness with me. Sometimes it meant, "Your father's silly, isn't he?" or "It's time for you to get to bed," or even simply "I love you." Regardless of its use, the signal was a private secret only we shared. The last time I saw her she smiled and touched her earlobe while driving past me on her way to the train station. Even though I was surrounded by friends waiting for the bus, I returned the gesture, a small memory that tempered any resurfacing sadness.

"...naturally began separating into two lines. One was clearly more crowded than

the other, stretching far into the distance until it blurred. In that line everyone radiated fulfillment. But from the much shorter line I felt a painful darkness…"

His time with Ethan finished, the man in the suit reappeared from behind the screen and trudged toward the exit. His eyes were vacant like he was sleepwalking.

"…later, a nurse told me I'd been dead for over a minute before the EMT brought me back. But I returned with their lives imprinted on me. They're a part of me now."

Dad and I were next. My heartbeat pounded in my ear like waves pummeling the beach. From the moment I'd directed Dad to the message board about Stuckey's gatherings I'd regretted my decision, knowing I was entering a game I had no control over. Now that I was about to meet Ethan, I was even more apprehensive. Something about the surroundings, Ethan's shadow, his voice—

"I think we're up."

Dad reached out. At first I thought he was going to take my hand, but instead he took the envelope containing Mom's picture. He held it by the corner with only the tips of two fingers. His face was so pale I thought he might throw up.

"Are you going to be okay?" I said.

"I'm not sure I can do this," he said, looking exhausted. "What if he tells me something horrible?"

The nakedness of his admission almost dropped me. It was the closest thing to honesty I'd heard from him in years. I wanted to hurry him from the room before Ethan could whisper his lies. But deep down, past the thick cord of betrayal wrapped inside like barbed wire, I knew this was what we both needed.

"It'll be okay," I said. "We'll do it together."

Burt gave the nod and we stepped behind the sheet into the bright shine of the spotlights. I held a hand to block out the light and saw the outline of Ethan sitting close. His dark form appeared to swallow the light around him. Without amplification his voice was a breathless wheeze.

"Come on over," he said. "I'm not that scary."

His laugh reminded me of a handsaw ripping through wood, and when my eyes finally adjusted I could see he was only partially telling the truth. Reports put him at thirty-three, but he could have passed for sixty. One side of his head was caved in like a dented fender. Short brown hair covered only half his scalp; the other side was nothing but a roadmap of scar tissue. His face hung slack as if sculpted of warm wax. I dug my fingers into my leg and tried not to stare.

"I'm Hank McCormick," Dad said, reaching out a hand. "This is my son, Will."

Ethan brushed Dad's hand aside.

"Do you have a picture?"

Dad hesitated, then dragged a finger across the top of the envelope. Without glancing at it, he withdrew the photograph of Mom standing on a hotel balcony. If he spotted it, Dad said nothing about the red "X" I'd drawn in Sharpie on the back.

Ethan took the photograph into his twitching hands. I held my breath. I was about to find out if I'd given too much trust to a man I didn't know. He studied Mom's picture for less than three seconds before handing it back. I thought I saw a faint smile cross Ethan's face when his eyes drifted to the mark on the back of the photograph.

He said, "Elaine McCormick worked as an actuary with Hutchison Insurance. On September 11th, she arrived at work at 7:53 wearing a black pantsuit she'd bought at Macy's."

Dad gripped my arm, burrowing his nails into my wrist. When I covered his hand with mine his wedding ring pressed into my palm.

"She was writing an email when the plane hit. The wing tore through her floor, destroying the entire office. The impact was so sudden she had no time to react and died instantly. Burning jet fuel incinerated her in minutes."

Dad's legs gave out and he sagged into me. I wrapped an arm around him and swallowed back the bile traveling up my throat.

"Is there anything else?" Dad said.

"When I saw her," Ethan said, "she was at peace standing in the long line. Elaine knew what awaited."

Dad's voice was a whisper. "Was she thinking of me or Will?"

"The dead don't think of the living," Ethan said. "That part of their life is over."

Tears raced down Dad's face. He exhaled, then wrapped his arms around Ethan, who bristled at the touch.

"Thank you so much," Dad said.

When Dad stood there was a faint light in his eyes, a small ember where I once thought only ashes remained. A brief image of the future, of Dad resuming a normal life and returning as my father, flashed in my head.

"We can go now," Dad said. He put his arm around me as we walked away. I leaned in, aware that a good deal of the weight I'd carried when we'd entered the building had now vanished. I'd done it, and I knew whatever guilt accompanied paying Stuckey two thousand dollars to tell my father exactly what I wished was worth it.

We were to the edge of the screen about to rejoin the others when Ethan called my name. I turned and he beckoned me, his thin hand pulling through the air. I tried to keep walking, but Dad stopped.

"What do you think he wants?"

"Let's just go," I said. "We've heard what we need."

"But maybe he remembered something else."

140

There was nothing I could do. The two of us started back, but Ethan said, "No, just the boy."

Dad shrugged, then told me he'd wait by the others.

Cold sweat trailed down my back. Ethan gestured for me to kneel. Heat radiated off his skin as if he were deeply fevered.

"Your father seems happy."

Not willing or able to meet his eye, I stared into the darkness over his shoulder.

"You're not the first one, you know," he said. "It's more common than you'd think. We're inclined to protect those we love."

"I can't pay you anything more, if that's what you want."

"It's true what I said before. You accepted certain conditions by coming here, and regardless of your intentions toward your father, I keep my end of the bargain."

I went to leave, but then his voice snaked into my brain, paralyzing me.

"For your fifth birthday, Elaine threw you a *Thundercats*-themed party and hired an actor to play Lion-O. On your ninth birthday, she took you and four friends to Coney Island for the day. Your friend Joey ate too much popcorn and threw up off the pier. You all watched the seagulls drop into the water to eat his puke."

My chest heaved, and I tried to slow down my breathing before I hyperventilated. Ethan didn't break his stare, and now he had a deep smile.

"And the last time Elaine ever saw you," he said, "you were at the bus stop as she drove away."

I couldn't move. Everything else faded until there was only his voice. I spoke into the darkness.

"Why are you telling me this?"

"Just keeping my part of the deal," Ethan said. "Elaine wasn't in her office when the plane hit. She was six floors down fucking Craig Hubbard on his desk. They'd been having an affair for over three years. He's the one who first showed her that charming sign you and Elaine shared. They would do the signal across the office when they wanted to meet later to fuck."

My mouth was dust.

"I don't believe you."

"It doesn't matter if you do or not," Ethan said. "When the ceiling collapsed, Elaine's back snapped, pinning her down. She watched the fire grow around her knowing she was going to die. Her last thought before her clothing ignited was how she had wasted her entire life."

Ethan's voice faded as if he were walking away in a dust storm. "When I saw your mother," he concluded, "she was with the others in the short line, radiating a shame and terror known only to those who realize they are damned."

141

I was still unable to move. The long hours, the overcompensation for her absences—somehow I knew. A light illuminated my memories showing the real events that had lived in shadow. Had she been with Hubbard all those nights she wasn't home? Were there others before him? Did she consider me part of that wasted life? The questions wouldn't stop.

"What am I supposed to do now?"

"Well, at least your father's happy, right?" Ethan said. "Isn't that what you wanted?"

Burt poked his head around the corner and cleared his throat. Ethan looked past me as if I wasn't there.

"Send in the next one."

I turned away and had to concentrate on each step just to walk. I emerged from behind the curtain feeling as if I were entering a new world forever altered. Dad waited for me, his hands out expectantly.

"So what did he say?"

He had wiped the tears away and now had a smile with real life behind it. A row of folding chairs stood between us. Aware of the newly drawn line separating us and weighed down by a burden I knew could never be unloaded, I forced a smile and began my new life in The After.

Ash Wednesday

by Lorne Dixon

Everything was a blur, my vision fading and brightening, until the pulsating colors and trembling shapes slowed their spin. I saw broken glass on asphalt, the swaying blue bristle tree line under the Santa Lucia Mountains, the twisting funnels of black clouds against a starless sky. I heard nothing except the hum of my inflamed eardrums. Rolling, standing up, wobbling, shaking, I turned back toward the fire.

I watched as a fireball ascended off the roof of the sprawling building. A line of flame ran across the *Morro Bay Private Mental Health Center* sign, curling the white paint, chewing down into the carved lettering. I snapped my dangling jaw shut and brushed myself off.

The explosion had caught us by surprise, knocking three teams of fire responders off our feet. Our Ladder's blitz line—two and a half inches of hose—danced on the parking lot like a snake. It struck a uniformed cop, bowling him over, slamming his unconscious body against the Chief's car. Half a dozen firefighters jumped to their feet and tackled the hose and held on until their combined weight and strength wrestled it under control.

The explosion meant the fire had reached the Sanitarium's boiler room. We'd contained it to the offices and Visitors Center up until then, but now it would spread fast.

"That's the game, folks," Chief Henderscott shouted.

A volunteer team member from San Luis Obispo ran to my side. He screamed over the fire's roar, "What's he mean by that?"

I shook my head. Only a few scraggly hairs on his chin, the kid couldn't have been more than twenty. I pulled his ear close. "It means the fire just won. We got nothing that can handle the sumbitch. Building's done."

Confusion crossed his face. "Then what now?"

"This just became a pure rescue mission," I told him, careful to lock his eyes on mine. He needed to understand what my words meant—fully understand. "We have to get in there and get those people out."

Confusion turned to panic. "But they're—"

He didn't say the word *insane* but it hung in the air just beyond his lips, almost audible.

"Yes," I said. "They are."

The same horrible thought fluttered through all of our minds, I'm sure, both the veterans of Ladder Six-Fifteen and the weekend adventurers from the eager volunteer squads that had raced to our town. The building was already partially evacuated. *Partially.* The first responders quit pulling patients out when a hallway ceiling collapsed, crushing three of the firefighters. I arrived just as they were regrouping in the parking lot.

Morro Bay divided its patients into three color coded wards. Green Ward was made up of the self-committed and the homeless. Yellow Ward was low-level criminals with mental health issues who had managed to avoid jail time in exchange for some time on a shrink's chaise. They were already gone, filed out and moved to the state hospital.

The violent psychotic incurables of Red Ward were still inside. A whisper echoed in my ear, an earlier voice warning me that some of the inmates had gotten loose in the confusion and that some of the staff were missing.

The Chief barked out orders, pairing up firemen with local cops. No one hesitated to follow the Chief's commands. The old man had gone to Korea and Vietnam, neither time on vacation, and his voice carried more authority than the stripes he had earned.

"You're with me," a voice said over my shoulder. I turned and saw Leo McNeiss suiting up. I'd known him since grade school, before he'd moved to the city and become a cop, before scandal had sent him back home to be a small town deputy, before the deep lines in both our faces. We had never been what you would call friends. As a kid Leo hadn't quite been a bully, but he wasn't someone you chose as an enemy, either. He pointed to the young volunteer from San Luis Obispo, "Both of you."

Shaking, the kid said, "My name's Fenley. Arno—"

"I wouldn't fling a link of monkey shit for your name, son," Leo said, strapping on his breathing gear. I doubted that he had ever used an oxygen unit before but he didn't need any instructions. That was just who he was. He handed over a pair of filtration masks. "We go in two minutes."

Fenley raced to a truck for more gear. Leo rolled a copper fire extinguisher over to me. Stepping in, he said, "We have a special task. I'm sure you remember the name Otto Weissmuller?"

I did. Five years ago, Weissmuller had been arrested and tried on seventeen counts of conspiracy to murder. He'd led a cult of drug-addled teens on a rampage through southern California, terrorized the nation, and kept the newspapers in business.

"This hospital has four wings, not three. The fourth is Black Ward. He's their star patient. It's a big secret. They don't want any of his *family* to try to bust him out." Leo cocked his thumb over at Fenley. The boy fumbled with the straps to his oxygen tank. "Don't want to say anything to him. Would spook him."

"He's already spooked," I said.

Leo attached the feed line to his tank. "Then maybe he's smarter than he looks. When we caught Weissmuller, he was an animal, filthy, long unwashed hair, three inch dirty fingernails—like talons. Barely human. He killed three cops with his bare hands at that roadblock. Bit one patrolman's eye right out of his skull."

"Christ," I muttered.

Fenley shuffled back to us as I jumped into my equipment. Inside our suits it must have been ninety degrees, but the kid was shivering. At that point he probably regretted ever volunteering for the Boy Scouts, let alone fire fighting. I wondered if he had caught any of our conversation. No, I decided. He was, after all, still standing.

We dropped the air masks over our faces and joined the procession of firemen and cops heading toward the Sanitarium's open front doors. Plumes of black smoke rolled out of the entrance in bursts. It felt like we were walking on a dragon's tongue toward its open mouth. Leo checked his service revolver and it reminded me that Fenley and I were armed only with fire extinguishers. The kid locked step and stayed close by my side. He did not even glance toward Leo.

A wave of swirling darkness reached out from the doorway and choked off our vision. We huddled together and pushed inside, walking blind, each of us with our free hand clenching the shoulder of the man ahead. The fire's fierce growl rumbled louder as our feet hit tile. Timber crackled and snapped. The building's foundation groaned as it weakened.

A rush of bristling hot air hit us and cleared out the smoke. A faint light crept in—the fire's orange glow seeping between shrinking wall panels—and the group separated into teams. Leo headed past the reception desk, walking fast, hands waving away lingering trails of smoke. Fenley and I hurried to stay close on his coattails.

A thunderous boom shook down from the hospital's roof and I drew the unsettling image of walking in a cavern deep underground while an earthquake raged in the rock overhead. I jerked my head up quick enough to see a section of the ceiling buckle inward. Grabbing Fenley's collar, I bolted for the hallway. The reception room's ceiling collapsed in a black shower of debris. I heard screams but didn't turn. I kept running, dragging Fenley along, until I caught up with Leo.

Glancing back, the reception room was gone, buried and smoldering. I understood at that moment the terror that miners must feel from inside a cave-in. A dark cloud hurled down the hallway like a fireball, covering us in soot. Fenley and I crouched down and followed Leo.

We passed through a set of double doors and the smoke thinned out. The fire lit room flickered evil orange and yellow hues. The nurse's station seemed to sway with the light, the floor and walls suddenly turned to rubber. My stomach turned as I stepped forward. Illusion or not, it felt like walking on a raft, the constant movement under my feet making each step a challenge.

We saw the first body as we made the turn into the disturbed ward. A nurse, stripped naked, stretched across the floor. Someone had wrapped her head in medical gauze, but not enough to mask the red stains over her eyes, flattened nose and mouth. In her blood, her killer had drawn a peace symbol between her exposed breasts.

Fenley took two steps back, pulled off his mask, and vomited.

Leo stepped over the nurse and continued down the hall. The doors on both sides had been forced open, some torn off their hinges. I caught up with him, careful not to look down as I hurdled the nurse's body, and peeked into the first room. An inmate sat on a bench against the far wall, his strait-jacket bloodied. He had been decapitated and his head returned to his neck upside down. The deep frown on his face had been carved into a crimson smile with two bloody thumbprints on his chin for eyes.

Fenley came up behind me, mask still in hand. I turned, blocked his view into the room, and shook my head. I saw his eyes glisten. The kid was close to tears.

I didn't look in the other rooms in that first hallway. Leo took the time to poke his head in each, a swift search, before returning to the hall. His face never gave any hint what he saw in those chambers. I shuddered at the thought that he might have seen worse.

Leo spun on his heels until he faced us, pointed to Fenley with one crooked finger, and barked, "Put the goddamn mask over you face."

Fenley obeyed. He brought the mask up to his mouth with shaking hands and rolled the elastic strap over his head.

Gesturing with the same finger, Leo continued down the hall to a set of double doors. Turning the handles, he found them locked, so he kicked them in. He was a stronger man than he seemed—and no one would have pegged him for a weakling. The doors splintered away from their hinges and collapsed inward. He stepped over the resulting debris into the highest security wing—Black Ward— and, God help us, we trailed along behind him, right down a steep flight of metal stairs.

Even in the dimming light I could see that Black Ward's walls were bare, not decorated with art school dropout oil paintings like the rest of the hospital.

The hallways were a cinderblock maze, a dungeon. But then, I thought, where else would they keep monsters?

More of the ceiling collapsed somewhere overhead—a hellish crescendo of splintering lumber, crackling masonry, and the whoosh of fire finding a fresh portal to the night sky. For a moment I feared the whole complex was pancaking down on top of us. I saw the drop ceiling over our heads plummeting down, followed by an avalanche of blackened debris. I raised an arm and ducked down, but the collapse was a trick of light, shadow, and my spinning head conspiring to bring my worst fears into my eyes.

Fenley's hand pushed between my shoulder blades, urging me to keep up with Leo and somehow my feet obliged, picking up speed, wandering into the dark. The last feeble trickle of light dissipated and I was blind. The concrete floor under my feet became a promise that I didn't dare trust—I expected to plunge down into an abyss with each clumsy footfall. I was shaking every bit as much as Fenley's hand on my back. All at once, I felt chills and hot flashes, freezing and burning.

Something was very wrong with me.

A door opened a dozen feet up the hallway and a flicker of firelight danced over the floor. We ran to Leo, standing in the doorway, gun drawn. As we passed through, I glanced up and saw that the fire had eaten away a corner of the ceiling, giving us that precious tiny light but also bringing the flames closer. I felt waves of blistering heat buffet down and suck the moisture from my pores. I continued to shiver anyway.

We passed a security checkpoint. The desk had been abandoned in a hurry, a cup of coffee and half a donut left behind in the rush to flee the building.

Leo pointed to a door at the far end of the short hallway. A clipboard hung under a small, wire-latticed window. Even from a few feet away I recognized the photograph that topped the medical charts and medication schedules. It was Otto Weissmuller, a few years older than the pictures in the newspaper after his arrest, but unmistakable: dark, wide-set eyes, thin, pointed brows, a receding hairline that rose like devil's horns.

Leo checked his gun, stepped up, and unlatched the door. I inhaled, held the oxygen in my lungs, and shadowed him inside the cell. My feet and legs had gone completely numb. An unsettling detachment flooded my senses and I watched myself move without feeling the floor under my shoes, or the ache of my bum knee, or the weight of the equipment on my back. It was an obscene freedom; it was sickening.

Silence greeted us inside the cell, as if even the noise of a collapsing, burning building refused to share space with the lunatic who lived there.

Otto Weissmuller sat on the corner cot, head down, face curtained by a few scraggly strands of dark hair. He rocked forward and stared at us. "Deputy

McNeiss, it's good of you to visit. Could you perhaps ask the ward nurse to kindly turn down the heat?"

Leo straightened his arm. His pistol's aim was locked on Weissmuller's pointed nose.

Fenley stumbled into the cell behind me, wobbling.

"Tell me, Leo," Weissmuller said. "Why exactly are there *two* firemen here?"

Leo lowered his gun and removed his breathing mask. "There was an inconsistency in the police reports. The initial report had you at five foot ten. The booking sheet listed six one."

Weissmuller cackled. "I'm six one."

Leo nodded, turned, and shot Fenley in the chest twice.

I scampered back toward the door, but my legs buckled and I fell to the floor. I began to reach for my outstretched legs but my arms went rubbery and dropped to my sides. I couldn't even raise my head off the concrete. Inside the mask I screamed—just for a moment, until my vocal cords locked up. I couldn't even blink.

Unable to turn my head or even shift my pupils, I watched Fenley's last breath escape his lips. His chest settled and the twin jets of gushing blood slowed to a trickle.

Leo appeared overhead. He removed my breathing mask, sliding it over my head and letting the elastic tug on my ears before it snapped free. "Sorry, bud. Don't try to move, you can't. I injected Pancuronium Bromide into your oxygen filter. It's a muscle relaxant. The disorientation you've been feeling is normal."

Weissmuller took my legs, and together they dragged me across the cell and propped me against the cot. Leaning down, Leo whispered into my ear, "His people have my daughter. What was I going to do? I help him escape, I get her back. Sorry you got put into play, man, but even as a kid you were an easy mark."

He tore off my clothes, balled them up, and tossed them into the hall.

Leo stood up. Weissmuller grinned. "You should Picasso up his face now, like my family told you. Just in case the fire leaves some flesh on him."

Nodding, Leo pulled back his fist and brought it down. Though paralyzed, I felt the blow, felt warmth spread across my face, felt my skull vibrate, shockwaves fleeing from the epicenter under his knuckles. The second and third blows came just as fast. After that, I lost count, unable to tell when the explosion of pain from one punch ended and the next began. I heard wet slaps. I saw his knuckles glisten with my blood.

He backed away and Weissmuller bent down and forced my mouth open with his thumbs. Reaching inside, he pried free my loosened teeth until my mouth was empty. Then he stood up, rattling them in his fist like pocket change before emptying his hands into the pocket of Leo's fire jacket.

Weissmuller smiled. His mouth was toothless, too. He reached under his pillow, retrieved his own teeth, and forced them into my bloody mouth. Cackling through his words, he said, "Now my dental records are your dental records. Like a gift on your birthday."

I wanted to spit his teeth out. I wanted to vomit. But nothing worked. I was an abandoned marionette dummy, a worthless human husk with severed strings.

As they turned away, Weissmuller pointed to Fenley's body with both index fingers. "Drag that shit into the hall, wouldn't you? Hate to have the clean-up crew think I kept a dirty cell."

Huffing, Leo bent down and wrapped his hands around the young firefighter's ankles. Still hunched over, he dragged the body out through the doorway. Weissmuller turned, flashed me duel peace symbols like Richard Nixon, and ducked out of the cell.

I listened to their footsteps travel down the hall.

A black spot grew on the ceiling as the fire burnt its way down. Grains of ash trickled down like fine black raindrops, building up like an anthill on the tile floor.

Four quick gunshot blasts echoed in the hall, close together—desperate, frightened, wild shots. Then there were screams, like wailing pigs, shrieks of absolute panic.

And then silence.

The anthill of ash grew into a small hill. The cell darkened. At first I thought I was passing out, but no, the padded walls were wilting from the heat.

I lay there waiting for a rain of fire to snake down through the hole in the ceiling and devour my flesh. So strange to panic when your heartbeat cannot quicken.

I heard the clatter of running feet and for a moment feared that Leo and Weissmuller were returning to torment me even more. But there was too much noise, too many feet.

They appeared in the doorway, twitching, heads jerking. Six men dressed in blue shirts and matching pants, each speckled with blood. I saw fear and frenzy in their eyes, but also hate and vengeance. I knew beyond question that these were patients from Red Ward.

Moving like an ape with his arms swinging, one of the men bounced over to me and smiled a wild, uneven grin. He had braces, and bits of red stuck in the metalwork. Reaching down, he picked up my hand and shook it.

Another of the madmen pushed him away and knelt down beside me. He never made eye contact, instead choosing to watch the mountain of ash growing beside us. "I wanted to meet you for a long time, Otto, and here we are, like synchronicity. Looks like they messed up your face real good, *shit*, but we took care of them. Jimmy, m'man, he bashed in that cop's head with a metal chair leg. So he ain't gonna hurt you no more, not with his head bashed in like that."

The room darkened more, but this time it wasn't the walls. It was me.

* * *

When I awoke we were in a van headed south. I don't remember being carried out of the hospital, but I *do* have a few hazy memories of the Red Ward boys carjacking the van. I don't know where we're headed, but I know that wherever they take me, I'll have to answer to the name Otto Weissmuller. I'd hate to think what they'd do if I told them any different.

Ghosts Under Glass

by Tracie McBride

Corey had discovered the first ghosts in a parked car near the bridge they usually slept under. David had run back to the stash of "treasures" he kept in a pilfered shopping trolley and had returned with a huge glass jar with a screw top lid. It was the kind of jar that looked like it should have a pickled fetus floating in it. "I'm gonna catch me one of those," he had said, patting the jar under his arm, "and keep it as a pet." They soon found more of them, all imprisoned within buildings or vehicles, but David had yet to get brave enough to see what would happen if he opened a door and let one out.

They walked past McDonald's, and Corey imagined he could smell fries cooking. He hesitated at the door. For no apparent reason, David started to laugh.

"What's so funny?" asked Julia, but Corey could tell that she didn't really care what the answer was. She was too busy eyeballing the ghosts tapping on the window.

A couple of the ghosts began to fling themselves against the door with all the strength they could muster, which was completely absent, and Corey took a step back. The ghost of a teenaged boy, his cap on backward, mouthed obscenities at Julia and gave her the finger. Julia reached out her hand and spread her fingertips against the glass. The ghosts flew into a frenzy, swarming across the window in a futile attempt to break through.

"Cool," said Julia. "Like one of those lightning plasma ball thingies." Her eyes shone in the light from the crackling ectoplasm. Corey couldn't stand to look at them for more than a few seconds at a time; they made him feel nauseous. He slapped her hand away.

"Don't tease them," he said.

"Why not?" said David. "We know they can't get out. It's the only thing we do know. That, and the fact that we'd better figure out where we're gonna find some food without having to tangle with those." He nodded in the direction of the ghosts and hefted his jar nervously from side to side.

"There's always vending machines…" said Corey.

"Glass," said Julia abruptly. "They're all behind glass. Could be the vending machines are haunted too."

"Nope," said David. "I've got it all figured out. Wherever there were people inside last night—and that was just about everybody—they were wasted. Wiped out. Nuked. Ghostified. Whatever you want to call it. We were safe, see, 'cos we were sleeping outside." He nodded, obviously pleased with himself.

Julia leant closer to the window and pressed her swollen belly against it. The ghosts froze for a moment, their phantom eyes stretched improbably wide, then renewed their assault on the glass, moving so fast they turned into a blur. David and Corey simultaneously yelled and pulled her away, one on each arm. The blur slowly resolved back into distinct shapes.

"For fuck's sake, Julia!" said David. "You don't know what effect those things might have on the baby." Julia pouted and looked away. Her gaze stopped on a small stuffed toy left lying in the gutter, and she wandered over to retrieve it, David's reprimand already forgotten. David and Corey looked at each other and sighed. Julia's baby might have been Corey's, or it might have been David's, or for all they knew its father might be floating behind glass somewhere. But they had taken responsibility for her. Julia was special, a genuine, free-spirited innocent, or at least that was how Corey saw her. The way her mind was wired up, she alone needed full-time attention. He didn't want to think about how they would cope with her baby as well. The boys trailed after her. It had started to rain again, and they scuttled between shop awnings.

"Look!" said Julia. "There's somebody else! A live person!"

David looked up, swore, and pulled her into a doorway.

"Sssh!" he whispered, clamping his hand over her mouth. "It's a cop!"

"Yeah, but it's a *live* cop," Corey whispered back. "He's the first real human being we've seen all day. Maybe we should all stick together—you know, safety in numbers and all that."

David gave him a withering look. "If you really believe that, then how come you're not rushing out there to greet him with open arms? Betchya it was some government conspiracy or fucked-up military experiment that did this, anyway."

Corey peeped around the doorway at the cop, silently conceding that David had a point. The cop crept down the street away from them, holding his gun outstretched in shaking hands. As he turned the corner, Corey caught a glimpse of his wide, manic eyes. He ducked back into the doorway until they could no longer hear the cop's footsteps. They stepped out of hiding and headed off in the opposite direction.

"So if we're not going to look for other survivors, what do you suggest we do instead?"

"Maybe we could hotwire a car and head out to the coast," David said.

"There's bound to be plenty of those million dollar beach houses sitting empty in the off season."

"And if they're empty, fuckwit," said Corey, "their pantries will be empty as well."

David scowled and kicked viciously at an empty Coke can.

"Or we could go to my folks' place," said Julia. Corey started; he hadn't thought she was listening.

"They went on holiday in Europe three weeks ago," she continued. She cradled a small purple teddy bear in her arms and stroked it as if it were alive. "They were supposed to be coming home on Sunday…anyway, Mum had a Natural Disaster kit, so there'll be plenty of tinned food in that."

David gaped at her. "I thought you said your parents were dead."

"They probably are now," she said, shrugging. "Every now and again they used to track me down. Give me some money, ask me to come home, tell me what's been going on with the family, shit like that." Corey nodded. Now that she mentioned it, he had seen her a few times talking to a well-dressed middle-aged couple, and once or twice seen money change hands, but he'd dismissed them as a couple of Christian do-gooders.

"So let me get this straight," said David. He had wedged his jar between his feet and stood leaning slightly toward Julia, his hands gripped together behind his back as if to stop himself from forming them into fists. "You had parents. Parents who were alive, and who loved you, and who wanted you to come home. And you're eight months pregnant, and living on the streets with a pair of losers like us. Why, Julia? Why didn't you go home?" He spoke gently, but he trembled with the effort. Corey groaned and tensed in readiness, just in case David's volatile temper flared.

Julia smiled sadly. Her hair had gone mousy and lank from the rain, and for a moment all her innocence seemed to drain away from her. She caressed her stomach, and muttered, almost too low for them to hear—

"Daddy's not getting his hands on this one."

* * *

The emergency kit at Julia's house proved to be more than amply provisioned, with the added bonus of a well-stocked freezer and a full gas canister on the barbeque. Corey and David finished off their meal with a generous slosh of cognac from the liquor cabinet. Even with the warmth of the alcohol suffusing his body, Corey felt weird sitting there with pictures of Julia as a child gazing down on him from the photos on the wall. It felt equally weird retiring to separate bedrooms to sleep instead of huddling together for warmth like they usually did. Corey sprawled on the bed and stared at the shadows on the ceiling. At some point he must have fallen asleep because the next thing he knew, David was shaking him awake.

"It's Julia," David said. "I think the baby's coming."

Julia's labour matched none of Corey's preconceptions. He had expected it to happen very quickly, and for there to be a lot of screaming. Julia was on her hands and knees on her parents' queen-sized bed, which was soaked with amniotic fluid. She reminded Corey of a cat he'd had as a kid who'd had kittens in his wardrobe. She stared blankly ahead, panting a little, and every now and again she would let out a quiet moan. Corey and David sat with her as the night melded into day. Sometime after noon she got off the bed and began to pace the room. Suddenly she stiffened, grabbed David by the shoulder, gritted her teeth, and yowled like a wounded animal. Blood trickled down her left leg. She drew a deep, shuddering breath and yowled again.

"Do something!" yelled David, wild-eyed with panic.

"What, what?" Corey yelled back. "What should I do?"

"I don't know—go get some towels, or boil some water, or something. Do whatever the fuck they do in the movies."

Corey fled the room. He huddled uselessly in the corner of the lounge and tried to block out the inhuman sounds coming from the bedroom. After one particularly long, loud, heartrending cry, the house fell silent. He crept back to the bedroom, afraid of what he might see.

Julia sat on the floor in the corner of the room with her arms wrapped around her knees. An umbilical cord snaked from between her feet, out across the blood-streaked floor to where it was attached to a tiny naked baby girl. The baby curled unmoving on her side as if still in the womb, her eyes screwed shut tight against the world. David stood with his back against the wall, clutching his jar in front of him like a shield. Before Corey's horrified eyes, the infant seemed to deflate. Its skin stretched tight over its frame, then disintegrated altogether, leaving only a mound of bones. Its rate of decay increased exponentially, until there was nothing left but a pile of fine, pale dust. A small, white cloud rose from the remains and coalesced into the shape of a newborn baby. Corey heard the squeak of metal against glass, and turned his head to see David remove the lid from his jar and launch himself across the room to scoop up the tiny ghost and slam the lid on. Momentarily the specter hovered in the jar, still curled in its fetal position. It raised its head and opened its eyes, glaring at them all through the wall of its glass prison with a malevolent expression of awareness. Julia crept toward David and took the jar from his outstretched arms.

"My baby," she crooned, rocking the jar in her arms. The ghost drew back its lips in a gummy snarl and hissed silently.

Corey smacked David across the ear with his palm. "What did you do that for, dickhead?"

"I couldn't leave it just flying around in here," David retorted. "Who knows what it might have done? Anyway, it's all Julia has. Surely it's better than nothing." He glanced at the dust pile.

Corey looked at Julia, still sitting in the muck of afterbirth, cuddling her macabre offspring.

"No," said Corey, "I think nothing would have been much better than this."

* * *

Between them, Corey and David managed to coax Julia into a bath and settle her into bed. She fell asleep almost instantly, still clutching the jar. Sleep came more slowly for Corey, and when it did, it was filled with disjointed dreams. He woke abruptly at 2 a.m. Someone was moving about in the kitchen. He got up and padded down the hallway.

Julia stood at the breakfast table, eating from a can of peaches by candlelight and humming snippets of "Rock-a-Bye Baby" between mouthfuls. The flickering light on her calm, composed face made her look like an angel. And there sits the devil, Corey thought, glancing uneasily at the ghost baby in her jar on the table.

"You know, Julia," he said, "maybe it's not such a good idea to keep your baby in a jar like that. It's a bit...creepy. Maybe you should bury her. It'll make it easier for you to let go."

Julia looked at him with wide, demented eyes. "What are you talking about? What kind of sicko would want to bury a baby alive?" She snatched up the jar and hugged it to her chest. "But you're right about one thing. I shouldn't keep her locked in like this." She put a hand on top of the jar and twisted the lid a quarter turn.

"No!" Corey lunged toward her and made a grab for the jar. For a moment they held it between them, Corey's large tanned hands over Julia's small pale ones, and then the jar slipped and fell, shattering on the kitchen floor.

"My baby!" Julia gasped. She stepped forward, slicing her foot open on a shard of glass, and bent over to pick up the infant ghost that now lay on the floor. A wave of nausea overwhelmed Corey, and he dropped, retching, to his knees. David came rushing through the kitchen door, clad only in grimy boxer shorts.

"What's going on? I heard a crash..." He skidded to a halt. The ghost baby slowly rose from its bed of glass until it hovered in the air a few inches above their heads. It turned in a circle, examining each of them, its little face oddly intent. Seeming to come to a decision, it flashed a predatory grin.

Then, the screaming began.

155

Sporting the Waters of the Bermuda Triangle

by Greggard Penance

Speculative Zone 28.499 N / 67.583 W

There is no sense of time or locale, just the sway of the boat to the ocean's violent fit. The water swells, pushes the craft up and bursts over the port side, then recedes, pulling it back. The shipmates keep their feet apart for balance, grab hold of rails, poles or equipment until it passes. Between these bursts, they move around, pause, anticipating the next jolt.

The midday sun washes the deck, but clouds tower in the distance to the front and port side. They stretch up from the horizon in deep streaks of charcoal and grey that split the day like the shadowed ridges of a canyon.

Blue light flickers across that blackness and charges the water, leaving a dome-shaped glow. Momentarily it is washed out by an outline of brilliant orange, which is followed by lime green. This bizarre electric storm has been brewing and becoming more pronounced as our boat approaches.

I have a full view of the port side and most of the bow. The captain's helm stands tall atop the bow, obscured from my sight by the edges of the rectangular slit that I've been given to see through. Across the deck stands another crate, I think the same size as mine.

A surge explodes over the rails. Mist roils the breeze and brushes across my viewing hole. My eyes should sting, but there is nothing. In fact, no sensation at all in my entire body, not even a tingle in my arms or legs. Perhaps the blood has constricted and my limbs have gone to sleep. Or worse, they might be dead. I'm confined so tight, it is as though I've been set in concrete to my nose. I'm also deaf. I can pick up their vibrations as the men shout at one another, but cannot hear them. Nor can I hear the storm.

The boat crew, burly men in rubber boots and raincoats, pace, industriously preparing. These are experienced seamen, who move with the boat as it responds to the swells that pound its port side.

During a calm moment, I study the other crate. Many rectangular holes in the side of it, and they are organized in precisely spaced columns and rows. These slits look to be the same as the one I view through, though I can't see what's behind them. The way the sun is positioned, shadows cover whatever might be looking out.

Flashes of blue, green and orange light trade off overhead, spider webs etching the ridges of the storm and the fierce sea. A skirt of shade overtakes the boat, and stars abruptly pepper the sky. We have passed through a gateway from day to night in an instant. Clouds do not exist inside, yet the electrical storm tears through the heavy air, making for the only light to see by, and the swells grow heavier, rocking the boat still harder.

The ship hands scramble, hurried by the deteriorating conditions. It is unclear what they are setting up, or what for. A powerful wave breaks over the side and one man is knocked down. The crewman gets up quickly and grabs onto a rail to brace for the next surge.

The boat changes direction, heads on into the swells. The men open cases, pull out equipment. It is somewhat recognizable, but I just can't place it. Memory of my own life is not only gone, but any education that would otherwise spur recognition of objects and activities seems to be damaged as well.

A violent flash of orange casts blinding light on the ship and illuminates the other crate. As the boat veers toward the center of the storm, the holes in the crate are angled to catch the light.

A massive swell appears ahead. The nose of the boat rises upward, and the hull rocks from side to side from the force. The men keep their legs apart, each bracing their stance as the surge of sea moves under. My box slides on the deck with the roll of the boat, changing my viewpoint. I can no longer see the bow, but instead the stern, though the other crate remains in my sightline.

The ship glows as orange lightning strikes nearby, and brightness washes over me. Consciousness flutters and something smothers my vision—I swoon.

Open eyes, vision gone. Brief blackness, then outlines appear. The hazy image like a Polaroid photo developing...

...through a window—no—a rearview mirror, a windshield. Night. Streetlights illuminate parked cars. Coming up on the lot, a building behind it, fluorescent with artificial light beaming up from below; a church with a tall steeple. Recognize the bell tower, the windows, the entrance. Come to an intersection, cannot read the cross-street sign but can recall what will be next. Cross the intersection, no more street lights. Narrowing road lined only by trees. The curves wind around in the blackness; can only

see two lanes, the broken yellow dashes, and the thick line of trees along the shoulder. A charm dangles from the rearview mirror. It swings along as the car leans one way, then the next. Just enough light from the dash. Can see what's on the charm.

A woman and a young boy. Her name, Mindy, his, Stephen.

A pickup truck turns out in front, leaves no time to brake. The driver swerves to avoid being rear-ended, but too late. Brakes squeal. Smash into the right fender, bounce off toward the trees. Will hit the trees. A thought burbles up—"too fast." See Mindy and Stephen alone, devastated. Feel the loss, the wrenching...

...back. I leave wife and son with no warning; they are alone.

Bright blue light flickers from all around. I wonder if Mindy has any idea what has happened to me. Where I am.

The electrical storm has engulfed the boat. The water lights up and unnatural splashes ensue. Giant fish surging along the surface; sea foam burbling in brilliant colors, reflecting the lightning that etches the sky. Soon I see that it is not just in the sky, but the water itself has become charged.

The crate in front of me catches a beam of blue light, and I see what's behind the first slit. Big, frightened eyes. They bulge in the darkness and light up with the storm, and they do not blink. The sky casts a new flash with an orange glow, and the lumen brightens, stretching across a few more slits, then the rest of the crate. Dozens of them, all pairs of eyes, all darting around, a pair for each viewing hole. Something's wrong. There are way too many slits, way too many pairs of eyes. There is no room for the bodies!

While the lightning charges the sky and branches across the sea, the water turns calm, churned only by the swarming fish or whatever sea life moves around just beneath its surface. The swells dissipate, and the boat settles. We are in the eye of the storm.

The deck hatch opens again, and two more men climb up from below, both wearing strange suits. They are covered head to toe with metallic material, and their heads have bubble-shaped helmets. The other men hand them the equipment and climb down through the same hatch.

One of the men picks up a stick. It is a fishing rod, but a massive one, thick and long. Constrained by the stiffness of the suit, he waddles to the stern, and carefully sits in a chair. The chair is bolted to the deck and it swivels as he straps himself in.

The metallic man works his way over to the crate. He shifts funny. It stirs in my memory images from TV of men walking on the moon. He pulls up a lid from the top of the box, and reaches in. Just below him a set of eyes turn up. He pulls something out of the crate and lightning flashes, enlightening a glass container that hangs from under his clenched palm and fingers. It looks like a two-gallon pickle jar. Inside it are the eyes, and behind them, the unmistakable contours and clefts of a human brain. The three parts float in a liquid, the eyes attached to the cerebral cortex with hundreds of strands of muscles and nerves. The man in the space suit holds the bottom of the jar with one silver-gloved hand, and the eyes stare up to watch as he twists the cap with the other.

A violent blast of orange light washes to yellow, and again my vision fails. I wait as the profile of a new scene takes shape.

A hallway. White walls line each side. Move forward, a woman in powder blue pulls the bed. She watches, encourages, "You're gonna be okay," but her voice is not sincere. Two metal doors fly open and she pulls me through. A man looks over the top of me from behind the gurney. "The surgeon is waiting in the OR," he tells the woman. "It appears that there are no head injuries."

The gurney is wheeled through another doorway. Two men standing in the middle of the room, gloves on and masks in place, rush to each side of the gurney and look down. They reach into the abdominal wounds, and one shakes his head. He looks at the other, turns and studies my eyes.

"He's in shock," the man says. He glances at the nurse and orderly who just wheeled me in and says, "That will be all." They nod and exit the room.

The other surgeon leans in close to my face, near enough to me that when he speaks, I can feel his breath on my cheeks. I wonder, in this trauma, how a sense so subtle remains possible.

"Well, it will all be for the best. The bleeding is terminal, the kidneys ruptured and his spine severed."

"He's got a donor card," the other says.

"Good, because we should certainly have use for the eyes. Let's see what else we can save."

...I come to and the man in the silver suit has one knee on the deck in front of the jar. He is now unscrewing the cap.

With the lid removed, he sets the jar down on the deck, reaches in with one hand and pulls the brain through the large mouth. As it glistens in the flashes of green, there is not enough muscle to support the weight of the eyes, so they dangle, staring down at the man's foot. He stands and walks over to the other man, who is waiting in his swivel chair, and stops at the rod. While still holding the brain in one hand he gathers a clear line attached to a hook in the other. It is an enormous treble hook, larger than his gloved fist.

He turns the brain over and digs the hook into the stem. The eyeballs shudder, from shock or incredulous pain. The man then takes the bait and turns it up as the seated man reels in the line, leaves approximately two feet between the tip of the fishing pole and the bait. The man who set the bait steps away as the fisherman cranks the pole back and with a powerful jerk swings everything forward, sending the brain hurtling, its eyeballs gyrating like protons around an

159

unstable atom. The bait disappears over the stern with a splash. Instantly, the water around it churns, and within seconds the man jerks. The hook is set into something powerful, and the rod rattles as the fight begins. The chair swings left, then right, and he reels hard. He lets up as his quarry turns and runs with the line. The drag on the reel whirs.

The electric storm lights the stage for some time until the man who is standing waddles over to the stern. He picks up a pole and turns it over the side. It's got a pointed aluminum gaff on the end, and he leans over the edge, in a prepared stance, holding it so that the hook faces out.

Green light illuminates something large as it rises up from the water, and the man with the hook lunges out at it. The man from the chair stands up, grabs a second gaff, stabs it into the fish from another angle. Both squat and strain to draw it in. The catch smacks the sidewall, its fierce fin or tail thumps three or four times, and a moment later a giant, fleshy creature slides over the rail and plunks onto the deck. It flops and squirms, and in the next flash of blue light, I see that it is not a fish. Nor is it an octopus or a sea lion. I've never seen such a beast. Ten feet long, this creature has smooth skin and blubbery flesh. It wriggles on the floor between two pairs of metallic boots. No fins, no features in the tail, and no face or eyes, it resembles a slug without antennae.

The man who reeled in the creature grabs another tool, a device that looks much like a pitchfork, only without the middle teeth, and he pins the monster, keeping its torso tight against the deck. The other man digs his boot sole flat against its squirming head, while the fisherman holds the midsection firm. He then pulls a two-foot-long pair of pliers from his belt pack. He leans toward the creature's snakelike head, turning about to get a look into the gaping mouth. With no further hesitation, he plunges the pliers deep inside the fleshy creature, past several rows of serrated teeth and wriggling gums. He digs around, causing the gums to flare and the long throat to swell and throb. Its six-foot length of tail recoils, unfurls, slaps the deck violently in an attempt to free its upper end, but the tool seemingly designed specifically to restrict this breed of monster does its job.

Seconds later, and the pliers are retracted. Out pops the brain and treble hook. He flips the bait onto the deck and the hook falls off to its side, a serrated chunk of cerebrum still attached.

He picks up his gaff from the deck and plunges it deep into the blubbery hide. Together, the two men drag the beast back toward the stern. One of them pulls open a hatch and they sling the giant thing so that it slides off into the compartment. The boat rattles again as the creature thumps the floor of the holding tank.

I turn my attention back to the sea-bleached brain as orange flashes from around the boat highlight its frayed and softened features. One milky eyeball lies next to it, a barely visible pupil gazing lifelessly into space. Again, a surge of blue energy engulfs the boat, and the eye twitches, turns up to look at me a final time. Then it goes blank in an eternal stare.

One of the men produces a push broom and uses it to brush the remains in short, choppy sweeps toward the stern. He shoves them through the scupper into the sea, while the other man washes the debris away with a bucket of seawater.

He hangs the bucket on a rail and ambles over to my crate. The skies rumble and beams of neon green creep in from above, as my roof is lifted. I turn my eyes up, and for the first time I can see the lid of my own jar and the metallic fingers finding their grip around it.

Skin

by Kim Despins

This thing wearing his sister's skin stands at the foot of Jeremy's bed, just as she has every night since he moved back into his father's house. When Jeremy asked Lisa to help care for their father in his last days, she hung up on him. Instead, this thing visits in her place. She whips the covers from his bed, and Jeremy's skin puckers in the cool rush of air.

He thinks she's changed her mind about helping with their father, but when he touches her, the skin slides over the thing underneath and he knows this can't be his sister. He tries to scream but nothing emerges except a soft moan. He pushes her away, but his hands caress that pale skin while something else pulsates just beneath its surface. His body refuses every command his mind issues. He's come to accept these visits, even enjoys them in some unnatural way. There's always penance.

His entire adult life has been penance. In the Peace Corps he taught English in a tiny cinderblock room to children who asked only the English words for food. After failing to feed anything more than their minds, Jeremy joined the seminary. His room there had a wood floor, plaster walls, and no starving children. As a priest, he enjoyed the overgrown garden behind the rectory. The trees hung low, denying the herbs sun and stunting their growth, but the air tasted fresh.

The priesthood had been his escape. The children, their minds hungrier than their bellies, arrived at Sunday school eager to learn. His parishioners responded to his counseling with appreciation. After almost thirty years of searching, Jeremy finally found a community, a family.

His father's illness has ripped him away from that family, and he aches to return. Jeremy waits for his father to die so he can return to his life in the church. His life with no starving children. His life without this thing wearing his sister's skin, and its unnatural hunger.

Lying rigid on his mattress, Jeremy promises when he returns to the church, he'll trim the trees and feed the herbs with sunlight. He can't confess something this unsavory, but he vows to pray every prayer he knows a dozen times. *Anything, he pleads with God, just make this thing go away.*

Every door is bolted, every window shut tight. Yet here she stands wearing the skin of someone he loves. This caricature of a woman is not his sister. Lisa lives thirty minutes away in Boston. Her partner and his religion are two of the many things they never speak about on the rare occasions they talk at all. During those conversations, Jeremy does the talking, and Lisa provides vague answers to his questions. Calling her his sister seems wrong, invasive. He barely knows her.

Would she notice, he wonders, that he replaced the Farrah Fawcett poster from his boyhood with a framed photograph of a pale yellow crocus, opening among the crystals of melting snow? The photo was a gift from a parishioner. Jeremy tried to tell Lisa that he'd burned the cache of dirty magazines he'd found piled in his dresser drawers, forgotten since high school. Her response had been a dial tone.

Jeremy called her three times the first week he spent in his father's house. Twice she hung up on him, and the third time her partner claimed Lisa was out even though he heard her voice in the background.

"Wait," Jeremy said, struggling to remember this woman's name.

"What?"

"Does she still like to catch lightning bugs?"

Lisa's voice came through the background. Jeremy pictured her standing next to her partner, one hand on her shoulder. "Tell him not now. I can't talk to him now."

"Don't call back." The partner hung up the phone.

The thing that looks like his sister unties her robe and lets it fall to the floor. Her skin glows in the moonlight. He wishes for the false safety of blankets, to curl up under the covers and pretend there's not a monster in the room. But his body disagrees. She climbs atop him, pausing to kiss his erection much the way Jeremy hopes to kiss the rings of the pope. Every night is the same, down to the hopes, regrets, and memories as she takes his willing body, and his mind pretends to fight from its cage.

* * *

At thirteen, Jeremy developed a painful crush on Missy Salinger when she pushed her bathing suit bottoms to her knees and showed him *hers* behind the boathouse. Jeremy put his family jewels on display for her, but she gasped and ran away, leaving him alone with his swim trunks around his ankles.

Thinking about the freckles on Missy's pale thighs and where they led, Jeremy hiked through the woods between his family's vacation house and the Salingers' cottage. Her voice reached his ears before he got to the edge of the woods. Crouched behind a lilac bush, he listened to Missy and Toni Wilson chatter about girl stuff while baking their skin in the sun. He ignored their words and drank Missy in with his eyes.

Her red hair, barely contained in a ponytail, shone in the sun. Jeremy imagined weaving his fingers through those curls. He untied his swim trunks and slipped his hand inside. Jeremy massaged his erection until Toni's words stopped him cold. The flesh in his right hand softened.

"You saw it?" Toni asked. "You really saw it?"

"Yeah, it was all shriveled and gross."

"So it was small? Where did he show you?"

Jeremy's skin burned to the tips of his ears.

"Behind the boathouse. I can't believe he really did it."

"Did you—"

"Ew! Of course not."

Jeremy sucked in deep breaths, but it didn't calm the anger flooding him. The word *liar* rested on the tip of his tongue. He breathed in a mosquito buzzing among the lilacs and coughed it out of his throat.

Both girls sat up on their towels.

"Who's there?" Toni called.

Crouched low, Jeremy ran back into the woods. Behind him, the girls giggled.

Missy's words followed him through the trees. "What a creep."

* * *

He's finally dying. A down comforter pins the old man to the bed, his outline faint. The rise and fall of his chest doesn't move the blanket, but the thick gasps tell Jeremy it's not quite over. Jeremy waits in a kitchen chair next to the drug-littered night table. Half-empty beer bottles stand among the prescription containers like trees. Jeremy gave up on taking away his father's vice when he found the Styrofoam cooler lodged between the bed and the wall. Instead he picked a handful of daisies and plunked them into a bottle. Now the flowers bend toward the floor, their white petals ringed in brown. His bags are packed and waiting in the car.

Dressed in his vestments, Jeremy reads his Bible. Matthew chapter five, verse thirty catches his eye. "If thy right hand offend thee, cut it off, and cast it from thee." His father tried that. The cancer started in his testicles. Doctors took those almost a year ago, but surgery came too late. The disease marched through his body to the lymph nodes, the bones, and finally to the major organs. Doctors removed every offending organ they could, but it was never enough.

His father struggles under the covers. Jeremy pulls the blankets off his chest and dabs at his sweaty forehead with a cool cloth while muttering meaningless words, telling his father it'll be all right. The old man grips Jeremy's wrist with the strength of a child.

"Forgive me, Father, for I have sinned." He gasps for breath, his toothless mouth a dark window into his diseased body.

Jeremy picks his father's fingers from his arm and looks away. "There's no need." Some things even a priest can't bear to witness.

The old man collapses onto the mattress, his uneven breath hitching into something that resembles a sob. He looks up at Jeremy, his eyes alert for the first time in days.

"Son?"

"I'm here, Dad."

"Remember when we went to Virginia Beach?"

Jeremy had been nine, Lisa six, Mom healthy. What Jeremy remembered best was that the cooler had been filled with soda instead of beer, and they'd built a sandcastle as a family. Dad drove them home before the tide washed it out to sea.

"I do, but then Mom died."

Jeremy checks his watch. It's just after eleven. The thing wearing his sister's skin usually visits around midnight. Part of him would like to be gone by then. Part of him will miss her when he returns to his life of penance. It's the most contact he's had with his little sister in years, even if it is with just her skin.

His father shivers under the sheet. Jeremy gets up to open the window and let in the cool air. When he turns back to his seat, she's at the end of the bed, robe pooled at her feet. Her toenails are painted glitter pink.

She raises one finger in the air and looks at Jeremy. Wait. He wraps his hand around the crucifix dangling from his neck. The cross is big enough to be hung on the wall, but he's always preferred the weight of it around his neck.

The thing that's not his sister pulls the sheet from his father's withered body. Somehow the old man has the strength for an erection. Jeremy tries to close his eyes, but they disobey. Heat gathers in his groin.

His father cracks open his eyes as she takes him in her.

"No more," he wheezes. "I'm sorry."

Jeremy's stomach churns. This thing has taken his father every night just before coming to his own bed. Jeremy tries to turn his head, but it remains fixed, his gaze on the two bodies.

She thrusts against the old man, making his body flop against the dirty sheet. The pungent smell of sex mingles with the odor of medicine and beer. His father coughs, gasps for breath, finds none. Jeremy sees himself shove the thing off his father, but his body makes no move other than to slip one hand into his trousers.

His sister—no, the thing wearing his sister's skin—makes no sound, she bounces against his father's hips, her gaze trained on the water-stained wall above

165

the headboard. Jeremy watches with one hand clasping his crucifix and the other caressing his erection, as his father expels a breath and falls limp. The woman runs her knuckle along the old man's cheek, then slaps him before slipping off of his cooling body. His head rocks to the side, his empty eyes fixed on Jeremy, whose hand is still in his pants.

She kneels in front of Jeremy, looks up at him with his sister's green eyes, and speaks with his sister's voice.

"It never bothered you before."

Jeremy extracts his hand from his trousers. She unzips them and takes him into her mouth.

Not my sister, Jeremy thinks. His mind chants the reminder, trying to take control of his body. *Not my sister.*

Jeremy focuses on his father's corpse, one age-spotted arm flung off the side of the bed. The yellowed nails are long because Jeremy forgot to trim them. He finds control of his own arms, they still have life. Jeremy grips the long end of the crucifix in both hands, rips it from the chain. He turns it upside down and thrusts it into the thing knelt before him. It slams into the base of his sister's skull.

Not my sister.

She gasps, choking on his member. Jeremy pulls himself from her mouth and brings the up-ended crucifix down again and again. In his hands, the metal cross pulverizes her spine. The sound of it reminds him of the crunch of gravel under his shoes on the rectory garden path. It reminds him of freedom. She falls forward, pushing Jeremy against the window. She curls into the fetal position, the blood darkening the wood floor around her head and matting her blonde hair. *Not my sister.*

Jeremy buttons his pants and starts to clean the mess. His erection refuses to fade until he has the thing wearing his sister's skin hidden away in the parlor closet.

* * *

Jeremy trudged through the house toward his bedroom where there waited a copy of a Victoria's Secret catalog he'd swiped from a neighbor's recycle bin. His father thumped down the stairs as Jeremy waited to go up.

"You been to see that Salinger girl," his father said.

"How do you know?" Jeremy braced himself against the wall as his father grabbed his shoulder to steady his balance.

"You been sniffing around that girl since we got here." He limped to his easy chair, collapsed into the flattened cushions, and exhaled. His father had installed carpet before arthritis settled into his knee, twisting it into a gnarled formation that looked more tree than human and bent about as well as wood. "That girl's nothing but a tease. She has no intention of putting out for you."

166

"But I don't—"

"Don't argue with me, boy." He dug a beer from the Styrofoam cooler next to the chair. "I was your age once."

"Yes, sir."

"If your mother was here, she'd say you was too young for sex."

Jeremy stared at his feet and nodded.

"She woulda kept both you and me on the straight and narrow like we should be." He twisted the cap off the bottle and threw it at the front door.

Jeremy climbed to the third step.

"But she's dead so you might as well grow up." He pulled the lever on the chair, popping the foot rest into place. "Boy your age needs to recognize that a cock-tease is nothing but a waste of time. Boy your age should be practical."

"Yes, sir."

"It's time to stop beatin' off to something you'll never have." He swigged his beer. "Got what you need practically right under your nose, too."

* * *

Old people he doesn't remember fill the house, cluster around their fallen friend. Jeremy imagines he can hear them praying, "Please, God, not me next." His father had insisted on a traditional wake in his home, even asked Jeremy to clear out the parlor in preparation.

Tired of hearing their stories about when he was "this high," Jeremy skirts the group. More often than not, he finds his back pressed against the closet door, palm on the doorknob, blood rushing to his groin, the smell of her lingering in his nostrils. Incense permeates the room, but barely masks her scent. Each time he compels his hands to grasp the oversized crucifix around his neck. It's bent, but he gathers more comfort from it now than ever. He scans the sea of blue hair for his sister's blonde head, then reminds himself that she refuses to step foot into this house.

Jeremy settles those still living into chairs, begins his father's wake. When it's over, he forces himself to the front porch, where he accepts their condolences to the music of crickets. "You're so brave to preside over your own father's funeral," one bent old man says. Jeremy nods, but doesn't feel that way.

The last car backs away and Jeremy means to follow, but he's left his Bible in the parlor. His father's casket dominates the room, surrounded by empty chairs and bouquets of flowers. His feet carry him past all of this to the closet. Exhausted, he surrenders, relying on the penance he'll do later.

It's inside. Cold and stiff, half standing against the back corner behind his father's fishing jacket. He lifts it, and his sister's skin slides across the body underneath. Jeremy's stomach roils, his member hardens. He lays her body on the carpet alongside the casket, brushes her eyelids closed, strokes her hair. Blood has matted it at the back of her head, but the front is still soft and white-blonde. Leaning forward, he presses his lips to hers. His excitement dwindles at the cold lack of response. His hand wanders between her legs, slips a finger inside. What was once damp like a summer day at the lake is now a dry riverbed. The memory is enough for him. Trembling, he stands and fumbles with his belt.

On the parlor floor, the body is sprawled, its torso stretched upward somewhat from rigor mortis, but legs wide and inviting. Jeremy looks away and opens his father's casket instead. Uncomfortable questions slide through in his mind.

What if someone finds the body?

What if I can never stop violating this thing?

Jeremy uses the pocket knife on his keychain to slice a V into his sister's skin on the thing's thigh. He fingers the tip of the V wanting to pull it back, but afraid to see what lies beneath his sister's alabaster skin. Afraid to know what has tempted him into such vile acts.

He yanks his hand away and leans over his father's casket, lets his forehead rest on his father's icy hands and sobs. "Holy Father, please forgive me." He repeats the plea until the meaning wanes and it becomes five words.

Lifting his head, Jeremy stares into his father's face. "You." His voice is thick. "It happened because of you." Jeremy slaps his father's wrinkled cheek, but the casket prevents him from hitting with any force. The blow leaves a smudge in the pancake makeup and rocks his father's head.

Jeremy clenches his hands into fists and pummels his father's face. Bones crunch under his punches. He steps back to catch his breath. The old man's lips sink deep into his mouth. Jeremy pries them apart. His dentures are now lodged in his throat. His nose sits at a crooked angle and a stream of embalming liquid drips from one nostril into his open mouth.

Jeremy wipes sweat from his face with his forearm.

He picks up the body, gently lays her on top of his father. The back of her head rests between his father's good shoes. He forces her stiffening arms to cross over her bare chest, and closes the casket.

* * *

Jeremy climbed the stairs, leaving his father alone in the living room with his beer and memories. Pausing at Lisa's door in the hall, he tapped and went in. She scrambled for a towel to cover herself, but he caught a glimpse before she wrapped her body in terrycloth. The cleft between his sister's legs reminded him of Missy. The sun had left a similar spattering of freckles across her thighs.

"What do you want?" she asked.

"Just bored. What are you doing?" He plopped down on her bed and pulled a pillow across his lap to hide the stiffness growing between his legs. A mayonnaise jar sat on her night stand. Despite the holes in the metal lid, a colony of fireflies lay on the bottom, legs in the air.

"I'm getting dressed. What does it look like?"

"Let me see."

"What?"

He tried the same line that had worked with Missy a week earlier. "Show me yours, I show you mine."

Lisa's eyes filled with tears. "Jeremy, no," she whispered.

* * *

The funeral is over, but Jeremy asks for a few minutes alone to say his goodbyes. The congregation has left and the pallbearers wait outside the closed church door. Jeremy runs his hand along the casket's lid. Now that the corpse is cold and stiff, the thing wearing his sister's skin has no more power.

He opens the casket and looks at her face. So like his sister, down to the scar splitting her right eyebrow. She was five, and Jeremy eight. He had her favorite stuffed bear held high in the air as she giggled and chased him through the house. Jeremy raced through the living room, but Lisa tripped on one of his trucks and fell into the glass coffee table. He runs his finger along the broken eyebrow. There was blood everywhere, splattered on the table, soaked into the carpet. Jeremy gave the bear back, but nothing would console his little sister.

Lisa wasn't in the church that morning. He looked for her face among the elderly, hoping for a glimpse of her, and found nothing but disappointment. No surprise, Jeremy thinks. She's been avoiding their father for years. He leans over the casket to stroke her hair, press his lips to her stiff mouth. She could have at least come to their father's funeral.

Reaching for the casket lid, he pauses. His gaze lingers over that V-shaped cut on her thigh. The point of skin has dried and curled.

Jeremy takes it between his thumb and forefinger. He holds down the leg to be sure he separates the skin from the thing underneath. He peels back the V-shaped tab. Under her skin are the ribbed scales of the evil that possessed his sister, forced her into sinful acts. He blinks and the scales are gone, replaced by strands of muscle and gobbets of fat. The only thing he finds under Lisa's skin is his sister's flesh.

Santa Maria

by Jeff Cercone

"Can you believe these people? What the hell's the matter with them?"

Rob ignored his friend and pushed his way through the crowd, bumping an elderly Hispanic woman in the shoulder. He started to apologize, but she was too preoccupied to notice.

"Santa María, Madre de Dios, ruega por nosotros pecadores ahora y en la hora de nuestra muerte..." She whispered the prayer, tears soaking her grizzled cheeks and her arms clutching what Rob assumed were her two grandchildren, who stared wide-eyed at the spectacle.

Dozens of people, the devout and the curious, had gathered at the underpass of the Kennedy freeway, positioning for a glimpse of the stain on the wall. A certain civility had taken hold despite the stifling Chicago heat and the decidedly unholy stench of exhaust fumes, sweat and urine.

Most kept a respectful distance, queuing up and allowing a few at a time, usually a family or a group of friends, to move up to get a closer look. Rob noticed, then felt guilty for pushing his way to the front.

"They're nuts!" Mitch said, not caring who he offended. "It doesn't look anything like her. It's a freakin' stain!"

"I dunno, if you stare at it long enough, it could look like her," Rob answered.

Behind them, people held their camera phones up to capture the image on the wall.

"So how do you explain the one that appeared in rust on the water tower in Des Moines?" Rob asked. "And then there was the other one that was supposedly just a random case of brown patch on that football field in Texas..."

"I had a rash once that looked like Danny DeVito if you saw it in the right light, but nobody was asking me for autographs," Mitch said, shaking his head.

"You're all class, Mitch," Rob said, chuckling inappropriately loud.

It was Mitch's idea to come here, not because either of them was religious;

170

he just thought it would be worth a laugh, and he suggested that Rob could get some footage for his film class. They had been friends all through high school and Mitch hadn't changed a bit, Rob thought. He wished he could say the same about himself. Iraq had done a number on him. But it was good to be home and among friends. And nice to be able to laugh again.

A small, middle-aged man in front of them turned and frowned.

"Show some respect, boys. The Virgin came to see us and all you can do is make jokes?" He shook his head, the brim of his fishing hat stained with sweat.

"Sorry sir," Rob said sheepishly while Mitch rolled his eyes.

A young woman was hugging the stain on the wall as her three little girls watched, the youngest with a beat-up plastic doll that was missing an arm and the oldest holding the leash of a large black lab who had plopped down in a mud puddle to cool off.

"Come up here and tell the Virgin your sins!" the woman barked at the girls, who approached the wall cautiously. "Ask for forgiveness."

They waited another twenty minutes for their turn, Rob only having to shush Mitch a few times. The man in the fishing hat was on his knees at the wall now, holding rosary beads in one hand, his other touching the stain. After a few moments, he struggled to his feet and put the beads in his pocket. He looked at Rob and Mitch and tipped his hat, then turned and walked toward the sidewalk.

As they moved closer, Rob took out his video camera and began filming the crowd, then swung around to follow their gaze. In front of the wall, an impromptu shrine had emerged, with a couple dozen or so glass candles, the kind they sold at the discount store on the corner, some with pictures of the Virgin, others with Jesus. People had left bouquets of flowers, cards, rosary beads, bibles and teddy bears. Rob noticed that the little girl had left behind the one-armed doll, probably at her mother's urging.

"Unbelievable," Mitch whispered. "Isn't it scary to think about how many desperate people live around you?"

"Come on, now. If they want to believe in something, who's it hurting?" Rob retorted, panning and tilting the camera on the stain. "It does look a little bit like her."

"You've been overseas too long, dude," Mitch said.

Rob zoomed in on it. If you stared at it long enough, it certainly looked like the outline of a woman wearing a robe, her head tilted slightly. He could sort of make out a feminine face at the top right and hands clasped in prayer above her chest. On the news, city officials were claiming salt runoff from the highway above caused the stain.

"Come on, dude. I gotta get back. I'm meeting Melissa for dinner," Mitch said, tapping Rob's shoulder.

"I think I'm gonna stay here and get some more footage."

"Whatever, Jesus Freak. Call me later, dude." Mitch said, then headed back to the car they had parked a few blocks away.

Rob waved the next group in line forward, then stepped back a little to give them some space, filming the whole time. The three old ladies didn't seem to notice him as they added to the pile of offerings against the wall and fell to their knees.

Rob was kneeling as well as he zoomed in on the women, panning from their feet and up over their hunched backs to the stain on the wall. He began to pan toward the shrine but doubled back to the stain. He was sure that he'd seen a pair of eyes open where the woman's face would be.

He focused again on the stain for a moment until he shrugged it off as his colorful imagination working and turned the camera back to the shrine.

He zoomed in to capture some detail of the gifts and felt drawn to the one-armed doll. He wondered if the little girl missed her doll or had already forgotten about it.

"It'd be nice if they can forget, wouldn't it?" a booming voice said behind his ear.

Rob jumped to his feet, almost dropping his camera, and spun around. There was no one within ten feet. He looked at the nearest person in the crowd, a bald man who was praying the Rosary.

"Did you say something?" Rob asked.

Annoyed at the interruption, the man shook his head, then returned his gaze to the wall.

Rob stepped around the group at the wall and resumed filming over their shoulders, zooming in on the stain.

This time there was no mistaking it. The eyes were open. And staring at him.

He lowered his camera and looked around, convinced Mitch was somehow playing a joke on him. He moved a few steps closer and stared at the stain with his naked eye and saw nothing staring back. He raised his camera and zoomed in.

Again, her face was alive. Soft and feminine and bathed in yellow light. Her open eyes followed him. Then she spoke.

"Your case will be heard tonight, Rob Tanziger. Be here at 3 a.m." she said, again in a deep, gravelly voice that reminded Rob of his drill sergeant.

He lowered his camera again and stared at the wall. Still nothing but a dark stain. But he heard the voice again, this time as if he were thinking it.

"Don't make us come find you."

Rob backed up, quickly making his way to the sidewalk, staring dumbfounded at the wall the whole time. Okay, he thought, that didn't just happen. You didn't just get threatened by a fucking stain on a fucking wall that looks like the fucking

Virgin Mary. Maybe you should call the counselor tomorrow. Maybe you need to talk about what happened over there in the desert.

"Watch it, man!"

The guy he ran into was solid as a wall. Rob groped around for his camera, then picked himself up.

"Sorry buddy, my bad," he said, gazing up at the tall, chiseled black man in front of him.

"You heard it too, didn't you?"

"Heard what?" Rob said. "What are you talking about?"

"She spoke to you too, didn't she? I can tell the way you're high-tailing it out of here."

"I don't know what you mean. Excuse me," Rob said, scurrying around the man and heading toward the bus stop.

"She said something about 'a case', didn't she?" the man said, his voice cracking. "What does she want? How does she know?"

For once in Rob's life, the Fullerton bus came just when he needed it. He boarded, took a seat, and gazed back at the man, who had his face in his hands and was weeping on the sidewalk. He seemed much smaller now.

* * *

Rob got off the bus at California and headed home, jogging at first, then sprinting the five blocks to his studio apartment, passing by the El Ranchero, where he usually stopped for a burrito.

He tossed his backpack and keys on the kitchen table, then headed toward his desk, fumbling the video camera out of its case.

"Watch out, Cletus," he said.

The fourteen-year-old cat held its ground, pretending not to hear until Rob put the camera bag down on its tail. Cletus gave him a dirty look before hopping to the floor in search of another cool spot to sleep.

Rob took the disk from his camera and began downloading it to his computer.

He grabbed a beer from the fridge, and noticed his hands shaking as he opened the bottle. Harry Caray shouted "Cubs win!" and it startled him. The voice was coming from the bottle opener his little sister had given him a few years ago, despite knowing he was a Sox fan.

He took two large swigs and settled down in front of the computer.

He watched as the scene he had witnessed earlier played back. The devoted followers. The gifts at the makeshift shrine. His lens focused lovingly on the one-armed doll. The footage was beautiful, he thought. Surely he could get an 'A' on this project.

Especially if he caught the stain coming to life on film. *But that didn't really happen, did it?* And to his relief, there was nothing on the tape. No eyes opening.

No Virgin Mary speaking to him. Just a dark stain on a freeway underpass wall that if you tried hard enough, you could see anything you wanted to in it. He'd done it plenty of times with little puffy clouds on clear days.

Okay, then you imagined it. Call Dr. Hammond on Monday and get your appointment moved up.

He'd almost convinced himself it never happened when he remembered the chiseled black man he'd smacked into. He knew he hadn't imagined that guy. The bruised shoulder he could feel beginning to throb was proof of that.

There was only one thing to do. He packed some fresh batteries into his bag and slid a fresh disk into his camera, then laid down for a nap. It was going to be a late night.

* * *

His dreams were vivid and intense, and, as usual, made little sense. He could see the one-armed doll, its eyes open, its mouth moving, but nothing coming out. He saw Cletus standing on two feet opening the fridge and asking Rob where his food was. He saw his sister crying and running from him when he tried to talk to her. Like she was scared of him.

Then he was back in Iraq. This part of the dream made sense. This part was always too real. The Humvee exploding in front of him, one of the doors tumbling to a stop near his feet. His eyes burning from the brightness and the heat of the noxious flames. Pulling his buddies out of the wreckage, one by one. Two already dead and his friend, Ryan, on fire, his skin smoldering as he rolled in the dirt...

"It's almost time. You should prepare your defense."

The voice jolted him awake and Rob jumped from the couch, his sweaty chest still heavy from the nightmare. He scanned the room, not realizing he was still clutching a pillow. Cletus stirred at the foot of the sofa, looked up at Rob, then closed his eyes again. There was nobody else there.

It was just part of the dream. Relax, he told himself. The clock showed 2:15 a.m. He'd hoped to head out much earlier. He cursed himself for not setting an alarm, put on his t-shirt and shoes, grabbed his camera and dashed out the door.

At least he was able to catch the last bus. He settled in for the fifteen-minute ride. He had the bus to himself, except for the homeless guy who got on at California and headed to the back row for a nap, his pungent odor eating at Rob's nostrils as he passed.

The bus approached the underpass. Rob pulled the cord and headed to the back door. He looked over at the homeless guy, who opened his eyes as the lights above the door turned green.

"Good luck," the man said before rolling over to go back to sleep.

"What did you say?" Rob asked, hesitating at the bottom step. The man ignored him. Rob could hear him snoring already.

"Let's go, in or out?" the driver shouted. Rob stepped down, the doors creaking shut behind him.

After the bus passed he could see the shrine across the street, bathed in a soft glow from the candles people left behind. The crowds were gone, but Rob could make out one lone figure kneeling at the wall.

He approached quietly, not wanting to interrupt anyone in mid-prayer, though he questioned why someone would be coming out in the middle of the night to pray to a stain on a wall, even if they were convinced it was the Virgin Mary. As he got closer, he realized that it was the large black man he'd run into the morning before.

The man was not praying, just whimpering.

"Please stop. I'm sorry. Please stop. I'm sorry," he said over and over, staring at the stain.

Rob thought about leaving. He had lived in the city long enough to know that it was not smart to engage crazy people on the street, particularly late at night. But he felt a need to help, so he eased up beside the man, who turned and looked at him, wild-eyed.

"Help me...I can't stop. Help me," he whispered.

Rob looked down and noticed the blood pooling around the man's knees and a pile of what looked like strips of old leather.

He followed the trail of blood up to the man's hands. He was holding a knife in his right hand and was cutting into his left arm, working the blade down from his elbow to his fingers, like he was peeling a potato. Most of his arm and hand was a pulpy mess, his fingers stripped to the bone.

"Please help me," the man begged.

"Jesus Christ, man, what the fuck!" Rob cried, then instinctively grabbed for the man's shoulder and elbow, hoping he could grip them hard enough to make him drop the blade.

But the man turned and slashed at Rob instead, getting off three quick swings, the first of which sliced through Rob's right forearm, though not too deeply. Rob backed off.

"Dude, you asked me to help you."

"I'm sorry...it's not me. It's not me..." the man cried, still slashing the blade in Rob's direction.

Rob grabbed his camera bag, figuring he could use it to deflect the knife while he tried to get hold of the man, but then another voice spoke.

"Do not interfere. His sentence is being carried out."

Rob turned to the wall, and it suddenly lit like a movie screen. The dingy highway underpass, stain and all, disappeared as the wall gave off a blinding, golden hue. Centered on the screen was a large, robed figure that looked part man and part...something else. It was large enough to fill most of the height of the screen, and had long, flowing hair with thick strands, each moving independently, like wriggling worms. It gazed down at Rob.

"Your trial will begin once we've completed with him."

"Who the fuck are you? What do you want?" Rob said, fumbling to get his camera out of his bag, hoping to capture this on film.

He did not answer. His face changed as the moments passed. He was an old man with a beard and mustache, then a young black woman, then the Virgin Mary again. The face morphed every few seconds, but the eyes, glowing with hatred and anger, never changed.

"What do you want from me?" Rob asked, stepping back and turning his camera on.

He looked through the lens, but this time all he could see was the same, dingy old wall. He lowered the camera and looked up into the light, shielding his eyes with one hand.

"You are accused of grave sins and you must be tried before this court and the throne of the Lord!" the thing shouted.

Behind the creature, a primitive courtroom scene unfolded on the wall. There was a witness stand on one side, next to a large, ornate throne in the middle facing the street. Both sat empty.

There was one row after another of wooden benches, filled with spectators turning to their right to watch. Some appeared human, some had wings...some had horns. All were focused on the man who knelt on the ground, flaying away at what was left of his arm. They cheered each time a strip of flesh fell to the ground.

The man, having done all he could do to his arm, took off his shoe with his good hand and started rolling his pant leg up, his face contorted in agony.

Rob turned his camera off and backed away slowly. Then he started to run.

"You cannot hide!" he heard behind him as he sprinted down the street, his heart pounding in his throat.

He didn't stop for several blocks, until he was too tired to continue. He realized he didn't even know where he was going. He rested, his hands on his knees as he struggled to regain his breath and orient himself. He took out his cell phone and called Mitch, hoping he was still awake.

By the fifth ring, Mitch picked up, annoyed.

"Dude, this better be important. I've got company."

Rob realized he had no idea what to say. All he could do was cry into the phone.

"Hey bud, what's goin on? Calm down," Mitch said.

"I think I'm losing my shit, man. I think I'm going crazy," Rob stammered.

"Okay, bro. Settle down. Where are you?"

"I'm not sure. I went the wrong way home," Rob said, looking around for a visual clue. "That looks like the Logan Square monument up there. I'm near Kedzie."

"Okay, can you make it over here? We'll talk it out and you can stay here. We'll call the doctor in the morning."

"Yeah the Blue Line is right over there," he said, his voice calmer. Mitch always had that effect on him. "Can you meet me at the station?"

"Of course. I'll see you in a few, bro. It's going to be fine, Okay?"

"Okay. See you there."

He hung up and took a moment to calm himself. He hit rewind on his camera, his hands still shaking, and then hit play. There was still nothing on the wall. Just the same dark stain. In the background, he could hear the man crying as he cut himself.

Rob turned the power button off and headed toward the train station.

Rob walked in, swiped his transit card at the turnstile, then walked down the stairs to the train platform. Despite the hour, there were plenty of late-night revelers still out.

He passed a group of men and women in their early twenties, all with either tattoos or lip piercings, some with both. They stared at him indifferently as he passed.

In the middle of the platform, a skinny, long-haired man was playing "Hotel California" on his guitar, and doing a fairly decent job of it. Next to him, a Hispanic man sang along with him, pumping his fist as they harmonized about not being able to "kill the beast." The singer didn't seem to mind the stranger intruding on his performance. In front of them, a guitar case sat open with a few dollars and a couple dozen coins scattered inside.

Rob opened his cell phone as he passed them to check the time: 2:59. He began to check to see if he had any messages when the screen went blank. A familiar golden light began to shine from it, then a face appeared. It was the thing from the wall.

"You cannot hide from us. Your trial begins now," the image announced in a grave tone.

Rob snapped the phone shut and threw it to the ground. It bounced and skidded toward the group of teens nearby. They turned and looked after it hit a tall boy's shoe. The kid picked it up and tossed it back to him, and Rob caught it.

"Sorry about that," Rob said, then hurried farther down the platform, stuffing the phone into his pocket.

The phone rang.

Impossible! There was no cell service down here. He took the device from his pocket, opened it, and the golden light glared out at him. He tossed the phone into a nearby garbage can then continued down the platform.

"Enough!" a voice boomed. Rob stopped in his tracks. The wall off his right shoulder lit up and the impossible scene from the underpass appeared. The creature emerged from the bottom of the wall, its wriggling hair crawling around its ever-changing face, and soon rose a good twelve feet above the rest of the courtroom spectators, who were staring to their left at the witness stand, where a young girl no more than five years old sat next to the still-empty throne. She appeared to be of Arabic assent, and by her headdress and blouse, maybe Iraqi. She sat nervously, eyes down, clutching a one-armed doll in one hand.

"Your trial begins now," the thing said again before turning its attention to the girl. "Of what doth the witness accuse this man?"

The girl looked up. Her eyes turned vacant and she slumped forward in her seat without saying a word. Another screen appeared above her and a scene began to unfold.

It showed the inside of a small, modest house. There were eight people in the room, four adults, three teenagers and a little girl. It was a tranquil scene of a family going about their daily life. Then a door was kicked open, breaching the silence and awakening Rob's memory.

Three U.S. soldiers entered the dwelling, shouting orders and pointing guns. The women and children in the house were screaming. A young man who Rob guessed was the little girl's father turned to run upstairs, but one of the soldiers opened fire, cutting him down from behind. The women and children went into hysterics.

"Sit down! Shut the fuck up! Shut the fuck up!" one of the soldiers screamed and Rob shuddered as he recognized that soldier. It was him.

The soldiers corralled the rest of the family, dragging them into the center of the living room and shoving them to their knees. The elderly woman fell to the ground hard and a soldier yanked her back up by her hair.

"Who did it? Who set up that bomb? Tell us!" a soldier yelled. Rob recognized him as his friend, Lieutenant Anderson.

In broken English, the old man said, "It was not us. We are no fighters."

"He's lying, man. It was one of them. It's right in front of their house for Christ's sake!" the other soldier said. Rob couldn't remember his name, and in fact it was their first time out together. "You heard that witness out there. He saw someone run inside just before it went off. What else do you want?"

"Just do him, man. Those are your friends all charcoaled out there," the soldier urged.

Anderson hesitated, then took the butt of his rifle and cracked it into the old man's nose. His frail face caved in on impact and he slumped to the floor. Anderson delivered two more blows to the man's head.

The women and children screamed louder. Anderson moved over to the only remaining male, a young teen, maybe fifteen or so.

"Was it you, you little fucker?"

"Come on man, he's just a kid," Rob saw himself say.

"That don't mean shit, man," the other soldier retorted. "I seen children and women blow themselves up just to take a few of us out. You can't trust any of em!"

"He's right. We gotta do 'em all. It could have been any of them. I ain't doin' this myself. You gotta help me," Anderson said, staring at Rob.

After a moment, Rob nodded his approval.

The soldiers moved behind the family, who sat cowering and crying on the floor.

Anderson looked at Rob.

"You ready?"

"No."

"Enough talk. Just do it!" the other soldier boomed, and Rob now recognized the voice. He had not heard it before that day and had not heard it again until today. It was the thing from the wall. Its eyes brimmed with hate.

Rob watched as he and Anderson pumped the family full of bullets, except for the girl, who was shrieking now.

"You gotta shut her up, man. Do her too," the other soldier urged him.

Anderson started to point his gun at her, but Rob pushed it away.

"We're done here," he said. "Let's check out the house next door."

The soldiers made their way out the front door. Rob stopped and looked back, making eye contact with the girl. Watching it now, he recalled hoping that she would be able to forget what she saw.

The door closed but the scene still played behind the little girl on the stand.

She ran up to her mother, whose face was frozen in a mask of horror. The girl prodded her, but realizing her mother wasn't asleep, slumped to the ground and started screaming again. The sound was drowned out by the gunshots next door.

Then the screen faded to black and the girl on the stand suddenly awoke. The creature and the spectators turned to face Rob.

"How do we find the defendant?"

"Guilty! Guilty! Guilty!" the crowd shouted.

"What should be the sentence?"

Rob snapped out of his trance and ran down the platform before they answered.

"Help me please. Help me!" he shouted to the other riders, who either stared at him or looked down at their shoes. It dawned on him that he now seemed like the crazy person that people should not engage in the middle of the night.

He slowed down and looked back. The spectators on the wall were still watching and shouting "Death!" but the people waiting for the train seemed oblivious.

Then he started running again, but he lost control of his motor functions, and his body turned back in the direction of the courtroom scene. He was running full speed down the platform, his legs churning forward despite his brain's orders to go the other way.

He heard a train approaching at the far end and saw its light appear in the tunnel. Passengers closed their books and gathered their belongings, some moving out of the way as Rob ran past.

He was picking up speed and was on a collision course with the train. The wall was dead ahead, and as he looked up, he could see the creature, its arms outstretched and its head turned skyward as it roared, the jury around it cheering. It looked down and locked eyes with Rob, as it morphed back into the Virgin Mary, its wild hair suddenly covered in white linen. It clasped its hands and bowed, as if in prayer, then grinned, two rows of sharp, black teeth stretching its mouth wide as its face began to morph again.

The train grew louder, its headlight burning his eyes, and Rob reached the edge of the platform, now nearly airborne, save one step. He closed his eyes as he leapt onto the tracks.

* * *

"What do you think it is?"

The woman rubbed her hands over the stain on the desk, then turned to the man next to her and took a sip of her coffee.

"I think it's exactly what it looks like."

He let out a nervous laugh.

"It does have some resemblance."

"Some?"

"OK, maybe more than a little bit."

"Has he seen it yet?"

"No, he hasn't been in yet, and it wasn't there last night."

"Who found it?"

"The lady from the cleaning service. She almost fainted. I don't know how we're going to keep her from telling people about it."

"Maybe *we* should tell people about it. I mean…these have been showing up everywhere lately. This is proof, isn't it?"

"Proof of what?"

"That he was chosen for this job."

"How do you think that would go over?"

"Well, I…wait, here he comes."

Footsteps and voices echoed outside the room. The door flung open and a man entered, trailed by a small entourage.

The man and the woman by the desk straightened up. The woman hesitated, then covered the stain with a pile of folders left on the desk before turning to greet her boss.

"Good morning, Mr. President."

The Healing Hands
of Reverend Wainwright

by Geoffrey L. Mudge

Another night, another show, another chorus of cheers and applause and unbridled joy that we will never hear. In the darkness and silence, only the rumble of the diesel engine roaring to life lets us know our part has been played for the evening. This night's showcase was relatively slow and tame. The only serious injury to come from the affair was a dislocated shoulder suffered by the blind kid, Augie. The sickening sound, somewhere between a pop and a crunch as muscle and bone tore apart, still echoes in my mind. There's not much to listen to in here, and the few sounds that aren't screams tend to linger a little longer than they should. The only other noise is the wet, hacking cough coming from Juliana's corner. I think she may have contracted emphysema or TB, but she won't live long enough to be bothered much by whichever.

However, experience, the harsh mistress that she is, has taught me that the good shows are tragedies in disguise. Having been here the longest, I've seen the patterns through a dozen of them. Through pure luck or divine intervention, I've survived longer than all those that were here when I joined. Most of the kids travelling with me now were picked up in Memphis and are generally unfamiliar with the ins and outs of the business. In my time with the Reverend I have found that slow nights are almost inevitably followed by horrendous ones. Those nights, the anguished cries reverberating in my skull make me long for the cavernous silence between one and another.

Joseph, chained closest to the heavy door, thinks he heard talk of moving to Wichita. Isn't that peachy? Kansas. The heart of the Dust Bowl. The land of polio and starvation. A visit to the festering wound spewing the misery that has been slowly eating America's soul may not end well for some of us. Frankly, I expect some deaths before we finish, and there are so few of us left. When I came in, there were a couple dozen of us, but now there are only six, and we all know the carnivorous tumor in Ralph's brain will soon finish him.

Though it's been quite a while since we picked anyone up, I couldn't say just how long. Time is extremely subjective with no way to track night and day. The occasional feeding and the never-ending shows are the only ways we have to measure the passage of time. In those terms, it's been twelve shows since Memphis, how long that is in normal people time, there's no way to know.

To be honest, the anticipation is almost worse than the performance. Almost. It's just so damn hard to sit in the hot darkness, afraid to speak to the only people who could ever understand this ordeal. But what would we say to each other? Speak words of hope that ring false and hollow the moment they leave one's lips? Talk of escape when metal and leather and malnutrition make it impossible? No, there are no words left in any of us. All the pleadings and prayers are spent. There is nothing for us but the sweltering silence of this dark oven.

And the show.

The goddamn show, it must go on.

* * *

The small fire spewed hot sparks and ash into the night sky as Abel hurled a fresh log into its embers.

"Hey! Watch out, you stupid bastard!" Lot yelled, beans and pork juice dribbling down his chin. Abel replied only by hanging his head and stumbling sullenly out of the weakening ring of light. Lot wiped his grimy mouth on his leather gloves. "Aw, hell," he muttered, "I guess I better go apologize to the big lout."

"Leave him be, Lot. He'll find a pile of dirt or a dead animal and he'll forget all about it." Adam's soft but powerful voice drew a hushed burst of laughter from the small group of shabby-looking men.

"Well, you're the boss," Lot sighed as he sat back down. "If you think he'll be okay, I'll get back to dinner."

"He'll be fine. Now finish that grub up quick, boys. We got a lot of work in front of us and you know the Rev hates to get behind schedule." Adam inhaled a last mouthful of beans and tossed the can toward the newly invigorated fire. The rest of the tired men quickly did the same. After much groaning and consternation, they eventually began to shamble toward the heavily loaded trucks.

"Where is the good Reverend this evening?" Jeremiah inquired as softly as he could without belying his utter dread of the holy man. "He didn't want to share in the vittles?"

"My sincere apologies for not joining in the sumptuous feast this evening. I acquired other accommodations and dined alone in the confines of my trailer." The reverend's deep, haunting voice and soft Southern drawl crawled through the

182

cool, dusty night air from behind the group of men. "Although, I must admit that I am slightly miffed that my presence was not inquired into until after the 'vittles' were no more than memories and grease stains." The last few words oozed from Wainwright's lips like a foul sludge and sent chills through the spines of every man who heard.

"Reverend! I...uh...that is...I mean..." Jeremiah tried to stammer some sort of coherent response, but as he turned to face the Reverend, their gazes locked and all his words seemed to slip away. Wainwright's eyes were all white with the exception of the pitch black pupils which pulsed and pinwheeled like a kaleidoscope. His direct stare was enough to make even the most resolute of men whimper, and Jeremiah involuntarily stumbled back a few steps.

The Reverend smiled coldly at his flock of miscreants. "Come now, dear Jeremiah, I merely sought to have a little jest at your expense. I am, all joking aside, glad that you are all well fed and eager to move forward. There is still so much work to be done. So much work. How go the preparations? Can we expect the main edifice to be erected soon?"

"The main edifice?" Adam interjected. "If you mean the big tent, we should have that thing up in a couple hours. As for the rest, Jeremiah here and Lot are gonna head to town at first light to start handin' out flyers. Me and the rest of the boys'll get the stage set up and Abel is gonna get the kids fed and cleaned up for the show."

Wainwright scowled up at the uncaring moon. "Abel, you say? You are aware we have several little girls amongst our family of flagellants, correct? We have traveled far and seen much together, Adam, but I swear to all that is holy in this world, if that half-witted pedophile touches even one hair on their sacred heads, I will castrate you both with my bare hands!"

Adam laughed nervously as he struck a match on his thick leather glove and carefully lit a cigarette dangling from the corner of his mouth. "Relax, Rev. Abel may be slow but even he isn't stupid enough to go after them girls." A casual glance passed amongst the huddle of men as the same shadow of doubt crossed each mind. Adam caught the look as it went around and sighed heavily. He dropped his smoke onto the hard earth. "Well, I gotta go, uhhh, check on some stuff. I'll be right back." Trying his best not to flat out sprint, Adam strode away from the group in the direction of the children's trailer.

Wainwright watched him for a short moment before turning his withering gaze on the rest of the workers. "Well, gentlemen, let's get to it, shall we? I have preparations of my own which must be attended to." The Reverend turned petulantly and walked away, darkness wrapping his tall, gaunt frame until it disappeared.

Jeremiah scooped the still smoldering cigarette butt from the ground and inhaled deeply. "This job gets a little more entertaining every day. What the hell does 'castrate' mean, anyway?" The men laughed nervously and made their way into the night, casting cautious glances over their shoulders for whatever demons might be following.

* * *

"Step on up, ladies and gents, and God-fearing children of all ages! For today, the just and holy Reverend Wainwright will hear all your pleas and grant God's mercy to even the most wretched amongst you! A nickel gets you in and a dime gets you a seat! Don't be shy now, folks! Claim your ticket now. They will go fast, and you've travelled so far, I'd hate to see you stuck out here with me when the service begins!"

Jeremiah's powerful voice rang through the crowd milling anxiously in the brown field. The blazing Kansas sun beat the life out of all below, and to most it was worth the nickel just to get in the shade of the tent. Of course, the Reverend's men had been diligent about spreading word of the healing service throughout downtown Wichita, and the assembled masses were almost all injured, sick or carrying someone who was. Bleak times often call for desperate measures, and hope in any form was a welcome relief from the pulverizing daily desolation.

It took only half an hour for the available tickets to sell out. Being the kind hearted doorman, Jeremiah let a few families slip in late with a wink and a grin. Lot came strolling out of the tent once they were in and secured the heavy leather flap.

"That's a hell of a crowd. How much did we get?" he asked as Jeremiah shook the box filled with silver and copper.

"Hooee, gotta be fifty bucks in there!" Jeremiah cooed. "Days like this make it all worthwhile." He put the heavy box on his shoulder and walked with Lot to the trailers behind the tent.

"So, did you get a look at the folks comin' through? There were some tasty looking dishes in there." Lot's eyes gleamed with a lunatic glare for half a second as the question fell out. Jeremiah licked his lips and tried not to think about it too much.

"Oh man, it's too early for that kind of talk. I'm starving as it is and I don't want to have to think about it all evening."

Lot laughed heavily, punching his friend on the shoulder playfully. "But isn't the anticipation half the fun?" Jeremiah frowned, staring at the sun as it crawled toward its tomb on the western horizon.

"For some, I reckon it is. Not for me, though. I like to stay focused on what's in front of me. Now let's get this loot counted up so we can have a smoke before the *real* show gets going. By the way, you seen Abel lately?" Lot shook his head and whistled a few bars of "Toreador," clapping his gloved hands as the two stepped into the shade of the hulking trailers.

184

Inside the big white tent, Reverend Wainwright had whipped the crowd into a frenzy. "Times are troubled, my friends," he crowed from his pulpit. "I can see it in your eyes, I can see it in your faces, I can see it in your hearts." His frenetic gestures rippled his long white robe as the light from a hundred candles danced in his dark eyeglasses. "I know your pain, dear people, God knows your pain. We have felt it in a hundred cities all across this great land. We've heard the countless prayers begging for relief, begging for mercy, begging for a 'surcease of sorrow', as a man wiser than I once put it."

Wainwright hopped down from the small stage and strode resolutely into the heart of the crowd. "But you know what? He hears you, and he shares with me all your prayers. All those cries that you think disappear unheard in the black of night do not go unheeded. I have come to this barren place for one reason today. I am here to take away your pain." With a heavy sigh the Reverend raised his arms to the Heavens. "Almighty Father! Smile on your dour children this day. Let your love rain on us and take away all the hurt Satan heaps on your flock!"

It took only one cry from the crowd to ignite the wild fire. "My daddy's got cholera! Can you help him?" Afraid to be left out of any miraculous proceedings, the mob began to shout as one. The pleading filled the tent and cascaded on Wainwright's back as he walked to the stage. He turned and gestured for calm. The wailing slowly tapered off until silence gripped the group in an anxious grasp.

"Please, my children, there's no need to grovel. As I said, your prayers have been heard and I am the answer to them. I will be here amongst you for as long as it takes. On this day the love of God Almighty will be felt by all! A lucky few amongst you will even have your ailments remedied by our most holy maker!" The crowd cheered and cried and gnashed their teeth in bliss. "Now, I see back in the back there, a child lying on the floor. Bring him to me."

A somber looking man in dingy denim overalls scooped the boy from the floor with the infinite gentleness and promise of protection that only a father can give a child. He carried the boy slowly to the front as the crowd parted for him like the sea for Moses. Pain etched the boy's face, but he bit back the stinging tears, wanting to be strong like Daddy but knowing he would soon break.

The man laid his son at Wainwright's feet. He removed his cap and spoke gently to the Reverend. "Please, sir, my boy, he fell down a well, his back is broken. The Doc says he ain't gonna make it."

Wainwright smiled warmly on the man as he put a soft hand on his forehead. "Your faith brought you here today and that faith will be rewarded, my son. Please take a seat over there and let the Lord do his work." Wainwright shook his hands and knelt down next to the boy, his back to the crowd.

"What's your name, child?" He asked as his gentle hands caressed grimy cheeks.

The boy gritted his teeth and forced a reply through his lips. "Joseph, sir." It was all he could manage through the haze of agony. Wainwright nodded calmly, and with a deep breath he removed his dark glasses and set his gaze on the boy.

A look somewhere between terror and awe crawled across Joseph's young face as he stared deeply into those hypnotic, dancing eyes. Wainwright lowered himself until the two were face-to-face. "Look at me, Joseph." He purred quietly. "Look deep and pour your pain into me. Give me all the bad things inside. Take the misery you feel and give it to me. All you have to do is let it go and you will be healed. Give me your pain."

The Reverend leaned close and pressed his hands to the boy's temples. Joseph gasped as Wainwright increased the pressure on his head until it felt like it might burst. He could feel every finger and nail digging into his skin, pressing and grinding like a vise. He couldn't look away from those hideous eyes, he couldn't fight back or break free. Even if he could, he had to admit to himself he wouldn't.

"Give me your pain."

Hot, rancid breath and small droplets of spittle fell onto Joseph's face. He could feel the bones in his skull flexing and tensing under the relentless pressure, and then there was a spark. The pain in his head dissipated and a pulse of charged energy leapt from his temples to his back like a heated wire.

"Give me your pain."

Like a black sludge, Joseph felt the ball of anguish slowly drain from his shattered spine. The bones mended and the nerves reassembled as Wainwright pressed his fingers harder into his cranium. The boy wanted to scream in joy, to jump up and dance a jig right there in front of the astonished crowd, but he was held by the Reverend's crippling gaze. Soon, the pain which had been collecting for days was being pulled gently away from him.

"Give me your pain..."

Joseph wanted nothing more than to give away his pain, his hurt, his memories of the furious, withering torture he had suffered.

"Please, take it away, take it all away."

He pushed all his hurt to the Reverend's healing hands. Wainwright's eyes spun and twirled and he smiled as the boy gave in and let everything be taken. Joseph had never felt so good, so alive, but even after the pain was gone, the electricity continued to drain him.

Fatigue suddenly fell over him and small twinges of fear replaced the joyous celebrations in his heart.

"Give me your pain..."

Joseph tried to shake free of the Reverend's hands, recognizing that something was wrong. He tried to speak, tried to tell his healer that he was all better, but he could not. The fanatical grin on Wainwright's face grew bigger as the boy tried to fight against his hold. Joseph's eyes glazed over and his will drained away. The Reverend smiled still, and pulled everything remaining from his victim, but was not yet satisfied.

"Give me your pain..."

* * *

I feel a gentle pressure and slight heat twisting the small of my back. So the show has begun and it appears that I shall be the first supplicant of the evening. I let out a little gasp as the pressure turns into a sharp pain grinding my vertebrae together. In the darkness, I know the other kids are looking at me wide-eyed, seeing little, but understanding everything. They know they are momentarily spared, but fear what may be ahead.

"Give me your pain."

I hear the Reverend's words scything through my mind. He must be in full swing now, the conduit open and the prostrated parishioner marveling at the miracle he'd brought to Wichita.

The sharp crack as my backbone gives out rings through the darkness like a gunshot. I would scream, but my voice was taken from me ages ago. I bend backward as my spinal cord tears and all the sensation drains from my legs like fluid. An icy chill grips my lower body, complemented by the fiery agony ripping into the rest of me.

"Give me your pain."

I try to imagine who is lying in front of the Reverend, slowly feeling their life return and their body becoming healed. It could have been anybody, really. We would never know the people Wainwright set his healing hands to, marking their existence only by the signature of their affliction. He took their pain all right, but he didn't keep it. He gave it to us. *Suffer the little children*, indeed. It could have been a source of solace to know that through our sacrifice, someone else was freed of their burden, but we know what else the Reverend takes.

When the families see the hollow eyes and hear the melancholy voice of the healed, they must understand as well. We don't really know how or why this reaper does his deeds, but in the guise of a holy man he draws the submissive to him like moths to a flame. For some, I guess, the end of agonies is worth the price of a soul.

As the echoes of my breaking back cease ringing from the dark walls, silence falls on us. Only, it's not silent, I can hear a slight jangling and the soft click of a lock releasing. A burning sliver of light blinds us momentarily before the door is flung wide open. The dying red sun envelops the huge frame of the man the Reverend calls Abel standing before us.

"Hello, Juliana," he whispers softly, his voice dripping like bittersweet poison. The sounds from the big tent waft slowly toward us. The door has never been opened during a show before and it is amazing to hear the cheers and exultations of the crowd. Taking a large revolver from his pocket, Abel climbs into the trailer and kneels carefully next to little Juliana.

"You an' me are goin' for a walk, girl." His shaky voice imitates calm and

187

caring, but seethes with hidden malice. As he waves the pistol in the girl's face, he asks, "Are you gonna' be a good little girl?"

Juliana's expression doesn't change, but she nods her assent. Abel fumbles with her locks, his thick leather gloves making the process almost comical. With a grunt, he finally gets her bindings undone and the last chain falls away.

Even after it's too late, the imbecile doesn't understand his mistake. At this point, my compatriots and I are no better than wild animals, beaten and starved, and to remove the leash of such a creature is both foolish and dangerous. Juliana springs toward her tormentor with a feral growl that chills even my screaming blood. Despite her atrophied and hunger-deteriorated muscles, she is on the big man before he can react.

With a hoarse yell, Abel falls backward out of the trailer, waving his gun wildly in the air. He understands the power the pistol carries, but not the operation that imbues that power. Juliana sinks her few remaining teeth into his wide throat and crimson liquid sprays the thirsty earth. The pistol falls from his fingers and he tries to yell for help but can only produce a gurgling whimper. The little girl, drenched in ichors and hopeless ferocity, steps back and picks up the heavy gun. As she aims at him, the two lock eyes. Abel holds his arms in front of his face in a futile attempt to ward off a bullet.

The big pistol wavers in Juliana's shaky grip. She looks back at us, tears leaving burning tracks on her squalid face. Her sad blue eyes lock onto mine and she says the last words I will ever hear her utter. "I'm free."

Juliana smiles as she puts the gun to her head and pulls the trigger. The horrifying impact spins her in a full circle as her pale face disintegrates into fragments of bone and brain. Blubbering and bleeding, Abel crawls to her and gently wraps her lifeless body in his massive arms.

The exultant noise from the crowd dissipates as the gunshot works its way through them. About a dozen of the more stouthearted revelers exit the tent to investigate. They immediately move to surround Abel, assuming the worst as he cradles the dead girl. Their cries for the harshest of justice fade to silence however as their mutual attention is drawn across the dusty field to our open cell. Their wide eyes and gaping mouths tell the story of the horrors we have become. They don't understand why we are here. They see only the blood, the bruises, the broken children in chains.

The Reverend bursts from the tent with Adam following close behind. After surveying the scene he waves hurriedly to Jeremiah and Lot. "I need you two to tend to the flock while I sort out this nasty bit of business. Jeremiah, you use that silver tongue of yours to keep the people distracted. Lot, gather the men and secure the tent."

The pair nod solemnly and move to their tasks. As they retreat, the Reverend turns his attention to Abel and the late Juliana.

With Adam in tow, he pushes his way through the small knot of dumbfounded onlookers. Unleashing a vicious snarl, Wainwright plucks Abel from the ground. "You fool! You damned fool! Do you realize what you have done?" He hurls the big man into the dirt with ease, leaving him whimpering and cradling Juliana's decimated corpse.

The Reverend sighs heavily. "Malaco—, sorry, Adam, I believe my work here is done. There will be no more miracles today." A look of pure disgust crawls across his craggy face as the band of men assails him with calls for Abel's scalp. "Clean this mess up, Adam. Let no word of what transpired today escape this plain." With barely subdued fury the Reverend takes Abel by the ragged throat and drags him, mewling and whimpering, away from the angry mob.

As Wainwright withdraws, Adam raises a gloved hand and waves at Lot. The large man waves back and motions to the entrance of the tent. A pair of men, one called Isaiah and one I do not know, hurry through to join Jeremiah. Lot secures the opening, tying it behind them with a thick strand of rope. The other hands move slowly around the circumference of the tent, similarly binding openings and weak spots. A murmur of worry and discontent begins to swell inside.

Satisfied with preparations, Adam grins, and for the first time I can recall, he bares what appear to be large fangs. His teeth are slender and razor sharp, like a mouthful of needles. The small group of men around him gasps and takes an involuntary step back.

Adam laughs, pulls off his leather gloves and reveals not hands but coiled tentacles hung with serrated hooks. They uncurl slowly, pulsing and twitching as they taste the violence in the air. Adam lifts his head and howls at the bloody sun, and from beyond my line of sight, his brethren howl back. In those shrieks the assembled crowd hears, whether consciously or not, the somber message. *All must die.*

The small crowd outside is strangely silent as Adam sprints into the heart of the throng. The black, pulsating tentacles hanging from his arms wrap around one unlucky throat and constrict, easily tearing through flesh and gristle. Adam roars and puts his teeth to his victim's face, ripping off a huge swath of nose and cheek. Blood sprays in a wide arc, drenching the closest of the stunned spectators. The torn man tries to scream in unison with his tormentor, but can force out only a thin whine and look of pleading desperation.

No one moves to help him, though; the huddled mass is frozen in shock and silence. Their minds still reeling from Wainwright's miraculous spectacle, the grotesque butchering paralyzes nearly all of them.

After a brief moment, a young man in a dark brown suit begins to shriek and babble. His fear spreads like a contagion, and the remnants of the mob scatter in a unified display of self-preservation. Adam instinctively leaps at the closest of them. Tearing a huge gash in the man's leg to prevent his flight, Adam quickly stalks to the next victim.

Foaming at the mouth like a rabid dog, Lot runs from his post at the entrance and smashes into the largest clump of fleeing parishioners, ripping and tearing everything in his reach. As he gnaws on a young man's skull, I see he has the same sickle dentistry as Adam, and the same barbed appendages shredding flesh and bone. Lost in a frenzied bloodlust, Lot drops the mutilated corpse and unleashes his fury. Blood and bodies whirl around him, chunks of gore and clotted hair hanging from his fangs and hooks.

The screams of those caught outside are soon echoed by those coming from within the tent. Jeremiah has apparently set to his task with the same vehemence and vigor as Adam and Lot. The tent's white walls are soon soaked through with muddy red stains and cries for mercy.

In the chaos, a few of the victims are able to escape the abattoir by wriggling under the hot, sticky canvas. As they scramble for whatever safety the baked earth has to offer, Lot and Adam give chase. Soon they are beyond where I can see and all I am left with are the sickening sounds of the hunt and the screams of the slaughter.

The waning sunlight is suddenly blocked as Wainwright steps into the doorway. "I am sorry you had to witness this, my children. Please do not allow this savagery to affect your work. When given the opportunity, we will again perform such great miracles." The Reverend sighs as he glances at the small girl with the massive exit wound in her head. "It is a great shame to lose Juliana. I quite liked her." He pauses to cast an accusatory glance at Abel, who stands behind him, head down and crying like a whipped dog. "Have no fear, though. We will find more friends for you before the next show."

We have no reply to give as Wainwright slowly closes the door. He smiles warmly, but his eyes speak the truth, they always have. He knows we will all take the same way out as Juliana, given the chance; he calls us his children, but we will never be anything but slaves. The heavy, metal door bangs shut, cutting us off from the atrocities of Reverend Wainwright and his acolytes. Once again we are left without any answers or hope of solace. Once again we are left with nothing but silence and dark.

And the show.

The goddamn show, it must go on.

Exegesis of the Insecta Apocrypha

by Colleen Anderson

"In the beginning, it was a shift, a flutter of orange and black that caught her eye and held it, pulling her into a new paradigm before she knew there ever was one. The opening of the butterfly's wings fastened her two-year-old gaze forever." Apocryphon [1]

The Apocrypha first appeared on the World Wide Web in the early twenty-first century. Their legitimacy as sacred writing was not considered for two decades, with arguments reiterating that class Insecta could never evolve to the state of written language, let alone into a mindset able to formulate histories and concepts of time. In light of the documented case of the child with compound eyes being born last year, as well as several climatic shifts that haven increased insect populations, the Insecta Apocrypha are being analyzed for new interpretations. Whether they are indicators of a convergence of evolution and intelligence to a new level is not in the purview of this paper.

What draws the eye immediately is the symbolism. Butterflies and birds have long been seen as forms of the human soul. Just as the Bible opens with Genesis, so does the Apocrypha begin with a genesis of sorts, and at the awakening of a child's consciousness begins the search for the meaning of soul. [2]

APOCRYPHON I—DISCOVERY

Ever since that first erratic flight, Libby's gaze followed minute forms of locomotion. Whether a larva wriggling, a beetle scuttling, a dragonfly flitting and hovering, or the leap of a grasshopper, she watched intently, tracing its path as long as possible. At the age of four, she squatted in the garden, staring intently at

---

[1] Alice Rothwell, ed. <u>Sacred Writings of the Modern Cult Movements in North America</u> (New York: Random, 2014) *All subsequent Apocrypha quotes are from the same publication.*
[2] Rachel Urghart and Roy Hammerschmidt, eds. <u>Exegesis of the Insecta Apocrypha,</u> Rabbi Joel Shapiro, Chapt. 1 "Interpretations of the Soul" (Numinous Press, Toronto, 2032) 14

something that shivered the long grass. Inhaling noisily, she wrinkled her nose at the cloying smell but stayed put.

Her father's words were less than a fly's buzz and her chubby little fingers itched to pick up one of the writhing white maggots that worked its way in and out of what was once a mouse. The grey brown fur was nearly indistinguishable under the moving carpet that gently trembled.

In that instant Libby understood that life was cannibalistic, feeding on itself, but taking different forms. Life fed on death, death generated life—an intrinsic cycle.

Early on, she noticed that people shied from answering her questions about death and decay. It disturbed them, especially when insects were involved in the decomposition. There was something about the mindless infestation of life feeding voraciously on the dead. A need was deposited in her, a small egg incubating, maturing the more attention she gave it, until it could eat its way out of her. The larval thought was curiosity, but it was inherently tied to watching life and death.

Her father buried the mouse and its white pulsing attendants, digging a hole so deep that Libby never found the spot again.

* * *

One humid morning brought mosquitoes swarming from the creek in the back field. Libby had been walking with her mother, who had stopped to take a few pictures of plants. She listened to the whine of mosquitoes and held out her arm. They alighted, a half dozen or so, their needle thin proboscises piercing her flesh. They sucked and fattened on her blood. Although it itched slightly, Libby didn't interfere with their feeding until her mother turned and said, "Libby, what are you doing!"

Her mother frantically brushed the mosquitoes from her arm and dragged Libby out of the woods, swatting the whole time. At home Libby found her arm swathed in calamine. She watched it throughout the next day, fascinated by the reddish bumps that arose. If she scratched them long enough they enlarged and seeped a clear liquid before blood oozed like small volcanoes erupting. She licked her wounds, feeling the heat of her skin and the slight sourness of the scabs.

She never shied from any insect, letting red-backed ladybirds and butterflies alight on her, moving her feet into the path of shiny, black carapaced June bugs, or walking into a spider's web to induce the arachnid to crawl across her. Holding her mouth open, she would stick out her tongue, letting a few brave insects land so that she could feel the soft dance of their feet. Bites and stings often laced her skin and left her parents bewildered.

Children have a natural curiosity and, like cats, they will watch anything that moves. They are sometimes considered cruel when, in their discoveries, they tear apart insects or hit another child with a stick. Libby's early experiences, when read without the fictional embellishments, are within the normal range of a child's development and expanding consciousness.

It is possible that this early infusion of insect venoms laid the tracery for Libby's later metamorphosis. Her next stage, in Apocryphon II, *began at the age of six. Libby actively investigated the insect world and was ready to learn the depth of what they could do.* [3]

APOCRYPHON II—EXPERIMENTATION

She found an orange striped kitten in the field behind her house. There was a small stand of alders near the creek and she stood under the fluttering leaves, holding the mewing kitten. Taking a string from her pocket, she tied one end around the cat's neck and the other end around a slender tree. Libby patted the kitten once, then walked away.

It took three days for the insect world and the mammalian one to intersect. Each day she strode quickly to the grove of trees and checked the kitten. The first day it struggled and mewed loudly when it saw her. She turned and left it. The second day, it lay on its side, panting, croaking out a feeble meow. Libby searched for insect activity and on seeing none, left. The third day, she bent over, peering at the prone kitten. Its eyes were open and glassy. The slightly matted fur did not move.

Libby settled herself in the grass, cross-legged, her elbows on her knees, chin in hand. Eventually, she noticed a minuscule flicker. She bent closer and watched fleas, which fed on the living, abandoning the carcass, some leaping off, some disappearing underneath, and even a couple of them crossing the surface of the corpse's blind eyes.

Next, the flies descended, buzzing and settling upon the creature, especially around its eyes, ears and nose. It had died with its mouth slightly open, the pink tongue showing swollen and dark. In crept a fly, glistening blue-black, and another, moving about, probing with insectile feet and mouth. The kitten's body crawled with insects, alighting and flying ellipsoid orbits. Libby removed the string from the cat's neck and returned home by dinnertime so as not to jeopardize her experiment.

Each day, she returned to sit and watch the insect activity. In just a few days, the orange and white fur began to move and ripple, like wind over grass. Glistening maggots tumbled from the mouth and eyes, feeding on necrotic tissue.

Eventually, ants and gnats and beetles crawled over the putrefying mass as

---

[3] Exegesis Shandra Radakrishnan, Chapter 3 "Psychoanalysis of the Messiah and Anti-Messiah in Relation to Major Religions" 39-46

the fur sloughed off, displaying the animal's liquefying organs. Libby held vigil through all of it, noting when flies grew bored with the carcass and when ants and spiders moved in to remove morsels. The kitten's body was a motel of activity. Only when the feeding slowed, with mostly bones and fur left, did Libby bury the corpse.

It was a couple of years later that she took a puppy into the same woods. This time she did not wait for death's slow claim but strangled the pup immediately, her hands choking off its whimpers as its black paws scrabbled in the air. When it stopped moving, she laid it on the ground, spreading out its silky ears.

Then she pulled a sharp kitchen knife from her pack. It glinted in the afternoon sun as she studied the black body of the pup. She placed the point against the soft, nearly furless area by the genitals and pushed in, sawing up through the skin to the ribcage. Only a small amount of blackish blood pooled out. Then she cut under the ribs in smaller strokes and across, forming a T. Pulling back the skin and opening the organs to the elements had already brought the flies. Her knife pricked the pink intestines that seeped a fetid black fluid.

Libby sat back as the flies settled upon her offering, humming their contentment. She twirled her wheaten hair, forgetting her hunger and almost missing the distant call of her mother. Scrambling up, Libby tucked away the knife and ran off.

Her diligence brought her each day to note earwigs and the black bowl of hister beetle backs moving in and out of the architecture of decomposing organs while maggots were born and grew fat on the meat. Within a few days the dog's black skin sloughed off the bloated body. Pupae from the flies eventually cracked their husks, emerging as a new generation.

Libby's interest only grew. Not far from her home was a two-story apartment building slated for demolition. The vacant shadows of the windows held only shards of glass. Plywood had been nailed up but vagrants and teenagers had pried them away. Libby had already explored the place, seeing what insects lived in dark and dank rooms.

* * *

When she was twelve she found a little boy of about five wandering down the street. He seemed to not realize he'd strayed far from the familiar. Libby gave him a cellophane-wrapped candy and as he popped it in his already sticky mouth, she said, "I've lost my puppy. Would you like to help me find him?" The boy nodded, pushing his stringy brown hair out of his eyes but not saying anything around the candy in his mouth. Gummy sweetness streaked his chin with brown and pink.

She took his hand and he followed complacently. It was easy enough to get him into the building and have him sit while she grabbed an old rag and some rope. She deftly tied him and before he could whimper, stuffed the gag in his mouth. He began to cry, soaking the rag with saliva and snot. Libby ignored him while she readied her tools; tweezers and scalpel. A few alert flies already circled the boy's face. From her pack, she withdrew several small jars, each holding a flickering, insectoid mass. In one she had scooped up beetles and earwigs and other ground insects. Another held the agitated buzzing of wasps, while a third showed the constant flutter of color from butterflies and moths. Two more jars contained flies and caterpillars respectively.

She ignored the boy's muffled shrieks, refusing to hurry.

After her experiments, Libby retied the gag on the unconscious boy, most of the insects having abandoned him, and threw a blanket over his body. He would be a better stew in the morning. She left and came back a day later, looking at his welted belly and peering at his crusting arms. Flies buzzed about the trickling snot on his face, landing and walking over his sweat-matted hair.

Libby continued for a couple of days, watching how the fly larva grew on living tissue. The boy stared vacantly, drooling, barely making a sound. When nothing more could be gained from her observations, she untied him and watched. He didn't move, just lay on his side. Maggots dropped off of his arms. There was no need to kill him. She packed up everything she had brought, removing jars, tweezers, scalpel and rope, leaving nothing behind. Libby walked away from the building, never to return.

Between the first Apocryphon *and the second, there is a shift of personality. What could be considered normal behavior for a child diverges wildly by the second writing, indicating sociopathic tendencies. Although Libby exhibits the escalation of brutality from animal to human subjects, she doesn't seem to repeat these offenses, which is atypical for sociopaths. However, her behavior in detachment and lack of empathy is typical. [4]*

Debate remains as to whether the Apocrypha only mark the first of each phase of Libby's experiments, or if indeed she only conducted one event at each stage. The first two Apocrypha remain nearly emotionless, whereas the third takes on a slightly different tone and it is believed that Apocrypha III and IV may have been written by Libby. Contention exists as to whether she wrote the first two, or if an unknown source fictionalized all of it. [5]

APOCRYPHON III—RESEARCH

She graduated from high school at sixteen and gained her doctorate in entomology by twenty-two. She became a forensic expert in decomposition and

---

[4] Exegesis Radakrishnan, 53-56
[5] Exegesis Carl Purdy, Chapter 5 "Interpretations of Voice" 76-78

the insects that populated the fleshy worlds of the dead. The microscopic realm of insect biology was as interesting as discovering that first maggot-ridden body.

Libby laid her groundwork well, knowing cell structures, the chemical interactions that drove ants, dragonflies, leafhoppers, moths, and the basis of different groups of social insects. Colonies and hives were fascinating in the caste structure of workers and drones. Not all ant colonies had only one queen and most workers were females, sometimes able to breed when necessary. Often drones lived only long enough to fertilize the queen before dying. In some species of wasps and bees the queens mated with multiple drones and stored the sperm, releasing it over time to fertilize the continuous cycle of egg laying at their discretion.

Libby stored the information, then began to study communication of hymenoptera; the bees, wasps, ants and their hives, colonies and social structure. She ordered yellow crazy ants from the Christmas Islands, Western honey bees and Buff-Tailed bumble bees, Asian giant hornets and German wasps. Besides hymenoptera, she brought in Kirby's Dropwing dragonflies from Namibia, Meadow Argus butterflies from Australia, ladybugs from Canada and a host of other species. She concentrated on the pheromone trails of ants and tried to see if she could colonize species that were not hymenoptera. She tried to form messages from light, from chemicals, from Braille-like forms. Diligently, for five years Libby tested many types of command or communication and searched for any effect on hive activity, caste structures or mating.

Her tests did not lead to any discernible change. Her research could have gone on forever. There were always many new paths to take in studying class Insecta. An estimated thirty million species were still unclassified, but Libby grew unsatisfied, feeling that she was not attaining her goal fast enough.

It dawned on her that though she had concentrated on hymenoptera for their social behavior that she herself was not social. How could she possibly understand such behavior unless she undertook the final phase?

First tidying her lab, Libby took two weeks off, leaving as many insects with the department as she took. After all, she worked alone and was known to keep to herself.

She went downtown and entered a department store. For the first time ever, Libby felt a bit displaced, as if she were an ant that had lost all pheromone signals to the colony. Bewildered, she stared at the array of cosmetics, jars and pomades, lotions, scents, eye and lip colors that surrounded her. Turning a slow circle, she could not pinpoint a place to begin until a clerk approached her.

"I want..." She made a motion around her face, struggling for what to say.

The clerk smiled and beckoned her to follow. "I know. You've not worn makeup before. Don't worry, I'll show you what you need. With your features, you don't need much but we can enhance and highlight what you have."

Libby sat through the experience, finding it alien, then proceeded to buy clothes that were more than utilitarian.

Always a good study, she had no problem in applying the makeup. She slipped on a slinky, red spaghetti strap dress that showed her long legs. Red stilettos added to her color and then she made her way to where males swarmed. The lights and music throbbed around her, pulsating off her skin. She danced awkwardly but it seemed to matter little to the men that grabbed her about the waist and pulled her close.

The first man offered to take her somewhere else. Libby freely gave up her virginity in a car. But she did not stay, exiting for the next nightclub. The second man took her in the restroom, and a third in the back alley where they went to "share a joint." At the end of the night, Libby went with five men, finally finding herself in a threadbare hotel room with a naked flickering bulb. She pulled the closest one to her and kissed him, undoing his pants. When he tried to push her head down, she pulled back and sat on the table, pulling up her dress to take him in. It wasn't long before the others followed.

Libby repeated the swarming for a week, collecting as many men's semen as she could. When she felt she had accomplished that task, now holding enough sperm to release thousands of eggs, she shucked off the mating colors and set to work in her home, which bordered a large, state protected park.

She brought out the terrariums with the various insects and arrayed them about her. From bees, flies, dragonflies, beetles, grasshoppers, moths, weevils, wasps and ants, Libby extracted eggs. She required special tools, often a microscope and careful incubation so that the eggs would not wither. Some she took from the hives about her place and others from the insects directly. When she had a good yield, Libby stripped off her clothing. Under a bright light, she made small incisions on her thighs, arms and abdomen, and inserted a different species' eggs into each opening. Although she felt the pain, it was an abstraction from the task at hand and it only aided her concentration. Overshadowing the pain was a flush of excitement, warmth that spread through her in ways sex hadn't.

As she laid each egg beneath her epidermis, she took out a glass case crawling with army ants. Pressing each bleeding wound shut, she applied the ants along the fleshy rim. The ants in turn seized the edges of the cut in their lightning fast jaws and locked on. Libby felt sharp pricks and then cut off the glossy black bodies, leaving the head and mandibles as sutures. She stood with her stitching of ant heads, and opened all containers holding insects.

A few variants of Apocryphon III *indicate that Libby prayed or cried at this point. These have largely been dismissed as additions by unknown sources that wished to humanize her actions. There is no indication in any Apocrypha that she ever showed intense emotion.*

197

It is argued that Libby was trying to become an insect and found the only way to communicate was to pass on her knowledge through her cells. Still others believe that she had in fact been imbued with the essence of Insecta from birth. [6]

APROCRYPHON IV-A—METAMORPHOSIS

Naked, Libby walked out her door and into the park. In the white heat of the day she stood beneath the trees, her bare feet burrowing into leaf mold. Feeling the slight ripples in the air about her, she spread her arms. It may be that she knew the secret language of insects and called her disciples unto her with the release of a pheromone borne on her words. In a high voice, she trilled.

They came, great black clouds of pixilating Insecta. The air rippled and thrummed with movement. The green bottle flies with their metallic sheen, the beetles with their chitinous clatter, the buzzing drone of bees, wasps and hornets, the flutter of moths and butterflies, the gnats, mosquitoes, the walking sticks and praying mantises. They came from miles around. Still they were only representatives of the greater horde, but one came of every type, thirty million strong.

Onto each pore and hair the smallest insects landed, followed by others, coating her arms, her legs, her naked torso, her face and eyes and ears. When nothing could be seen but the pulsating cluster, it rose into the air, higher and higher, like an enormous runaway swarm. Lifting to the heavens like a gyrating, buzzing black host, it grew smaller and then…dispersed, scattering insects like seed pods.

APOCRYPHON IV-B—METAMORPHOSIS

Libby walked naked amongst the trees under the moon's silvering light. Like Lilith in the Garden of Eden, she moved with confidence. The air seemed to blanket her as she raised her slim, bare arms to the heavens and she cried out in a voice like the chirrup of locusts. Into the skies, boiling from the ground, the myriad host arrived on the pheromone trail, the Insecta in their glory of gold and red, gunmetal black and blue, jarring green and earthy brown, a scintillating mass of color, of forms soft and furred, hard and chitinous. Sound rose like a roar, a thunder, an unearthly humming.

Those who heard the cacophony of wings and legs, and clatter of millions of mandibles thought the end was near. The insects came from all around, swarming up her legs, onto her head. Then they burrowed, chewed and crawled within her. Some crept in her nostrils, others into her eyes, while flies and gnats filled her ears. Other vermin and plump larvae wriggled up her legs. All made their own way and she said, "I am of the hive. Eat of me and understand."

---

[6] Exegesis Purdy, 112-115

She did not scream nor run, but stood, her form limned in an odd moving pointillism. When an hour had come and gone the insects pulled back as if one and departed. Where they had been, nothing remained; not bone, nor hair, nor flesh, nor sinew. It was as if she had never been.

* * *

Her name could have easily been Deborah or Melissa or Mariposa, as would befit a benefactor of insects. Swarmings happen from time to time near urban centers yet no specific incident can be pinpointed in North America where a woman was consumed by insects. There is no extant evidence that she existed under any of these names; that she wasn't a myth generated for a troubled world of the new millennium.

Is this a metaphor in which Libby imparts her knowledge to the insect race, raising them up to the next level of evolution? Indeed, praying mantises have been known to lose wings and then regain them in a single generation—a startling discovery even before the Apocrypha were created.

More disturbing is a concept in which few scientists give credence (indeed, they refuse to even look at it), that Libby did indeed pass the mantle of a superior thinking race onto insects, and that homo sapiens' days are numbered. The aforementioned child with compound eyes supports this belief. She not only exhibits the ocular anatomy of Insecta, but displays disturbing digestive traits as well as the ability to communicate and direct insects in hive activities. However, this mutation also supports the argument that due to climatic and environmental changes the human race is evolving into something...else.

There are only four Apocrypha (Discovery, Experimentation, Research, and Metamorphosis), *which coincidentally compare to the four stages of insect growth: egg, larva, pupa and imago. Since the appearance of the first* Apocrypha, *global warming and pollution have seen the extinction of many amphibious species that kept insect populations in check. As well, entomologists have recorded a change in hymenoptera hive and colony organizations and structure, as well as the evolution of some other orders into new, highly organized social structures.*

The question most debated about the Insecta Apocrypha *is who wrote them? If Libby did exist and if she did not write them, then the only living beings that saw her deeds were the insects.* [7]

---

[7] <u>Exegesis</u> Shapiro, "Conclusion" 198-220

Jerrod Steihl Goes Home

by Ian Withrow

Traffic on the corner of Brisbane and Montgomery is light this morning, more so than it has been in a long time, and Jerrod Steihl feels peace in the relative quiet. The air is chilly; it tastes like smoky fireplaces, or snow that has not yet fallen, and the sky is as white as empty paper. Jerrod slips his hands into his sleeves and waits for his school bus to arrive.

"Might snow a shake," he says to the vacant street corner and smiles, because the words aren't his. They feel funny coming out of his mouth.

He walks in a small circle, careful not to lose his footing on the frost-covered sidewalk. From somewhere close by, a few blocks maybe, there is the squealing of breaks followed by the roar of a diesel engine. The recognizable yellow of the school bus rounds onto Montgomery and accelerates toward Jerrod's street corner.

Jerrod hops a few times. Pulls at the shoulder straps of his camouflage backpack, adjusting the weight. He likes his backpack. It makes him feel cool, tough, and when the others see the swirling turns of black and army green they know that Jerrod is someone not to be messed with. Or at least they will after today.

Mr. Williams pulls the bus up to Jerrod's corner and the screeching of the breaks is much louder, almost deafening. Now the air only tastes like exhaust. Jerrod frowns, glances at the mountains on the far side of the valley. The exhaust reminds him of gas stations and lawn mowers and summer days on Aunt Jennie's speedboat. It doesn't remind him of home. The glass and metal door yawns open and Jerrod sees Mr. Williams. He's wearing his Seattle Seahawks coat, the blue one with the puffy sleeves and the ripped collar. Mr. Williams must be a pretty big Seahawks fan. He wears the coat every day.

"Good morning, Jerrod," Mr. Williams says and waves a gloved hand. He's smiling. Jerrod can see three black teeth and the large gap where four others had once been. Brenden Marshall says that Mr. Williams chews beer cans for dinner and that's why his mouth looks this way. Jerrod's mom used to say it was tobacco. Jerrod isn't sure what to believe, but he thinks his mom was probably wrong. Jerrod has chewed gum before. His mouth doesn't look like that.

"Good morning," Jerrod says back. He climbs the three massive steps. Mr. Williams closes the door behind him.

"Should have a hat on, it's too cold for naked skulls this morning," Mr. Williams says.

"I forgot," Jerrod says and starts down the aisle. He doesn't mind talking with Mr. Williams, but doesn't like it either. Mr. Williams smells bad, like old milk.

"Well," he calls after him. "Better find something. Hurry up and grab a chair. Running a little late today."

Jerrod ambles through and, holding his backpack on his lap, slides into an empty seat. The artificial leather is cold; it seeps through his jeans and numbs the backs of his thighs. Someone behind him says something and Jerrod hears his name. A few of the kids begin to snicker. Mitch Schroeder is sitting across the aisle. He offers Jerrod a slight smile and waves. Jerrod hugs his backpack against his chest and looks out the window. He doesn't mind Mitch as much as the rest. But Mitch is still a kid, and as Jerrod knows, all kids can be dangerous if pushed in the right way. The diesel engine rumbles and roars as Mr. Williams guides the yellow monster down Montgomery.

The view from Jerrod's window is a familiar slideshow of single-family homes and two-car driveways. Some of the houses are still decorated with plastic ghosts and rotting pumpkins, some have changed over to turkeys and pilgrims, and one or two have skipped all the way to reindeer and assorted lights. All are covered in the thick and unwelcoming frost that comes every year before the first flurry of snow.

The bus pulls next to another street corner and two more children, Bennie Holliday and Karli Millstein, climb aboard. There is plenty of room beside Jerrod but the two pass by, offering only cautious glances. Jerrod leans his head against the icy glass of the window and sighs. The bus roars on.

Soon, the neighborhoods give way to vacant fields that are overgrown with yellow, reedy grass and littered with fast food wrappers and empty beer cans. Behind the fields, mountains stand tall and stoic, like guardians of some ancient place. A column of smoke rises up from the tallest mountain as if a great fire is burning there. Rolling and melting into the paper-white sky in a season too late for forest fires. Jerrod stares at the mountains. He wonders if anyone else can see the smoke, if anyone else can hear the Voices. That single word repeating again and again:

Home.

Wadded notebook paper flies into Jerrod's seat from somewhere behind him, dividing his attention and bringing him back into the bus. Someone bursts out laughing. It's a girl's laugh. Nicki Waters. She's always been one of the meanest.

"Saw that," Mr. Williams says. "I see it again, you'll walk the rest of the way to school." The laughing stops, but the snickering is still there. The snickering is always there.

Jerrod cautiously turns his head and looks at the paper that has come to rest beside him in the crevice of the seat. He uncurls the wadded paper. At first he thinks it may be blank, that it might be one of those "infinity snowballs" the kids sometimes throw at him. Then he turns it over and sees the message:

"Dear Jerrod," it reads in bubbly, circle-dotted writing. "We don't like you. We hate you. You smell bad and you are a fat fatty fatso. You have boobs and you are a boy! Why don't you just die because all you do is take up space? Sincerely, Mrs. Rider's class plus Bobby Pinken and John Sears. P.S. You SUCK!"

Jerrod stares at the note, rereading the words until his vision blurs and tears roll down his face. Wiping his eyes, he risks a glance across the aisle. Mitch hasn't noticed. He is busy fogging the glass with his breath, drawing superheroes with his finger. Spiderman first. Then erasing with the sleeve of his jacket, re-fogging, and drawing what looks to be the claws of Wolverine next. Then Spiderman again, crude and ugly in the misty residue of his breath.

"Spiderman always knows when to run," Jerrod says.

Mitch doesn't answer. He continues to draw.

Crumpling the paper back into a ball, Jerrod drops it on the floor and kicks it under the seat in front of him. He hears his name again. Whispers, then the words, "fat ass" and "weirdo." He clutches his backpack, this time feeling the hard, rectangular presence of the Book.

Not anymore, the Voices say. Not after today.

"All right," Mr. Williams says when the bus is stopped in front of Lewis and Clark Elementary. "I'll see you guys in a few hours." He swings the door open and kids file out, giggling past Jerrod as they go. Jerrod pretends not to notice and picks at an imaginary stain on the front of his sweatshirt. When the bus is finally empty, Mr. Williams says, "Come on, Jerrod. Time to move on."

So Jerrod does, thanking Mr. Williams politely as he descends the stairs. He steps onto the frozen concrete sidewalk, crosses the schoolyard and takes his place at the back of Mrs. Rider's line, where the rest of the third graders are already waiting. Mrs. Rider is at the front, asking the Farley twins how their evening went and if they had any troubles with their math homework. Her hair is black with stringy, gray highlights. Her eyes are brown and warm. Jerrod loves Mrs. Rider. Feels he can tell her things he wouldn't tell anyone else. If he had a choice, Mrs. Rider would be his grandmother, instead of the boney-bodied, wispy-haired old woman he is forced to kiss each Christmas and every other Easter.

The bell rings and everyone gets quiet, and for a moment there is only the wind and the brittle leaves scraping across the playground, and the diesel roar of the school bus driving away. The chatter of other classes as they line up in other areas of the playground. Jerrod hears none of these things. He looks over his shoulder at the mountains. The column of smoke continues to writhe into the sky. He watches it, and smiles.

"I know," he says. "I'm coming."

* * *

Belinda Rider stands before her class, silently counting as her students wait for her command. She has twenty-four this year. It's a big number—the biggest she's ever had. Eight more than she ought to have considering the size of her classroom and the curriculum she is expected to cover. She knows this will become an issue in the spring, when the prospect of summer ignites the souls of all children, sending them into early afternoon frenzies that are almost impossible to control. But for now, in the cold morning air, she doesn't mind the number. They are quiet and pleasant, and as she sees their rosy cheeks and running noses, and their wide, obedient eyes, she can't help but feel love for them.

"Okay, class," she says, turning to the side and extending a hand to guide them. "Let's head inside. Remember this is pizza week. You're only two good days away, so no fooling around."

Shoes scuffling over pavement, the children head inside. They are mindful of their spacing. Their lips are tightly sealed. No one wants to be the one to ruin the monthly pizza party for the class.

Belinda smiles down at them as they pass. Karli Millstein with her ladybug barrettes. Kurt Rowe in the Grizzly football jersey he has worn every day since his birthday. Nicki Waters, lips always turned up as if she just got away with something, or is about to try. Belinda's eyes linger on the girl, and she wonders which of the two it is today. Maybe neither. Probably both.

Then Nicki is gone and Mitch Schroeder is there, head down, untied shoelaces tapping the ground with every step.

"Good morning, Mitch," she says.

"Morning."

He still has the bruise on the back of his neck—a thumb-sized purple smudge in a halo of yellow, just below the hairline. Seeing this makes her smile fade away, makes the cigarette burns in his jacket all the more noticeable, and she suddenly recalls the glazed look in his father's eyes at the parent-teacher conferences. The stink of alcohol on his breath.

"Is everything okay?" she says, because it's all she can think to ask, and makes a mental note to check back in with the counselor. She tries to remember where she put the forms, the ones all teachers are required to fill out whenever suspicions of abuse arise. They're somewhere in her desk—probably the bottom drawer, behind the detention slips, the confiscated bubble gum, and her throat lozenges.

Mitch answers without looking up. "Yeah. I'm fine." Then, like the others, he vanishes through the doorway.

She is about to follow when she stops. Her instincts are telling her she has only seen twenty-three faces this morning. Someone is missing. She turns around and sees him, a snowman of a child in a gray sweatshirt standing at the far end of the painted line. His backpack hangs low on his back. The straps swallowed up by the cotton of his sweatshirt, and the soft flesh of his chest. To Belinda, it looks as if he's carrying the weight of the world in there. He is looking over his shoulder, and he's giggling.

"Jerrod," she says. "We're going in now."

Jerrod says something that isn't directed at her.

"Hey, Jerrod." She starts down the painted line. By the time she reaches the boy she is limping, the cold infecting the bone-on-bone grind of her arthritic hip. She smiles through a wince and puts a hand on Jerrod's shoulder. Heat radiates from under his coat. He flinches and looks up at her.

"It's time to go," she says. "Your classmates are already inside."

"Okay," he says, hopping to adjust the weight of the backpack, and starts for the door.

"Who were you talking to back there," she asks, limping along beside him.

"No one," he says. "I'm moving today."

"Are you?"

"I have a new home, now. My parents said no, but I'm going anyways. They can't stop me anymore." He hesitates before going through the door and whispers. "I only have one more chore before I get to go. Like a test."

Belinda frowns. "Who says so? Your parents?"

Jerrod doesn't answer, and as he steps through the doorway, Belinda decides to alert the counselor of this child as well.

* * *

"Sit down, everyone," Mrs. Rider says when they've all entered the room. "And take out your journals, please. You know the drill. I want you to write about the best thing that happened to you last night and the worst thing that happened to you last night. You have ten minutes."

Jerrod unzips the large pocket of his backpack, pushes the Book aside, and retrieves his spiral-bound notebook. He opens it to the proper page, grabs a pencil from the metal lip just inside his desk, and begins to write.

He's good with words, has been since he was very young, and is able to construct the new letters with relative ease. They're more difficult than the cursive *q*'s, *z*'s, and *y*'s he learned last year on Mrs. Morey's ice-cream paper, but after practicing at home these past few days, the new letters are coming out quite nicely.

"Five minutes," Mrs. Rider says from her desk. "Start wrapping things up, please."

Jerrod finishes early. He puts his pencil down and stares at the wooden surface of his desk, at the things that had been carved by students who must be grownups by now. There is the smiley face with the red-inked eye, the etching of the name *TuRnER*, and the letters *F-U-K*. Jerrod has never been able to figure out the last one, because it isn't a word he's ever heard of. *F-u-c-k* he's heard of, but not *F-U-K*. He thinks the letters might be initials, or maybe something from the Book that he hasn't gotten to yet.

"Time's up," Mrs. Rider says. "Now, who would like to share with the class?" She scans the room, passing over Jerrod once. Twice. It makes him nervous, because he didn't write about his evening. She passes over a third time, then says, "Mitch? How about you?"

Mitch Schroeder shakes his head. His eyes are wide.

"Yep, come on...up to the front of the class."

"Mrs. Rider, I didn't write anything," Mitch says. He covers his paper with his arms.

"I know for a fact that you did, Mitch. Now, come on. Everyone has to share sooner or later. Might as well get it over with today."

Mitch sighs. He gets up and drags his feet to the front of the class, shoelaces tapping all the way. Once there, he twists from side to side, holding his journal in front of his face so all Jerrod can see is a bushy tuft of red, curly hair blooming from the top of Mitch's notebook. Mitch begins, reading each word as if it is its own sentence.

"The worst thing that happened last night was my dad got mad and yelled at my mom and left and my mom cried and yelled at my brother and me and we didn't get dinner. The best thing was my mom took us out for ice cream later and I got to have a large peanut butter cup sundae to myself."

He lowers his notebook, moves quickly to his seat. His face is red and when he sits down he puts it into the fold of his arms so that only the back of his head and neck are showing.

"That was very nice, Mitch," Mrs. Rider says. She opens a drawer in her desk, shifts a few things around, and pulls out a pink sheet of paper. "I'm jealous of your peanut butter cup sundae. Was it good?"

Mitch nods, but doesn't lift his head. Jerrod watches as Mrs. Rider writes on the pink paper. He is barely aware that his fingers are stroking his own paper, smudging the letters. Making them warm.

"Okay," Mrs. Rider says, still finishing her writing. "I have to run to the office for a minute. Who's our policeperson? Karli? Aren't you in charge this week?"

Karli Millstein nods and lifts her paper badge into the air.

"Good. I'll expect a full report when I return. Remember, class. It's pizza week." Her eyes linger on Nicki Waters, then she stands and leaves the classroom, the pink paper waffling in her right hand.

For a while, the class is quiet. Jerrod looks down at his paper, at the letters he has carved there with his mechanical pencil. The writing isn't finished yet, but he has to wait. Write. Read. Write. Read. That's the pattern. Write. Read. Write. Read. It's what the Voices say.

Then Nicki is out of her desk, moving to the front of the room. "I'll read," she says, as if she's doing the class a favor, and stands primly beside Mrs. Rider's desk.

"The best thing that happened to me last night," she says, "was when I got to go to my Nanna's house and watch the Hannah Montana concert on cable."

The class stirs, and the anticipation is thick in the air. Jerrod can feel their eyes on him. Watching. Waiting. Nicki glances at Jerrod. An evil grin spreads across her face.

"The worst thing that happened to me last night was when Jerrod Steihl farted and I smelled it all the way from my Nanna's house."

The children erupt in full-blown hilarity. Nicki doesn't waiver, doesn't move. She is glaring at Jerrod. Waiting for Jerrod to cry. For once, Nicki Waters will be a stupid jerk that doesn't get what she wants.

The laughing continues. The jeers begin. Like Nicki, they are all leaning, watching, waiting, hoping for the moment in which Jerrod Steihl finally snaps. They do this in the way that Jerrod's father once slowed while driving past a traffic accident, or the way that his mother used to cling to her cell phone when hearing a juicy bit of gossip about a neighbor or fellow church member.

He bends down and reaches into the large pocket of his backpack. The cover of the Book is made of smooth leather and feels nothing like the harsh, cold seats of the school bus. He tightens his grip and pulls it out, setting it on his desk beside the notebook. He flips pages until he finds the first of his two bookmarks: a Richie Sexson baseball card. Not the Seattle Mariner Richie Sexson, but the Milwaukee Brewer Richie Sexson. It's the better Richie Sexson, so said Jerrod's dad.

Here the writing is still in English, though it isn't the English Jerrod has been learning these past few years. The English in this Book is different, full of strange words, like *thou* and *thy*, and larger ones that are too complicated for him to pronounce. He scans down the page. The jeers become crueler, angrier.

"Are you going to cry, Jar-head?" Jerrod hears one of them say. "Are you going to squirt some?" Jerrod's eyes roll across the words until he finds the tiny note he left himself the night before. *READ HERE—You have to do it three times*, it says in his familiar chicken-scratch scrawl. He nods, as if it was the page telling him to do this rather than his own handwriting, and then begins to read.

He speaks quietly, barely able to hear himself over the ruckus around him.

It doesn't matter; the Voices didn't say anything about the words being heard, just that they must be read aloud. He repeats this phrase twice more, closes the Book, and picks up his pencil. He has to work quickly if he is going to finish before Mrs. Rider comes back.

"Look at his tongue," says Bennie Holliday. "It's like he's going to eat his own face."

Jerrod realizes Bennie is right, feels the wetness of his tongue on his lips. He doesn't withdraw it. He is focused and this is his focused face. Something has awakened within him. He writes as if he has known this language all his life. The tip of his pencil swoops and spins, etching the intricate new letters into the page.

When he finishes, he rips the paper from the notebook. Holds it in front of his face, staring in awe at the alien script. There's an electric feeling in the air, shockwaves rippling up his arms and across his chest. It's a feeling Jerrod has never experienced before, and now that he has it, Jerrod never wants to let it go.

"Oh man, he's going to eat the paper," someone says.

"Probably," says another. "He eats anything."

Everyone laughs.

Jerrod turns his head, stares at them, and the laughter quickly dies.

"I'm *supposed* to eat the paper," he says quietly, and devours it, stuffing it into his mouth and tearing away large chunks. At first he has a hard time chewing. Then his saliva softens it into pulp, and the paper tastes good. It tastes oh, so good.

The students gape at Jerrod with wide, unbelieving eyes. One of them is able to mutter, "Geez…" And Karli Millstein, seeing as she is the policeperson, is brave enough to say, "That's disgusting." But as he thrusts the remaining bit of paper into his mouth, no one makes a single move.

Jerrod swallows and relishes the feeling as it slides down his gullet. The edges of the paper have made small cuts in the corners of his mouth, and he thinks he might be bleeding. But he doesn't care. A warm sensation is growing in his chest, and, for the first time in his life, he is aware of his potential strength.

Almost, he thinks, and reaches again for the Book.

This time he opens it to the second bookmark, a third place ribbon he earned for one of his poems during last year's county fair. He pushes the ribbon aside. *Now you read this*, his handwriting says in the margin of the page. *But only once. DO NOT READ IT TWICE.* Reading it twice would be bad for everyone— the school, the neighborhood, maybe even the entire town. Reading it once was only bad for Mrs. Rider's classroom. Once is enough. For now.

The Voices grow louder, chanting Jerrod's name from faraway places. Smokey places. Snowy places. These are the Voices that called Jerrod into the yellow-grassed fields nearly two years ago, the Voices that led him to the secret hiding place of the Book, buried there, deep down in the earth. Jerrod doesn't know why they spoke to him then, or why they speak to him now. All he knows is that the Voices are sweet, pleasant, and he believes everything they say.

Leaving his belongings on his desk, he zips up the pockets of his backpack, puts it on. The backpack isn't necessary for the thing to work, but it is camouflage. He stops beside Mitch Schroeder's desk.

"Hey, Mitch."

Mitch doesn't say anything. He keeps his head down. Jerrod can see a doodle on Mitch's journal entry. It's Spiderman, better than the window drawings, hanging from the corner of the page.

"I like Spiderman, too," Jerrod says. "He always knows when it's time to run away." It's the best he can do for the boy who was almost a friend. Then Jerrod is walking again, and the Voices chant on. They don't want Jerrod thinking about Mitch Schroeder. Not with work to be done.

Jerrod doesn't go all the way to the front of the room. He stops in the corner where Mrs. Rider keeps the overhead projector and the rolled up maps the class uses during their Geography period. Jerrod figures this spot is as good as any. Close enough to the door. Close enough to the middle of the room.

"What's he doing?" Karli Millstein says. No one knows.

He raises his arms above his head and he can feel the bottom of his gray sweatshirt lift up, revealing his rotund, pale belly. Any other time on any other day, this would've left Jerrod wide open to verbal attack. This time, on this day, no one notices Jerrod's exposed flesh, veined with purple stretch marks. They seem more concerned with the floor of the classroom. It's starting to shake.

The warmth in Jerrod's chest becomes hot. Sweat beads and drips from the corners of his brow. He closes his eyes. In his mind, he sees a small, black seed. The seed is smooth, perfectly round. He can feel it with his mind, the way he can taste a cheeseburger before he takes his first bite.

"Grow," Jerrod says and scrunches his face in concentration. "Come on... *grow.*"

The seed in his mind begins to pulse, ripple like a pregnant belly. A tendril bursts from one side of the seed. A second explodes from the other. Then a third. Then a fourth. Jerrod hears something from the corner of the room. It's Nicki. She isn't crying yet, but her eyes are wide and her once mischievous face is vacant and pale. He watches. Waits. The floor splits and the Voices cry out. As Karli Millstein's paper badge flutters away from her grasp, dancing through the air like a late-autumn leaf on a winter wind, an exhilarated and guttural cackle boils up from the depths of Jerrod's core.

* * *

Belinda Rider feels the bone-on-bone grinding deep within her pelvis, shooting daggers of pain throughout her abdomen and down her left leg. Her hip is begging her to stop, but she won't. She can't. She needs to get back to her students.

She had already left the office when the building began to shake. At first she thought it nothing more than a small earthquake, which this area receives every so often. She could recall three distinct tremors during her tenure at the school, none of which resulted in any damage.

But a moment ago, as she walked past the gymnasium, the halogen lights began to quiver in their housing and she grew worried. By the time she reached the cafeteria, a fire extinguisher had fallen off the wall and the power had gone out, and she was afraid.

Now she is terrified, hobbling as fast as her body would allow in the worn support of her orthopedic shoes. She ignores the pain erupting in her hip. Barely notices the commotion of the classrooms to her right and left as colleagues instruct their students. Everything is a muted jumble of sights and sounds.

A screeching static bursts from the overhead speakers. Principal John Winter's voice pours down from above. "Do not panic. This is not a drill. Please proceed with School Lockdown Procedure. I repeat...this is not a drill. Please proceed with School Lockdown Procedure."

She hears, "Please get under your desks..." as she passes Mr. Thompson's room; sees a child run out of Mrs. Harrington's room, eyes wide, as Mrs. Harrington chases after; hears ."..No, Brian, I don't think this is a terrorist act. Now, plea..." as she passes Mrs. Bowe's room. The entire building feels as if it is tearing in two.

Her right foot slides on the waxy surface of the floor and white pain explodes just below her waist. She cries out and almost collapses, catching herself on the cool porcelain of a nearby drinking fountain before falling to the floor. She lifts her eyes. She can see her classroom at the end of the hall. The door is open. Incandescent light is pulsing inside the room. And from within that light, obscene and writhing shadows spill out against the hallway walls.

She grits her teeth and starts moving again. She is close enough now to recognize the faces behind her student's screams. She can hear Marissa Potts calling for her mother. The Farley twins sobbing in near unison. Sammie Hayes pleading for help. Just ahead, daytime janitor Terry Bahl emerges from the adjacent hallway. He stops when he sees her. He starts running toward her but she stops him. Shaking her head. Pointing to her classroom.

"The children," she screams. "Terry, get to the children!"

He nods, his face simultaneously determined and heroic, and runs for the pulsing light. Much younger than she, he moves with such vigor that she almost feels relief, as if his youth alone is enough to end whatever harm is coming to her students. The building continues to shake; lockers have opened and their contents pour into the hallway. She sees a flash of orange plastic and recognizes it as Brenden Marshall's water gun, the one she had ordered him to take home.

Up ahead, Terry reaches the open door and stops. He stands for a moment, his face a mixture of shock and something else she can't identify—astonishment, maybe terror. Then he springs into motion, youthful limbs flailing wildly as he runs down the hall, escaping whatever horrors might be lurking inside her room.

"Terry! *Terry!*"

She starts forward and her right foot catches on some of the debris from the lockers. She goes down, crashing onto her left side amidst fluttering papers and scattered, brownbag lunches; there is a loud pop in her hip and the feeling of something foreign floating around in her pelvis. For a moment she is lost, her vision swamped with starry blackness, and she feels nothing but pain and the urge to vomit.

Her classroom is so very quiet.

Belinda moans and pulls herself down the hallway, dragging her legs behind her. She can vaguely make out the sounds from other classrooms, teachers consoling children who are both excited and scared. She can hear nothing from her own classroom. She is about to call to her students when Jerrod Steihl walks out into the hallway.

His shaggy, brown hair is dripping with sweat. His gray sweatshirt holds dark circles beneath each arm. Tiny trickles of blood ooze from the corners of his mouth and his face is blotchy and red. There is a wildness about him, some new and powerful thing lurking just beneath the surface. He is holding Karli Millstein's paper police badge in his hand.

"Mrs. Rider," he says. "I'd like to go home, now."

"What's happened, Jerrod?" She's still crying and has to speak between sobs.

His tongue darts out between his lips, then he says, "Spiderman's the best because he knows when the bad things are about to happen. It's the Voices, that's what I think. The Voices telling him to go home." He shrugs, then winces. "My head really hurts. And my tummy doesn't feel very good. I don't care if it's pizza week. I just want to go home. Can I please just go home?"

"Tell me what's happened. Why aren't they talking, Jerrod? What's in there?"

Jerrod's eyes narrow. "They're done talking." Then he turns and walks down the hallway.

"What's in there?" she screams after him. He doesn't stop. She watches the boy until the final strap of his camouflage backpack disappears through the heavy doors that lead outside. Then, pulling herself to the open door way, Belinda looks into her classroom.

Most of the desks have been turned on their sides and pushed into one corner of the room. The fissure in the floor is wide. The linoleum tiles are like broken teeth around the rim. Belinda blinks once. Twice. Unable to comprehend the giant tree that is occupying her room—the thick, organic trunk rising up from the fissure, the serpentine branches spreading out in every direction. The thorns covering the branches are long and ugly, like claws—and hanging among them like bunches of overripe fruit are her students.

There is Marissa Potts dangling above Belinda's desk, the blood seeping from a dozen puncture wounds in her chest and stomach. There is Brenden Marshall, propped up against the base of the tree, his head lulled to one side, bones bulging like a fist through the skin of his neck. Nicki Waters hangs near the ceiling, a particularly long thorn protruding from her gaping mouth. And there are more, so many more—her entire class, up in the branches, their blood raining down. No, not raining. Floating. Like the ash of a great fire. Like snow.

Belinda tries to back away from the door, screaming, snot and spittle and tears all mixing together in the lower half of her face. A small boy is lying face down just inside the door. His head is turned away, but the purple smudge is there, on the back of his neck. A branch is protruding from the middle of his back, as if it caught him trying to run away. As if he almost made it. Then the bruise moves and she has time to think, *My God, he's still alive*, before her mind gives up and her eyes roll back in her head.

* * *

Outside, Jerrod Steihl walks across the frost-covered playground toward the yellow-grassed fields on Montgomery Street. He clutches the shoulder straps of his backpack and smiles. He doesn't think about Mrs. Rider's third grade class, nor his parents, in their house back on Brisbane, snowing down from a tree of their very own. Beneath the white starkness of the almost-winter sky, the distant mountains are jagged and snow-capped and wonderful. The Voices are still there, and they are calling to him.

It's snowing, not enough to stick but just enough to notice. "I told you it might snow a shake," he says to no one in particular, and his smile widens. He veers from the familiarity of Montgomery and starts across the fields. He is heading for the mountains and the pillar of smoke that maybe no one else can see.

He is going home.

The Immolation Scene

by John F.D. Taff

"From near his heart, he took a rib.
All fires have to burn alive to live."
"All Fires"—Swan Lake

Ashes...

It's snowing, the flakes are red, like snow in hell, and Corey thinks they taste of cinders. That's what spills down his throat when they melt, leaves his mouth raw.

The warehouse before him is in full conflagration, flames leaping from its roof, flicking like reptile tongues from its burst, shattered windows, between the skeletal remains of its façade. He stands apart from the chaos, the twisting hoses, the intent firemen, spinning red lights, far enough to avoid being consumed, close enough to consume it—the roar of the flames, the avid heat, the burning grit.

He can also smell the rich scent, scummy and thick on the ash-laden air, of boiling human fat. He wonders if anyone else smells it, knows what it is.

They were here tonight. The Immolation Scene. I can feel it. I'm getting closer to them.

To her...

* * *

Amy.

She had come to fix his laptop. He'd been typing at home late the night before, trying to finish a report. Nodding off, fire had squirted from his fingers, singeing the Q, W, E and R keys, melting the A, S, D and F keys.

He was still wondering how he was going to explain it when she came in.

Amy's hair was upswept in a '40s movie star style. It was red, the unnatural red of crayons, traffic lights and fire engines. She wore a dark, prim skirt and a severely plain, long-sleeved white blouse that revealed tattoos beneath its shifting edges. Each ear boasted three earrings, and there was a discreet nose piercing that

212

glittered when the fluorescents hit it. Her heavily chewed fingernails were painted dark eggplant.

Corey was as uncomfortable with her quirky beauty as he was with the fact that he had dated her for a while a few months back. The attraction had been instant, over drinks at a departmental party at a nearby bar. Their relationship was swift, torrid, the chemistry definite and mutual.

But after six months, most of which Corey thought were pretty good, she abruptly broke it off. There were arguments, tears...so many tears...

He didn't understand at the time, still didn't.

I love you, he told her. *Isn't that enough?*

Her answer was *No.*

You're not willing to really love, to give yourself to it, let it change you. You're not willing to let yourself feel anything.

It had been uncomfortable for a while, after the split, working at the same company. But the office was large enough that they didn't see too much of each other.

"Umm...hi. Someone's computer not playing nice?" she said, standing in the entry to his cubicle. She carried a small gray case before her, slung around the corner of his desk, holding it before her like a shield.

"That'd be mine, I guess," he said, blocking her view of the keyboard.

"Mind if I take the captain's seat?" she said, flicking her gaze across him.

"Sure," and he leapt to his feet. They stood face to face for a moment; he looked into her eyes, eyes that he still saw in his dreams, eyes that were a beautiful, deep violet...the Technicolor of Elizabeth Taylor's eyes in old photos, or of bruises, of twilight.

Then she was sitting and he was shuffling behind her, gritting his teeth wanting her to say something. "Usually I get Devon," he said, as much to fill the silence as to offer a silent thanks to the Gods of IT for sending her instead of Devon (of the too-tight pants and the body odor that smelled of equal parts Big Mac and Axe body spray).

"Well, it looks as if you fell asleep smoking at the keyboard, which is generally considered a bad thing. Not as bad, I guess, as falling asleep in bed smoking, but..."

"You know I don't smoke," he said awkwardly.

"Ummm...well, that's good, actually, because the company pretty much frowns on employees who burn up their laptops while smoking menthols. I'd probably have to report you or something."

Corey realized that she seemed more nervous than he felt. He saw she was rolling up the right sleeve of her blouse, doing so conspicuously, as if wanting him to notice it and not her words. A magician's misdirection in reverse.

Her arm was thin and gracile, lovely. The skin was smooth and pale, freckled with moles. Corey was a sucker for moles and freckles.

213

Then he saw *them*, and he froze. His mouth went dry and he felt it...that feeling he got when it came...when the fire came...

It was a tingling, a little ticklish buzz just beneath the skin, like the first electric pulse you feel on your lips before you get a cold sore.

She had a few small, red, circular welts across the smooth inner flesh of her forearm, grouped like crop circles.

You might think they were cigarette burns, especially given her hair, the tattoos, the piercings. And you might not be altogether surprised.

But he knew her, knew what he was looking at.

And he *was* surprised.

He had seen every inch of her closely, carefully. Why had he never seen these before?

Corey grabbed his own arm, felt the first pulse of fire push outward from his skin, singe the hairs there, felt its heat push against the cotton sleeve of his own shirt.

He saw her take notice, watch a small brown pinprick of heat scorch the fabric.

Grabbing the computer, she stood, almost frantically, stepped away.

"I'll have to replace this," she blurted, pushing past him. "I'll move your files to the new one. I can get it to you in about an hour or two, if that's okay...well, even if it's not okay."

Moving into the hallway, she turned, eyed him uneasily.

He slapped at his arm, patting the flame out, patting the flame back into his body.

"I'll call when it's ready."

Corey watched her walk to the elevators, his laptop clamped under the arm still exposed by her rolled-up sleeve.

Corey waited, but she didn't return.

He went home and sat on the couch, picked at the toppings on his frozen pizza. In his peripheral vision, the images on the television jumped and bucked, shifting colors, shifting lights.

Numb.

On his arm, he coaxed a small flame into being—crisp blue at its base, yellow-white at its flickering tip. He watched it bob and weave there, a tiny dancing wraith, burning his skin, tickling his mind, pleasant and unpleasant.

He thought of her, the burn marks pocking her arm.

Why hadn't she said anything before?

When he looked back, his entire forearm was ablaze. He saw the skin turning pink beneath the gaseous blue sheet of flame that engulfed it. He stared at the fire in awe for a moment, never having let it come out this far before. He felt the delicious hotness of it atop his skin, beneath it...

214

...in it.

It was burning him, devouring his flesh, crisping the fine hairs.

He leapt to his feet, waving his arm over his head as if dispelling a cloud of bees. Slowly, the flames sputtered, faded.

Corey breathed heavily, shocked at how far he'd let the fire go. The skin was unbroken, mildly red as if sunburned. He smelled something acrid in the air, saw that all of the hair on his forearm was gone, burned away.

Quietly he went into the bathroom, let cold water run over the scalded skin, then applied a daub of burn ointment from his medicine chest.

When he went to bed that evening, that skin—new and pink and sensitive, burned to life by destroying the older layer above it—felt everything.

* * *

The coffee from the café downstairs sloshed out of the Styrofoam cup. He grabbed a few napkins to keep it from touching the new laptop that sat in the middle of his cluttered desk. Mopping the coffee away, he noticed a small white envelope addressed to him in a loopy, girlish hand.

Corey took the envelope and, impulsively, smelled it. A faint air of flowers hung about it, made his skin tingle. A small card tipped into his palm when he ripped the envelope open.

If you're still interested...and I am...meet at this address Friday at 9 p.m. We can talk more.—Amy.

Without realizing, he rubbed the new skin of his arm beneath the sleeve of his business shirt.

It was going to be a long week getting to Friday.

* * *

Corey steered through a section of the city he'd never been in before. It was almost 9 p.m., and the streets were lit only by the orange glow of dusk-to-dawns perched high above the pavement.

A figure stood beside the closed door of the building that matched the address on the card. The man barely looked at him as Corey pushed the heavy door open, stepped inside...

...a carnival, for that is what it seemed.

The space was enormous, industrial, dark. It seemed to recede into shadows that were moving, punctuated by lurid, red bursts of light. People filled the space, easily 100 or more, men and women of all ages, races, and shapes.

And the smell...the smell he would associate forever with them, the Immolation Scene. Like any bar, it smelled of close bodies, stale beer, the tang of lemons and limes, cigarettes. But there was something more, something at the back of all this, behind it, yet looming in its presence.

It was heavy on the air the way a campfire or fireplace is if you're sitting too close; piney and vaporous, as if you were inhaling the soul of what had burned, a thing too tenuous to carry with it an actual aroma, only a hint.

Below this, the scum, the oily smear of *something*...

To his left stretched a bar, slick wood and dirty brass. She was there, at the bar, draped over a seat. He noticed her bare arms atop the slick, dark bar, noticed the numerous small dots of red that freckled her flesh.

Her violet eyes sparkled like amethysts.

"You came," she said, and it sounded to Corey less like surprise than a simple acknowledgement.

"Sure," he said, sidling up to her. "You thought I'd stand you up?"

"No," she said, her smile enigmatic. "I knew you'd come."

"How's that?"

She said nothing, reached to him, took his arm in her two pale hands. He shivered a little as her nails touched the skin of his wrist, undid the button of his shirt cuff, peeled it back to reveal the skin of his arm, still raw, red from the other night.

Exposed, he could feel the goose bumps she raised with her breath, the dangerous sharpness of her nails as they raked his flesh. She ran her fingers in a slow, looping curve up the swell of his forearm, and Corey nearly gasped in pleasure.

His arm twitched, and she giggled, letting loose of it so slowly, so gently he almost felt as if she were reluctantly passing its ownership back to him. He blinked, rolled the shirtsleeve back down.

"How's *that*?"

A hand drifted up, pushed at a curl of hair near her temple, toyed with it in that most common of flirtations. Corey smelled the hint of her perfume, violets perhaps...or roses, gentle on the air in the narrowness between them.

He chose to believe, for no other reason than the color of her dense purple eyes, that it was violets.

"How come you never told me...never said anything?"

She considered that for a moment, toyed with a drink on a coaster, sighed. "How come you didn't?"

A thousand answers flashed through his mind. Instead, he asked, "So, how did you know?"

Amy stirred at the slumped, yellowed ice in her glass. "Not too difficult, really. Just look for melted laptops. It's a sure sign. Besides, there were those flames on your sleeve." She nodded toward his arm. "It feels a whole lot better if you do it with someone else. Believe me, I know."

Corey's brows gathered in the center of his smooth forehead.

"Wikipedia defines spontaneous human combustion as 'the burning of a living human body without an apparent external source of ignition.' That frakked up computer, those burns on your shirtsleeve," she let her voice fade.

"Yours, too?"

She smiled. "Wikipedia also says its victims are mostly lonely people," she looked down at the bar, swirled a finger atop its pitted surface. "Are you? Lonely?"

Corey considered that for a moment. He had friends, a life. Since he'd split from her, he'd been out on the occasional date. But he also thought of the evenings at home on the couch, the cold meals, the long nights alone in his rumpled bed.

From all of these, it was her that was missing.

"So what is this place?" Corey swallowed, flexed his still tingling arm, looked around.

Amy tilted her head. "A place."

"Does it have a name?"

"Not really. It's just a place we meet. We meet at a lot of different places." She shrugged, lifting the glass and tilting a melted chunk of ice into her mouth.

"Who's *we?*"

Watching him carefully, certain that he was paying full attention, she pushed the chunk of ice to the front of her mouth with her tongue, caught it between her teeth. Another tongue, this one of fire, darted from her mouth, melted the ice cube almost instantly. A puff of steam escaped between her lips, and she smiled, giggled again.

"People who want to *feel* things…*feel* life. You know…one of *us.*"

"*One of us?* What are you? Magicians? Carnies?"

Amy laughed hard at that, taking in the dregs of her drink, and setting the glass onto the bar. "Are *you* a magician? A carnie?"

Corey shook his head.

"Then you're one of us," she said. "We're, like, made for each other." She looked up suddenly, her violet eyes dark as wounds in the dim light of the bar. "But I'm tired of the tears, Corey. So, how far?"

"How far what?"

"How far are you willing to go…this time? How much of yourself are you willing to give?" Her eyes focused on him. "How much are you willing to *feel?*"

Corey blinked, not sure of what she meant…then *sure* of what she meant.

"As much as I need to, I guess."

She considered this for a minute, weighed it.

"Okay, buy me a drink and I'll show you around."

* * *

Amy led him, her arm entwined in his, and she felt soft and warm. The new skin of his arm tingled as she rubbed against it, maddeningly painful and sensual at once. And she seemed to know, because she held her body close as they negotiated the crowd.

She seemed to have a destination in mind as she pushed through the crowd, leading him. As they progressed, Corey took in his surroundings.

Here, a man stood on a small platform, shirtless, bearded. A blazing ring encircled his head, forming a crown that burned white and gold. From his eyes, flames guttered. His hands were outstretched, palms facing the crowd, more flames, blue and violet, dancing atop his fingertips. He was talking, reciting poetry, his voice sonorous, enchanting over the rush of the conflagration. His gaunt appearance and blank eyes were startling, like a prophet of the apocalypse.

There, a woman, also topless, hair swirling as if caught in an underwater current. A necklace of fire crawled across her chest, her shoulders, a thin string of blue flame beaded with balls of orange the size of marbles. The whole thing moved, orbited her body, rolling across her flesh. Her face was raised, rapturous eyes cast to the dark ceiling. Corey could see their whites.

Barely visible through the crowd, a man and woman stood nude on a slightly raised dais, entwined, the entire circular platform rotating slowly, affording the crowd a changing view of the couple.

Amy's tug on him lessened, and he realized that she wasn't watching the couple, she was watching *him*...his reaction.

The couple was completely enshrouded, burning fiercely. Flames rose from their heads, squirted between their lips, followed the line of leg, the curve of hip. Rose-colored, amber, orange, jet-blue tinged with jade green, the blaze moved about them, sensuously, avidly, sinuous and alive.

Corey could feel the heat from the performance, could hear the flames crackle, the whoosh of the air that fed them like an open, uncontained furnace.

He turned to Amy, leaned into her, the sounds, the permeating smell of ash, the greasy smell of roasting flesh overwhelming his senses. She reached to touch his face.

He sensed, rather than saw, the corona of flames that surrounded her hand, felt its heat as it neared his face.

As if she had drawn it forth, a tuft of fire erupted from his cheek, guttered there in anticipation of her fiery hand.

When it came, when her enflamed hand softly caressed his cheek, the entire side of his face burst into luminous blue-green, covering it like a caul.

He watched her through these flames, watched her smile, watched her close her eyes and move in to kiss him.

Only then did he feel the heat...*really* feel it.

He pulled away from Amy, thrust her roughly from him.

Corey brushed at the flames. The skin of his cheek stung, throbbed.

Amy's eyes searched his; something deep, pleading swam in them. He allowed her to press against him, allowed her to find his lips again. They were chapped, hot. He felt pressure building inside his skin, but willed it to stay down, stay inside.

218

They kissed, and this time he kept his eyes open.

They kissed and he saw the couple on the stage, now extinguished, saw them naked of their fire, saw the burns and scars and weals that covered their bodies, the raw, red skin, the charred flesh of thigh, of palm, of chest.

They kissed again, and Corey closed his eyes.

* * *

When he awoke, he stared at the ceiling for a minute, trying to figure out where he was.

Amy's place. He recognized the crack in the ceiling, the muted street sounds through the closed window of her apartment.

He felt it as he moved, the sheets sliding over his body...that tingling, pain/pleasure sensation that raced electrically across him, across his new skin...

...new skin burned to life from the old.

He quietly rose from the bed and padded into the bathroom. The door closed with a gentle click, the light came on with another.

What greeted him in the mirror caused him to gasp, clench the edge of the sink.

The face that stared back was tight and shiny, red, scalded. His eyebrows were gone, his hairline scorched. His lashes, too, were gone, melted. His eyelids were red, puffy, filled with fluid.

His chest, his arms were burned, deep enough to make his skin feel stiff, drawn. The hairs on his chest, under his arms were gone as well, as neatly as if he'd shaved them. Burns trailed further down to his stomach, his groin, his thighs...

Corey gasped, not in shock, but in feeling...all of this new skin, all of this exposed skin brought with it overwhelming sensation. Over the pain, there was an almost euphoric sense of *feeling*, as if for the first time.

He felt the edge of the countertop press his legs, the shivery coolness of the porcelain sink, the stir of the air conditioner...all of them, all at once, and it was almost too much.

Trembling, hands shaking, he fumbled open the medicine cabinet, raked across its contents, sending them spilling into the sink, clattering onto the tile floor. He found a tube of burn ointment, twitched its cap open, squirted a thick dollop of it into his palms.

She pressed into him from behind, and the contact, the silken warmth of her body conforming to his, made his eyes roll back in his head, his hands clench on the sink and the tube of ointment.

It was as if someone had pressed a bare electric wire to his spine.

"What are you doing?"

He thought of the woman, the one with the flaming necklace, how she had raised her head to the ceiling, her eyes white with rapture as the fire burned her skin, burrowed a groove in her flesh.

"The burns…got to put something on them," he gasped, pushing her away. Cool air flooded the space between them, making every remaining hair on his body stand on end.

"Why?"

Corey took a deep breath.

Was she kidding?

He turned to face her, was not surprised to see that she, too, was covered in red, scalded skin. Some of her hair was singed, her eyebrows. There were raised, red burns across her breasts, the flat of her stomach.

"We burned each other. Here, let me…"

Amy looked at him sadly, slapped his hand away, spattering the blob of ointment against the wall.

"No!" she said. "That's *what* we do…*who* we are. I'm not going to cover all the new skin we've burned off. It lets me feel so much more. It lets me feel *you*."

She stepped closer, put her palm against his red chest.

"Don't you feel it? Don't you feel me?"

He *could* feel her, the coolness of her palm, the moisture. The enlivened nerves of his new skin seemed to triple, quadruple the normal feeling of it, sent it slamming into his brain in a rush, a sensation that threatened to incapacitate him.

Corey took her hand gently, pulled it from him, held it. He saw the pads of her fingertips, the wrinkled moist palm, all red, all burnt. He thought again of the couple they'd seen at the warehouse, entwined, enrobed in sensuous, living fire. But then he remembered how they looked after—the seared flesh, twisting scars, melted skin.

"Look at us," he croaked, through blistered and cracked lips, through lungs that felt sere. "We'll burn each other to death."

"No," she said, beginning to cry, trying to get close to him, to touch his skin with hers. "No, don't think of it like that. Think of it like we're burning away the loneliness, burning away the empty evenings, the lonely nights. We're not burning to death…we're burning to *life*. A new life together."

Corey looked at her, and despite his love for her, all he could see were the burns, the angry flesh, the swelling. All he could think of was the pain, the fluids rushing in beneath the appalled flesh, flushing away dead cells, trying to heal that which had been hurt.

"No," he said. "It's too much…I can't do this…"

She cried harder, her breath hitching, tears trailing down her cheeks, across her naked breasts. "You said you would…give as much as you needed to…this time."

Corey wanted to reach out, to hold her, to tell her that he loved her. But he saw his own hands, shriveled, burnt, and drew them back.

"Not this way."

She looked away. "I should have known…this is just like last time."

"Jesus Christ! You're asking too much of me. Too much!"

She stepped away, let him pass.

They did not touch.

Corey sat on the edge of her bed, put on his clothes slowly. As he drew them over his skin, each movement was a symphony of sensation. His breathing quickened, his pulse became erratic, thready.

When he was dressed, he turned to her, standing still, silent in the bathroom doorway, limned by its colorless light.

She said nothing, and her face was in shadow, but Corey heard her sobs.

"I can't do this anymore. I won't cry for you anymore." She sniffled. "This is it."

Within the darkness of her face, a small flame appeared, centered on her right eye.

It flared there, intensely bright, as violet as her eye.

Just as quickly, it went out.

He heard her gasp.

He heard a small *pop!*

He heard something drip to the tile floor...*plipplipplip.*

He was horribly sure that it *wasn't* her tears falling. But he could think of nothing to say, to do.

So he turned and left, silently, carried away on the scent of violets, of burning flesh...

* * *

Months passed, Amy disappeared, quit her job, left her apartment. No new employer noted, no forwarding address left. And for a while, that was fine with Corey.

...for a while.

He went back to long days at work, longer nights at home, eating alone, sleeping alone.

Numb.

Old skin had grown over the new, insulated him again from feeling anything.

Numb.

Until he thought about *The Immolation Scene.* That's what it was called on the jewel box for the movie soundtrack CD. The name fit, so Corey took it, used it for her group.

The Immolation Scene.

He watched the movie on his DVD player over and over, because that scene came the closest to showing how it actually felt.

Or maybe how he *wanted* it to feel...

In the movie, the antagonist *(or was he the protagonist here?)* sprawled atop

221

the dark beach—injured, defeated, a river of magma flowing past him like a hot line of hate; a sky of lurid, blackened clouds boiling overhead. Fire all around him, in the air, the ground, the river...

When his body erupted into flames, though, those flames came from *without*, Corey thought, not from *within*, like his own fire.

Corey always believed that his fire was something else, something different...a wick tapping into some deeper fuel, a fuel that burned only the grace from him. He could relax, not worry about it consuming him; not worry about losing himself in it.

But that man there on the screen? It didn't just consume him, it changed him, altered his soul as he lay on that black sand beach. You knew because the movies were made out of order; you already knew, going in, what the fire *did* to him, what it *made* of him.

He had thought all of this *then*, but *now*...well, *now* he knew better...since he met her...lost her...*again*.

Now he paid more attention to the fact that the character in the movie had also let the flames make of him what they would.

And for what?

For hate.

She had asked him to do the same, but for love. And he had resisted that, misinterpreted it.

Just as that character had.

You're not willing to let yourself feel anything.

If someone's willing to do it for hate, he told himself, *you should be willing to do it for love.*

Corey thought about that as he watched a tiny bloom sputter atop the pores of his left arm, let it roll down to his hands, crawl up his fingers. The fire was white hot, radiated heat in great pulses that he could feel on his cheeks.

He had never let the fire get far enough for that, though...

...not even for her.

Numb.

No more...

He let the fire go, to make what it would of him.

To make him feel.

And he did...the heat grew until it sent tendrils of pain down his hand, into his arm. He smelled the ash, the charring skin, the cooking meat.

First one, then another of his fingers fell to the floor, sloughing embers like cigar stubs.

Corey fell to the floor, too, on his knees, weeping, *feeling...feeling it all...*

He had to find her.

He had to tell her that he *felt*, show her how he *felt*.

* * *

Glass…shattered glass.

Corey stoops to pick up a piece that sparkles in the swirling lights, the twitching firelight. It has melted its way into the soft asphalt at his feet, like a small meteor hurtled to earth, and he must pry it from the gummy material.

How many more of these warehouse fires will I have to visit before I find her?

He needs to find her; he knows that now.

He needs to tell her, he understands that now.

It isn't sharp, jagged like shattered glass should be. Its edges are blunted, blackened. It is as smooth as a pebble worn by water.

The size of a quarter, it is egg-shaped, perhaps a broken piece of something larger, probably a window in the building that is completely engulfed. Corey turns it in his hands, his hands smudged by the black ash that slicks its surface, and thinks that it looks familiar.

He is close…so close now…

As he rubs the ash aside, Corey sees a flash of color within the glass. Perhaps the window bore a painted sign, the name of a lawyer or the logo of some pharmaceutical firm.

But it's not that…it's not a piece of a window or a cocktail glass. He realizes this as he holds it in the ash-smudged palm of his ruined hand. It pulses with deep purple light, the color of violets…

Amy's eye.

His heart lurches, his hand bursts into white-hot flame. He feels it scorch his palm, melt the glass fragment to slag, which drips to the pavement between his remaining fingers, *plipplipplip*, like the original that this glass one had replaced months ago.

Another tear, shed for him.

She wants him to find her.

He is close…so close now…

He *feels* it.

He feels everything.

Open Mind Night at The Ritz

by Shane McKenzie

The Ritz was the best place to see flesh-benders in the whole city. And Sunday was the day to go, because it was Open Mind Night. Caleb had been showing up for months, planning to show off his Talent, but could never persuade himself to actually get on stage. Especially when he'd have to follow Radical Raymond. Nobody could follow that.

Caleb's hands were slippery and began to shake. He shoved one hand into his pocket and rolled the cube of flesh between his thumb and forefinger. It was a piece of his dead aunt's corpse. The funeral had been a few weeks back, and Caleb had cut a perfect square from her neck; nobody noticed. He'd reached into the coffin, making like he was stricken with grief, then sliced it away, a portion under the collar of her dress, covered it back up before anyone was the wiser. He kept it in his freezer in a plastic baggie to keep it fresh, but every week, he'd fish it out and take it to the Ritz with him, the meat cube thawing out in his pocket. The smell got slightly more potent every time. But he brought it each Sunday, hoping to take it on stage and bend it for the crowd. But he couldn't do it. And every time, as he watched the magnificent display before him by a man that was nothing short of his idol, he knew he'd have to dig deeper into himself than he'd ever had before to find the courage.

Caleb leaned against the bar with his martini in hand, staring at the stage. The condensation on the glass dripped over his fingers, so he wrapped a napkin around it and took a sip. Radical Raymond was putting on quite the show. Caleb could only dream of being as good a flesh-bender as him. He'd known he was meant to be one for a few years, but never had the guts to actually show off his Talent. Not that his Talent was anywhere near Raymond's. None of the flesh-benders he'd seen over the years were as good as Raymond.

Caleb jammed his hand into his pocket to feel for the cube of flesh again. He knew it was there, but his obsessive compulsions guided his hand into his pocket every few minutes or so, just to get that reassurance it hadn't fallen out or that he hadn't been pick-pocketed. His fingers collided with the firm, cold flesh cube, and he fondled it for a moment as he downed the rest of his drink.

"Another martini, friend?" The bartender looked more like an overgrown boy than a man—mid-twenties, gelled hair, tattoos covering his neck and forearms. Caleb nodded and set his glass down. The bartender watched the stage as he prepared the drink. "He's damn good, ain't he?"

"He's amazing."

Radical Raymond sat on a stool at the back corner of the stage, shadows covering him like a second skin. Some of the less Talented flesh-benders held their hands up to their foreheads; some had their digits digging into their temples, trying to look dramatic. But not Raymond. His hands were folded in his lap, one eyebrow raised as he bended the flesh in the middle of the stage, in front of the awestruck crowd.

"He's the best there ever was," Caleb said in a dreamlike state. He turned to find a new drink in front of him and that he'd spoken to himself. The tattooed boy-bartender was flirting with a girl at the other end of the bar, paying no attention to Caleb.

Raymond stood from his stool and plucked his piece of flesh from the stage floor, then bowed to the crowd. They erupted with applause, whistles, stomping, and shouting, all praising the man that had just wowed them with his unequalled ability. Caleb was still reeling from the beauty of the man's art.

The host jumped back on stage, his portly belly stretching his Ritz t-shirt, a mustard stain just above his belly button. His labored breathing was obvious when he spoke. It made Caleb uncomfortable just to watch him.

"How bout that Radical Raymond, huh?" His sweat gleamed under the stage lights, and he took deep breaths to recover from his previous sentence while the crowd gave another round of applause. "And now my friends, we open the stage to you aspiring flesh-benders out there. Don't be shy now."

Caleb willed his legs to move, but they refused to cooperate. They were pillars of stone, bolted to the ground, refusing to obey his brain signals. But to Caleb's relief, an attractive, petite Hispanic girl got on stage.

She bowed to the crowd and stretched her mouth into a smile that dug into Caleb's chest and tunneled to his heart. The girl was breathtaking, intoxicating to look at. Caleb was more than impressed, not only with her beauty, but with her courage to get on stage and follow an act like Raymond's. She'd really have to do something special—none of the old clichés he'd seen a million times. Flesh-bending was an art, and too many wannabes figured they could jump on stage and do it without putting enough thought into it; this wasn't something that just any Joe Schmo could do. You'd have to have the Talent, of course, something given to those special few at birth, but along with that, you had to have creativity, inventiveness.

Shane McKenzie

Caleb's mouth hung open as the girl peeled her shirt from her torso, wearing nothing underneath, and shook her tits at the crowd. Perfect roundness with big, dark nipples, swaying as she tossed the garment into the audience. She bent down and her breasts hung, and when she stood back up, she held a silver knife that she'd unsheathed from her knee-high leather boot.

Then she plunged the blade into her chest. She sawed at the flesh, cutting around the left breast until it ripped free and plopped to the floor, jiggling like molded Jell-O. Blood pumped rhythmically from the gaping wound, yet she only smiled. A real pro, this girl. The crowd reacted with applause, and Caleb wanted nothing more than to be engulfed by her body, swallowed whole by her sex. And not just because of her beauty, but her genius. She was going to bend her own flesh, something Caleb had never thought possible. His pain tolerance was that of a child's, but this woman, half his size, had severed her breast and hardly flinched. She began working at the other.

"Not bad, huh?"

Caleb jumped at the voice beside him, but couldn't peel his eyes from the girl mutilating herself in the name of her Talent.

"It's astounding," he answered back.

"You can say that again."

Caleb had to tear his eyes away from the stage, like a Band-Aid from a festering wound. His level of frustration was on red as he turned, ready to show his displeasure with a hard scowl. But he didn't want to miss a moment of the show; he wanted to continue his gluttonous drinking-in of the gorgeous female bleeding before him. He spun to face the voice, and found Radical Raymond leaning against the bar beside him, sipping the last of a drink, sucking in an ice cube and chewing on it. He turned to Caleb and held out a hand.

"Raymond, nice to meet you."

Caleb almost buckled under the pressure, but he threatened his hand—in his mind—that he would cut it off and bend it on stage if it didn't do his bidding. Thankfully, the hand cooperated and clamped around Raymond's.

"C—Caleb. I'm a huge fan, Mr. Raymond."

"My name isn't 'Mister,' okay? And don't call me 'Radical' either. I didn't come up with that stupid fucking name, the Ritz did. Just Raymond if you don't mind," he said, slamming his empty glass on the bar.

Caleb felt his face glowing like a Christmas light. "Sorry. Can I buy you a drink, Raymond?"

The man raised an eyebrow, one of his signature moves, and looked Caleb up and down. "Just so you know, I like pussy, okay?"

"Yeah, good...I mean...so do I. I'd love to meet that girl," Caleb said as he shifted his attention back to the stage. The girl sat on the same stool that Raymond had, blood still pumping from the open wounds, covering her body like a crimson jumpsuit. She'd bended the flesh of her breasts into a full-sized man and a woman, and her nipples became their sex organs. The man's dark, hard cock pointed at the crowd and they shouted their approval. The other breast, now a woman, lay on her back, the place between her legs as dark as the man's dick. She grabbed her ankles and spread her legs so wide, she could have ripped herself in half. The man reached down and stroked his hardened member, which began sprouting arms and legs as he rubbed it. What was a bulging vein a moment before peeled away and became an arm, sprouting a tiny hand on the end.

Raymond laughed. "Yeah, I'm sure you would, Caleb. She's damn good."

Caleb heard Raymond talking, but his eyes were moths to the bright light on stage. This girl could flesh-bend as good as Raymond, if not slightly better.

The man on stage had a full-blown fetus for a penis, and he got on his knees and plunged it into the woman who shouted her pleasure with each pump. Her stomach began to bulge, more and more with each pelvic thrust from the man. And when her belly was to the point of bursting, the man pulled out, a dark void where the baby-dick once was. The woman reached up and grabbed his head, then shoved it into her sex, all the way to the shoulders. The man's body went limp as she stuffed him in further, opening wide to take his body into hers.

Caleb was speechless with the beauty of it. He glanced toward Raymond to get a glimpse of his reaction.

"She's very Talented, huh, Caleb?" Raymond said, sliding his tongue across his teeth.

"Oh God, yes. I've never seen anything like this…no offense to you mister… uh…Raymond." Caleb shot Raymond an apologetic look. But Caleb's eyes were sucked back to the stage. "You've always been my favorite. I could never bend flesh like you…or her."

Raymond emptied his drink, and as he set it down, the boy-bartender had a fresh one waiting. It seemed as though Radical Raymond was a vodka tonic kind of man, and Caleb pointed to the bartender. "That's on my tab as well."

"You got it, slick."

"So, Caleb. You're a fellow flesh-bender, hmm?" Raymond grabbed the drink and reached into the glass for a cube of ice, which he tossed into his mouth and rolled around before chewing it. "Why haven't I seen you here before?"

The left breast devoured the man with her vaginal maw, but had doubled in size. She stood, facing the crowd, the size of a Sumo wrestler. Dark brown udders ran down the front of her torso, squirting milk at the crowd in pearly streams. They loved it, every one of them, some opening their mouths to catch the precious liquid and taste the art.

"Oh, I've been here before. Lots of times. Just don't think I'm good enough to actually get on that stage," Caleb said, glancing at Raymond. "Especially not after someone like you."

Raymond laughed, slapping the bar and knocking over some of the other patrons' drinks. But none of them noticed; they were hypnotized by the artistic smorgasbord before them.

"Let me see it," he said, slamming his drink in a single gulp.

"I'm sorry?"

"The flesh, give it here."

Caleb already had his hand in his pocket, flicking the cube back and forth from nervousness. He pulled it out and handed it to Raymond.

"You see, this is the problem, Caleb. I can smell the damn thing a mile away. Dead flesh is no good."

The massive woman on stage reached behind her head and unzipped herself, splitting her front wide open. The gorgeous girl on the stool, the genius at work, scrunched her brow, causing the breast-woman's entrails to burst out and whip around like streamers caught in a strong wind. The chaotic flailing ceased as quickly as it began, and the intestines reached out to the crowd, tickling the people in the front row under their chins.

"But…I've always been able to bend it at home…I mean…when I'm practicing alone."

"Yes, Caleb. And I could buy any old cheap pencil for a dime and still draw a picture, right? It's all about the flesh, my boy."

Caleb grinned so hard he nearly tore the corners of his mouth. His idol, the great Radical Raymond, giving him flesh-bending advice. "Thank you so much! But where do I—"

The crowd burst into deafening applause, and when Caleb turned to face the stage, the flesh had morphed back into the severed breasts. The gorgeous artist walked forward and plucked them from the floor, then twisted them back onto her body as if they were jar lids.

A firm grip took Caleb's shoulder and he turned to find Raymond staring intently at him. "All in the flesh, Caleb."

As he said the words, his mouth oozed from his face like melting candle wax. The rest of his body began to liquefy and pool onto the floor, his sparkly stage clothes floating on the surface. A few people in the crowd noticed the commotion, mouths gaping, gasping and murmuring to one another.

Caleb tried to explain that he had no idea what had happened, but his jaw moved up and down with no words to accompany it. He turned to the bartender, ready to accuse him of poisoning the vodka tonics.

But his eye caught the Hispanic female on stage, the girl who had outdone Raymond in her flesh-bending, outdone any person Caleb had ever seen with Talent. She grabbed the skin of her face, wadded it up in her fist like silk, and pulled outward. The crowd turned their attention away from Caleb to witness this miracle of artistic beauty.

She pulled away the skin, discarding it on the stage floor, piled up like soiled linen. And Raymond stood there, stark naked, facing his adoring fans with open arms.

"Amazing," the boy-bartender said from just behind Caleb on the other side of the bar. He'd been slicing limes as the miracle of flesh-bending had unfolded.

Caleb was proud. He knew Radical Raymond was the best there ever was or ever would be. Caleb's smile never left his face, only stretched wider, and he caught Raymond's eye—just the quickest of glances—and he winked.

"He's the greatest," Caleb said, and then reached across the bar to seize the knife from the bartender, pulling it from his slack fingers as he continued to gawk at Raymond, who took his well-deserved bows.

Caleb couldn't let him down. He had to go on stage. Show Raymond that he had true Talent. That he was a flesh-bender. Caleb slammed his hand on the bar and severed his left thumb at the knuckle.

The pain was beautiful.

Footprints Fading in the Desert

by Eric J. Guignard

The footprints in the sand should have been impossible.

And yet they weren't. They were the imprints of bare feet, and Lisa shook her head, groggy and perplexed at their appearance.

She first thought it must be a hallucination, an early morning dream or desire for rescue projected onto this desolate land. But then she crouched down and ran a slender finger through one of the shallow marks. The soft ravine her finger carved in the sand crossed over the footprint, disrupting the indentation of its heel, and then curled up to each toe print, remarkably preserved in that coarse, white grit. The tracks were of human feet, just a little bigger than her own. The left footprints stepped in a normal linear direction, but the right footprints had an odd angle, with slight drag marks at each step, as if that side were lame. The prints were fresh, and she scanned the wide desert for their source, but the steps only shrunk away from her, fading into the soft line of the horizon. Conversely, searching for a destination in the other direction led to the opposite horizon.

Lisa's vision had never been strong and she normally wore gold-rimmed glasses, which were now gone. Her view, already fuzzy, was further hampered by the constant blowing sand, tossed howling and furious through the sky by a hot wind that rarely lulled. Could there be refuge nearby? Some place just beyond her field of vision, close enough that someone could romp about this expanse of barren earth without shoes? She couldn't fathom that was possible, yet those footprints came from somewhere and led elsewhere, against all common sense. Lisa considered the chance of those tracks passing by and then wondered if it were not just someone else stranded in this wasteland as she herself, a misplaced socialite plucked from hotel-top cocktail parties in an irony of the cosmos.

Lisa decided that whether the person was lost, crazy, or just enjoying a midnight stroll while she had slept, she must find the walker. Anything was better than withering away alone under the wreckage.

Fifty feet away lay the twisted and burned remains of the Cessna 172 aircraft. The shattered rear fuselage, resting underneath the shadow of one severed wing, had been her home for the last three days. Away from that (*not far enough away, though she had been too hysterical to go any further*) were two mounds, covered with sand and rocks, each projecting a pair of feet like grim armaments. One grave contained the Cessna's pilot, a salty old redheaded man with bristly whiskers and stagnant breath. He was brought on as a replacement for the regular pilot, who coincidentally also crashed in the desert just the week before; a bad omen indeed for Lisa's flight. The second grave contained her husband, Phil Strancell, entrepreneur and owner of Strancell Technologies. The impact of the crash had split Phil nearly in half, from crotch to neck. Somehow, he lived for almost a full day after the accident, strapped into the co-pilot's seat looking like a snapped turkey wishbone, his organs and arteries held together miraculously by the same portion of torn fuselage that had also performed his grotesque bisection.

Lisa knew she was in the Great Basin Desert, somewhere between Idaho and Nevada or, as Phil likened it, *halfway between Hell and Hades*. The Cessna had nosedived into an ancient fissured lakebed, blanketed under wind-swept sand. There shouldn't have been a mark of civilization for hundreds of miles around to disturb the dotting sagebrush and rolling dunes, yet, looking down at those footprints, Lisa saw hope. Whoever left those tracks came during the night, walking obliviously past the wrecked plane. The desert night was as dead-black as the Cessna's melted tires, and it was impossible to see more than a few feet away.

Within that forsaken land, she'd discovered that another person existed; one who limped past while she fitfully slept. Each night since the crash, she'd rolled back and forth in haunted slumber, dreaming of rescue from her worsening nightmare...though the actualization of her dreams had all the substance of a mirage: The trail of a barefoot man or woman wandering the desert through the dead of night? But the prints were fresh, and they led away from her aircraft crypt. To Lisa, that was motivation enough, and she knew she must follow them.

The morning was young, but time was against her. Lisa would have only a few hours to pursue the tracks until the summer sun began to crush her with its choking, heavy heat. She lacked a thermometer but guessed the daily temperature rose above one hundred ten degrees, and her only comfort was to curse each searing day with a creative lexicon she didn't know she possessed.

She dashed back to the mangled Cessna and packed to leave. Fashioning a hobo's knapsack by looping a cloth seat cover around two broken poles and tying it in place with electrical wire, she filled the sack with the meager food and clothing she'd been able to salvage. She also carried a thin blanket and, most importantly, two plastic eight-ounce water bottles, the last of her one-a-day rationing.

By the time Lisa returned to the footprints, they were already beginning to fade, melting to ghostly imprints that cut into the flat, gritty earth. Wind blew a steady mist of sand, covering the line of tracks as it covered everything else. Lisa jogged quickly along the trail, each of her footfalls leaving marks that mirrored the ones she followed. She looked back only once at the wrecked aircraft, bidding a silent farewell to the graves she was forever leaving behind.

It had been only three days since Lisa's life was split abruptly apart, much as her husband's body had been split. Three long and desolate days of cooking under the desert sun, her skin once moist and fresh, now turning brown and cracked like dried jerky. Before the crash, she'd been napping quietly in the rear passenger seat until a sickening drop in the plane jolted her awake, and her face slammed against the metal ceiling. The plane fell, and she bounced backwards behind the seat in slow motion while trying to remember how to scream. She saw only the backs of Phil's and the pilot's heads. Like Lisa, Phil was silent. He was frozen, and his hands clenched into claws upon the armrests of the co-pilot's chair. The pilot screamed into the radio, "*Oh crap, oh crap, oh crap,*" as if that were the latest lingo for a mayday request. The plane shook apart as it fell from the blue sky. The pilot pounded on dials and struggled with the throttle and almost seemed to bring the craft under control, just before it slammed into the sandy earth below. Lisa blacked out.

Waking groggy, she found herself buried under her seat, a cushion of space surrounded by crumpled metal and fiberglass. Her left shoulder was sliced to the bone, her body a map of swollen bruises. Pulling herself up, the first thing Lisa saw was a large hole in the plane's windshield. The pilot had ejected through it, leaving behind streamers of red flesh across the jagged shards of glass. Her husband still remained, buckled in, and Lisa crawled slowly between the twisted alloy tubing to his side. In shock, she found him alert and staring at her, his chest cleaved into two halves. Even through his injury, Phil could speak and calmly inquired as to Lisa's own health, before politely asking for a drink of water. She tried to unbuckle him, but the crevice in his chest began to split wider open. The seatbelt running crisscross over Phil's body acted as a tourniquet, holding his torso together so its insides didn't spill out like a burst sewage pipe. When he drank the water Lisa brought him, it bubbled out from under his shirt. She shrieked, and Phil spoke, calm and reassuring to the end. Clenching her hand, he declared that someone would come for her, she would be rescued...

Lisa shook her head now, telling herself to focus on the footprints. They were becoming fresher, more pronounced in the sand as she shuffled across, although after hours of walking, her stamina began to falter. She grew weak while the sun grew strong. Heat waves rolled upon the land, blurring her thoughts and vision in watery mirages. The wind, too, punished her, a ceaseless beast that gusted in unnatural flurries like small dervishes. It was not a strong wind, but it blew enough to fill the air always with sand, to scratch her face and dull her vision, and to produce strange ghostly images. The wind was also enough to blow away the footprints she followed, if she did not hurry.

Lisa staggered further until exhaustion forced her to rest. Three days since the crash, with little to eat or drink, had crippled her vigor, while despair chipped away her resolve. She'd followed the footprints into the roasting afternoon, but they still cruelly outpaced her; she couldn't catch up to whoever left them. She wondered if they might stretch forever across that forsaken land, one mysterious leg dragging tirelessly behind the other.

Scattered along the trail, thick sagebrush sprouted from the searing desert, and Lisa selected the largest one to rest beneath. She draped the seat cover from the Cessna atop its grey-green needle branches, creating a semblance of shelter, and collapsed under it. Sipping a water bottle, she moaned lonely bleats and closed her eyes, remembering…

Phil's final hours after the crash had been ones of agony. Not agony for Phil himself, who bore his death sentence as serenely as a Zen monk, but agony for Lisa, who helplessly watched her husband fade away. She wept and lashed out at the wreckage in frustration, and imagined that the vultures circling high in the sky were helicopters searching for them. Phil and she each had cell phones that were shattered and useless, and the plane supposedly contained an emergency beacon that transmitted in cases such as this, but what that really meant, or if it even worked, Lisa did not know. All she knew was that no one came for them. Dying, Phil drifted in and out of consciousness, repeating the same simple message, urging her to stay calm.

"Someone will find you…you will be rescued," he whispered between gasps. "Just stay here. Someone will come to you. People don't go missing in the desert forever."

Phil had said someone would arrive to rescue her, and he'd been right.

As Lisa lay under the sagebrush, a veil of shade passed above her, blocking the burning bright light. Her eyes fluttered open, blinking at the shadow's unexpected presence. Before her stood a man dressed in ragged clothes, tattered as if he'd been pulled through a cyclone. His pant legs were ripped at the knees in long drooping angles, and his waistband held up loosely by frayed suspenders. He wore a button-down shirt, once white perhaps, but now torn and blackened from grime and age. A wide-brimmed hat drooped over the man's head, casting murky shadows across his face. The hat was pockmarked with holes, as if chewed upon by worms and moths.

The man stared down at Lisa, the features of his face fuzzy under the brim of that rotting hat. Sand coated his skin and seemed to float off him like drifting snowflakes. He spoke to her in quiet earnest, his words monotone, yet sincere in their desperation.

233

"My family needs help."

The man's plea left Lisa feeling sick. It was as she feared: the walker was as lost in the desert as she herself. She replied, "I'm sorry...I'm lost out here, too. Our plane crashed and my husband is dead. What—what happened to you?"

With a slow shake of his head, the man spoke in a whisper. "We lost the trail. We was travelling to Oregon territory from Missouri. Gonna farm wheat in the Multnomah Valley, but got turned sideways in a great sandstorm. That was a long time ago. We ain't got no water left, and my children are thirsty."

The man's voice drifted as if borne upon the wind, and dissolved across the vast expanse. Each word formed slowly and creaked from his mouth with a rough texture like coarse gravel grinding upon itself. Lisa shuddered, bewildered. She thought of the impossibility of two lost people finding each other in that desolation, and a sobbing grimace broke free as she imagined the answer.

"Oh, God, am I dead?"

"Dead? No, Miss, sunstroke must be getting to you. Please though, I need your help. My family needs your help."

Lisa coughed hoarsely, suddenly feeling foolish for having asked such a thing. She uncapped a water bottle and took a delicate sip, sucking tenderly at each drop. She looked back to the man, struck again by his face, fuzzy and dark with dirt, outlining foggy eyes that gazed upon her with such appeal. Hesitantly, she offered up the bottle.

"I just have a little bit left, but you can have a drink."

"No, but thank you, ma'am. If you can spare some, please save it for my children."

He stood there, solemn and motionless, staring at her, and she stared back at him, confused and contemplating, until he reached a hand out to help her stand. The movement made Lisa flinch. She declined his assistance and stood on her own.

"Come with me," he said. "They're this way."

The man set off, walking through the sand, and only then did Lisa note his feet. They were bare and gnarled, blistered from treading unprotected over the burning earth. He walked with a limp, and she observed as he strode away how each footprint in the sand was formed. The thousands of empty prints she had followed were now filled. The left leg stepped strong, compensating for the weaker right leg, which twisted slightly and stepped at an odd angle. After several yards he paused and turned gravely back to her.

"Please, we must hurry."

That voice again, gravelly and hoarse, flat as the desert land, but whispered light as the air. Apprehensive, Lisa followed.

They walked for hours. Lisa proceeded slowly, staggering under the pounding sun. She needed to rest often, and the man always waited for her. He never seemed to need rest of his own, and only after several minutes of her sitting motionless, would he quietly urge her on again, pleading that she must hurry. They continued hiking under the blazing sun and through the clouds of sand. Lisa followed each footprint that formed in front of her, until fatigue wore her down.

"I can't go on," she panted.

"We're almost there. They're waiting over yonder."

He pointed to a steep dune rising before them. Lisa grimaced, but commanded her legs to keep moving, forcing each to lift just one more time, and then once again after that. She plodded up the dune behind him, trembling in exhaustion.

Rising over the crest of the dune, she saw wagons below. They were skeletal remains, as if beached whales had inexplicably rotted away in that dry land. Bleached bows rose like arched ribs above the desert floor, their wood cracked and withered from exposure to the elements. The wagon carcasses sat in a semicircle, three of them decaying in unison, with each frame tilted low and borne by many-spoked wheels. Lisa knew those wagons were very old, like the Conestogas pulled by oxen or horses she often saw in spaghetti western movies. The man walked down the dune to the nearest one and motioned for her to join him.

Lisa trailed him to the wagon and saw four skeletons propped against its slumped sideboard. Each skeleton was smaller than the one to its left, as if a row of children were lined up in successive ages. She cried out in sorrow.

Nearby, another skeleton, this one full-sized, lay sprawled on its back and half-buried under the drifting grit. It wore the tattered remains of a calico dress, and Lisa could only imagine the mother's grief of watching each of her children wither away and die like poisoned flowers. The skeletons were rotten and crumbling with age, but each skull was positioned so that it looked expectantly at the dune Lisa and the man had just climbed over.

"Please, can you help them?" he asked. His voice sounded again as a haunting whisper drifting on the wind.

"Them?" Lisa replied, pointing in horror to the collected bones waiting in the sand. "This is your family?"

"Yes, they need help. They need water. I swore to them I would come back, that I'd bring help."

Lisa covered her mouth to stifle a rising scream and backed away from the strange, pleading man. Past the first wagon's remains more battered skeletons lay in similar postures of demise. They wore chaps and boots, all with hollow eye sockets staring sightlessly at the crest of the dune, waiting for the man's return.

She staggered from the wagons, struggling through sand that sucked at her feet and blew into her eyes. Clawing at the air, Lisa tried to flee, only to abruptly trip upon something half-buried in the earth. The scream escaped then, as she fell. Her ankle twisted with a sickening pop and, attempting to rise, she found her leg could no longer support her.

When Lisa saw what tripped her she screamed again, scrambling at the ground to crawl away.

Another skeleton protruded from its grave of sand, although it was not as ancient as the others. Aviator goggles hung around its serrated neck and a torn leather cap adorned the skull, resembling a World War One pilot. Like the dead of the wagon train, this corpse stared toward the crest of the dune, one bony white arm raised above its brow, forever shielding from the sun's blinding rays as it lay waiting.

Lisa wailed at her crippled ankle while a gust of sand blew past, then cleared. She dropped her head and crawled on hands and knees from the pilot's bones. She moved like this until her hand pushed upon another skeleton half-screened by the bleached earth. The sob that broke free as she jerked away was equal parts disgust and despair. The carcass was dressed in high-waisted jeans, with chains and cuffs rolled up to showcase two-tone Keds sneakers, baking under the endless sun. Patches of its crisp dark hair remained, piled high in the style of Elvis or James Dean.

A wild frenzy overtook Lisa. She wanted to flee, to escape this scene of horror, though her impulse for flight was immediately countered by a sense of submission, as she wondered where she could possibly go. Behind her, the strange man did not give chase, but remained motionless by the first wagon, watching her without expression. Lisa's mind raced to understand, to unravel this puzzle. How could an aviator and a 1950s greaser be found amongst a wagon train from the 1800s? Had others become lost in this terrible land by coincidence and wandered upon the wagons' remains, only to perish there themselves?

As if in response, the wind calmed and the flying sand cleared, and she saw there were many more.

Beyond the Elvis-kid's remains lay another skeleton, this one slender and wearing lime-green pedal pushers and a tarnished peace symbol necklace. Past that were row upon row of the dead, circling around the wagon train. She saw one corpse finely dressed in a tattered pinstripe suit that fluttered in the breeze to reveal an old gangster's revolver. Another body wore the unfortunate attire of a Victorian-era's stiff velvet dress. To wear drapery like that out here was madness... yet nothing about this desert made any sense. The next skeleton wore the fatigues of an infantry soldier, while beside it lay bones in a prisoner's uniform, serial number etched across its breast.

The worst was a dead man in Bermuda shorts and polo shirt sprawled on his side. He was not a skeleton yet, and Lisa could still make out mottled features, partly hidden underneath Oakley sunglasses. The corpse was in the process of decomposing, and the rotting flesh cooked under the sun while insects and lizards feasted on it.

All the dead stared at the crest of the dune, each waiting for the man she met to bring back help. He calmly appeared next to her, his quiet stride betrayed only by clouds of dust kicked up by each step.

He asked, "Please, can you help them?"

"I can't help them, I can't help them!" Lisa sobbed. "I'm dying too…I need help, don't you see? I'm dying out here, like all of them—" She broke off with a wail.

The walker's expression changed. He looked down at Lisa in grief, sympathizing at her incapacity. She too needed help, and her words repeated the unendurable plight of his past. His sinking eyes flickered black and white, and he knelt to her. The man took Lisa's hands solemnly into his own, so that her fingers were buried deep within his firm and gritty grasp. She felt sand moving beneath his skin, flowing deep through the veins and arteries of his being. It was cold, unlike the sand of the desert that burned hot to the touch.

"Please, then you must wait here. I will go out and find someone to help us." He gently brushed back a loose lock of hair that fell across her brow. "I make this oath to you, that I will not rest until I have found rescue for us all."

Lisa nodded, gazing into his face, her only hope.

"I must leave now to search. Wait here. I'll be back, and I will bring help. I'll return over that rise." He pointed at the crest of the dune he so recently had led her across.

"I swear it," he whispered solemnly, and Lisa knew he was a man who kept his promises.

The man stood, sand dripping from his arms, dust floating from his mouth, and turned to trek back up the dune. Lisa wondered how many times before had he left? How many times had he sought rescue in others, only to find they too were lost and wandering in hopeless despair? How many years of searching the desolate wasteland had it taken to wear off the very boots he once walked in? Someday he would find help, he would never cease until rescue was brought to her and those others lost in the desert.

The man walked away, slowly and eternally, his twisted right leg dragging with each limp step. He left a fresh set of tracks in the sand as he departed, rising up and over the dune's crest. She lay there waiting, as the sun melted to moon and was born back again. She lay there staring at the dune and watched as his footprints faded in the desert.

The Vulture's Art

by Benjamin Kane Ethridge

Taking the baby to the desert wasn't crazy. Hardly surprising, Jeff's family thought differently. Since that terrible night in the delivery room, emotional family members tiptoed around his feelings, the nonconfrontational avoided him completely, and the bewildered offered tough love. Yet, with the baby, everybody was on the same page: he wouldn't be able to raise her alone—just look at the stupid decisions he was making already.

People treated the psychologically wounded with an odd xenophobia that granted them license to say things like, "This too will pass," "This will not kill you, but give you strength," "It'll be hard, but you'll weather this storm," and of course, Jeff's mother's favorite speech, "You have little Rose to think of now. Remember her. Remember that baby has a whole life ahead of her and you need to be there. Kim wouldn't have wanted you to mope around forever."

It hadn't been forever, though. Not even close. The baby was only five months old. And Kim was only five months dead. With the world outside the tragedy, there were no in-betweens. Extremes were in abundance, though, and frankly, Jeff had had enough of those to last him a lifetime.

During his annual vacation, he didn't want to stick around the condo where all of Kim's belongings sprung out of closets to sabotage him. And he didn't want to go on the cruise with his parents—he and Kim did that same Mexican Riviera deal for their honeymoon. Jeff just wanted to take Rose somewhere left untouched by the world. The cabin had running hot and cold water, heater and A/C, filled refrigerator, cable TV, and a bed. The property manager also set up a crib in the guest room.

For over a month Jeff had daydreamed about those boulders lit pink from the setting sun. Anza Borrego had been his favorite place as a kid, and he hoped that any memories Rose formed would plant the same naturalistic awe deep in her mind.

Maybe later. For now, the baby slept peacefully in her car seat.

The cabin was eight miles off the main road outside the state park. Jeff worried whether the road's increasingly deep ruts would wake Rose. She'd had two restless nights (along with Jeff) and this was finally the sleep she needed. Luckily the cabin soon came into sight. A turkey vulture glided around the area. *Great,* Jeff thought. Hopefully whatever died wasn't close enough to stink up the house.

He put the car in park and glanced back. Rose's head remained cocked to the side, a diamond of slobber in the corner of her mouth. Lord, she was heartbreaking. Seeing her sound asleep made him worry about whether she was still breathing or not. At home he'd woken her a couple times when he nervously pressed his ear to her chest, questioning the obvious pulse of her heart. To think, without the frequencies of that little organic pump, that relatively simple muscular device, his own heart would surely twist shut—there would be no need to go on.

As quietly as possible, he got out and detached the traveler car seat with Rose in it. She stirred slightly as he climbed the dusty wooden steps. It took him a minute to find the key that management had given him. The lock and hinges had been oiled and the door opened without a sound.

The cabin was nice and big. Upstairs were two neatly arranged bedrooms with no frills: bed, dresser and wastebaskets, and an adjoining bathroom. The living area was warm looking—a rustic carpet, solid wood furniture, fireplace and big screen TV mounted over the mantle. The kitchen had black and white checkerboard tile and pale marble countertops.

He placed the car seat down by the coffee table. There was a pine candle near the edge, so he moved it to the table's opposite side, away from the baby. He went back outside. The brand new Expedition, now road-filthy, hummed and clicked as its engine cooled. The back hatch sighed as he lifted it. With great care, he moved the aluminum suitcase with the shotgun to the back seat. His brother Bill had talked him into the gun after frightening him about snakes invading the house. Jeff had never seen a snake out here in his many past visits, but it was worth the protection. He loaded up his arms and turned back for the cabin.

The vulture from earlier lighted nosily on a cell phone tower. The tower was made to look like a scraggly palm tree, possibly to preserve desert aesthetics. It was a sturdy tower, and Jeff was confident even large carrion-eaters could do it no harm. With the vulture watching him, he went back and forth with several loads. On his last trip, box of diapers and toy bag in hand, he halted a moment, studying the bird. The vulture's face was indistinct, just a slash of red atop black shoulders, and the beak wasn't apparent at this vantage. What was apparent was a bulbous paunch that hung low from the bird's midsection.

"Good eating around here," Jeff said.

The vulture lowered its red head, slowly.

Five days here will be enough, he decided, shutting the door, bolting it. A missed text had come through an hour earlier from his mother. Jeff scrolled down. It was a link to an article about the rise of delivery deaths from amniotic fluid embolisms. She always sent him this shit. It wasn't that his mother was purposely insensitive, but she wanted him to feel less alone in all this. She didn't realize that he wanted to feel alone, if only for a week.

Jeff unzipped his duffel to take out a new pair of jeans. Rose rocked inside the traveler. Her gray eyes fluttered open and a smile hit her lips with a suddenness that had him smiling also. They stared at each other for a moment, father and daughter, the only thing that mattered now. Rose licked her lips and glanced around. She had on her hungry face. He was starting to know those faces well.

"One bottle coming up."

On his way to the powdered formula, he stopped cold. He'd forgotten the nursery water. It was on the passenger seat.

He went down the porch and almost slipped on a small gray thing. A hatchling desert tortoise struggled to swim through the brown-red sand. It had a pattern on its shell plates that almost resembled a smiley face.

Jeff moved his eyes to the pseudo palm tree. The fat vulture wasn't there anymore.

Rose made a long mumbling sound from inside. He had to hurry. He moved the tortoise off the road into the shadow of a rough surfaced rock. *Taking care of all the babies around here.* Jeff dusted off his hands and made for the Expedition.

* * *

Watching the video monitor brought to mind the baby shower in Victorville. Kim hadn't wanted to put the baby monitor on the store registries, because it was too expensive, and especially since it was presumptuous this child would actually come to be, after four other miscarriages. But Jeff bought the monitor anyway because he believed with every loss, Kim gained determination. It'd been a struggle to get pregnant, a struggle to carry a child past the second month, and the last pregnancy had ended in the third trimester. He didn't think anyone, including himself, could bounce back after that, least of all a woman who insisted on blaming herself. But that day, Kim's face had turned to him, apple shaped with high cheekbones ripe with blush, and her eyes nearly misted. *Nearly*, because Kim would seldom cry. "You got the monitor?" she'd said.

God, how that moment had made Jeff feel good. He'd done the right thing, the best thing possible. After years of being with Kim, he'd realized that was difficult for a man to do. Too dumb or too oblivious, he never felt as though he could do anything right.

A thrashing against the cabin scattered his thoughts. Jeff shot up from under the cool sheets. He leaned over to the windowsill. There was a bright halogen light on the porch. Under its manipulation, the desert floor crawled like gray television static. A shape moved off the hood of the Expedition, then was gone. Jeff waited a few minutes, trying to see. Probably that damn buzzard. After a moment, he drew away from the window and dropped back down in bed.

A feeling of panic tightened around him, as it always did now when he couldn't go straight to sleep. Time to face it—that's what coming out here was all about. Jeff would raise the baby alone. He'd have help, but largely, it all rested on his shoulders. *Alone.* He knew the terror of that reality would subside when he went to sleep. Kim was in his dreams, and in them her being alive seemed so... natural, like the idea of her death had been precisely sliced from his mind. Yet sometimes he had flashbacks to that hallway in labor and delivery. Things crashed down; terror and misery and a resounding numbness that dubiously questioned it all. When Kim had started to code, some doctor in blue scrubs, a powder blue assassin, pushed him out the door, incomprehensible words flowing beyond that surgical mask, from which later, in that hall, that horrible fucking hall, Jeff would try—for the love of Christ—to derive meaning.

He never had.

"Stop," he muttered and breathed slow to calm his heart. "Just stop it... stop."

What if it had been both of them? Rose and Kim.

Stop it. Just stop!

What if you'd refused to try for another child? Kim would still be alive.

The pillow under his face was wet. He refused to turn it over, though. He'd like to sleep in his tears for a while longer. They were for Kim, and in a way, for the grayscale baby gently sucking her pacifier on the monitor's screen.

Jeff wasn't as strong as Kim. But now he had to be. His whole life would be for Rose. Raising her the right way, yes, that would get him through this pain. He'd get out of debt with the life insurance and save for Rose's first car, her college, and maybe the down payment on a house when she got married.

The last was too depressing of a thought to endure. Losing Rose from his life someday. His last piece of Kim. He'd be so much less useful when Rose had someone else in her life. He'd be the old gray face that showed up on holidays and birthdays, and then afterward he'd be alone in his empty house. How else could it be? He didn't have the courage to ever marry again; he knew that better than anything else. Solitude was his destiny and such ideas put Jeff over the top.

And so he slept.

* * *

In a riptide of diaper changes, bottle preparation, and naps, the next day pulled into dusk. Rose had taken only catnaps and her sleep would be deep tonight. No early morning surprises like yesterday when she'd taken a Thanksgiving Day shit.

That reminded Jeff that he needed to get his anti-bacterial gel from the car.

At once, he heard a tearing sound from outside. It was abrasive, like packing tape being pulled off. Jeff squinted, not believing his eyes. Off to the side of the car, in the scrub, a large tortoise rested upside down, leathery legs splayed. The turkey vulture dipped its beak down and ripped a piece of snotty flesh from the side of the turtle's sagging head. The shelled reptile looked withered and ancient, and from what Jeff knew of tortoises, that could mean over one hundred years old.

Repulsed, he stormed loudly down the stairs, threw his arms forward and shouted, "Blah!"

The vulture's gait shifted only a little and it went for another bite.

"Blah!" he said again.

With that the bird flew off. It glided back to the cellular palm tree, which seemed to be its home.

Jeff approached the tortoise and shook his head at the massacred throat and the black rheumy eyes. "Poor old guy," he said. "Live all those years, for this." *Could this be a female?* Maybe that little baby from yesterday had crawled out of her eggs nearby. Pretty old looking tortoise to have children, though.

He managed to turn it over but it was too damned heavy and awkward. Lifting the tortoise into the dumpster would not be possible, he soon found out. The best he could manage was covering it with an old blanket. He'd have to report it to the property manager and have them deal with it. Once he was certain the edges were tucked under securely, he grabbed his hand sanitizer from the car and squirted some into his palms. Thinking about it now, that tortoise had the same smiley face pattern on its back that the baby had. Perhaps they were related after all.

Rose was awake when he got back inside.

* * *

During naptime the next day, he woke from a dream about Kim's funeral. It seemed like a retelling of that day, but that turkey vulture was there, perched on a headstone in the old section of graves. The bird had gray dust on its beak. Jeff awoke as he connected the idea that Kim had been cremated.

He was still dwelling on the dream later that evening. After a bottle of chardonnay, he wasn't really asleep yet, just drifting, listening to the monitor, to the breathing, soft baby snores, and the whispering. The words were sharp but light, bladed feathers falling into the eardrum, seesawing on the air, razor-slicing the ear canal as they fell.

Jeff cracked an eye. On the monitor, something dark covered the screen. "What the shit?" He slid off the couch and slammed his funny bone on the table. Gritting his teeth at the deep pain, he scrambled upstairs. The door was not shut completely, only cracked—he rushed through. Over the baby, talons wrapped around the cherry wood frame, the vulture perched, beak inches from Rose's ear. Jeff grabbed the first thing he saw, a Grover doll, and hurled it. The vulture had already turned for departure and the doll struck it in the back as it flew for the torn screen. A few black feathers came loose as it awkwardly regained itself and flapped off into the desert void.

Softly whining, Rose twisted back and forth. She'd somehow burst free of her swaddling blanket. Jeff pushed out the torn screen and slammed the window shut. He carried the baby into his room, a safer room. She was getting so heavy lately. Growing so fast. He imagined Kim yelling at him in that cracking, stressed-out voice she'd sometimes harness, *Why aren't you checking the baby? Check the baby!* Jeff put Rose down on his bed. Her eyes were open and expression perplexed. Jeff checked her for bleeding. His handling made her cry but his mind raced too fast to hear her pleas. He'd wanted to bring her out to the cabin because nobody gave them time alone. They all thought he wanted their company. But Jeff only wanted to be alone so he could deal with this...this goddamn calamity his life had been made into.

And to do that he'd brought Rose into a dangerous place. Why did he leave that window open? *It was a warm night. No! You don't leave windows open! You were drunk and stupid.* Yes, he was a fucking idiot.

"I'm so stupid, I'm sorry, so sorry, goddamn it if you're hurt," he told the baby, who'd stopped crying and acutely regarded him through tear-streaked eyes.

Something was wrong with her.

Something about Rose had changed. Her eyes were no longer gray—they were a deep brown. She had hair. Lots and lots of hair, blonde like her mother's. Jeff took a step back, hand quivering to his mouth, mind questioning his drunkenness. Rose's body was even larger. He hadn't noticed at first, not in his hysteria, but it was plain.

The baby on the bed looked over a year old.

* * *

Jeff had nearly everything packed in the car before sunrise. The desert, once his special childhood refuge, had the look of a wasteland about to dissolve under the final blow of atomic war. Hot red energy from the escaping morning sunlight struggled in each rock and boulder. Something evil had come into Rose's bedroom and now he had to answer for it. But how?

He called his parents, and when that didn't go through, he texted them. They were floating on the Mexican Riviera, oblivious. Jeff had inspected Rose almost every waking moment since the attack and he saw no other change. His mind started questioning reality. He didn't know much about babies, but he knew his daughter. He could tell when diapers changed scent or when her eczema scarcely changed. This wasn't natural. He knew that. But if he could just find someone to tell him he's crazy, he'd feel so much better. Maybe Kim's death had happened much longer ago—maybe he'd mentally buried months in his emotional trauma.

Whatever the hell this was, he'd assembled and loaded the shotgun right away and kept it close while he packed. Rose hadn't figured how to walk yet, but rocked sideways on a quilt in the living area, intrigued by her newfound muscle power. It had taken him over an hour to feed her. The formula wasn't cutting it. He was hoping she'd knock out but it wasn't the same as with five-month-old Rose.

They were ready to go just as the sun passed over the top of the hills. The driver's side door screeched as it opened. *Cheap steel.* Rose hardly fit in her traveler car seat, legs dangling over the side, arms pumping her body up and down in the restraints like a lunatic. What had happened to his baby girl? What had that monster done to her?

Jeff took off down the road, furiously kicking up pebbles and dust. He eased off the gas a little. The engine struggled. Gradually the temperature gauge sped up into the red zone. They got about a mile down the road when the SUV seized and rolled to a stop.

"Of course this would happen," he said and fought a nasty curse at the back of his tongue. Rose had her hand in her mouth. She suddenly cried when she bit herself with her new teeth. "Hold on baby." He reached under the dashboard and popped the hood.

Jeff knew nothing about cars. The Expedition's inner workings were a mess of dusty mechanical things he didn't plan to ever understand. He struck the side of the car with his palm. The engine compartment had looked so clean at the dealership. The desert dirt must have kicked up and made the mess—but some of the dirt looked crusty and old.

"Fuckin new car. Nothing's made good anymore. Nothing!"

The baby squealed and he clenched his eyes together at the sound. He went for the owner's manual. The glove box dropped open quickly and he noticed cracks in the plastic. After inspecting the contraption for a long moment, he looked around. Like with the glove box, there were cracks up and down the leather upholstery, and a piece of vinyl peeled away from under the dashboard. Confusion took his breath away. He dragged his eyes to the odometer. 333,657 miles. He blinked and shook his head, then reflexively glanced at his watch.

He popped up in his seat when his cell phone blared. *Unknown caller.* It could be Billy, who had a landline with caller ID shutoff, or it could be his parents from Mexico. He answered and got a voice cloaked in static.

"Mom?" he said. "You're breaking up. I need help. Help me please. I'm at the cabin, just down the road. I'm going into town. Something's wrong with Rose—"

The voice on the line warbled and droned for a moment. Then he heard the chanting. The whispers he'd heard through the monitor the night before. The vulture's whispering…Jeff pulled the phone away from his ear, aghast, then yelled into the phone, "What is this? Who is this?"

A piece of plastic nearly caught him in the eye. The cell phone's frame crumbled to pieces in his hand; the screen grew long cracks and the circuit board and other components fell into his lap. He hadn't even put any pressure on the device.

In the rearview he noticed bold gray streaks at his temples. He leaned closer. Several forehead wrinkles he'd never seen before had cut into his flesh. Jeff adjusted the mirror, slowly, to get a view back to the cabin. With a casual expansion of its shadowy wings, the vulture took flight off the cell phone tower.

* * *

Jeff hadn't convinced himself earplugs would protect them from the vulture's unutterable sounds, but it was better than nothing. Rose immediately pulled hers out. They hadn't really fit inside her small ear canals anyway. Jeff put a pair into his ears and thought about what to do next. The shotgun rested across his lap. It was surreal to see it out, assembled, in his hands. Jeff hated guns. Hated that people could easily hurt other people and animals. Take lives. But this was necessary. It made him feel alive and good, not resolved from his recent failings, but good.

They would head out on foot at first light with a backpack filled with water bottles. The park was less than ten miles away. It would be a hike, and it would be difficult with Rose, but it could be done.

Jeff would shoot every bird that came near them.

Rose was sobbing. Following one fit of disoriented planning, he'd left some of the formula in a box on the porch. It was stupid, he knew, but at the time he just wanted to get them through the door. Rose's volume increased. That trek from the Expedition had been terrifying. He figured the vulture would swoop down and peck out their brains, right there. Then when they got inside, he wondered if that thing could chant to the cabin and make all the wood rot, bringing the roof down on them. Rose screamed in confused terror. The baby's pleas echoed off the cabin ceiling, stabbing his eardrums. The vulture had destroyed his car, his phone—made them brittle with age. *It's bringing us closer to death and it closer to mealtime.* Jeff scrubbed at his eyes as Rose whimpered before another scream. The bawling sounded like calls from the slaughtered. Jeff had carried weakness with him almost nonstop for five months now.

"All right!" he cried out suddenly. Rose's screams had penetrated through the invisible walls he'd put up. Because he'd never before grown frustrated with her, she responded to his panicked tone by frowning deeply and wailing. Jeff held her, her heart beating with his. "I'll go out and get your formula, okay, but you're not coming little girl."

Before he could talk himself out of it, he carried Rose to the closet, put her in a sitting position under a few old lady coats hanging there. There was no lock, so he grabbed a high back chair from the table and tucked it under the handle, just in case she figured out the knob. She was particularly quiet, which concerned him.

Better get moving before you traumatize her, asshole.

Shotgun over his arm, Jeff went outside. The can of formula was in sight, along with a sleeping bag and some other stuff he grabbed in his terror. As he made his way over, he caught sight of something moving in the night. Jeff opened his eyes to their limit, tried to soak up the darkness, process it, read the evil in it. The vulture was there. It was picking at the blanket covering the dead tortoise.

He took each stair, careful not to make a sound. He had to get close enough. His brother had taken him out to the fields to shoot before. Jeff hadn't liked it at the time, but now he felt the experience had served him well. Closer, he went on, the vulture scuttling a bit to the side, perhaps aware of him. Jeff took his chance. He aimed at the feathered thing. He squeezed the trigger. The kick sent him back a few steps and a stinging bruise instantly formed in his armpit. Thankfully the earplugs saved his hearing.

Darkness spread out in front of him. He hurried to see if he'd hit it. There was a wash of blackness around the heap of blanket. Hopefully there were scattered feathers and blood. Jeff approached and peered over the side of the tortoise's shape. Something shattered in the cabin. Three stabs of pain went from his bicep to his neck. The vulture had landed on his shoulder, its beak parted, black tongue clucking inside, the alien chants rolling out with lethal swiftness. *Toptoptoptop-teep-toptoptop-teep-toptoptop.* His earplugs hardened and burst and the hideous stream of words ran into his soul, just as that doctor's voice had that night when Kim left him. That which had denied him a part of his life was doing it again. So deadly and familiar.

He snatched the bird by its throat, and swung it over his shoulder, slamming it to the dirt. There was a loud snap of bone, and a half-squawk, and the vulture went silent. His reaction surprised him but the result didn't satisfy him. He'd dropped his shotgun in the struggle, but now he ripped it up from the ground, desert dirt coming with it in his hand. He drove the stock down into the tiny head, three wet times. The air smelled like a barnyard of forged copper, moist feathers, and standing blood.

The cabin window suddenly exploded in yellowed, brittle shards, like glass from the window of a long dead cathedral. Dark shapes flapped up through the jagged opening. His mind reeled. He ran. The word *no* beat into his brain. He couldn't think to breathe but his body needed it. The coughing fit tasted bloody. The taste didn't register.

Two obese vultures hunkered at the closet. One stuck its beak down at the bottom of the door, chanting…chanting…chanting. This one's voice a bit deeper. *Topetopetope-toop-toop-topetopetope.* He didn't want to think about how the words sounded like tumors growing, as though that could even have a sound. Not just tumors. All cells, every cell. The expansion made him want to scream until he blacked out. The other vulture suddenly pulled at the stuck chair at the closet with its fine, flesh-tearing beak.

Jeff yelled through the chanting words but the strength of their cadence overwhelmed any sounds that came from his throat. Each syllable ripped something away from his spirit. He took aim.

The first shot simultaneously killed the closest bird and maimed the other, sending it backward on a feathery surf of gore. It squawked and thrashed, grounded for life, on the way to its death. It opened its beak, *teeeeeep*—buckshot blew it apart, peppering the wooden stairwell. Jeff took another shell from his pocket. Filled the barrel. Finished the other vulture.

The second shot rang loud in his naked ears. A woman's scream peeled out from the closet. The gun thumped on the wooden floor and he choked on his terror. The sound of the scream overwhelmed him. His stomach turned over. She made incomprehensible sounds, the mewling of a trapped animal.

"Rose," he breathed, his body quivering. He kneeled before the closet and dropped his forehead against the door. Some of the coats in the closet screeched on their hangers as Rose backed away from the sound. Jeff mumbled and sobbed and fought with his own mind. It took him a long time to gain control.

Sometime late that night, Jeff limped to the closet and let the woman out.

The Happiness Toy

by Ray Garton

The woman standing on the porch carried a large black satchel, and although Lisbeth had never seen her before, she smiled as if they were old friends.

"Hello, there!" she said in a voice as sweet as her round face. Bright blue eyes perched atop apple cheeks and white teeth glimmered between smiling red lips. Her golden hair was short and bobbed and she wore colorful clothes. She was quite plump, with red nails on her pudgy fingers. "How is your day going?"

Lisbeth felt her brow tense in a slight frown. "I'm...good. Are you selling something?"

"Only happiness."

Lisbeth nodded. "You come to tell me about Jesus, then?"

The woman's smile faltered. "Jesus? Oh, no, no, not that. I don't do religion. No, I meant what I said about happiness." The smile returned as she lifted the bag and patted it with her hand. "I got it right in here. Do you have a few minutes?"

Lisbeth had no interest in buying anything, whatever it was, but she was tempted to invite the woman in anyway. It would be nice to have a conversation with someone, to hear a voice that wasn't on the TV or the radio, or that wasn't Mama's. But Mama didn't like having strangers in the house.

"I, um, really don't think so," she said apologetically.

"Oh, come on, I won't take much of your time, I promise. And it'll be fun." The woman tipped forward and lowered her voice to a conspiratorial whisper. "Don'tcha wanna see what I got in the bag?"

"Well, I, um...I—I—I—"

The woman looked serious for a moment as she reached out and put her hand on Lisbeth's shoulder. Lisbeth saw it coming, but the contact still made her jerk. She wasn't accustomed to being touched. By anyone. "Look, honey, no offense, but I can tell you could use a little happiness." She dropped her hand. "Besides, I'd appreciate a cold drink. It's awfully hot out here."

248

It wouldn't hurt to bring the poor woman in out of the miserable August heat for a little while. She stepped aside and said, "Come in."

"Thank you," the woman said, entering the house. "I'm Sunny."

You sure are, Lisbeth thought.

As Lisbeth led her toward the kitchen, she noticed Sunny looking around the room with an arched brow. They never had guests, so it seldom occurred to Lisbeth how odd and even creepy the decor was—all the crucifixes and pictures of a dying Jesus, especially the big one over the fireplace with all its bloody, gory details.

"I hope I didn't offend you when I said I don't do religion," Sunny said as they entered the kitchen. "Because someone here obviously does."

"No, you didn't offend me. Would you like some ice tea?"

"That would be wonderful!"

Nodding toward the table, Lisbeth said, "Have a seat."

They were soon facing each other at the table over tall glasses of ice tea.

"Mama's pretty religious."

"Your mother lives with you?"

"Well, it's more like...I live with her. She's old and pretty sick. I take care of her and...everything else around here."

"What's wrong with her?"

Lisbeth paused to listen for the sound of Mama moving around. She had a habit of quietly leaving her room, hobbling through the halls and sneaking up on Lisbeth when she least expected it. When she heard nothing, she lowered her voice and said, "What's not wrong with her? It's a long list. She's old. She had me pretty late in life, and I was...unexpected."

"I'm sorry. Like I said, you could use some happiness, darlin'." She winked, reached down and opened her bag on the floor. "You don't have a boyfriend."

Lisbeth sniffed, sipped her tea, then shook her head briefly.

"And you don't date much."

She stared down at her drink, not sure how to respond. She didn't want to come off as pathetic. But it was probably too late for that. When she was a teenager, the girl who lived next door used to say that Lisbeth had a "cloud of pathetic" floating around her, like the dust that followed Pigpen everywhere in the *Peanuts* cartoons. The other neighbor kids always had a laugh at that.

"I know, I know. You've never been on a date." Sunny reached across the table and patted Lisbeth's forearm comfortingly. "That's okay, honey."

Lisbeth began to feel uncomfortable. These weren't questions. She glanced at Sunny, wondering if perhaps they'd met, if they knew each other from somewhere.

"Know what I sell? Toys. For grown-ups. Do you know what I mean?"

Lisbeth frowned, squinted slightly and shook her head again.

Sunny giggled and lowered her voice to a whisper. "Sex toys."

Lisbeth's frown deepened as she tried to imagine what a "sex toy" would be. She knew it was something that would send Mama into a rage because it included the word "sex," but beyond that, she was at a loss.

Sunny said, "You know...dildos? Vibrators?"

Lisbeth's frown did not waver. She slowly turned her head from side to side.

"You're not familiar with sex toys? At all?"

"No, I'm afraid not. And if Mama wakes up and decides to come out of her room, you'll have to go, because if she hears us talking about sex, she'll get really upset."

"Don't worry about Mama, honey. This is none of her business. This is just for *you*." She sipped her tea, then locked her hands together on the table and her thumbs fidgeted with one another. Finally, she said, "You're 31, right?"

"How'd you know?"

"I'm very perceptive." Her eyes moved over Lisbeth's face and upper body.

It made her self-conscious. She knew what she looked like. Depending on her mood, what she saw when she looked in the mirror fell somewhere on the spectrum between plain and hideous. Since Lisbeth had been a teenager, Mama often said, "It's *good* that you're ugly. Salvation will be easier if you're ugly. Beauty brings temptations. Pretty women are sinful women. God did you a favor when he gave you that cleft palate at birth. The scar it left behind will keep the men away. And that's as good as keepin' the sin away."

Sunny said, "Have you...well, *ever* had a boyfriend?"

Lisbeth shook her head.

"Not even in high school or college?"

"I was home-schooled. And I didn't go to college."

Sunny pressed her lips together as her eyebrows rose. "Well. I won't bother with my usual spiel then. We'll just get straight to the hard stuff." She chuckled. "So to speak." She set her drink aside and lifted the black bag onto the table. "I don't show this to everyone. I'm very...intuitive, you might say. I know—I just *know*—who needs what I'm selling." She reached into the bag and fished around. "And *this*...is what *you* need."

She removed from the bag a smooth, flesh-pink tube of floppy rubber that was flat at one end, rounded at the other. It was about six or seven inches long. Even though she wasn't in the room with them, Lisbeth could hear what Mama would say:

Get that thing out of here! That's a phallus! That's the root of all evil, not money or the love of it! Put it away right this second!

"Now, I bet you can guess what this is for," Sunny said, smiling playfully as she held the ersatz organ in her fist and flopped it back and forth.

Lisbeth could imagine. But the very thought made her face feel hot and her chest tighten with guilt.

"You masturbate, right?" Sunny said.

Lisbeth averted her eyes.

Sunny giggled. "Darlin', it's nothing to be ashamed of. We *all* masturbate. Even the people who say they don't. That includes your mama, believe it or not."

Lisbeth already knew that. In the last year, she'd caught Mama playing with herself a few times. She blamed it on Mama's worsening dementia. Lisbeth had been masturbating since she was a girl. Discussing it bothered her far more than actually doing it. She found it difficult to feel guilty about something that felt so good. It made no sense that God would condemn feeling that way when he'd included it in the physical design of His creations. But then, a lot of things about God didn't make sense, so Lisbeth just didn't think about them.

"This is a dildo, and it's for masturbation," Sunny said, offering it to Lisbeth. "*But*—it's unlike any other dildo ever made."

Frowning, she hesitantly took it in her left hand. Its surface was smooth and featureless.

Sunny reached into her bag again, removed a small plastic bottle, unscrewed the cap and offered it to Lisbeth. "Put a few drops on the dildo, then rub it all over."

"What is it?"

"Just plain old lube. Any lubricant will work."

Lisbeth tipped the little bottle and dribbled some of the clear, thick fluid onto the dildo, then put the bottle down.

"Go ahead, rub it on," Sunny said.

Wincing slightly, Lisbeth spread the liquid over the soft surface, closed her fingers around the dildo and rubbed the length of it until it glistened. Then she gasped and jerked her hand away as if she'd been burned.

She'd felt the shaft begin to stiffen and swell.

Sunny grinned. "Don't stop. Keep rubbing it."

As Lisbeth kept stroking it, the phallus continued to harden, thicken and even lengthen. The flesh-pink tone darkened gradually as veins rose just under the surface. She made a whimpering sound because it was—

"Exciting," Sunny said. "Isn't it?"

Lisbeth didn't take her eyes from the dildo as she continued to stroke. Her breathing changed as her heart rate increased. She tucked her lower lip between her teeth and rubbed it with the tip of her tongue as she felt the penis throb in her hand. It actually *throbbed*. It had become so warm, hard, and fat. She imagined feeling that swelling and throbbing inside her...as she had imagined so many times...with such bitter frustration and need. For so many years, she'd yearned to have something inside her...to slide luxuriously...to pound her mercilessly. Not her fingers, not the handle of a hairbrush, but something hard and fat wrapped in flesh. A man.

This wasn't a man. But it was flesh. It was impossible, of course, but that was what she felt as she slid her hand up and down. It was longer now, harder, and it was, however impossible, flesh.

"Like I said," Sunny whispered, "it's not like other dildos. I call it the Happiness Toy. Because that's what it brings. You can't buy it anywhere else. Only from me. Honey, that thing will give you the best orgasm of your life, but it does so much more."

Lisbeth barely heard her over the sound of her own heartbeat in her ears as a moist burning grew between her legs.

"When you use it...it changes you, Lisbeth."

"How?"

"In wonderful ways." She chuckled. "It would be useless to try to explain it. You wouldn't believe me. You'd just have to...experience it. For yourself."

She imagined how it would feel...in there...moving in and out, as it grew hotter and harder...

"Lisbeth! *Liiisbeth!*" Mama's shrill voice cut through all of it like a gnarled talon. Even though she was in her bedroom at the other end of the house, it felt to Lisbeth as if she were screaming in her ear.

She dropped the dildo onto the table and her chair scraped over the tile floor as her legs stiffened reflexively, pushing it back. Her breasts rose and fell as she panted. She looked at the clock on the wall. It was time for Mama's afternoon pills. If she didn't take a glass of apple juice in there right away, Mama would be hobbling through the house in no time.

"Do you want to see what she wants?" Sunny said. "Then we can—"

"No, you'll have to go. But...but..."

"Yes?"

"How much is it?" Lisbeth whispered.

"Well, if you're going to buy it, we need to discuss what it'll do when you—"

"*Lisbeth!* Time for my *pills!*"

Lisbeth's voice was tremulous with fear as she said, "No, I don't have time. I've got some money hidden away. Tell me how much. Then you have to go."

* * *

She handed Mama the glass of apple juice and waited as she took her pills.

It was hard to believe the powerful voice that carried through the entire house came from such a scrawny, bent old woman. Her arms and legs were knobby sticks, her torso a narrow, ribbed tube, and her wrinkled, sagging skin covered only bones, with no sign of any muscle tissue. As she watched Mama go through the painstaking process of swallowing each one of her pills with apple juice, Lisbeth wondered how they got down that skinny neck without becoming hopelessly lodged.

Mama sat up with her back against a pile of pillows. A nasal cannula rested above her upper lip and the large, thick glasses on her nose made her eyes look huge and distorted. Her toothless mouth was a withered hole in her face. Wiry hair the color of old bones spiked in all directions on her head. She had her large-print bible on her lap, which she read occasionally. Usually, though, she preferred to have Lisbeth read it aloud to her, interrupting her now and then to say, "Amen!" or, "Yes, Father!" or to tell Lisbeth what a wretched sinner she was.

"Have you had a man in the house?" Mama said after taking her last pill. She always spoke at a level near a shout, her voice scratchy and harsh, and now, as usual, her entire face was pulled toward the center in a deep, bitter frown of suspicion and disapproval.

"Of course not."

"I heard the doorbell."

She couldn't hear half of what Lisbeth said while standing directly in front of her, but she could hear the doorbell while closed up in her bedroom in the back of the house.

"It didn't ring," Lisbeth said, ignoring the pang of guilt that blossomed in her chest at the lie.

"I *heard* it."

"No one's been here."

Mama's enormous eyes squinted at her through the thick lenses. "Well. Guess not. What man would come to see you?" She laughed, but it sounded like she was coughing. "*No* man would come see you. Unless he was blind."

She took the empty glass from Mama. "Can I get you anything else?"

"Let the cat in."

"Missy's gone, Mama."

"She ran away again?"

"She died."

"*When?*"

"Three years ago."

"What about Lulu?"

Lulu had been their collie. "Last year. She got hit by a car and died."

And now it's your turn, Lisbeth felt another pang. But the guilt wasn't as strong as it had been when she'd begun thinking such thoughts. She was waiting for Mama to die, even looking *forward* to it. Lisbeth had made peace with that. But she didn't know what she would do with her life once Mama was gone, only that she finally would be able to do *something* with it.

Something besides taking care of Mama—feeding her, bathing her, changing her diapers and constantly being available to do her bidding. She left the house only to take Mama to the doctor or go to the grocery store or pharmacy. Whenever she went out on her own, the temptation not to go back home was always powerful.

But her anticipation of Mama's death was not entirely self-serving. After all, Mama was miserable and was steadily losing her mind. Death would be a relief for her. That was what Lisbeth told herself, anyway, to soothe that pang in her chest.

Mama considered the deaths of Missy and Lulu, which were always news to her. "Do we have *any* pets?"

"Not anymore."

"We should get a cat. Go get a cat, Lisbeth."

"I'm not going to go get a cat, Mama."

"Then tell your father to go get one!"

"Daddy left when I was eight, Mama. Remember?"

Lisbeth went to the door, then turned back and said, "You don't need to shout for me, Mama. Use the intercom. Just push the button and I'll come."

But she wouldn't remember. She never did. The next time she wanted something, she would shriek Lisbeth's name like a madwoman.

Lisbeth went back to the kitchen and put the glass in the sink. She looked at the dildo on the table in the cloth bag Sunny had given her. She'd included the little bottle of lubricant as a bonus.

She'd walked Sunny to the front door. Before leaving the house, she'd turned to Lisbeth and leaned so close that her lips touched Lisbeth's ear. "It's only for you," she'd whispered. "*Tell no one.*" Then Sunny had left her lips there for a long moment, her breath hot on Lisbeth's ear. It had sent a delightful tingle down her neck.

Sunny had left the house as Mama continued to shout. Lisbeth had started to close the front door, stopping just before it latched to pull it open a few inches so she could look out and watch the woman go down the front walk.

But Sunny was already gone.

* * *

Lisbeth checked to make sure Mama was sleeping because she wanted to be left alone for a while, then went to her own bedroom and locked the door.

Holding the dildo and lube in the cloth bag, Lisbeth stood at the mirror and looked at herself. Her mousy brown hair appeared unwashed, but it wasn't. It simply had no life. Her round cheeks were pocked by the ghosts of teenage acne so bad that her face used to bleed. The scar left behind by her cleft palate slanted upward from her top lip. She'd been slender in her younger days, but a sedentary life and careless diet had made her doughy and shapeless.

She ran her fingertips lightly over the acne scars, then touched her limp, flat hair. Normally, she spent very little time looking at herself because it was depressing—and doing this was depressing her now. She had not come to her room to brood.

Walking to her bed, she removed the dildo from its bag. She sat on the edge of the bed and put the lube and dildo on her nightstand, with the empty bag beside them. She undressed and pulled back the covers, got into bed, then uncapped the small bottle and dribbled lube onto the dildo. She held it close to her face in her left hand and watched the thick fluid run slowly down the sides of the rubber penis. Then she ran the tip of her forefinger through it, slowly dragging it the length of the shaft.

She made a quiet whimpering sound as it began to thicken before her eyes. She found it amazing...and terribly exciting.

Lisbeth stretched out on the bed as she stroked the dildo and watched the veins appear and the color gradually change, and she felt it swell in her fist. She had never seen a real penis, not in person. But she'd seen pictures. And that was what the rubber shaft became—a real penis. Then she noticed something she hadn't seen in the kitchen with Sunny.

At the rounded end of the dildo—which was now a defined mushroom-like cap—there was a slit, and from the slit oozed a small droplet of clear fluid. At first, she thought it was the lube, so she wiped it away, then continued to stroke the shaft. A moment later, another droplet emerged from the slit.

Lisbeth squeezed the dildo—

It's not a dildo, she thought absently, *it's a penis. It's a...a...*

—and more of the fluid came from the slit in the head.

"A cock," she whispered to herself, frowning at the discharge as she tingled with naughty delight at saying the word out loud. Sunny hadn't mentioned that there was anything *in* the dildo.

She rubbed it across her right breast slowly, back and forth, leaving a glistening trail, then down over her belly. With her right hand, she reached down and stroked herself with one finger, then two. She'd been wet since Sunny had first shown her the dildo and her fingers made moist smacking sounds.

She slid the toy between her lips and pressed it against her clitoris, then rubbed it back and forth as she released a long, trembling sigh.

No, it wasn't a dildo. Not anymore. It was flesh against her, warm and alive.

She kept moving it on that same spot until the sensation moved throughout her body. She gently pressed the tip against her opening and slowly slid it inside. Eyes closed, her mouth opened wide as her head tilted back and her body shuddered with pleasure.

The toy swelled inside her, pressing against her inner walls as she moved it in and out, feeling it grow.

The sound of her own voice startled her at first, and then she lost track of it as she slipped downward into the sensation. Time dissolved along with her surroundings. She was accustomed to tingling feelings in various parts of her body when she masturbated, especially as she neared orgasm, but this brought something new, a growing burning sensation in the soles of her feet and the backs of her thighs. The burning intensified, but then she lost track of that, too. Of everything. Soon, the bed beneath her was gone and she was suspended in darkness. Her ears thrummed with the sound of her blood rushing through her veins as all her attention focused on what had become the very center of her existence: The throbbing, disembodied cock pounding into her. She forgot that she was manipulating it with her hands because she no longer had hands ...or arms... or legs...or feet. She existed only as an engorged vulva and the pulsing, wet tissue that squeezed the cock as it grew within her.

The entire universe exploded in blinding, agonizing white light.

She did not hear her own cries as her orgasm seized her, or the screams they became as the orgasm continued relentlessly, roaring through her like a train in flames. She felt only the cock, which exploded inside her, punching her like a fist, impossibly wet, connecting with exposed nerves previously untouched.

Pounding...pounding...pounding...

On the door.

"—beth! Lisbeth! *Lisbeth!* What's *wrong* with you?"

Gasping for air, Lisbeth rolled to her left to get off the bed, but she had no control over her body yet. She was fluid that spilled over her bed, directionless and without form. It was the floor that finally restored her to solidity when it rose up in a rush and slammed into her.

"Open this door, Lisbeth!" Mama shouted. "Right now, young lady! *Open it!*"

Lisbeth rose up on hands and knees as the pounding continued at the door. Her vision was blurred and her ears were still filled with the rushing of blood, but Mama's voice pierced everything and tore a long trench in the surface of her brain. For a moment, she wanted to rush out of the room, pounce on Mama and snap her brittle, scrawny neck.

She stood and stumbled around the room looking for her clothes, but couldn't remember where she'd put them. Her bathrobe was tossed over a chair. She clumsily slipped it on and went to the door, clutching the lapels together at her throat, still panting. Mama stood crookedly on the other side in her yellow flannel nightgown, back hunched, her wheeled oxygen tank standing on her left, aluminum quad cane on her right.

"What have you been *doing*, Lisbeth?" Mama demanded. "I've been standing out here—" Mama froze and gawked up at her with misshapen owl's eyes, her toothless mouth hanging open. She stumbled backward a step, leaning heavily on her cane. "Whuh—what...who...who *are* you?" Her hushed voice sounded not unlike the old garbage disposal in the kitchen.

Lisbeth leaned heavily against the doorjamb and her head fell forward a moment. "It's me, Mama," she said.

Mama's face only grew more confused and frightened. "But...but...no, it's…not. Lis…Lisbeth?"

"Go back to your room, Mama."

"What…what's happened to you?"

"I said, go back to your *room*, Mama."

Her entire small, frail body began to tremble. Her already lined brow wrinkled further with a frown and her chin jutted indignantly. "This is the work of the devil," she said with quiet gravity.

Lisbeth rolled her eyes behind closed lids. She was simply not in the mood for any of this and felt herself getting angry fast. "Go back to your room, Mama, and I'll—"

"Get thee behind me, Satan!" Mama shrieked.

Clenching her fists at her sides, Lisbeth shouted, "Shut up and go back to your room!" Then she slammed the door and locked it.

She flopped onto her bed and spent some time enjoying the interrupted afterglow of her orgasm. After a while, she got up, tossed the robe back onto the chair and began to dress. She stopped when she glimpsed herself in the mirror across the room. She stared at her reflection for a long moment, then approached it slowly, cautiously. She felt a chill as goose bumps rose on her arms and back.

Her hair fell in waves over her shoulders, shiny and full.

It's unlike any other dildo ever made.

Her face was smooth and had narrowed, her pudgy cheeks flat beneath high graceful cheekbones.

Honey, that thing will give you the best orgasm of your life, but it does so much more.

Her double chin was gone and her neck was slender.

When you use it…it changes you, Lisbeth.

But the most amazing thing—the thing that made Lisbeth gasp when she saw it—was her upper lip and the skin above it. It was smooth. Unblemished. Unscarred.

In ways you can't imagine.

She stumbled backward as she began to cry, until her legs hit the foot of her bed and her ass dropped to the mattress. Lisbeth smiled as she sobbed.

* * *

When she took Mama's dinner to her, the old woman cowered in her bed and stared fearfully, carefully watching her every move. She didn't speak.

Mama refused to have a television in the house, so Lisbeth usually spent her evenings listening to music and reading. But she spent that evening locked in her bedroom, lying naked on her bed, giving herself orgasm after orgasm with Sunny's Happiness Toy. Each time there were improvements, but they were small compared to the initial change, which had been drastic.

With each use, the dildo's penile features lingered a bit longer. By midnight, they did not go away. It remained a thing of flesh and veins.

Lisbeth did not get to sleep that night until the early hours of the morning. And then she slept deeply.

* * *

The next morning, Lisbeth woke feeling better than she had in…as long as she could remember. When she took Mama breakfast, the decrepit old woman stared at her in silent fear, but Lisbeth smiled and wished her a good morning. She had errands to run, and for once, she looked forward to going into town.

It was a gorgeous day outside, sunny and hot. She'd dug deep into her closet and pulled out a pair of shorts and a little top she hadn't worn since she was 19. At first, she felt self-conscious in them, especially when she noticed at the grocery store that people were staring at her. But then she realized it was only *men* who were staring, and they seemed to do so with approval.

She got her groceries, then picked up Mama's prescription refill at the grocery store's pharmacy. The woman at the register gasped when she realized who Lisbeth was.

"Lisbeth!" she said. "You look so…*different!* Have you lost weight? Changed your hair?"

Lisbeth blushed and stammered for a moment, then stopped, smiled and calmly said, "Just taking better care of myself."

At the checkout, the bagboy—in his mid-twenties, though, so he was hardly a *boy*—ogled her as he bagged her groceries. Lisbeth had been shopping there for years and he'd never so much as noticed her before. In the past, whenever he asked her if she'd like help to her car, always without making eye contact, she'd said no, and she would have done the same this time—if he'd asked. Instead, he put the last bag in her cart, smiled and said, "I'll help you out," pushing the cart toward the exit.

Outside, she pointed to her car in the lot and said, "Right over there."

He kept looking at her on the way, always smiling. It made her feel vaguely uncomfortable, but she reminded herself, *you don't look the same anymore.*

"I don't think I've seen you in the store before," he said.

"Then I guess you haven't been paying attention." A heartbeat after speaking: *I can't believe I just said that.*

He was quite handsome, with full, dark hair and bright blue eyes, broad shoulders and a creamy tan. He was the kind of guy Lisbeth typically hoped would *not* notice her. But today, she felt differently. And she enjoyed it.

"You shop here often?" he said as he stopped the cart behind her car.

She opened the trunk. "I do *all* my shopping here. Have for years."

He took a bag out of the cart and stopped to look at her closely, frowning a little. "Really? Then I *haven't* been paying attention." As he put her groceries in the trunk, he said, "Looks like you're shopping for two people." The way his voice went up at the end, it was *almost* a question.

"My mother. I take care of her."

"So you're not married, or anything?"

She grinned so hard that she felt a little embarrassed. "No. Or anything."

He put the last bag of groceries into the car, then closed the trunk and took his cell phone from his pocket. "Why don't you give me your phone number and we can get together. A drink, maybe? Since I haven't been paying attention, I can make up for lost time."

Her hands were still trembling as she drove home. She'd never been asked for her number by a man before and she kept replaying it in her mind. Over and over. He actually wanted to go out with her!

Mama will be furious. She'll want to know where I'm going and why and with who and how long I'll be gone. She smiled to herself. *And I'll lie.*

As if she were being punished for the thought, Lisbeth's front left tire blew out. She struggled to maintain control of the car while trying to pull over to the side of the road. Instead, she drove up onto the curb.

"Damn," she muttered as she backed up enough to get off the sidewalk. She had never changed a tire before, but over the years, Lisbeth had discovered that she was a quick learner because she had to do things for herself.

She got out of the car and took a look at the tire. She would have to move the groceries from the trunk and put them in the back seat so she could take out the jack and spare tire. Sighing with frustration, she went to the rear of the car and opened the trunk. Before she removed the first bag of groceries, a car pulled over and parked in front of hers.

Before the driver could get out, a second car pulled up behind hers.

Both drivers were men. She did not have to change the tire herself.

* * *

Lisbeth couldn't help giggling as she carried groceries into the house. She had to make two trips, but she didn't care. She was too happy to be bothered by anything—even Mama.

As she unpacked the groceries, she thought of the two men who'd helped her change the tire. One had asked her out, the other waited until the first had driven off and then had asked for her number. It was a deluge after a lifetime of drought, and it was a bit dizzying.

She thought again of Mama and how she would react to Lisbeth having anything that resembled a social life. It would infuriate her. But she was hardly in any position to do anything about it. And how much longer could she last?

Mama was probably upset that Lisbeth had been gone so long—more than three hours—but she simply couldn't find it in herself to be concerned about that. As she put groceries in the refrigerator and cupboards, Lisbeth allowed herself to imagine what her life would be like after Mama was gone.

Before Sunny's visit yesterday, she'd found it difficult to imagine being alone and had no idea what she would do with her life. Now she seemed to have something of a future. She had been smiling so much, her cheeks ached.

Once the groceries were put away, she started on Mama's lunch. It was twenty minutes to one and Mama liked her lunch precisely at twelve-thirty, so she was going to be cranky. She made Mama's tuna salad sandwich on white bread while a kettle of water heated up for tea. Several minutes later, she took the lunch to Mama's room.

The door was closed. It was usually open a crack, but Mama had closed it completely.

"Lunchtime, Mama," she said. She put the cup of tea on the plate with the sandwich and used her free hand to turn the knob.

It was locked. Mama never locked her bedroom door.

"Mama? Why is your door locked?" When there was no response, she knocked on the door. "Mama! Are you all right?" No answer. "Mama! *Answer me!*" She heard nothing in the bedroom and her chest tightened. A surge of fear and guilt made her guts twist into knots.

Lisbeth rushed back to the kitchen and set the plate and tea on the counter.

"The key, the key," she whispered to herself, trying to remember where it was. She'd never needed it before.

She opened one of the drawers under the counter and rummaged through the junk—pens and pencils, loose scraps of paper, screwdrivers of varying sizes, a padlock, a couple of old Christmas cards, a book of obsolete postage stamps, paperclips and rubber bands. But no keys.

It was an old door and an old lock. Lisbeth wondered if she could kick the door in if she tried hard enough. Then she remembered some old keys in one of her dresser drawers.

She hurried into her bedroom, went to the dresser and checked her drawers. It was the third one down. There were two rings of keys there, none of them labeled. She would have to try all of them. Snatching the keys up, she rushed toward Mama's room, but stumbled to a halt when something caught her eye.

Her nightstand drawer was open about an inch. She knew she had closed it—right after she'd put the dildo in that drawer in its cloth bag.

She walked to the nightstand slowly, her feet heavy, legs numb. Opening the drawer all the way, she found the cloth bag. The dildo and lube were gone.

A chill erupted inside her chest and spread throughout her body. Clutching one ring of keys in each hand, Lisbeth went to Mama's room. She talked as she tried the keys, one at a time.

"What're you doing in there, Mama? Why aren't talking to me? Why is the door locked, Mama? *Why?* What have you—"

One of the keys turned in the lock. She pushed the door open slowly.

Mama's bed was empty, the covers thrown all the way to the foot. The dildo lay on the mattress, the sheet stained with dampness around it.

"Mama?"

She stepped inside and saw Mama standing at the window, looking out at the strip of lawn beside the house as she slowly brushed her hair. But something wasn't quite right. Mama was different.

"Mama, why wouldn't you…say…something…when I was…knocking?"

Lisbeth felt a wave of nausea.

Mama's hair was no longer grey. It was dark now, smooth and shiny. She stood erect in her flannel nightgown, her back straight.

"Muh-ma…ma?"

Mama stopped running the brush through her hair and slowly turned around. Her face was smooth and unlined, even pretty. Her eyes were clear and alert. The corners of her mouth were turned downward.

"You've been gone a long time, young lady," she said in a clear, full voice. A healthy voice. "I hope you've got a good explanation for yourself."

Lisbeth heard a small, childlike whimpering sound, and a moment later, realized it was coming from herself. Her knees felt weak, her throat tight and something like a fist seemed to be squeezing her heart.

Mama would not be dying anytime soon.

Follower

by Danny Rhodes

I.

It was already the end of November, and Morris understood the risks of what he was about to do. His plan was to hunker down overnight in the bothy at Helm's Pass and set out for Fell's Edge the following morning. The sun was shining when he set out from Black Fen but there were reports of storm clouds accumulating in the West. If the forecast was to be trusted, he'd have most of the day to complete the ascent. He'd return to the bothy afterwards, wait for the storm to pass and then head home. There were posts on the message boards saying he was a fool for tackling Fell's Edge so late in the season, but none of the others had been through the six weeks he'd endured. They'd not had to deal with it all.

He would negotiate Fell's Edge, complete the 'Fifty Peak Challenge' in a single season and gain recognition amongst his online peers in a way nobody had managed before. His name would be legendary.

He left his car and started his trek upward. When he looked back over the landscape there wasn't a sign of man's mark in any direction, save for the ribbon of road that stretched away towards Saddlemoor. And even that looked different from this height, more downtrodden earth than tarmac, as if he'd stepped out of the present into another time. He shrugged his shoulders and pressed on over the escarpment. The test, as always, was to access the peak in the traditional style, to be able to look back at this conquest when he was an old man and know he'd done it the hard way, having truly earned it. He couldn't dream of Everest anymore, but he could still find his own little place in history.

Morris trudged on, trying not to think about the accident of six weeks earlier, and the lingering pain in his torso. He'd been lucky, that was the long and the short of it; lucky to escape with just a cracked ribcage, though he hadn't felt that way at the time. The pain had been excruciating.

He'd been in the Cairngorms, descending Ben Macdhui in driving sleet.

The terrain had become uncertain underfoot, like greased glass. He'd not been careful enough.

He reached Middle Beck and stopped to rest. His side was aching. He took two painkillers with a swig of tea and munched on an energy bar. The vista presented him a view of the valley all the way to the sea. Clouds were still massing over the water but they were not threatening. Not yet. A shaft of sunlight pierced the gloom. He watched it sweep across the landscape, casting its beauty on the estuary, on Saddlemoor, forever onwards until, for a few brief moments, he was warmed by its glow. He tipped his head back and closed his eyes. Wasn't that why he did this, to experience moments where the hum-drum act of living was interrupted by some greater understanding, to experience moments of, dare he even think it, grace?

He took his planned ten-minute break, letting the tea warm him through, sucking in great lungsful of air. He popped a dextrose tablet into his mouth and let it dissolve on his tongue, then checked his map. The route he'd chosen, rather than confound him as many had suggested, seemed to be a tame enough beast, even in November.

He was tightening the straps at his waist, standing upright and shifting his position to get everything comfortable, when the man first came into view. He was way down in the valley, following the route Morris had taken some three hours earlier. Morris took out his binoculars and asked himself the usual questions. Hiker or climber? Amateur or serious? The stranger had his hood up so Morris couldn't see his face. He studied his gait instead, the speed of his ascent, the equipment he was carrying, the clothes he was wearing. It was possible to understand so much about a man from his clothing, especially in a sport like this. But, accounting for distance and magnification, the man's clothes were hard to pin down. They looked a little heavy, a little cumbersome. His boots looked bulkier than necessary, the leggings thicker, the jacket stiff and inflexible. The colours, sombre hues, brown and beige, suggested another era.

There it was again, that feeling of lacking anchor in the world, of time shifting in this most timeless of places. Morris touched the outcrop beside him and stroked the cool stone.

It spoke to him, as it always had.

II.

The bothy was situated halfway up the mountain, a small wooden structure at odds with the barren world around it. There was no smoke coming from the chimney. Morris turned to look behind him along the ridge, and raised his binoculars. Sure enough, his follower was there, a dark silhouette against the blazing sunset. Morris imagined the stranger's gaze falling upon him, and oddly,

263

felt a tiny shred of fear whittle its way into his bones. He took solace in the fact that there would be others at the bothy.

But, when he arrived, it was quiet. The door opened with a gasp. A musty smell met his nostrils. The wood burner was cold to the touch. As he set about making a fire he thought of his follower.

He shivered.

He had imagined this room filled with others, men like him who lived for the outdoors. Men with stories to share.

He picked himself a bottom bunk and hung his jacket from the bunk above so that he could cocoon himself from the room. He poured some tea from his flask, munched on a biscuit and waited.

He pondered the silence and sullenness of the place: the coarse blankets, the stained sinks, the cracked and warped furniture. Where there might once have been a map there was now just a rectangular outline on the wall, a mark to suggest something longstanding had been removed.

Intermittently, he moved to the door and looked out to see if his follower was approaching. But the man did not materialise. Morris wandered around to the side of the building and looked towards Fell's Edge, hoping to see a posse of men coming back down.

The trail was empty in that direction as well.

As dusk passed he started to wonder if something might have happened to his follower, if the guy might have fallen or injured himself. But, what could Morris do? Should he go out looking for him? Put himself in danger? No. It was best to stay put, tend the fire, keep the place warm for others in case some should arrive.

It was pitch black outside when Morris completed his final recce. Seeing nothing, the feeling of absolute isolation set in. Unusually for him, a man experienced in detachment, he also felt the silent chill that accompanied it. For whatever reason, despite what the hostel association had told him, he would be alone on this night. No brash Americans, no quiet Scandinavians. There would be no company at all.

He thought about the man on the ridge, his follower. Perhaps he'd found himself a place to hunker down. He contemplated this man, who wore such strange attire. The guy could be ex-special forces, who preferred solitude, or perhaps just a recluse, someone who couldn't interact. Might his follower be sleeping on the mountain purely to avoid having to share the cabin with another human soul? Morris sat on the steps at the entrance for a long time, staring out at the hulking shadows of the mountain and the grey hue of the clouds.

The silence was all-encompassing.

Etiquette suggested he leave the door accessible, but before bed, convinced as he was that nobody was coming and full of irrational fears, he propped a chair under the handle. He later felt foolish for doing that, and couldn't sleep, so he took the chair out again. He lay staring at the door. The flames flickered. Shadows danced on the ceiling. He climbed off the bunk, took out his map and studied it inanely. There was nothing he didn't already know. When the flames of the fire started to die, he propped his flashlight against the wall to create a tiny alcove of light in the bottom bunk, a place of refuge.

Just for a little while, he told himself. *Just until I'm ready to sleep.*

He tried to get comfortable, but now his injured ribs protested. Whichever way he lay he could not shake the pain. He took two painkillers from his pack, swallowed them and waited for the numbing effect to kick in.

He closed his eyes.

It was later, somewhere in the dead of night, that he opened them to find the electric torch still on, its power diminished to virtually nothing. He switched it off. The room was overtaken by darkness. Morris, for all his years and all his mountains, had never known pitch black like this. The sound of a creaking floorboard dragged him into wakefulness. He stiffened, too terrified to breathe. He lay like that until his muscles started to ache and his chest burned. Then he exhaled slowly and drew in another deep breath. Pain shot through his ribs, causing him to wince and grit his teeth. The floorboards creaked again. Had somebody entered while he was sleeping? *Had* he been sleeping? He couldn't remember.

He smelled something different, something old and waxy. He told himself it was the blankets, the sheets, anything at all, but he knew it was none of these things. It was the smell of whatever had entered the bothy. Morris didn't dare move. He had the torch in his grip but he couldn't bring himself to switch it on.

He did not want to see.

And so he lay under the sheets with his eyes closed, telling himself he'd imagined it all, that there was nothing there, that the creaking floorboards and waxy smell were in his head. He started to drift back to sleep. That was when the breathing started—the harsh, gravel-like sound of a man struggling to inhale and exhale. Morris pulled himself up into the corner of his bunk, grabbed the torch and turned it on. For a while it blazed bright. He guided the beam around the place. There was nothing. He climbed out of the bunk and shone the light in every corner.

Empty.

He shone the light at the other bunks.

Empty.

There was just him.

But the smell returned when the torch light faded, and soon after he climbed back under the sheets he heard the breathing again. Or perhaps it was the wind in the eaves. Yes, it had to be that, air working its way inside, circulating in the roof-space somehow, confusing him. And the creaking, it could be the timbers settling down now that the fire was out. The smell? The smell could be the fireplace, or perhaps his own sweat-soaked clothing.

Logic wrestled with imagined threats.

Morris pulled the blanket tight to his neck and forced himself to sit upright, fighting the urge to sleep. He was a child again. He sat like that until the first threads of morning pierced the edges of the shuttered windows. Then, only then, did he allow himself to tumble into dreams.

III.

He woke with a feeling of panic working its way up from the pit of his stomach. He'd had a nightmare. He was negotiating the summit of Fell's Edge, heading for the marker that would signal the culmination of his year's endeavours. He'd come over the final ridge to discover his follower at the marker waiting for him. The man turned to look at him and then crumbled to dust before his eyes.

Morris fell out of the bunk and dressed. He didn't bother with breakfast. He dumped all of his food, save for a cereal bar, on the floor beside the bed. He'd collect it all on the way down. He shook his flask, realised it was half-full. He did not have time to light another fire and boil water. He was frantic with worry about beating the weather. He forced the door to the bothy open and gasped when he saw where the sun was positioned amongst the mountains. He pulled on his boots, secured them with hurried knots and slammed the door behind him.

In the distance he could see the clear outline of Fell's Edge.

It looked eons away.

The sun was warm for November. It vindicated his decision to make the ascent, and relaxed him a little, but his mood remained dark. He could think of nothing else but the man on the mountain. There was a path, of sorts, a discernable route, but his feet unseated random pieces of slate, causing them to skitter off the trail.

Morris stared ahead. The sunlight hurt his eyes but mercifully the route to the summit looked empty. Perhaps his follower had left the mountain the previous evening. Perhaps he never was a threat. But the clothing he wore, the metronomic way he walked, his ceaseless encroachment, all these things spoke to Morris differently. He couldn't risk it. He had to press onward, leave nothing to chance, regardless of the risks.

He was halfway up the gradient when he spotted the man. To his relief, his mighty relief, he saw the figure was behind him, a dark smudge in the valley. The man was standing outside the bothy, sort of lingering there. It unsettled Morris to see him like that, waiting at the cabin as if there was something to wait for.

Morris took out his binoculars. He focussed in on the grey clothing, the hood and the dark shadow contained within it. He watched the man enter the building, reappear a minute later and move towards the trailhead, adopting the same metronomic rhythm as if this were a rehearsed performance.

Morris put his binoculars away and continued his climb. Above him, beyond the angle of the mountain, was Fell's Edge, his Valhalla. Way off to the west, rolling in off the sea, was the storm predicted for that evening. Behind him, climbing the mountain, was his follower.

Morris hurried on. Ridiculously, no matter how much he increased his pace, the gap between him and his follower did not widen. If anything, despite his efforts, the gap seemed to contract. Had it become a race? The man was too far away to reach the peak ahead of him. It was physically impossible for any man to breach such a distance so quickly. And yet the gap was dropping at an alarming rate. Morris was tiring too, physical exertion exacerbated now by a draining of his mental capacities as he sought some explanation for the events taking place. There was something else too, a fear gnawing away at his mind. If his follower caught up with him, would he cause Morris harm? He knew this was a fatal combination. A man could not allow himself to grow tired or confused on a mountain. He cursed himself for not eating, for not drinking, for allowing fixation to overcome preparedness. And the danger signals were already raging, the loss of clarity, the feeling of disorientation, anxiety. He took a mouthful of tea. It was tepid. He spat it out. He looked down the mountain and picked out a tarn amongst the nothingness. As still as glass, the bleak mountains, the wide-open sky and the billowing clouds were reflected on its surface. He imagined himself hiding behind an outcrop, striking his tormentor with a rock as he passed, dragging his unconscious body to that place, and drowning him there. But a cloying mist rolled over the mountain, and he lost sight of the pond within it.

The mist soon enveloped Morris and everything around him. It only added to his anxiety. He couldn't see his follower anymore. He plodded on, trying to keep to the route, not daring to stop. On and on he went, blindly into the mist until, to his absolute terror, he heard the sound of footfalls behind him, the distinctive crunch of boots on shale. Steady, metronomic footsteps, growing louder. Morris fought to increase his pace. Each time he placed a foot on the ground a shot of pain emanated from his damaged ribs. And with each step he was finding it harder to ascertain height and distance, the space between footfalls. Behind him, the footsteps seemed closer than even the moment before. He imagined a gloved hand reaching for his shoulder...

Focussing on too many things at once, the footsteps, his follower, the encroaching storm, Morris lost his footing.

It wasn't like before, when he'd cracked his ribs. He had slid then, on his haunches. Though he'd been unable to stop himself, a protruding outcrop had saved him. This time he fell more awkwardly. His left knee turned in an unnatural direction, sideways and outwards. The pain was instantaneous. He felt something tear inside it and give way. He felt bone gnaw against bone. He dropped in such a manner that his weight, supplemented by his backpack, shifted onto the other leg. It wasn't strong enough to support him. He tumbled off the side of the ridge and fell through open air. For a brief second he felt weightless, without burden, and then there was impact.

He woke to the realisation that the injury was a bad one. A furtive glance at his legs confirmed his fears. Both were crumpled underneath him, impossibly so. He tried to put the image out of his mind. Curiously there wasn't much pain, but then there wasn't much feeling either. His ribs were worse. Each time he tried to move, a searing jolt shot through them. The very act of breathing was agony enough. He'd fallen six or seven meters, vertically, with nothing to break his fall but his backpack. He understood he would need help very quickly if he were to have any chance of survival. He stared upwards along the ridge, through the mist, into the white orb that was the sun, then in the direction of his follower. Surely it was only a matter of time before the man appeared behind him. Relief surged through him, and he basked in the irony of it. His relentless tormentor would become his saviour.

But time seemed to stretch as Morris lay stricken on the ledge. What could be stalling his follower's climb? What had become of those incessant footfalls? A cold chill came over him. What if the man had turned back, perturbed by the encroaching mist, the gathering cloud? And then another thought. Might the fall have knocked him unconscious? If so, how long had he been out? Might his follower have already passed while Morris lay prone on the ledge? Passed without glancing in his direction, eyes focussed solely on his next step, as Morris should have done.

When the fog loosened he tilted his head back and looked at the inverted horizon, at the clouds amassing beneath it. He saw what they were, their purple hue, the weight of them. Even without the fall, those clouds were a threat. If he'd made it to the summit, and immediately headed back towards the bothy, would he have completed his return before the snow started to fall? For it would fall, there was no doubt about it. It would come up the side of the mountain, blowing and scudding, and it would bury him. He had to pray that the man who had been closing in on him all morning was almost to the ridge, that somehow he would discover him there.

It was much later when Morris thought he heard the steady crump and clack of boots on rock. He looked up at the ridge, hoping to catch a sight of the man in the ebbing mist. For a time there was nothing, just the grey shroud and the sound of the footfalls crushing the shale, but then a shape appeared on the edge of the ridge. A hunched form, the shadow of a man's body angled against the slope.

Morris called out. "Hello!"

The figure continued up the ridge.

Morris called again, mustering what little strength he had. "HELLO!"
Pain exploded from his ribs.

Did the figure check his stride for an instant? Did he look about himself? Or was he just drawing breath before heaving himself on again?

"Down here. I need help," gasped Morris, but his voice was weak and feeble now.

The man was almost to the point where Morris had fallen. In another few seconds he'd pass by. Morris reached for a rock, fighting the burning, agonised protests of his broken ribs and flung it in the direction of the man's feet. It came up short and bounced away down the mountainside. Morris made to shout one last time, but because of what his eyes beheld, the words never escaped his lips. Instead, he shrieked, his broken body reverberating in pain.

"Gnnnnrrrrr."

The thing appeared to him through a momentary thinning of the mist. It stood there perched on the escarpment above. He noticed the man's clothing, its age; the sheep skin jacket, the heavy boots, the threadbare ropes around the man's middle. And when the man turned to look at the congealing clouds Morris caught a brief sight of the face inside the hood.

Neither the cutting wind, nor the wet mist were what caused his weakening body to shudder.

The gaunt face, dried out and mummified, its skin stretched tight, its eye sockets empty, the lips drawn back, revealing sparse teeth loosely held at odd angles by gums that looked like petrified rubber. The nostrils spread wide, where the skin had stretched and torn them open...

The thing that had once been a man turned and shuffled onward along the ridge. It scaled the shale another few meters. And then something happened. Its boots dislodged a rock, which tumbled away and down the mountain. Morris's follower, the thing that had haunted him since the previous afternoon, tumbled after it. With the fall came a high-pitched scream, one that contained more than the fear of falling, and a sound far beyond a mortal cry of terror. There was desperation and frustration in the cry, which could only come after years of torment, of having something coveted within one's grasp but letting it slip. The dark shape dropped past him over the ledge, down the mountain and out of sight, to be replaced by an even more terrifying entity.

Silence.

Morris closed his eyes. He tried to tell himself he'd imagined all that had occurred, that he was losing his senses, going into shock. He tried to tell himself he was hallucinating. But he knew he wasn't suffering from any of those things.

Not yet.

Night fell quickly on the mountain. The angry clouds brought their snow. Trapped on the ledge, unable to move, Morris scraped away at the rocks beneath his shattered legs and rolled himself into the indentation. He tucked himself up in a ball in that place and tried not to think about the freezing wind. But it was futile. The gusts whistled through the cuts of rock and came at him from all angles. He felt parts of himself, exposed extremities, turning numb.

He dragged his rucksack from underneath him and took out the flask of tea. There wasn't much left. He remembered tipping a good three mouthfuls away during his rest stop, and he wondered how many hours three mouthfuls of cold tea might add to a man's life in a crisis such as this. Well, he'd wasted those hours as he'd wasted almost all of his life, achieving nothing, going nowhere. At least if he were to die here on the mountain he would be remembered for it. In some perverted way he found solace in that. He imagined the message boards brimming with life as the news broke, the furious conversation, the sympathetic obituaries, the "I told you so" admonishments.

Morris meandered through the eventualities, his mind playing tricks. He saw images in the mist, curious forms approaching from beyond the ledge, things floating there and fading again, things without faces, things that were not human.

For a while he was in the bothy again, lying in the darkness, his jacket hanging off the top bunk, creating the wall he hid behind. But he wasn't alone. There was something in the bothy with him. The sound of scraping and shuffling on the floorboards, the sound of laboured breathing, the acrid smell of tobacco, the clink of a brandy glass, the rustle of a map, a cough. Even in his mesmerised state, Morris felt the blood run cold in his veins at those sounds.

The pain came in waves. He was free of it one moment and then ravaged by it the next. It was all-encompassing. He screamed against the mountain, agony echoing through his broken body as his voice echoed off the surrounding walls. When the pain gave him respite, he tried to close his mind to his fears, to remember where he was and think of a future spent in a place other than this. But all he could think of were mountains, bigger and bigger mountains with higher and higher peaks.

He wasn't ready to die.

He woke intermittently throughout the night, once to see the clouds had moved away, and the night full of stars. He felt as though he could reach out and touch them. Later, he roused to see the sun rising from behind the mountain. He turned to look along the ridge and there they were, all of them, each and every member of the climbing forum. They had come to save him. Ahead of them, striding purposefully towards him, was the mountain rescue team, the lead climber making his way steadily along the precarious section of ridge, turning to look in his direction, but changing form, losing colour, becoming an eyeless man in one hundred-year-old clothing, stopping above Morris, exposing that drawn, taut face, walking on, stumbling, falling off the side of the mountain to indeterminable depths.

Again and again and again.
For a century.
Forever.

IV.

Morris couldn't feel his legs at all. His fingers were useless appendages. Clarity was cracked and splintered ice. Pain ebbed and flowed, emanating from his ribs. As he succumbed to it, he tried to cling to the knowledge that he'd be remembered, that his name would live on. It was all he had left, the hope of leaving a legacy.

He grinned at the thought, imagining a photograph of himself to accompany the dedications on the message boards: one knee raised, his boot planted on a rock, his hands on his hips, the vista of a mountain range behind, sunglasses, bronzed skin…a confident, life affirming smile. He was Steven Morris, a legend in his own right, the first man to complete the 'Fifty Peak Challenge' in a single season.

Almost.

It was only at the end, as he slipped towards unconsciousness for the last time, that Morris endured the final realisation. The thought crashed into his mind like a dislodged boulder.

He didn't know his follower.

Then came the terrifying understanding. Perhaps they would never find him. There would be no epitaph, no shrine to remember him by. He was a faceless name on an impersonal message board. He would be forgotten as his follower had surely been forgotten, plunged into damnation, forced to clamber up Fell's Edge in freezing November mists while a man from the past pursued a similar folly behind him, forced to endure this fate day after day, for all eternity.

Contributors' Notes

Colleen Anderson

Colleen Anderson has published nearly 200 pieces of fiction and poetry in such places as *Chilling Tales*, *Evolve*, *Horror Library* and *Cemetery Dance*. She has been poetry editor for the *Chizine*, host of the Vancouver ChiSeries, co-editor for *Tesseracts 17* and *The Playground of Lost Toys*, as well as a freelance copyeditor. She has been twice nominated for the Aurora Award, longlisted for the Bram Stoker Award, received honorable mentions in the Year's Best anthologies and been reprinted in *Imaginarium*. New works for 2015 are in *Nameless*, *Second Contact*, *Our World of Horror*, "OnSpec," "Polu Texni" and *Exile Book of New Canadian Noir*. See more at colleenanderson.wordpress.com or facebook.com/colleen.anderson.9699

• *Exegesis* was conceived when I attended the Center for the Study of Speculative Fiction novel writing workshop in Lawrence, Kansas. While we were all workshopping our novels, Kij Johnson mentioned an exegesis several times, which means the critical study of a text, especially referring to scripture. Other stories we talked about had apocryphal tropes and styles. These are big words with a lot of meat behind them. I had this image in my mind of a woman standing in a field, her arms out, covered in a myriad of insects. I'm also disturbed by and intrigued by a sociopathic mind. To be so alien in a human body—it's what I explore here—is she sociopathic or is she an insect in a human body? Insects (as far as we know) have no emotions. They don't worry about biting us. They do it to survive, mindless yet single-minded.

Michael A. Arnzen

Michael Arnzen loves to experiment on the dark side. He has won the Bram Stoker Award for a serial killer novel, a monster story collection, a mutant poetry collection and even an email newsletter. His writing has been adapted to film, music and refrigerator magnets. His Stoker-winning novel, *Grave Markings*, was recently re-released by Raw Dog Screaming Press, in a special 20th Anniversary Edition. Mike currently teaches in the Master of Fine Arts program in Writing Popular Fiction at Seton Hill University. You can find him on Twitter @MikeArnzen or gorelets.com

• As you might guess, the concept for **Guarded** was sparked while I was waiting in the security line at the airport. I saw the TSA guards going back into a secret room. They were probably just taking an innocuous break, but I, of course, began to imagine the worst. It's a little weird having a dark fantasy while standing in such a policed position—you start to get a little paranoid. I think those feelings really came out when I wrote the story, shivering on the plane ride home.

Rick J. Brown

Rick J. Brown is a horror and science fiction writer whose work appeared in the horror anthologies *Horror Library Volume 1*, and *Butcher Shop Quartet II*, both by Cutting Block Press. He has received two Honorable Mentions from *Writers of the Future*, the top international writing contest for science fiction and fantasy writers, and has written screenplays in professional workshops with Hollywood writer/producer Glenn Benest, an ex-collaborator of Wes Craven. Rick's screenplay, *BLOOD BROTHERS*, was deemed "masterfully written" by Twilight/Protagonist Pictures. He is a professor of psychology at Citrus College in Southern California. Updates on his work can be found at rickjbrown.com, and you can connect with him on Linkedin: linkedin.com/in/rickjbrownwriter.

• History is replete with the darkest horror, but only a few of us have felt its suffocating grip. When writing **The Puppet Show**, I asked the following question: "What is one of the worst possible scenarios that one might have to endure?" We live in a universe over which we have very little control. And while there is often a yearning for understanding why we suffer, the answer never comes.

Kealan Patrick Burke

Born and raised in Dungarvan, Ireland, Kealan Patrick Burke is the Bram Stoker Award-winning author of six novels, over a hundred short stories, six collections, and editor of four acclaimed anthologies. Kealan has worked as a waiter, a drama teacher, a mapmaker, a security guard, an assembly-line worker at Apple Computers, a salesman (for a day), a bartender, landscape gardener, vocalist in a grunge band and, most recently, a fraud investigator. When not writing, Kealan designs covers for print and digital books through his company Elderlemon Design (elderlemondesign.com). To date he has designed covers for books by Richard Laymon, Brian Keene, Scott Nicholson, Bentley Little, J. Carson Black, and Hugh Howey, to name a few. A movie based on his short story "Peekers" is currently in development as a major motion picture through Lionsgate Entertainment. You can find him on the web at kealanpatrickburke.com and Twitter @KealanBurke.

• I'm always fascinated by the after-effects of trauma, how memory (or the corruption of memory) affects us, and how insanity manifests itself as an alteration of perspective. At the time, the theme of school shootings was a topical one. Unfortunately, that hasn't changed in the intervening years.

Michael Louis Calvillo

Practically born with a book in his hand, Michael Louis Calvillo had an obsessive love affair with books—mostly of the horror and science-fiction persuasion. From an early age, he constantly read, recounted movie and book plotlines to anyone who would listen, and wrote with equally unbounded excitement—even publishing a post-apocalyptic short story at the ripe old age of 12.

His true love, however, was his family, which served as the inspiration for his writing. In spite of the gruesome content threaded throughout his work, Michael's family life, with his wife Michelle and daughter Deja, was remarkably sweet in an unbelievably '80s family sitcom fashion. This probably explains why, if you look beneath the gory surface, all of his works are dripping with relentlessly schmoopy expressions of love. In addition to his true love affair with books, Michael was also passionate about teaching high school English, infusing pop culture and rap music into his lessons to infect the next generation with the same deep appreciation he had for literature.

If you want to know more about the author, he is revealed subtly, and sometimes not so subtly, in each of his works, which you can check out at michaellouiscalvillo.com. As a prolific author who wrote faster than a speeding bullet and more powerful than a locomotive, he has left us with an amazing repertoire. These include his first novel, *I Will Rise*, a collection of short stories, *Blood & Gristle*, and a novella, *7 Brains*, all of which received nominations for the prestigious Bram Stoker Award. Other works include his novels, *Lambs*, *As Fate Would Have It*, *Death and Desire in the Age of Women*, a novella, *Bleed For You*, several poems, an autobiographic blog, and a feature-length screenplay, *Athena*, which is currently in production.

(Ed. note: Michael Louis Calvillo passed away in 2012 and his story, **Consumed**, appears courtesy of his widow, Michelle Stockdale.)

Jeff Cercone

Jeff Cercone is a writer and editor living in Chicago. His work has appeared in the Late Late Show webzine and he is the former editor of the Down in the Cellar webzine. He has worked in journalism for 25 years and currently works as a digital editor for the *Chicago Tribune*. You can follow him on Twitter @jeffcercone.

• Working in media is like having your own weird-story idea generator. I came to Chicago in 2003, and a couple years later the *Tribune* reported on people flocking to a see a salt stain on a Kennedy Expressway underpass that they thought looked like the Virgin Mary. I guess it did if you squinted hard enough, but dozens of people were quite convinced and crowds visited for weeks.

So I wondered what if it were something masquerading as the Virgin Mary, sent not to inspire the faithful but to punish the sinners? At the time I was writing the story, anger over the Iraq War was at its peak and I wanted to write about that, so those two ideas merged into the story here. The stain on the underpass isn't really visible anymore but people still leave flowers there and somehow it has its own Yelp page.

Charles Colyott

Charles Colyott lives on a farm in the middle of nowhere (Illinois) with his wife, two daughters, cats, and a herd of llamas and alpacas. He is surrounded by so much cuteness it's very difficult for him to develop any street cred as a dark and gritty writer. Nevertheless, he has appeared in *Read by Dawn II, Dark Recesses Press, Withersin Magazine, Horror Library* Volumes III, IV, & V, and *Zippered Flesh* 1 & 2, among other places. He also teaches a beginner level Tai Chi Ch'uan class in which no one has died (yet) of the death touch. You can get in touch with him on Twitter @charlescolyott or email him at charlescolyott@gmail.com. Unlike his llamas, he does not spit.

• I wrote *The Steel Church* as a reaction to the increased partisan polarization in America. It was a weird time. The Iraq War was in full swing, people were taking bulldozers to Dixie Chicks records, and the word "traitor" got thrown around with alarming frequency. My brain, being the bizarre creature that it is, just extrapolated from that to create a future America where civil war had been the norm for generations. It was a strangely fun story to write, though, and I've thought about returning to that story world several times. Hopefully someday.

C. Michael Cook

C. Michael Cook is the author of "The Boys of Bald Cave." It appeared in *Unspeakable Horror*, which was nominated alongside the *Horror Library* Volume 3 for best anthology at the Bram Stoker Awards. Both were also shortlisted by Ellen Datlow for the year's best horror.

His other published short—"Unto the Sons, the Daughters"—was nominated for the Pushcart Prize in 1998. It's available on his website at cmichaelcook.com. You can also follow his blog cmichaelcook.blogspot.com

• One summer afternoon in 1998 I was struck by the image of a man in a hospital, severely underweight and malnourished, but refusing all food. He was in restraints and sedated because he had tried to bite several doctors and nurses, and been sent there originally because he'd done the same thing to a neighbor's dog. I thought solving the mystery of what was wrong with him might make a good story, and imagined him finally confessing that he couldn't eat anything dead, that he could only bear to eat things that were still alive, and that he was *starving*.

I approached *The Living World* from several different angles. One involved telling the story through a series of 911 calls, hospital reports, and therapy session notes and transcripts. None were very successful, and eventually it went fallow. A lot of ideas come to me this way. An image or mood or observation hits me and I then try to build a satisfying story around it. Too many fall by the wayside for want of a beginning, middle and end.

I picked up the idea again in the fall of 2007. I'd taken some time off to write, and it was one of the more promising of several stalled projects. I don't remember exactly how or why I decided to make all the characters women, or to tell the story from Melissa's perspective—perhaps it was sheer frustration that nothing else seemed to be working—but those two changes jarred the rest of it loose. If I remember correctly, the bulk of the "first draft" (or more accurately, the umpteenth) came together over the course of an afternoon and evening. The story wasn't fully polished when I pitched it to R.J., but near enough to know I had something that might be worthwhile.

It seems I publish a bit more, and a bit more successfully, every ten years. With any luck, 2018 will bring good news about the two novels I'm working on.

Kim Despins

Kim Despins has published a number of short stories and a novel. She also collaborated with a group of talented writers to create a mosaic novel called *Tales from the Yellow Rose Diner and Fill Station*. One of her favorite stories, "Momma's Grave," is forthcoming in the *Cemetery Dance* anthology, *Shocklines: New Voices in Terror*. You can follow her on Twitter @kdespins.

• This story originally started out as a piece about a Catholic priest struggling with his human urges and his past sexual encounters with a former girlfriend. Religious imposed celibacy has always struck me as unnatural, and my opinions did a little more than just peek through in the story. I could never get it to stop being so damned didactic. So I kept the first paragraph, dropped the rest and started fresh. The story took a new and completely unexpected turn and eventually became **Skin**. After the first draft, I sat back and thought to myself, "where did *that* come from?" That thought was quickly followed by "what is wrong with you?" During revisions I dropped the original opening paragraph as well. Nothing of the original story remains. Trust me, that's a really good thing.

Kurt Dinan

Kurt Dinan is a high school English teacher in Cincinnati where he lives with his wife and four children. His debut novel, *The Water Tower 5*, is scheduled for publication in April of 2016. You can follow him on Twitter @ KurtDinan.

• ***Into the After*** is one of the few stories that came to me while brainstorming What If? scenarios—What if a parent was so grief-stricken that his son decided to go to terrible lengths to help him? I'd just read an article about people profiting off the 9/11 tragedy, which helped me focus the story some, but I was struggling with tying it all together. It wasn't until the third or fourth draft of the story that I came upon another What If? that helped me finish the story—What if someone the reader thinks is a charlatan isn't? Once I had that idea, the rest of it finally fell into place.

Lorne Dixon

Lorne Dixon grew up on a diet of yellow-spined paperbacks, black-and-white-monster movies, and the thunder-lizard back-beat of rock-n-roll. His novels include *Snarl*, *The Lifeless*, *Eternal Unrest*, and the upcoming *Blue Eel*. Five of his short stories have appeared in volumes of *+The Horror Library+*. You can follow him on Twitter @LorneDixon

- *Ash Wednesday* is an example of "situational horror," a naturalistic approach to the genre that does not rely on the supernatural for its foundation. The moral question posed in the story, whether it is honorable to risk a good man to save a murderer's life, allows a plausible scenario to serve as cautionary food for thought. Inspired by the Blackwell Island asylum fire of 1858 and the Frederick Mors prison escape.

Benjamin Kane Ethridge

Benjamin Kane Ethridge is the Bram Stoker Award-winning author of *Bottled Abyss*, along with *Black & Orange*, *Divine Scream*, and other novels.

His short fantasy and dark fiction has appeared in numerous magazines and anthologies. For his master's thesis he wrote, *Causes of Unease: The Rhetoric of Horror Fiction and Film*, available in an ivory tower near you. You can contact Mr. Ethridge via Twitter @bkethridge or Facebook.com/benjamin.kane.ethridge

- On *The Vulture's Art*: Parenting a child really changed me. The things that used to bother or scare me transformed when I suddenly became in charge of another life besides my own. Losing a child to something tragic seemed an obvious jagged emotional edge to me—just horrible and unthinkable, of course. But about what losing one through the normal progression of time? What about the idea that our children will age and become adults, and that small life we took care of really does vanish over time? How awful would it be if there was something that could rob those precious years away? It's bad enough that time passes on its own and those golden moments are distant memories, but what if you aren't given the chance for those memories? For me the concept was appalling enough to put it down into story form.

Ray Garton

Ray Garton has been writing novels, novellas, short stories, and essays for more than 30 years. His work spans the genres of horror, crime, suspense, and even comedy. His titles include *Live Girls*, *Ravenous*, *The Loveliest Dead*, *Sex and Violence in Hollywood*, *Meds*, and most recently, *Frankenstorm*. His short stories have appeared in magazines and anthologies, and have been collected in books like *Methods of Madness*, *Pieces of Hate*, and *Slivers of Bone*. He has been nominated for the Bram Stoker Award and, in 2006, received the Grand Master of Horror Award. He lives in northern California with his wife, where he is currently at work on several projects, including a new novel. Visit his website at RayGartonOnline.com or Facebook.com/ray.garton.3 or Twitter @RayGarton

• Technological advances have made everything "smart." We have smart phones, smart cars, smart appliances. There's a lot of talk about the development of artificial intelligence these days. Human beings are advancing themselves into obsolescence. It occurred to me that it might be interesting to apply these advances to sex toys. What would a "smart" dildo be like? The result was *The Happiness Toy*.

Stephen R. George

Mr George is the author of 14 horror and suspense novels published in the 1990s and early 2000s. He has also written under the pseudonyms Jack Ellis and Valerie Stephens. He was born in Aberdeen, Scotland, and moved to Canada when he was nine, in 1969, and has lived there ever since. He has worked in advertising since the mid 1990s, first as a freelancer and then as a full time copywriter and IT guy in an agency, and he still does contract work for an agency or two. He also teaches Web development courses at the University of Winnipeg, and runs a small web development consultancy.

• I always found writing short fiction to be more difficult than writing novels and, so, *Chainsaw Execution* is one of only a handful of short stories I have written.

Eric J. Guignard

Eric J. Guignard writes dark and speculative fiction from the outskirts of Los Angeles, and his works may be found in stacks of disreputable publications haunting back alley bazaars. As an editor, Eric's also published the anthologies *Dark Tales of Lost Civilizations* and *After Death,* the latter of which won the 2013 Bram Stoker Award. Read his novella, *Baggage of Eternal Night* (a finalist for the 2014 International Thriller Writers Award), and watch for forthcoming books, including *Chestnut 'Bo* (TBP 2016). Outside of the glamorous and jet-setting world of indie fiction, Eric's a technical writer and college professor, and he stumbles home each day to a wife, children, cats, and a terrarium filled with mischievous beetles. Visit Eric at: ericjguignard. com, his blog ericjguignard.blogspot.com, or Twitter @ericjguignard

• *Footprints Fading in the Desert* is one of my earliest short stories, written in July, 2011. Ultimately, that isn't very long ago at all, but I only decided to pursue writing in February of that year. When I made that decision, my goal was to write two short stories a week, which I maintained for some time. Unfortunately, most of those tales were—and remain—awful! This one, however, turned out well, and I'm still proud of it. 2011 was a tough year, as I'd just lost another job in 2010, and was floundering as a displaced sales rep in a downsizing economy. My wife and I had a young son, and I was cashing out retirement accounts to pay bills. I'd recently attained my master's degree, and the only work I could get was hanging Christmas lights in shopping center courtyards. The old maxim came to mind to "do what you love" and I understood its truth; prior, I'd worked lucrative jobs I didn't enjoy, but suddenly they were gone, the money was gone, and I felt I'd wasted a decade for nothing. I'd wanted to be a writer in high school but was told not to misuse my time and to pursue business instead, which I did...oh, to do it all over. But enough sour grapes. I turned to creative writing in early 2011, and it tangentially led to a new career in technical writing, which was quite serendipitous. I don't have much to say specifically about the process of writing **Footprints Fading in the Desert**. Ever since I was a boy, my favorite reading has been of survival stories. I started sketching out the opening scene, but didn't know what to do with it. My wife and I were visiting somewhere, and I started pacing in a lonely room, and the storyline and ending just sort of "popped" into my head. Thanks Muse!

Kurt Kirchmeier

Kurt Kirchmeier lives in Saskatoon, Saskatchewan, where he splits what free time he has (never enough) between writing fiction and photographing nature (he has a particular fondness for birds). Kurt's stories and poems have appeared in numerous print and online publications including *Abyss & Apex*, *Murky Depths*, *Shimmer*, and *Weird Tales*. You can find him on Twitter @saskwriter and his website kurtkirchmeier.com

• My inspiration for writing **Obsidian Sea** came from a prompt I received in one of the many timed-writing challenges I used to take part in before switching my focus to novel-length works. What exactly the prompt was, though, I can't recall.

Bentley Little

"Bentley Little" is the pseudonym of a U.S. diplomat who must remain anonymous lest his writings adversely affect United States foreign policy. Because of his regrettable off-duty behavior, he has been permanently banned from attending the World Horror Convention and from entering the country of Japan.

• When I was little and traveled with my parents between Arizona and California, we would always stop at a Texaco gas station on the outskirts of Desert Center in the California desert. A new highway was built in the late 1960s or early 1970s, and the entire town was bypassed, but over the years I looked out the window of the car at the old road and watched as the gas station changed owners, went out of business, became festooned with graffiti and gradually deteriorated. Several years ago, I saw a special about singer/ songwriter Carole King and, amazingly enough, she was shown filming a music video at that same abandoned gas station. The idea of a famous person at the gas station gave me the idea for this story.

John Mantooth

John Mantooth's first book, *Shoebox Train Wreck*, was released in 2012 from Chizine Publications. His debut novel, *The Year of the Storm*, came out in June 2013 from Berkley. He lives in Alabama with his wife, Becky, and two children. You can follow him on Twitter @busfulloflosers.

• Many years ago, I drove a school bus. I quickly learned there are only two options for school bus drivers: allow the screaming kids to drive him insane or block them out by losing himself in thought. Naturally, I chose option two and used the time to tell myself stories. As a result, almost all of my early stories were set on a school bus. This one was no exception. I do think it might be my only story where the bus driver was a robot, though. Still, I have to wonder which is safer? Insane robot driver or distracted (and possibly insane) human driver? It's something to think about, but don't think too hard, especially if you have kids who have to get on a school bus in the morning.

Tracie McBride

Tracie McBride is a New Zealander who lives in Melbourne, Australia with her husband and three children. Her work has appeared or is forthcoming in over 80 print and electronic publications, including *Bleed, FISH* and the Bram Stoker Award-nominated anthologies *Horror for Good* and *Horror Library Volume 5*. Her debut collection *Ghosts Can Bleed* contains much of the work that earned her a Sir Julius Vogel Award. She helps to wrangle slush for *Dark Moon Digest* and was the vice president of *Dark Continents Publishing* (2010—2014).

Visitors to her blog are welcome at traciemcbridewriter.wordpress.com or Facebook.com/tracie.mcbride. Goodreads or Twitter @TracieMcB or email traciemcbride@hotmail.com

- *Ghosts Under Glass* was originally conceived in a dream; a nonsensical non sequitur featuring three hungry teenagers, one of them carrying a purple teddy bear, roaming deserted streets while ghosts menaced them through the window of a McDonald's. Who were they? Where were they going? And what was up with those ghosts? Re-reading the story some years on from its construction, I'm aware that I never fully answered any of those questions.

Ron McGillvray

Ron McGillvray is a writer from Ottawa, Canada. His writing credits include the short story "The Garbage Collectors," which was published in *Horror Library Volume 2*. His story "Big Boy" was produced as an audio version by Pseudopod and his story "A Night Out" was published by *Dark Fire Fiction*.

Two of his film scripts, *The Storm* and *The Goodbye*, were both produced by Cellardweller Projects. *The Storm* was chosen as one of the films to be screened at the 2007 World Horror Convention. It also screened at the Shocklines Film Festival in New York City. His story "Head Case" was made into a film produced by Columbia College in Chicago. His film script *Magic Man* was optioned by Hyde Park Media. His Stage play *The Line* was picked up as part of the reading series by the Saint John Theatre Company.

- My story *The Garbage Collectors* came about in a roundabout way. My wife decided it was time to do some spring cleaning and had me start throwing out unused and useless stuff of mine. One of these items was a lamp I'd had since high school, under the light of which I'd written many of my earlier unreadable stories. After putting it at the curb for garbage pick-up the next day, I thought about that lamp as I was getting ready for bed. I looked out our spare bedroom window and saw the lamp sitting at the end of the driveway. The thought popped into my head, I wonder if it is out there wondering what it had done wrong to have been thrown out with the trash? Even though I knew it was silly, I went back outside and rescued my lamp and hid it away in the basement. Did I mention the lamp didn't even work? Afterwards, lying in bed, I tried to rationalize it and wondered what would I do if I had to decide which of my children I had to put at the curb for the local garbage collectors? That was the germ of the story you are about to read, and I hope for your sake you never have to make that same decision.

Shane McKenzie

Shane McKenzie is the author of *Muerte Con Carne, Pus Junkies, All You Can Eat, Addicted to the Dead, Fat Off Sex and Violence*, and many more. He writes comics for Zenescope Entertainment and screenplays for LucahGore Productions. The first chapter of his novel *Muerte Con Carne* was adapted into a short film called *El Gigante*, and production for the feature-length film will begin in late 2015. He lives in Austin, TX with his wife and daughter. You can follow him on Twitter @ShanePMcKenzie.

• Getting into one of the *Horror Library* anthologies was an early goal of mine when I first started trying to write. I wasn't ready to try novels yet, so I focused completely on short stories. It was a really great way to learn, not only the craft, but how to stand out from the crowd, not to mention the ever important toughening of my skin. Because more than anything, I was receiving rejections. And that's what I deserved at the time. I wasn't trying anything new, wasn't taking any risks. My ideas were always strange, but I was too timid to really trust my instincts and I was instead writing and submitting "safe" horror. Well that wasn't working and it never should. *Open Mind Night at the Ritz* was the first time I really trusted myself and just let my imagination loose. Didn't hold back, no matter how weird it seemed at first. Not only did I get an acceptance and meet a very early goal of mine, but I learned how to make an editor take notice, and I've been doing it ever since.

Geoffrey L. Mudge

Geoffrey L. Mudge is a writer of horror and dark fantasy. He has very few published works, but he hopes to rectify that problem in the indeterminate future. He spends most of his time, during which he should be writing, chasing ghosts and looking for money in holes in the ground. Mudge currently resides in New Mexico with his wife, Brandi, and their dogs, Hazel and Moxie.

• Strangely enough, the inspiration for ***Reverend Wainwright*** came from my wife. She was suffering through some severe medical issues and was in a great deal of pain almost constantly. As we lay in bed one night, she was squeezing my hand and crying and I asked myself what price I would pay to take away her pain. Once that seed was planted, the character of Reverend Wainwright began to grow. Unfortunately for me (depending on your perspective), I'm cynical enough that even in my imagination the person that could help would only do so for nefarious reasons. Wainwright was immediately more interesting as the antithesis of a healer, abusing the hopes of the terrified to extract his toll.

The initial incarnation saw Wainwright as more of a shady snake oil salesman. However, as the scope of the story grew, I wanted to be able to bring more people to him than one might imagine a salesman could draw. The choice to make him a faith-healer came quickly and was much more satisfying. Using the trappings of religion to pervert it allowed Wainwright more freedom in his actions and also let me hint at his backstory without delving into any significant details.

Of course, he would need helpers as he traveled and I knew I didn't want him to collect his troupe from the captured children. Without giving away too much (I am most certainly not done exploring these characters), there is a definite connection between the Reverend and the hands and there is one small, and seemingly insignificant hint hidden in the story as to what they actually are.

I actually knew how I wanted the story to end before a lot of the other details were in place. Right off the bat, I decided that this narrative would not be about a regular "day on the job" for the Reverend, but rather a worst case scenario where the system breaks down and the true nature of the characters is revealed.

Daniel L. Naden

Daniel L. Naden has always been a writer. It's an affliction, a blessing, a curse...a dominant part of his life for as long as he can remember. He has published work in the areas of politics, humor, philosophy, and of course, fiction. Dan's stories explore the irony in life, through the lens of horror, suspense, & sci-fi. His writing has appeared in great anthologies such as *Horror Library Volume 2*, *Our Shadows Speak*, and *Dark Distortions*, along with top-notch markets like *Dark Recesses Press*, *Astounding Tales*, *Ragged Edge Publishing*, *Montage*, and *Pajamas Media*. In 2013, Dan's short story, "Loss," won the Best In Show, Short Fiction Story in the metro-wide Art@ Work competition, put on by the Arts Council of Metropolitan Kansas City. In 2014, Dan took top Art@Work honors once again with his story, "Just One." Dan and his wife Paula reside in Gardner, Kansas. They have four grown children and two grandchildren. You can follow him on Twitter @AuthorDanNaden

• They say you're supposed to write what you know and as a parent of four, the challenges of raising children seemed like a good fit for a story about a little girl with a frighteningly large talent. Like a lot of my stories, *Drawn* got its start from a simple *what-if.* What if a little kid had the power to grab whatever he or she saw, with just the power of wanting it to come? Simple as that, an idea that popped into my head one day, then exploded as my writer's mind began turning the concept over and over, trying to figure out what it would mean, seeing the story spin itself out around it.

What intrigued me the most about the idea behind *Drawn* was how much more complicated would be the process of raising an infant who had the power to take what she wanted, whenever she wanted it. I found it interesting how adding a little thing like seamless telekinesis to a child's development could turn the normal joys and challenges of parenthood into something more of a nightmare. And how we could find just how big little Anna's power actually is.

Marc Paoletti

A former journalist, Marc Paoletti holds a master's degree in fiction, and writes copy for the top advertising agencies in the world. He is the author of *Scorch*, a thriller that draws upon his experiences as a Hollywood pyrotechnician, and co-author of *The Last Vampire* and *The Vampire Agent.* His acclaimed short fiction has appeared in numerous anthologies. Visit him online at www.marcpaoletti.com, and follow him on Twitter @MarcPaoletti.

• I wrote *Apple* quickly, and I'm not sure I'm comfortable with that. Don't get me wrong—I stand by the story. I'm just a bit disturbed that such nihilistic material would flow from my fingers so easily. In fact, the story put me off writing horror for quite some time. Editors R.J. Cavender and Boyd Harris were kind with their praise over beer and BBQ in Chicago, but I'm pretty sure that's because they're dark bastards themselves. I say that with respect, of course, and realizing it takes one to know one. I felt similar pride/revulsion when I heard the story had earned an honorable mention in *The Year's Best Fantasy and Horror.* I hope people enjoy the story, darkness and all.

Greggard Penance

Greggard Penance spends most of his creative efforts writing nonfiction for small magazines. He has no public persona, and likes it that way. Every blue moon, he cuts his true muse loose, and gets his horror on. His dog only sleeps in his bed when he's not home.

• A number of experiences find a way to express themselves in most of my works. *Sporting the Waters of the Bermuda Triangle* is no different, though nothing is more primal to me than the depths of an ocean. We don't know what's down there, and that has always worked my spine into kinks. Then, you mix in other elements, such as an eerie place like The Bermuda Triangle, a central character who is in the predicament that he is in, and throw in a crossover into other dimensions, and my brain twists trying to remember how this whole thing came about.

I've never felt safe in open waters since watching the film *Jaws* as a teenager. I think the story has been brewing since then. I read Michael Crichton's *Sphere* sometime after that, and wanted so much more from it. I wasn't invested enough to write a novel on such a strange mix of images that were haunting me, and besides, this story wouldn't translate well into one, so I began it as a short piece. I saved the unfinished manuscript on my hard drive not long after 9/11, and like many other works, it sat there for a good while. Then I read a haunting short story that took place in deep waters a few years later, and that prompted me to dig my story out and blow the proverbial dust off.

Cameron Pierce

Cameron Pierce is the author of twelve books, most recently *Our Love Will Go the Way of the Salmon* and *Bottom Feeders* (with Adam Cesare). His work has appeared in *Dark Discoveries, Gray's Sporting Journal, Giallo Fantastique, Letters to Lovecraft, The Barcelona Review, LitReactor*, and many other publications. He is also the editor of four anthologies, including *The Best Bizarro Fiction of the Decade*, and head editor of Lazy Fascist Press. He lives in Astoria, Oregon with his wife. You can follow him on Twitter @ CameronPierce.

• *I Am Meat, I Am in Daycare* was written under the influence of Bentley Little, sleep deprivation, and *The Day the Country Died*, the seminal album by the British anarcho-punk band Subhumans. At the time I wrote it, I was living in San Luis Obispo, on the coast of central California, taking college classes and working as a paperboy. Often, after delivering papers all night, I would go to the 24-hour doughnut shop on S. Higuera and write, or I'd go home and write until I passed out from exhaustion. This was the most normal short story I wrote during that period. Several years after appearing in *Horror Library Volume 2, I Am Meat, I Am in Daycare* appeared in my first short story collection, *Lost in Cat Brain Land*, which was awarded the Wonderland Book Award for best bizarro collection of 2010.

Danny Rhodes

Danny Rhodes's short stories have appeared in numerous publications and anthologies, most recently in *Black Static* and *Crimewave*. A future story is due to appear in *Cemetery Dance Magazine*. He has written three novels: *Asboville, Soldier Boy* and *FAN*. Visit his website at dannyrhodes.net, on Facebook, and Twitter @danrhodesuk

• *Follower* was initially inspired by a photograph of the body of George Mallory, a climber who took part in the first British expeditions to Everest and who ultimately died on the mountain in 1924. Mallory's body was lost for 75 years until its discovery in 1999. Due to the mountain's climate, the body was incredibly well preserved. There wasn't much of a journey from witnessing that photograph to the imagining of a story in which a modern day adventurer, lured by social media, competition, the chance of flirting with fame, and blinded by a sense of indestructibility, might suffer a similar fate. The pursuit of Morris up the mountain by a being from another age was my attempt at administering the sort of quiet, unrelenting unease MR James mastered in some of his classic ghostly tales.

Sunil Sadanand

Sunil Sadanand lives in New York City. His work has been featured in *Chizine, Flesh & Blood*, the *Horror Library* anthologies and other small press publications.

• In many cases it's difficult for me to pinpoint the origin of a story idea. Usually they come from nightmares, or some burst of inspiration where two or more unrelated ideas come together. In this case, I remember specifically when the concept for *Trapped Light Medium* came to me. I was in a summer camp, and someone gave me a magazine devoted to gruesome subject matter. I've no idea what the title of the magazine was or where he got it from. That such a thing existed fascinated me. That there was audience for this type of stuff was even more interesting. There were graphic photographs of victims of car accidents, biker brawls and other seemingly random acts of violence. Close-up gunshot wounds and stabbings. A full page spread devoted to torture camps in Kenya, where victims were purportedly raped by dogs trained specifically for this purpose. I was sickened and numbed and disturbed. Then I started thinking about who took those photographs. Who went around snapping off pictures of the bodies? How did he know these things were going to happen? How did he know?

Alan Smale

Mr. Smale's short fiction has appeared in *Asimov's*, *Realms of Fantasy*, *Abyss & Apex*, and numerous other magazines and original anthologies. His novella of a Roman invasion of ancient America, *A Clash of Eagles*, won the 2010 Sidewise Award for Alternate History, and the first book in a trilogy set in the same universe, *Clash of Eagles*, appeared in *Del Rey* in March 2015. You can find him online at alansmale.com, Facebook/alansmale, and Twitter @alansmale

• The high-walled schoolyard in *Bound* is a gritty but faithful recreation of the playground in the northern England primary school that I attended until I was seven. (The devastated surroundings, less so.) And even though I wrote *Bound* ten years ago, I can still vividly recall all kinds of details about its world that never made it into the story.

Joan Berniker

Sara Joan Berniker lives, writes, and reads in Peterborough, Ontario. Her fiction has appeared in *Cemetery Dance*, *Playboy*, and *Albedo One*, among others.

Jeff Strand

Jeff Strand is a four-time Bram Stoker Award finalist, and zero time winner. His 20+ books include *Pressure*, *Dweller*, *A Bad Day For Voodoo*, and *Dead Clown Barbecue*. You can visit his Gleefully Macabre website at jeffstrand.com, follow him on Twitter @JeffStrand, or friend him on Facebook at JeffStrandAuthor.

• I can't usually pinpoint the moment of inspiration for a short story or a novel. Often, it's a very uninteresting, methodical process of brainstorming that leads to a story idea. In the case of *The Apocalypse Ain't So Bad*, though, the inspiration came from reading Brian Keene's novel *Dead Sea*. Now, I'm not copping to ripping off *Dead Sea*. It has the nihilistic tone that's common in zombie/post-apocalyptic fiction, but what struck me in Keene's book were the discussions about, "In a world ravaged by the undead, why should we even bother trying to stay alive? What's the point?" The answer, as provided by the novel, is: "There is no point, and we shouldn't bother." That mega-bleak world view made me think that it would be funny to write a story about a character who feels the opposite. The apocalypse would suck, sure, but unless you got bit by a zombie or lost your reading glasses, there would be an upside, right? Part of you would have a blast on the post-apocalyptic wasteland. It's okay to admit it.

John F.D. Taff

John F.D. Taff has more than 75 stories in publication in such markets as *Cemetery Dance, Deathrealm, Big Pulp, Postscripts to Darkness, Hot Blood: Fear the Fever, Hot Blood: Seeds of Fear,* and *Shock Rock II.* Six of his shorts have been selected as honorable mentions in Ellen Datlow's Year's Best anthologies over the years. His short story collection, *Little Deaths,* was named the No. 1 horror collection of 2012 by Horrortalk. *The End in All Beginnings,* his recent collection of five novellas published by Grey Matter Press, has been very well reviewed and was called "the best novella collection in years" by Jack Ketchum.

Books of the Dead Press will bring out two of Taff's novels this year, *Infestation* in the spring, and *The Orpheus Box* later in the year. Grey Matter is also publishing a standalone novella, *The Sunken Cathedral,* this spring. You can follow him on Twitter @johnfdtaff

• *The Immolation Scene* began a long time ago as an idea for a story on spontaneous human combustion. I remember reading about this as a child and seeing a wonderful black-and-white picture of an old woman's support hose-clad leg near a charred recliner—all that remained of her after she apparently ignited. There the idea sat, though, until I read the liner notes, of all things, for the soundtrack to the movie S*tar Wars Episode III: Revenge of the Sith,* specifically Track 12, *The Immolation Scene.* Great title, I thought. And though the story takes nothing from that (admittedly not great) film other than this, it got me thinking about my long dormant idea. Sometimes you just need a catalyst to make an idea work, and this was mine. The story came together pretty quickly and easily after this.

Ian Withrow

Ian Withrow is the author of several short stories. A graduate of Princeton University and the Stonecoast M.F.A program at the University of Southern Maine, he currently resides in western Montana, where he worships good music, great books, and spends his nights with every limb tucked safely beneath the covers. You can follow him on Twitter @withrow406.

• I was thirteen years old when ***Jerrod Steihl Goes Home*** first spewed out of my head. Two hundred words of my handwritten scribbles composed for a homework assignment that had been given to my seventh grade English class. Because why not give your teacher a story about a student unleashing unworldly hell on his school? To Mrs. Burnette's credit, though, she gave me nothing but encouragement. 'Keep writing,' she said. 'Don't ever stop.' Fifteen years later, the story returned. Again, the result of an assignment, this time as I was working toward my MFA. It was longer than it had been before—new characters emerging, aspects of the setting subject to change— but deep down, the heart of it was the same. If you let it aerate for a while, keeping the book open so the story can breathe, you'll taste the influences at work: Shirley Jackson, H.P. Lovecraft, and the ever-potent King. Mostly, though, there's Jerrod. Finally at home in these pages, the seed-planter of inky trees.

Made in the USA
Lexington, KY
01 December 2015